Best
Short
Stories
&
More

By AZ Writers

Copyright

Fogarty, Pat, ed. *Best Short Stories & More*. By AZ Writers. Prescott & Dover. Granite Publishing January 2019 Print

ISBN 978-1-7328121-1-6

Granite Publishing
Prescott & Dover

9 8 7 6 5 4 3 2
First Edition

Printed in the United States of America

Cover Design Mariah Sinclair
Cover inset Photos
Eric Anderson Book One
Jared Verdi Book Two
Cathy Severson Poetry Book

HBBXN 1551065906

Reviews

"Best Short Stories and More by AZ Writers is an impressive collection of stories and sonnets written by an eclectic group of Arizona writers. You'll laugh, you'll cry and more importantly, you'll enjoy the book. The wide-ranging subjects hold your interest and make the reader eager to continue. It's well worth your time."
— *New York Times Best Selling Author Mike Rothmiller*

"Not much is assured in life or literature, but here's one guarantee you can count on – in this collection of stories and poems you will find several that will make you glad you bought the book. AZ Writers have produced an impressive body of work. One story made me laugh aloud, another brought back nearly forgotten memories, and one touched my heart. So, your favorite stories and poems, the ones that will reach out only to you, are waiting for your discovery."
—*Sam Barone: Best Selling Author of The Eskkar Saga Series & The Empire Series.*

Dedication

The AZ Writers Collection of Best Short Stories & More is dedicated to the memory of Edgar Allen Poe, Emily Dickenson & Walt Whitman. Edgar is considered by many to be the Father of the American Short Story. Whereas, Emily and Walt are considered by many to be the Parents of American Poetry.

Acknowledgments

Without the collective efforts of a fine group of writers and poets, this compilation of *Best Short Stories & More* by AZ Writers would never have become a reality. I would like to thank each author who contributed to this project. A special thanks to Roger Antony, Dan Mazur, Sandy Nelson, Greg Picard, Bill Lynam, Mark Wenden, Bruce Paul, Dennis Royalty and Sherrie Lyons for their extra efforts to bring this multi-genre collection to fruition. This collection of Stories and Poems started as a project by *The Professional Writers of Prescott* and its Board Members; Joe DiBuduo, Toni Denis, John Maher, Steve Healey and myself—Pat Fogarty; who all worked together to get this collection published. We also thank Jerry Lincoln who unselfishly filled the gap with her expert knowledge of publishing and distribution. And, I especially thank my wonderful bride Susan for her organizational skills, common sense advice, and encouragement. Pat Fogarty: Editor

Preface

This collection of "*Best Short Stories & More*" by AZ Writers contains seventy-seven captivating stories written by 47 noted authors possessing an outstanding range of talent. In this book, the reader will experience the writing voice and style of many authors. Whereas in most other collections the reader is confronted with a dozen or more stories written by one author who writes stories with the same voice, the same style, and usually with the same plot, which after a story or two, become quite boring. Or, as in some other collections, the reader will find Stories written 100 years ago by authors who are no longer with us. In "*Best Short Stories & More*" by AZ Writers, the reader will find a contemporary multi-genre collection of stories by dozens of authors who are still, as of this writing, on the green side of the grass. *Best Short Stories & More* by AZ Writers includes memoir stories, historical fiction, creative non-fiction, and many other well-written pieces that will amuse, intrigue and mystify the reader. A few of these stories may make you laugh, and a few may bring a tear to your eye. You will also find well-crafted stories with irony, sarcasm, adventure, mystery, crime, and a couple with a bit of romance. What you will not find in this collection are mature content and inappropriate language. The "More" section of "*Best Short Stories & More*" features a concise selection of 44 non-abstract poems created by 25 established and emerging poets who, in their own poetic style, have written poems that tell a story.
Pat Fogarty: Editor

"Those who tell the stories rule the world."

—Hopi American Indian proverb

"The most powerful person in the world is the story teller. The story teller sets the vision, values, and agenda of an entire generation that is to come."
—Steve Jobs

El Toreador
By Greg Picard

"YOU WANT IN ON THIS, BOSS?" Tom Seaton had a raised brow, with a questioning turn to his face. Mr. Spock, on the bridge of the Enterprise, would have been proud.

"Why not, I haven't had my daily dose of stupid yet." Ranger Chris Becker obviously wasn't happy at the moment. "I would just like for once to have an ordinary day with happy park visitors and nice weather. No drugs, no thieves, no cars crashed, and no lost persons…and all the upper management in Headquarters on vacation. Is that too much to ask?" He slapped his computer mouse down on the desk and scrunched his Stetson on his head and said, "Might as well look the freakin' part for this. Whose place did this come from?"

"Lots of the horsie set start out that way, but the only guy I know that's raising livestock down there is over in Rattlesnake Canyon. Jack Hammond."

"Bulls! For Pete's sake, it's like a damn Merrill Lynch commercial with the stupid thing running down the middle of Highway 79."

"Don't forget your red cape!" Seaton was at full smirk.

"Oh yeah, really funny! At least Dick Savage isn't in town. I don't even want to think what the park superintendent would do with this one. Do you think Earl Martin is around now?"

"His horse concession is shut down for the winter, but if he and his wife aren't visiting their daughter, I expect he's there taking care of the horses."

"Did you notify highway patrol?" Chris asked Tom.

"Yeah, they have a bullfighter on the way." Seaton taunted as they tromped down the stairs and through the receptionist's office.

"Jane, would you see if you can find a number for Jack Hammond and call and tell him we've got a bull that we think might be his running on the highway just north of Oakzanita. Then see if you can get Earl

Martin. Fill him in and see if he'll meet us down there. Maybe we can get him to help us. He knows more about animals than anybody I know. The guy's trained bears and God knows what else, surely he'd know what to do with an adult bull," Becker said as they slammed the office screen door behind them.

As an afterthought, he pulled the door back open and shouted to Jane, "And call Frank from fish and Game and tell him to bring a grizzly-sized rifle ASAP."

When they got to the south boundary parking pullout, there was a crowd of cars parked. Though it was a light traffic day, a line of vehicles was starting to back up down the highway. People were trying to turn around, but some were just spellbound lookie-loos. Becker was spellbound as well. It wasn't a bull. They were looking at the nearly five-foot shoulder height of a 1,500-pound male buffalo that was alternating charging a now battered Chevy and a school bus and stomping the ground. The bison probably couldn't hurt anyone in the big bus, but the screams of the children were unnerving.

"Where's Clint Eastwood or Gil Favor when you need them," Becker mumbled as he whipped the patrol truck back out of range. People had begun to wave and holler at them to do something.

"I think I'd rather have Geronimo, boss."

"Bring the shotgun, Tom, and load it with all the slugs you can."

"I think that's gonna just make him mad." Seaton practically squeaked it out. The rage of the bull was even making him nervous.

"There is that possibility."

"'Course, he already looks kinda mad at that school bus. I don't blame him much. I never liked riding in one."

"I wish we could get all these people out of here somehow." Becker pulled out his belt radio and thumbed the transmit button. "Montane, C537"

"537 Montane," Jane answered from the office.

"Did CHP give us an ETA on their units?"

"They should be there by now from what they said. They had two units coming from Alpine."

Tom turned to Chris, "Maybe we could take the patrol truck and turn the siren and lights on and distract the thing…maybe herd it toward the East Mesa Road up toward Oakzanita trail. That's probably how it got here anyway."

Becker was reluctant to try to shoot this monster with all the people around, and somehow even though it was likely destined to be burger patties by the rancher, he just felt bad about killing it. The press would have a field day with it, and Park Superintendent Dick Savage would blame Chris.

"O.K. let's give it a try."

"I sure hope we can keep him from goring us. Savage will have a cow if we mess up the truck," Tom muttered.

"Cows? Let's not get any more livestock involved in this than we have to, OK," Becker laughed.

Seaton took over driving and brought the truck up close to the traffic jam and flipped on the lights and siren and kept hitting the horn. At first, the buffalo took no notice and was still hammering the bus, but as they moved to the front, he suddenly stopped and stiffened his forelegs and dipped his head as he moved to face them.

"Uh oh, I think he's figured out we're here," Seaton said as he flipped the wheel to circle around the bull.

Chris cradled the shotgun out the passenger window and said, "See if you can make him follow us toward the fire road. Besides, he'll do a lot less damage to our back bumper than the front or sides of this thing."

As they were weaving in circles and dodging the bison's charges they took several hits to the rear step bumper and bed. It would have been comical if it hadn't been so dangerous. It wasn't looking good, but at least they were moving the bull back toward the fire road entrance. As they struggled to tease with the snorting bull, Chris caught movement out of the corner of his eye. Charging at them full tilt was Earl Martin on the biggest white stallion Becker had ever seen. He wore thick chaps and was swinging a lariat over his head as his horse dove toward the rear of the buffalo. As he threw the rope the loop snagged one of the bison's rear legs and the horse pulled up short snapping the rope tight. The bull was surprised and positively annoyed. When it turned to face the rider, Tom took the opportunity to turn and charge the beast with the truck. Confused, the animal couldn't figure out who to attack and stood still snorting with its head down. Martin took advantage of the distraction and backed the horse to tension the rope. Finally, the animal made a decision and turned to charge Earl.

Chris raised the shotgun thinking he'd have to shoot the bull for sure, but it seemed Earl was prepared for this and dropped his rope turning his horse to the fire road entrance. The bull followed full speed.

"Go, he's got him on the fire road, let's box him in from behind and keep him moving."

"Damn, I hope Earl's faster than that bison, I don't think we're going to have to do much to keep him moving."

"Did you see the size of those horns on that thing?" Becker said as he kept the shotgun at the ready. Becker hadn't had much time to marvel at the power and majestic size of the bison or its horns, but he was wondering about the fate of the bison in America as they tried to remove this one. Millions had roamed the central third of the United States for millennia. They kept the plains soil tilled and fed and clothed long lost Indian civilizations. It seemed a shame to kill this example in a park dedicated to the preservation of nature…not to mention the bad PR it would engender and all the nagging he'd have to hear from Dick Savage.

Seaton glanced at the rearview mirror, "Take a look behind us boss, I think the rest of the posse just arrived."

Becker turned to see two fish and game Broncos bouncing and fishtailing in the dust cloud behind them. "Well, at least they'll have a rifle that can reliably drop this bull if we need to." Again, it bothered him to think of shooting the bison.

Seaton was fighting the wheel in the rutted road, "When is this animal gonna get tired of running! We'll be at the Oakzanita trail junction in a minute. I hope Earl sticks to the fire road, so we can follow. That trail won't get the bull back to Jack Hammond's place."

Becker sighed, "I can't believe I'm chasing a buffalo in a pickup truck on a Tuesday morning. Whoever heard of herding with a pickup anyway? OK, when we get near the trail split-off, you back this truck way off and let the bull focus on Earl. I just hope he knows where he's going and what he's doing."

The turning point was at an oblique angle, and Martin didn't even slow as he peeled off left to keep to the fire road.

"Either he wants maneuvering room, or he's got a plan and knows where he's going," Seaton hollered over the engine as he gunned it to close the distance back up behind the bull and keep it moving.

As they rounded the next bend, they were joined by another rider approaching from the opposite direction. When he saw Earl Martin and the bison, he kicked his horse forward at a canter and rounded on the bull. The animal faltered for a moment and then charged the new rider. The rider was purposeful and appeared to know what he was about. Chris guessed he wasn't a casual recreation rider and must have been one of the ranch hands or Jack Hammond himself.

"Do you recognize that guy?" Becker asked Tom.

"I met Hammond once, and it's not him, but I'm betting it's one of his hands."

Between the two riders milling back and forth and the park service truck noisily gunning and blaring its siren, the bison finally seemed confused about its mission. As Chris watched the tiring animal stall and paw the ground, the ranch hand slipped his rifle out of the scabbard and shouldered it in one fluid motion. Before Chris could blink, he had fired two shots.

The bison shuddered and stumbled. It took two steps and turned toward Chris. At that moment as the huge brown eyes looked at the two rangers, Chris felt a sense of sadness he couldn't quite explain. The buffalo was just doing what it was made to do, running free and mounting a defense under what it perceived as a threat, and chasing predators from a herd that had already vanished 150 years ago. It was sad that a magnificent animal like that and his male brethren were to now be only sperm donors for future hamburger patties at Safeway, and BBQ steaks at yuppie parties.

The hand stepped off his horse as the buffalo dropped to its knees and crashed onto its side on the ground. Its great hairy head blew two snorting breaths that raised puffs of road dust...and then nothing.

"Looks like you guys have been having an interesting day," the warden behind them said as he slammed the door to his vehicle and walked up to Chris and Tom. "Everything OK here?"

"Looks like. Thanks for coming, Frank," Becker said. He had forgotten all about the wardens following them.

"Shame you had to kill it," the other warden said as he walked up from his truck.

"Naw," the ranch hand said as he walked past the dead bison, "the owner, Mr. Hammond, was gonna give up on the bison meat business anyway. Not enough demand yet, and the bulls are just too hard to manage. Too much investment in fence. He's gonna go back to cows. Lots better dispositions."

"You got a plan for this one?" Chris asked.

"Yeah, I'll bring up the bucket loader, and we'll haul it out. Take me a bit to get it here though. You guys mind watching the carcass for a bit?"

"Yeah, we'll stick around," Chris said.

The wardens eventually took off, and Chris thanked Earl Martin for his help. He told Tom to take the truck, finish his camp check, and tend to the park. After they left, Chris waited in the stillness with the dead bison. He wondered what it felt like to see a prairie filled with these magnificent beasts as far as the eye could see, and what skill it must have taken to kill one for food and its hide with only primitive weapons like spears and bow and arrow. He'd read somewhere that they sometimes chased the herd and drove dozens of bison off a cliff to their death below. In some ways, it was little different than the white settlers and hunters coming with their efficient big bore rifles. Where there was a demand, mankind sought to fulfill it. Perhaps the Indians would have eventually decimated the bison as well. Sustainability was a concept that even now was a hard sell in modern America.

He felt like hiking once the bull was hauled off, and he walked the trails the rest of the morning back to his office. He couldn't get the look in the bull's eyes out of his head.

Breaking In
By Dennis Royalty

"PROGRESS IS CRISIS-ORIENTED," a wise man once told me. It's a great saying, so often true. I only wish I'd heard it prior to 1966, when it might have offered some consolation to a fuzzy-faced teen working at Schnaible's Drug Store in Frankfort, Indiana.

Schnaible's was my first job unless you count delivering *The Denver Post* when we lived in Colorado.

I'll get to the crisis part in a minute. First, the setup. This story begins when my parents urged me to earn money for college during my junior year in high school.

With minimum wage pay at 75 cents an hour in 1966, being able to save 75 cents for each hour I worked was realistic in 1966. I lived for free at home. And, there wasn't a whole lot of things I needed to spend money on. And if I did buy a pack of baseball cards or a Hersey bar, they were a nickel each. My pal, Andy Mitchell, already was a stock boy at Schnaible's—so there was added incentive to work there.

"Stockboy" actually was "do-anything-boy" on nights and weekends. We added price tags to everything, from aspirin to shoe polish, and carefully positioned new stock behind the old as we shelved items in neat little rows. But the job also required everything from bagging for the cashier to working the register when Marguerite took a break, to cleaning the stockroom and the bathrooms, and--very important to owner/pharmacist Fred Schnaible—helping customers with a smile.

Smile I did, but I also tilted toward harmless smart-alecky at times. This behavior was limited, usually, to shoppers I knew as they entered Schnaible's with a "help me find it" expression.

"Looking for Alka-Seltzer?" I'd say.

"See that Coke machine back in the corner?"

"It's nowhere near there." (Fear not: I quickly steered folks to their quest. No harm was done, and a little boredom lifted for me.)

Excitement came to Schnaible's every six weeks or so with the arrival of the Kiefer-Stewart truck, bringing sales merchandise ahead of our ad in the *Frankfort Morning Times*.

That's when Andy and I had to hustle. We needed to unpack what the truck brought to the stockroom, then get it marked and displayed before the ad hit *The Times*.

I'll never forget Bon Ami cleanser, priced at 9 cents a can. Kiefer-Stewart unloaded what seemed like hundreds of the round containers, each invariably coated in a flour-like cleanser. We got them priced and shelved on time but wore Bon-Ami powder for the rest of the shift.

Andy and I stacked Kiefer-Stewart boxes floor-to-ceiling in the stockroom. One day, we giddily yanked open a large container marked "Superballs" that had been precariously stacked atop other boxes, within reach but at least 8 feet up.

A cascade of bouncy orbs ensued in all directions. Dozens hopped about as if they were alive, making such a commotion that Mr. Schnaible abandoned his post to check out the noise.

This was one of the rare times when Fred Schnaible looked over his bifocals at us, red-faced and exasperated. The rubbery balls not only caromed off his legs but, worse, some bounced beyond and into the store.

Who knew Superballs didn't come in individual packaging?

The Superball episode aside, Mr. Schnaible was tolerant, forgiving, and kind. He and another good-natured pharmacist, Dave Decker, not only managed the pharmacy but ran the entire store, dividing a seven-day workweek. In their eyes, I was a conscientious worker, arriving on time, a self-starter. Schnaible's seemed a perfect fit for me.

Until, that is, pharmacist Steve Decker arrived—Dave's younger brother.

Mr. Schnaible had another store in Lafayette to look after, so needed more help. Steve was tall (maybe 6-3) and thin, with a drill sergeant-looking crew cut and personality to match. The fact that the pharmacy area (off-limits to anyone but pharmacists) was built a couple of stairs higher than the rest of the store made him seem all the more intimidating.

The honeymoon was over for Andy and me. Me, especially.

"DEN-NIS." "Oh, DEN-NIS!" Steve's voice carried to the supermarket next door and the parking lot beyond.

A task hadn't been done to his satisfaction. I was in the crosshairs as I hurried to his pharmacy perch.

How long had I been working here? What else did I need to have explained to me? On and on he went. Before Steve, coming to work was pleasant. His demanding style changed that. And it kept me on edge.

I can't blame what happened next on Steve Decker. But in my defense, I was doing a lot of looking over my shoulder when he ran the store, my confidence wavering.

And so, it was when I confronted the dreaded routine of refilling distilled water bottles.

Frankfort was well known for its hard water, so distilled water sales were high. Schnaible's carried one-gallon glass bottles that were returned after use. It fell to Andy and me to peel off the old labels, affix new ones, and refill the bottles.

Refilling them meant pouring water into each bottle from sizable 5-gallon glass jugs.

At this point, I must confess that arm strength has never been, well, a strength for me. When a 5-gallon glass jug was full, it was all I could do to hoist it in the air, aim it at a glass funnel placed in the mouth of an empty bottle on the floor, and pour in a gallon's worth.

Once the empty was full, I'd remove the funnel, cap the newly-filled bottle, and repeat the same hefting chore until enough one-gallon distilled water bottles were ready to restock the shelves.

Along came a Saturday morning where things weren't going well. Andy was off, and I had much to do. Leaving the distilled water refilling to his next shift wasn't an option. Naturally, when it came time to refill empties, the 5-gallon jug was completely full. This maximized the degree-of-difficulty for me.

I placed the glass funnel into the mouth of an empty and lifted the large jug, staggering under its weight. Distilled water surged forth, slopping beyond the funnel. Suddenly I was off-balance, grappling with a-now-slippery 5-gallon jug.

Out of control and out of my hands it went, like a dirigible crashing to earth. Only, in this case, the massive jug slammed into the glass funnel and glass bottle below, smashing them to pieces.

A resounding crash brought pounding footsteps from the pharmacy section, just outside the stockroom.

Steve Decker's eyes caught me at my worst, fumbling to retrieve hunks of glass but skidding on a flooded floor.

"IDIOT! IMBECILE!"

"Clean up this mess right away! Get the rest of those bottles filled!"

But then Steve realized there could be no more distilled bottles filled this day, or any day in the near future. That's because our glass funnel was in shards on the floor. Schnaible's had no other suitable funnel for the task.

"Now you've done it," he thundered. Only an influx of customers at the pharmacy counter halted the onslaught. And prevented Steve Decker from seeing tears in my eyes.

It didn't take Mom and Dad long to realize something was up when I got home. After some blubbering and consoling, Dad produced hope.

"I think we've got similar funnels at work, let me check."

Back he came from the National Seal plant with not one but two funnels, a glass one, similar to what I'd broken, and a same-size plastic funnel. A godsend!

I couldn't wait to get back to the store. Steve was alone in the pharmacy area when I rushed up to him.

"Look what I've got," I said meekly, pointing to a paper bag I carried.

"What now?" he said, descending the stairs.

Triumphantly, I reached into the bag. I would show him!

Inside, I had sleeved the funnels. I grabbed one and whisked them out, triumphantly.

"Here you go," I beamed.

But I was gripping only the top edge of the plastic funnel.

From beneath it slipped the glass funnel.

Which plunged to the tile floor, end over end.

And smashed into pieces.

Teeny, tiny pieces. Glass everywhere.

I froze.

Steve did too, eyes bulging.

Finally, I managed a gasp, incredulous. And awaited Mount Vesuvius to explode.

He did. But in laughter.

Loud, belly-grabbing, raucous laughter. Recognition of the absurdity-of-it-all kind of laughter.

And then he touched my shoulder--not to send me reeling, but in a caring way

Steve Decker wasn't laughing at me, he said.

Things happen.

Everything will be OK.

"But how about getting a broom and a dustpan, to clean this up?"

Things were never the same between us after that. Instead, they got better, much better.

We still had a plastic funnel. He even thanked me for bringing it in.

So, from the apparent worst, progress. Crisis-oriented progress, to be sure.

But a good kind of progress, as progress so often is.

Uncle Harold
By S. Resler Nelson

I GUESS LOOKING at it now, my Uncle Harold was a softhearted guy, but he never showed it, except for the last time I saw him. And even then, it was only a glimpse. I had stopped by his farm in Arizona on my way home from college like I had several summers before.

I watched him toil in the hot sun, his face wet with sweat, and his hands cracked and dry as the ground. He looked up and saw me coming his way and drove his tractor on, in the blazing heat and white dust. I admired him when he labored like that, because he knew farming so well, and it was his life.

He stopped in a bit and shut down the rumble of his old Ferguson. He wiped the pouring sweat from his face with his sleeve and leaned back, stretching his hunched shoulders.

I put down my suitcase and looked up at him from under the brim of my baseball cap.

"When did you git here, Joe?"

"Just got off the bus at Hopkin's Corner a while ago and walked here," I said.

"That's quite a ways. You seen Aunt Bess yet?"

"No, I just got here."

"School out for the summer?" he asked and wiped sweat from his eyes with a tattered rag.

"Yeah," I said. "You want some help?"

"Naw, why don't you go and keep Aunt Bess company? Tell her I'll be along for lunch purdy soon."

He always worked alone. He knew how he wanted things done. He started the tractor and I walked towards the house. Across the field, I could see the weather-beaten gray barn and leaning fences. Near the barn was the old, white two-story house. The paint was faded and peeling, and the weeds were high.

I looked back at the golden oats ripening in the sun, and in a barren field Uncle Harold furrowed up the dry earth into clouds of dust.

Aunt Bess saw me coming and waited on the porch. She wiped her hands on her apron and waved. It was good to see her again, as it had been a year. Her small round face smiled.

"We've been expectin' you, Joe. When did you git here?"

"Just a while ago," I said. "Uncle Harold says he's about finished in the field."

"He's workin' too hard, Joe. He's gittin' so thin, and his back bothers him a bunch. He's not young anymore, and with the boys gone, I wish he'd get some help."

"I offered to help him," I said.

"I know, but he don't want no help. He's gonna kill hisself workin'."

"You look good, Aunt Bess."

She stood back and sized me up. "Let me take a look at you, Joe. You're growin' so tall. Is that college teachin' you anythin'?"

"Yeah, I'm going to be a writer."

She frowned and didn't comment, and I followed her into the house. She moved some papers from the table and a cat from the chair, and I sat down. The kitchen was full of fruit and vegetables, canning pots and jars, and dishes not done. She worked as she talked.

"It's been lonesome around here since the boys left."

My two cousins had joined the Army. They told me they wanted no part of farming, and I figured that gnawed at Uncle Harold a lot. But then, I didn't want to work the farm either.

"How's Mary Anne?" I asked.

"Oh, she's fine. Has another boy, so we got three grandkids now."

"That's good. Anything else new?"

"Harold bought a horse."

"A horse?" I said, surprised.

"Uh-huh, traded a couple tons of oats for him last winter." She stopped what she was doing and came to sit near me.

"He's an Appaloosee," she drawled, "but he didn't color out. Harold got him from a rancher near Gilbert. He was thin and had his winter coat, but Harold knew he'd look good in the spring, and he does. He's so shiny now. Real proud and full of hisself."

"I'd like to see him," I said, being fond of horses. There was something about them, and Appaloosas were a fine breed. I remember the old, big-boned plow horses Uncle Harold had when I was a kid. Even they were beautiful to me.

"Harold's colt is so purdy in the morning when we put him out. He trots around with his tail up like a deer and snorts at everythin'. Harold stands and watches him for the longest time before he goes to work."

We strolled out into the sun, and I could see the Ferguson parked in the field and Uncle Harold starting for the house. We walked the worn path to the corral by the barn. Birds lined the water trough and katydids buzzed in the weeds. The air was stifling, and the sun burned high overhead.

The colt was stretched out flat on the ground, his back to us. He was good sized, maybe a two-year-old, a dark bay, muscled and sleek. He didn't stir when he heard us coming.

"He's restin'," Aunt Bess said. "He played hard this mornin'."

She stood at the gate and tossed a pebble that bounced in the dust beside him. The colt didn't move, and she said, "Get up, boy. Come on. I want Joe to see ya."

He still didn't move.

She opened the gate, and I followed her into the corral.

"Well, I don't know. Maybe he's sick," she said. "He's never done this before."

Aunt Bess walked slowly around him, and I stepped where I could see him better, too. His mouth was ajar, and his lips pulled back from his teeth. His eyes were open, staring through a blue film.

"He's dead!" she cried and ran past me through the open gate. "Harold, the colt's dead!"

She came back with Uncle Harold. Tears streamed down her face, and she grasped her apron.

Uncle Harold walked around the colt, and Aunt Bess stood beside me.

"He was fine this mornin'," she said. "I saw him when I went to the garden. He was just standin' there."

Uncle Harold looked long and hard, and I did, too. The colt had a fine-boned face and a long neck. His legs were clean and straight, and his hooves small and trim. There were marks where he'd thrashed on the ground and a disturbed place in the dirt where he'd tossed his head around.

Uncle Harold took off his hat and threw it in the dust. "Damn! Everythin' round here goes bad."

He turned and walked away.

Aunt Bess sobbed, "Why did he die, Joe?"

"Maybe a twisted gut," I said. "I've read where horses die suddenly from that. No good reason for it, either."

"Did we do somethin' wrong?" she asked in a trembling voice.

"No, the colt looks like he's had good care. A horse has a hundred feet of intestines, so as big and powerful as they are, they have a sensitive gut, and things can go wrong. You and Uncle Harold aren't to blame."

I knew a twisted gut, if that's what caused his death, could be aggravated by eating too much sand, and there was plenty of that in the valley. Or he could have had an unexpected bowel obstruction.

Saying something that would lead her or Uncle Harold to blame themselves would only make them feel a whole lot worse than they already did. I could tell they both loved the colt, and whatever happened wasn't from neglect. It was just a freak of nature.

Aunt Bess put her arm around me and then went to the house. I stood by the gate for a long time, listening to Uncle Harold's tractor chugging in a distant field. My uncle wasn't one to talk much or express his feelings, but I knew this colt's death was tearing him apart.

A rendering truck came an hour or so later, as I waited near the horse. Flies swarmed around the bay now, and I tried to shoo them away, but it was no use. Aunt Bess stayed inside, and Uncle Harold's tractor was so far off I couldn't hear it anymore.

The truck driver put a cable around the colt's neck and winched him up the ramp towards the truck bed. The colt inched slowly like he didn't want to go, and his legs hung up a couple of times on the slats.

"Nice colt," the driver said when he was done. "Don't mind picking up an old one or crippled one, but this here's a nice colt."

I tried not to think about it, as the truck rolled through the weeds and out to the dirt road. I watched until it disappeared beyond the cottonwood trees.

My visit was shorter than in summers past, and Uncle Harold died that winter. Aunt Bess moved into town to live with her daughter's family. And the farm was sold in the spring.

All Quiet on the Bureaucratic Front
By Dan Dražen Mazur

PETER WAS A QUIET MAN living in a quiet neighborhood in a quiet town. Life was quiet but a bit boring. He had no relatives, no family of his own, no friends and no pets. The only thing he had going for himself was his work, and now this has changed as well because his company was downsizing. For years he worked as a salesperson at a stationary store of a neighboring town, traveling every day back and forth about thirty miles each way. There, Peter was appreciated because he seldom complained about crazy scheduling. He agreed to work weekends, afternoons, and he was available to fill in on short notice. He was taken for granted a bit and taken advantage of a lot. However, seniority made Peter the highest earning sales-person on the floor, and the company would save money by letting him go. He was replaced with two entry-level part-timers.

The new situation hit Peter quite hard and he spent a week in quiet desperation, and then picked himself up and made a few weak attempts to find another job, to no avail. The economy was not at its highest, and Peter was too old and quiet, so someone would always beat him, either by being younger, having better credentials, or leaving a better job interview impression.

Peter gradually became depressed, and after thinking of different options, decided to commit suicide. Peter, being who he was, choose a different pathway of departure, from what many other, serious, committed suicide candidates would do: after selecting when's, where's, and how's to do it, then writing a goodbye letter, be on their way by jumping from a bridge, laying down on railroad tracks, hanging or shooting themselves, or simply overdosing on a bunch of over-the-counter sleeping pills. No, Peter was too quiet, too mild, too modest, and much too law-abiding citizen. He knew that taking one's own life was not permissible, and to make it legal he decided to get a permit to do it.

So, Peter went to the county Public Works Department and waited his turn for a prolonged time. He then approached the clerk there, inquiring about the paperwork for a permit to commit suicide. The clerk said they had no such forms and directed him to the Department of Public Safety in the State government office building. The State building was in a neighboring town, where Peter used to work, and Peter postponed his visit to the next day. He drove there the following morning, only to be told that such forms are not available there either, this could likely be a federal matter. He was told to address his issue to the GSA department, which stood for General Services Administration. Luckily, the federal building was close by, and after waiting for employees to come back from an hour and a half long lunch, he was told that there was no specific form for his request. The clerk there was very nice and suggested he should write a letter of request, but to submit it to the county government. The courteous federal government clerk went further and continued that he should be prepared to wait for their response because they were swamped with high priority cases, and short on personnel, which is why she recently switched jobs from there and came to work for the federal government. The county situation was crazy, and she was much more relaxed now.

Peter agreed and drew up a letter of request on his computer. He couldn't print the letter right away and had to go back to the stationary store he used to work in, where he was greeted by his fellow worker and store manager. He needed to purchase a Magenta ink cartridge for his printer. Oddly, his printer wouldn't print in black ink, although there was plenty of black left in its respective cartridge, but the Magenta ink cartridge was empty, and there you have it. Color cartridges were expensive, and Peter figured out this was a way the cartridge makers were cleverly but unfairly making extra money.

When the letter was printed and looked good enough for submission, Peter decided to avoid a long wait in line and sent it through the regular mail. He kept a copy of the letter, frequently reading it, and found that several improvements could be made to it, but it was too late. The letter was entitled, To Whom It Might Concern, and titled Request for a Permit to Commit Suicide.

Several weeks passed by, and finally, Peter got the notification that his Request was denied due to failure to pay a filing fee. The letter did not specify the amount of the filing fee, and Peter went there in person where he discovered, after a nominal waiting time, that not only filing fees need to be paid, but also a penalty fees for non-compliance. The amounts of both were not too bad, but they accepted only cash or official checks. The clerk kindly explained that credit cards were not accepted because credit card companies take a chunk of every transaction, which lowers the amount left for the county. As far as personal checks were concerned, there were too many bounced checks in the past, and it was a nightmare to collect the monies again, including the fees that the bank charged for bounced checks.

Peter went to an ATM and withdrew cash, returning to the office. After waiting some more, Peter realized that there was another clerk there. Since Peter had not brought their letter, this nitpicky clerk couldn't identify the case without the number they'd assigned to it. The fact that earlier the different clerk had no problem to locate Peter's case without any letters and numbers didn't help. So, Peter had to drive back home to get that letter. All this driving back and forth was quite exhausting, and Peter became mildly irritated and tired of this runaround.

He was mildly speeding, trying to get back to the county office before closing time, and wouldn't you know it, he was stopped by the police and given a speeding ticket. This put Peter in a bad mood, and when he arrived at the County Clerk's office, he was already irritated with the situation and was kind of short with that clerk, who found Peter's behavior less friendly and less submissive than he was used to. The clerk immediately took it personally and took a defensive posture. He was agitated with such aggressive customer behavior and refused to offer any help with Peter's request.

Consequently, Peter's stamped, and fees-paid request wound up at the bottom of a huge paper pile. Peter feared it would take a while for his request to be considered. The clerk was exulted for not telling Peter that in case of the address change he should report it within ten days, otherwise if the post office returned their mail with the Permit, there would be no attempt to locate the party's in question current address.

Peter didn't know that and indeed moved to a cheaper place. He failed to report the new address within ten days. He waited and waited, and little by little got used being in limbo for so long. He even quietly began enjoying life, food stamps and other conveniences the government provided to poor people. He even started quietly singing when taking a shower. Life was good, and Peter looked forward to living a long and happy quiet life before receiving the government's Permit to Commit Suicide, if at all.

Not that the story need be long, but it will take a long while to make it short.
– *Henry David Thoreau*

The Thumbprint
By Sue Favia

SHE HAD THE BIGGEST HOUSE, the biggest yard, the best food, and a swimming pool in her own back-yard, and of my three aunts, Aunt Doll was my favorite. All our relatives would come to Aunt Dolls and Uncle Joe's house for every holiday and any other occasion that called for food, wine and plenty of beer. But, the most memorable visit was on the Fourth of July.

Neighbors, friends, and relatives all brought their dishes to add to my aunt's dishes, and the entire day was spent eating and swimming. After a few hours of drinking my father and uncles would begin throwing us kids in the pool while my aunts would hover over each one of us making sure we came up for air.

Every time we stepped out of the pool my Aunt Doll would stop one of us kids to go into the house and bring out another utensil or plate of food. The yard was long and narrow, maybe one hundred and fifty feet or more with the house and pool almost at opposite ends of the property.

"Oh, honey, would you bring out that serving fork on the stove and bring me the rest of that sausage in the green bowl," or, "sweetie, there's some more olives in the frig and then grab the block of cheese in the square container on the second shelf on your way out, and put this in the sink on your way in, would ya', Hon'," she cheerfully instructed.

My sisters and I made a game about who could get past Aunt Doll without being summoned to bring out another plate of food or carry in an empty one, and then we'd laugh and tease the one who got caught for the next kitchen run.

The food was placed on long banquet tables in the yard near the pool. The cuisine was mostly Italian from the men's side of their family, and Lithuanian cuisine from my aunt's side of their family, in addition to all the traditional American food from neighbors and friends. When the entrees and side dishes were exhausted, and cleared away, the table was once again filled with delicious sweet desserts lasting into the night.

For the entertainment, my Uncle Joe and his friends and neighbors would pool together their firework collections. When the sun fell low in the sky, Uncle Joe and his two brothers would clear a safe place in the yard to set them off. For hours, we would be awestruck, watching the sky dazzle with brilliant streaks of colors and intermittent blasts of cherry bombs and silver salutes. When the fireworks ran out we kids would light sparklers and run through the yard as they flickered in our hands, making circles and figure eights in the night.

Aunt Doll was a large woman with a great presence and a loud contagious laugh, yet another side to her I found to be intimidating. Do as we were told and all was well—cross her and there was trouble to pay.

Aunt Doll was married to my Uncle Joe, my father's younger brother and had six children. Uncle Willie, my father's older brother, was married to Aunt Annie, who also had six children, and the eight of us made twenty, so there was no room for any of us getting away with anything and Aunt Doll cut no slack and played no favorites. She was stern, but in a fair and loving way. While she enjoyed us all, she didn't allow misbehavior, disrespect or making a mess in her house. Most of all she didn't allow waste at any meal.

"Take as much as you want," she'd say, "but eat every bite." Her food was the best we'd ever had, and we never left a crumb.

Often in the summer, after one of our warm weather occasions, my cousin Patty and I would plan ahead to stay overnight at Aunt Doll's for a few days, so we could play in the pool and hang out together. Patty was a year younger than I, and the daughter of my Aunt Annie and Uncle Willy.

The pool was above ground, but it was still the biggest and deepest I'd ever seen, in anyone's yard. At my age, I could barely keep my mouth above the water level. I had to stand on my toes and bob up with each inhale to make sure I wouldn't take in any water.

During one of our visits, after playing in the pool all morning with my cousin Patty, my Aunt Doll called us all in for lunch. I had smelled the food coming through the window for the past hour and was starving. Aunt Doll said she was baking ham and she would make us sandwiches for lunch. I believe her entire day was spent in the kitchen, at least through the summer months.

"Time for lunch—come on in. Dry off first, and bring your towels in to sit on," Aunt Doll instructed through the screen door. There was thick sliced ham with Swiss cheese, potato salad, and for dessert, all the watermelon we could eat. As Aunt Doll passed out the plates to her boys first, Patty and I munched from the bowl of chips on the table. When Aunt Doll set my sandwich in front of me I shuddered at the sight on my plate. There, like a crater, was her large thumbprint, deeply imbedded in the soft white bread. I sat at the table staring at it in dismay, contemplating my options. This was definitely going to be a problem. There was no way I could eat that thumbprint.

I began with the undamaged half of the sandwich, then I ate the potato salad and chips. I knew the watermelon would have to wait. I had to approach the other half of the sandwich with careful consideration.

Slowly and systematically I began eating my way around the oversized thumbprint, avoiding the depressed area completely, thinking I could dump the contaminated portion in the garbage when my aunt left the room. But, no such luck, Aunt Doll was having more company over for dinner that night and had a pot of spaghetti sauce cooking on one burner and another pan of sausage and green peppers on the other. She wasn't leaving that stove, not for a minute.

"You kids need to finish up here, I've got to get started on my Jello molds and I need the table." Aunt Doll said.

Aunt Doll was the queen of Jello molds. Whenever there was a family gathering, she would make her famous fresh fruit creation, mixed with cream cheese and strawberries, sometimes pineapple or orange segments, stacked high with fresh whipped cream.

My cousin Patty was making great strides with her lunch, and Aunt Doll's two older boys were already finished and running out the back door to the pool again.

"Hey, Jodie, get back here," she yelled, as the door slammed behind him. "I said finish everything—and that means your milk, too." Jodie ran back in, chugged down the rest of his milk losing much of it down his bare chest, and almost in the same sweep, scrambled back out the door to beat his little brother Mark to the pool.

Patty and I sat at the table, as my aunt, all too often, glanced at our plates. As my sandwich was getting smaller and smaller, it seemed as if the thumbprint was getting bigger and bigger. If she forced me to eat it I knew I would gag, or possibly worse. I'd never be able to come back again—ever. My mother once forced me to drink the rest of my 7-Up after I allowed some birthday cake to back-wash into the last remaining few inches of the bottle. I gave a warning signal with some gag reflexes which, unheeded, led to the entire contents of the pop, cake and recent lunch ending up on the floor. The thumbprint had inevitable possibilities. I couldn't bear the humiliation, but even more, Aunt Doll being angry with me. Would she understand? Would she know it was about her thumbprint?

I knew this was not normal. It's not like I saw her lick her fingers or pick her nose. At home, whenever my mother left an imprint in my food, all I had to do was remove it from my plate and drop it on the floor and Blackie would take care of the rest. With ten of us at the table, who would notice anyway? But Aunt Doll did not have a dog and it was only Patti and me sitting at the table. I couldn't tell Patty about the thumbprint, she'd think I was crazy—nor would she understand—I'm not sure I did.

I sat there, now, looking at the circular mound on my plate, nibbling as close as was safe to the edges of the imprint, so it wouldn't appear so large.

Patti had finished and was nudging me to hurry up, we could both see that our aunt was becoming impatient. The longer I stalled the more attention was drawn to the thumbprint, that was now beginning to look like the size of a hubcap.

Patty stood up and stared at the odd remnant on my plate, then Aunt Doll turned around looking at my plate as well. The two of them stood there watching with puckered eyebrows, as if it were a science project and they were waiting for it to move.

It seemed as if time stopped—as well as my breath. Tears welled up and rolled down my face as I sat in my anxiety. Without turning her head, my aunt somberly said to Patty,

"Now you go on outside and play, hon," she said, with her eyes still fixed on my plate.

Oh, my god, she wanted no witness. I wanted to yell to Patti, "don't go—stay outside the screen door."

Now, I envisioned myself on the floor in a half-nelson, with Aunt Doll prying my mouth open to force feed me this vile mutation of what had seemed like, a lifetime ago, just a sandwich. I had just learned in school that the human jaw was the strongest muscle in the body—so even given the size of her hands, I knew there was a good chance that if I didn't scream, nothing was going into my mouth. I was shocked out of my visions as her large hand reached over my shoulder, picked up my plate and allowed the thumbprint to slide into the trash.

As she gave me a half-wink and nudged me out the back door I thought I almost saw the corners of her mouth ever so slightly turn up.

My own experience is that once a story has been written, one has to cross out the beginning and the end. It is there that we authors do most of our lying.
– Anton Chekhov

Irish Resentments
By John Maher

THE IRISH ARE NOTORIOUS for holding their resentments. Just study Irish history and that green land's 800-year resistance to the English occupiers. The Irish rebelled and lost fifteen times until they won their freedom in 1922. The Irish don't stew, plot revenge, or carry on vendettas. We're pragmatic. We wait because we know that what goes around comes around. We don't forget. As Robert F. Kennedy, one of America's most prominent Irish-Americans once stated, "Don't get mad. Get even."

In 1920, when my father was ten years old, and head altar boy at St. Michael's Roman Catholic Church in Flushing, New York, a young priest arrived from Ireland as a new member of the parish's clerical contingent. He was "Lace Curtain Irish," meaning his people were property-rich in Ireland. Most of the Irish parishioners of St. Michael's came from "Shanty Irish" stock. Their people had been "dirt-poor" tenant farmers in Ireland. These parishioners regarded The New Priest with measured contempt. His custom-tailored black priest suits, his own personal altar vestments, his ornate gold chalice, and his aloof persona heightened their disdain. But it was the pride he had for a book that heightened their animosity. The book was his special Missal, the liturgical volume encompassing the words and gospels a priest uses to celebrate Mass. Pope Pius XI himself in Rome had blessed this special Missal, and The New Priest acted as if its glorious status added to his self-importance.

The New Priest's Missal was a prodigious book with a sumptuous tooled leather cover and binding, gold embossed lettering, rich illustrations, and parchment pages. Many St. Michael's parishioners quipped that it wasn't a Missal at all; it was a reproduction of the Book of Kells, the famous 1,200-year-old Irish manuscript displayed at Trinity College in Dublin. The Missal was maybe a foot thick and weighed approximately twenty pounds. The New Priest venerated his special, Pope-in-Rome-blessed Missal. To many of his parishioners, he had greater esteem for his book than his flock.

Every Sunday, in keeping with his head altar boy position, my father served the main 10 o'clock mass. A bulk of parishioners attended this mass weekly, including my devout grandmother, Nana. Born and raised in County Limerick, Ireland, she immigrated to America in the late 1890s, another one of the boatloads of Irish girls used as domestics. As she did every Sunday, she sat in the second pew on the right. She was there not only to pray and celebrate the mass but to gaze with joy as her oldest child, and firstborn son served mass, in her judgment a harbinger for what she believed would be his destiny as a priest. Shortly after The New Priest's arrival, he said the main 10 o'clock Sunday mass for the first time.

At the appointed time in the mass, the altar boy moves the Missal from the left side of the altar to the right. As my father commenced doing this, hugging the immense book to his ten-year-old chest while negotiating the maneuver, he stumbled on the hem of his oversized black cassock; the ankle-length clerical robe altar boys wear under the white surplice. And he tumbled headlong down the three steps and off the altar. He landed in a heap on the marble floor just inside the altar rail. The Missal arrived nearby a millisecond later with a resounding *splat*.

At the explosion of the Missal landing, the priest halted mass. He turned on his heel, looked over the wreckage that had unfolded below him, and bolted down the three steps towards my father sprawled on the marble floor. Everyone in the church assumed he intended to minister to my father's possible injuries. Instead, he seized my father by the arm, jerked him to his feet, and smacked him in the back of the head with a vicious roundhouse right. The *thwack* echoed throughout the church.

Then, the priest went over to his special Missal and gathered it, and its brass stand off the marble floor. Caressing it to his bosom as if it were a mistreated puppy, he carried it back up the three steps to the altar. He ignored my father still standing dazed by the altar rail. Once positioned again at the head of the altar, he tenderly set the Missal and brass stand on the right-hand side. Then with indifference, he returned to the mass as if nothing had taken place. Dead silence permeated the church.

In the second pew right-hand side, my Nana's piercing blue eyes scrutinized the goings-on with seething fury. Because she held clerics in the highest esteem as required of a good, respectful Irish-Catholic, she said nothing to the priest then or ever regarding his mistreatment of her child. But from that moment on, she seldom spoke to the priest. She avoided any dealings with him if possible, and never allowed him to hear her confession, always going to one of the other priests for her weekly visits to the confessional. This occurrence led to two developments, one two hours afterward, the other in thirty-five years.

At roughly high noon on that Sunday in 1920, after my father had completed his chores as head altar boy, he withdrew The New Priest's special, Pope-blessed Missal from the sacristy, the place where clerics and altar boys assemble for mass. Cradling the twenty-pound book in his arms, he plodded up the six flights to the top of St. Michael's belfry. Once there, he opened a small access door in the belfry that faced onto Union Street, one of the major avenues in Flushing. Then, he threw the Missal out into the open waiting air. It sailed fifty feet to the pavement below, where on impact it exploded like an IED, albeit a holy one. The book's spine snapped in several places, scattering its parchment pages over Union Street. My father suffered no guilt in doing this. In fact, he felt quite satisfied.

Thirty-five years later, on a hot, muggy July 1955 Sunday morning, my Nana walked the half mile from her home on Avery Avenue to St. Michael's Roman Catholic Church. As she had every Sunday for fifty years, she would attend the main 10 o'clock mass. At seventy-five years of age, she was built like a small draft horse, short, thick, boxy. She wore a Navy-blue rayon dress with a string of pearls around her neck. A matching blue pillbox hat with a veil nested on her head. Black Oxford shoes with squat heels squeezed her swollen feet. Midway up the front entrance to the church doors, her heart gave out, and she collapsed on her back there on the steps.

Concerned parishioners gathered around her. The New Priest, now The Monsignor and head of St. Michael's, happened to be present. His routine every Sunday demanded he receive his flock in his custom-tailored black priest suit and spit-polished brogans to glad-hand or browbeat them as they attended mass. He rushed to my Nana's side and kneeling asked, "Nellie, do you need The Last Rites?"

My pious grandmother, though dying, drilled her piercing blue eyes into the eyes of this man she had despised for thirty-five years and said, "Not you, ya bastard." She glanced up at the crowd hovering near her and said, "Get me another one." The priest who was to celebrate the 10 o'clock mass was called from the sacristy. He arrived flustered in full liturgical regalia, along with a flock of nervous altar boys also dressed to serve mass. He knelt on the steps and gave my grandmother The Last Rites. And then Nana died.

*This story is a tribute to my grandmother and my father. It illustrates my belief that much of who we are and what we are is the product of the people who came before us. I carry and cherish the spirit of my father and my grandmother.

Most of the basic material a writer works with is acquired before the age of fifteen.
– Willa Cather

One Bronx Morning
By Pat Fogarty

WHEN I WAS A KID, *Leave it to Beaver* was my favorite TV show. The black and white sitcom focused on the life of a young boy whose nickname was Beaver. He and his family resided in an unspecified town somewhere in suburban America. The weekly episodes set in the late 1950s and early 60s totally captured my imagination. But; I never understood why I enjoyed the show so much. The only thing Beaver and I had in common was our age. We were both ten when I started watching the show. As a youngster growing up in a crowded south Bronx neighborhood, I used to dream of being raised in a home like Beaver's. He owned a bike, lived in a nice house and every week his parents gave him a generous allowance. I guess I became a bit envious. Yet deep down, I knew the allowance deal and the cookie cutter house in suburbia was not going to happen in my world.

The earliest memory I have of making a few cents was when my friend Tony Biaggio and I collected empty bottles in vacant city lots for the deposit money. Tony was an only child and the only Italian kid I knew who didn't go to Catholic school. He and his mother lived with her parents in a private house nestled between two five-story apartment buildings. Tony never spoke about his father and I never asked. His Grandmother went to Mass and received Holy Communion every morning, but I never saw his mom or grandfather attend Church.

Although Tony was my age, most people took him to be younger because of his size. He may have been small, but Tony was a tough kid and a real hustler. He knew all the best places to search for empty beer and soda bottles. Most Saturdays, Tony and I would make the rounds scavenging in alleyways and litter-strewn lots for our treasure. I had an old rusty red wagon that I pulled behind me for hauling stuff. We got two cents for the twelve-ounce bottles and a nickel for the quart-sized ones. All the bottles were made of thick glass and the stores would only pay the deposit if they were clean. Tony's grandpa let us use his garden hose to rinse the bottles near the curb in front of his house. That was about as close to Tony's home as anyone ever got. None of the kids on the block were allowed to set foot on the front steps leading to his residence. His grandparents didn't speak English and they preferred not to associate with anyone on the block.

One Saturday morning while Tony and I were washing our collected bottles, Mr. Rosen, who lived on the first floor in the building adjacent to Tony's, stuck his head out of his living room window and said, "How would you guys like to make a quarter each?"

Wow," I thought, "That's a lot of money."

Candy bars cost a nickel apiece, so I figured I could buy a big Hershey bar every day after school for a whole week. Tony turned off the water to the hose, brushed his black gypsy-like hair away from his eyes and said, "Yeah, what do we got to do for it?"

The old man pointed to a little red Volkswagen parked across the street and said, "Wash and dry my car and you'll each get a quarter. But you've got to do a really good job."

Tony turned to me and said, "What do you think? Should we?"

I shrugged my shoulders and said, "Sure, why not?"

The arrangement turned out to be the start of a full-time Saturday business for Tony and me. We were a good team and it wasn't long before some of the other car owners on the street asked us to wash their cars too. I remember making two dollars in one day that spring. I thought it was a fortune and so did my mom. She brought me to a bank on the Grand Concourse near Yankee Stadium and helped me to open my first savings account.

Tony's grandpa would stand on his porch smoking a thin twisted cigar while we used his garden hose. You could tell he was proud of his grandson, and even though he never spoke a word to me, he nodded when he saw me on the street. Getting that little bit of recognition from him made me feel important.

Mr. Rosen and his red Volkswagen became our best customer. We washed his car every week. He could see exactly what we were doing from the living room window of his street-level apartment. I didn't mind him watching us but Tony didn't like it. If Mr. Rosen noticed a spot or some part that we missed, he'd poke his head out the window and holler something like, "I think the driver's door still has a smudge." Or he might say, "Hey guys, how about redoing the hood?"

I didn't mind the criticism. I figured he just wanted his money's worth. Mr. Rosen and his wife were older than my parents and never had children. On weekdays, Mr. Rosen left for work about the same time I left for school, and as soon as he would leave his apartment building, Mrs. Rosen would holler something out the window to him. In my mind I still have a vision of her—half hanging herself out of the living room window in an oversized pink terry cloth robe and yelling, "Stanley, don't you forget my cottage cheese. Do you hear me? Don't you forget the cheese."

Without slowing his stride, he'd cringe his shoulders, turn his head back towards her and say something like, "Yes Silvia, I won't forget. I promise I won't forget."

Most evenings on his way home from work I would see Mr. Rosen carrying a package or two. If I saw him struggling with a couple of sacks of groceries, I would offer to assist him. If he let me help, I'd usually get a nickel.

I remember a time when he was having trouble trying to manage a grocery bag in one arm and some dry-cleaned garments on wire hangers in his other arm. I asked if I could help and he said no. As he entered his building, the thin plastic covering the garments got caught on the front door and when he tried to free it, the groceries spilled out all over the place. It was a mess and I kind of felt sorry for him.

On Fridays when Mr. Rosen arrived home, he'd change clothes and then, he and his wife would get in the Volkswagen and drive away.

One morning, after I got to know Mr. Rosen and realized he was a fairly nice man, and curiosity got the best of me. When we crossed paths on my way to school, I said, "Hey Mr. Rosen, where do you and Mrs. Rosen go on Friday nights when you and her get all dressed up?"

He stopped for a moment; put his hand on his chin like he might not want to tell me, and then his face turned into a big smile and he said, "We go out for dinner. Silvia loves Chinese food. She can't get enough of it." Then he gave me a quizzical look and said, "Why do you ask?"

A little disappointed, I looked up at him and said, "Oh, I told Tony you probably went dancing somewhere downtown."

He shook his head and said, "No, we don't dance anymore. Now, get going before you're late for school."

When the school year ended in June, I anticipated that the car washing business would take off—I was wrong. 1960 was a drought year in New York. That meant, during the summer, Tony and I could only wash cars on certain days. I remember the cops driving around the neighborhood making sure that none of the big guys or parents opened fire hydrants for kids to cool off and play in. Tony and I had to adjust our car washing schedule. It was inconceivable to even think that Tony's grandfather would break the law by allowing us to use his garden hose on a forbidden day.

By the middle of July, we started getting plenty of rain, and by the beginning of August, the city reservoirs were almost full. The drought restrictions were lifted, and Tony and I were almost back to our old schedule. But; there was a new problem. We were getting too much rain and most of our customers didn't want us to wash their cars if it was supposed to rain that day or the next.

On Saturday morning, August 13, 1960, I got up early and listened to the weather forecast on my mother's kitchen radio. They were predicting a hot muggy day with temperatures reaching the low 90s. They also mentioned a possibility of some afternoon thunderstorms.

I met Tony at 8 a.m. in front of his grandfather's house. We decided; we had better go knock on Mr. Rosen's door and check with him before we started working on his car. It took a long time for Mr. Rosen to answer, but when he opened the door, he acted as if he was glad to see us. We explained our doubts about washing his car and he said, "Don't worry about the rain. Just go ahead and do a good job."

That was good news for us and we went straight to work washing his little red Volkswagen. We were about halfway finished when a police car came speeding up the wrong way of our one-way street. It stopped right where we were washing Mr. Rosen's Volkswagen. Before the cops had time to get out of their patrol car, another squad car came racing down the street from the other direction with its siren blaring and its cherry red bubble light spinning. For a split second, Tony and I both thought they were after us. I figured, maybe I misunderstood the watering rules. When the police arrived, Tony's grandfather was standing on his front porch with that thin stogie in his mouth. He casually walked down from his porch, looked around, rolled up his hose, and walked back up his steps. The four cops didn't even glance at him. They went straight into Mr. Rosen's building. Within minutes, several unmarked police cars arrived with detectives and the big brass. A crowd of people gathered on the street in front of Mr. Rosen's building. Everyone was trying to figure out what was happening. Two police officers stationed themselves by the front entrance of the apartment building. The cops were polite, but they wouldn't answer any questions. After a while, I noticed a commotion going on in the building's vestibule. We could tell something was up. Just then, two burly detectives emerged with Mr. Rosen wedged between them. He wasn't cuffed. I heard one cop tell another that they were taking Mr. Rosen to the station house in order to get a statement.

When Mr. Rosen saw Tony and me standing by his car, he said to his escorts, "Hold on, I owe these two boys some money for washing my car."

All of a sudden, everyone's eyes were on Tony and me. Mr. Rosen reached into his pocket and pulled out his wallet. He ruffled through the billfold, withdrawing two bills. He handed a one-dollar bill to each of us and said, "You guys deserve this. You do nice work."

As soon as the two beefy detectives and the other patrol cars left with Mr. Rosen, the crowd outside the building disappeared. Tony and I noticed one of the unmarked cars remained parked near a fire hydrant. So, we knew at least a couple of detectives were still in the apartment with Mrs. Rosen. The Venetian blinds in the living room had been lowered, but there was a space on the bottom that didn't touch the windowsill. Tony and I both wanted to peek under the blinds into the living room, but he wasn't tall enough to look in without me giving him a boost, so I said, "I'll look first and if there's anything to see, I'll hoist you up for a look."

Tony said, "You promise?"

I said, "Yeah sure, I promise."

I went to the window, stood on my tippy-toes and saw Mrs. Rosen sitting motionless in a large stuffed chair with about ten plastic dry-cleaning bags wrapped around her head. Her mouth was wide open, and she looked as if she was about to scream. Tony pulled the back of my shirt and said, "Hurry, there's a police wagon coming down the block."

I backed away from the window and Tony said, "What's in there? What'd you see?"

I felt like puking but managed to say, "Nothing Tony. I didn't see a thing."

By the look he gave me, I knew he could tell I was lying.

The police wagon had the words "County Coroner" stenciled on the doors. As the two attendants were removing the body of Mrs. Rosen from the apartment, Tony heard one of them say to the other,

"Yeah Scott, can you believe it? Her husband swears it was a suicide."

The Hike
By Toni Denis

"WELCOME TO THE SUNDAY church service," Morty said to the first arrival at the trail, a woman named Penny who had signed up online. She wore a confused look. "This is as close as we get to it, anyway."

The name "Atheist Hiking Club" started as a joke when Ed and Morty first bumped into each other early on a Sunday morning on a Phoenix hiking trail during the winter. They lived in the same neighborhood and had a passing acquaintance.

"Looks like all the atheists are hiking today," Morty said. They laughed.

"I'm more of an agnostic," Ed said. He swiped at a bead of sweat trickling down his nose. "But either way, Sunday is the only day I have to spend out in nature. Saturdays are for errands and my sons."

Morty, a wiry man with Einstein-like white bushy hair and a mustache, nodded sympathetically, even though he'd never had children. "My schedule is full of volunteer work since I retired, but I always make time for a hike on Sundays."

They hiked together up the mountain, Ed slowing his usual blistering pace so that they could talk along the way. The next Sunday, they met up at 7 in the morning and hiked together again. Soon friends began to join them. After a few months, they decided to try some new trails, and friends of friends came along. Finally, so many people were interested, they began coordinating the hikes via email, then on social media, so when they posted online, they needed a name. They decided to call the group the Atheist Hiking Club. Within three years, more than 100 people were on their list, though no more than a dozen usually joined them on an outing at one time.

Morty had lost his wife to cancer several years earlier, so he was always available for a Sunday hike and enjoyed the company. Ed's wife Calista liked having time to herself for her arts and crafts on Sunday, so he was often available for outings, too.

The two men became good friends, spending an evening a month at dinner together, sometimes with Calista and a friend Morty brought, whether it was Kyle his college-aged renter or a couple he'd known for years from his prior work at a publishing company. He hadn't gone out with anyone since his wife's death five years earlier.

"Would you like us to set you up on a date?" Calista asked over dinner one night when it was just the three of them.

"I couldn't imagine being with anyone other than my dear Miriam," Morty said. "I don't have the heart."

Much of what he and Ed talked about had to do with hiking, from overnight plans to which boots to buy and gear to bring. Arguments broke out over which sock brands were best and what snacks provided the most energy for hiking. While the goal was to travel as light as possible, Morty couldn't resist carrying a large backpack full of snacks and water, a lightweight thin plastic rain slicker, a small fluorescent flashlight, a camelback full of water that he could suck through the rubber tube, an empty water filtration bottle and a first aid kit, among other emergency goodies.

Since he liked to navigate and could use a compass with ease, Morty became the leader of the group. His overfilled backpack made everyone turn to him for any need they had, especially since novices often neglected to carry enough snacks or water. Aside from his walking stick, he always carried a buck knife on his hip, which he'd found useful for digging, cutting briars and as protection. Plus, he liked how it made him feel like Tarzan of the Jungle, he'd joke.

By the end of April, Phoenix mountain hikes were too hot to endure, so Morty and Ed decided to start driving a couple of hours upstate to the mountainous regions of Arizona with altitudes of a mile or more, where the temperatures were cooler and the breezes steady. Far fewer hikers joined them because of the time it took to leave at dawn to get there and then to head back in the afternoon.

Their regulars ranged in age from 20s to 70s. Morty was one of the oldest members, having reached 78 that year. Once a woman in her mid-80s joined them, but she never returned to hike again because she'd had too much trouble with her knees. Morty had descended with her to make sure she made it down the mountain, but it took twice as long as it normally would have.

Today they were hiking a trail called Spruce Mountain, the tallest point in a forested area on the edge of Prescott, one of the earliest Westward settlements in Arizona. The regulars who were there included Colleen, who'd retired as a nurse, a couple in their 30s—Brian and Maisie—who both worked in a prison; Penny, a woman in her 50s who led spiritual retreats for women, Ed and Morty.

"Let's get a move on," Morty said when he counted the attendees.

"Almost everyone who RSVP'd is here. We're only missing two men from this area—wouldn't you know, they have the shortest drive."

As he finished speaking, a car pulled into the parking lot. Two gray-haired men, tall and fit looking, got out.

"Is this the Atheist Hiking Club?" the man wearing neon green and purple shorts asked. Everyone replied "Here!" as though it were a roll call. The man on the driver's side bounded out, wearing a red t-shirt and black running shorts and got their hiking sticks from the trunk. Most of the hikers wore camp shorts with pockets, hiking boots, canvas rimmed hats and kerchiefs or headbands to catch the sweat.

Morty stood in front of the group holding a map. "This is a straightforward hike, as long as you stay on the trail and pace yourself," he said. "It's a three-hour climb, accounting for ten-minute breaks each hour. I expect we'll stop for a bite to eat at the top. Everyone stay with the group, follow my lead and you won't have a problem. Any questions?"

"Do you know the trail?" the neon shorts man asked.

"What's your name?" Morty asked him.

"Tom."

"How about your friend?"

"I'm Dallas," the man in the red t-shirt said.

"OK, folks, we've done this trail once before. All I ask is to stay away from mountain lions and bears!" The regulars laughed. "I have copies of the map in case you want to explore and don't want to get totally lost. This trail travels up to a height of 1,700 feet through a pine forest. Mostly the Douglas fir, not spruce. It's a misnomer. At the top is a ranger station used for spotting fires. There are several large boulders on the way, a stream to cross and areas of rock fields. If you have hiking sticks or poles, I suggest that you bring them. It will keep you balanced and possibly prevent any slipping. Any questions?"

"Yeah," said Dallas. "You mentioned bears. Have you seen any?"

Ed chortled when he caught Morty's eye. "Nah. There aren't many bear attacks, but you can't be too careful. We did come across a bobcat once, but he was more afraid of us than we were of him. You need to watch out for mountain lions, though if you stick to the group you should be fine. They like better odds than eight people—maybe just one or two."

Dallas's eyes widened. "What do you do if you see a mountain lion?"

"They're attracted to green and purple shorts," Morty said. "I'd change if I were you."

Dallas began heading toward his car.

"He's kidding!" Ed said. "Just don't run away if you see one, that'll kick in its prey drive."

"You want to get everyone yelling at it and it'll go away," Morty said.

"Oh," Dallas said, rolling his eyes.

"Ed will start the hike, so follow him and I'll bring up the rear." Morty winked at Colleen, who shook her head. The two latecomers walked ahead of them and Morty and Colleen started up the trail.

"You shouldn't tease the newbies so much." Colleen chided Morty as she hiked slightly ahead of him on the narrow trail. "They might decide it's not worth the risk."

"What's the harm?" Morty said. "It's good for them. Gets the heart rate up and prepares them for the climb."

The two were silent as they moved quickly up the trail. The best speed was one in which hikers could talk at the same time they were moving, but Morty liked to stay close to the group, so he quieted down as they rapidly climbed during the first leg of the hike. They stopped when Ed pointed out an owl's nest in a tree.

"Funny, I don't think you and I have ever had a real conversation during a hike," Morty said when they started moving forward again.

Colleen squared her jaw. "That's because you're always too busy chiding everyone and playing the leader. How come you're not in front as per usual?"

"Feeling a bit tired today," Morty said. "I told Ed he needed to lead for a change. I didn't sleep well last night. It's one of those days."

"Your conscience bothering you?" Colleen asked.

"Nope. More like my back, my knees, and my feet. Aging sucks."

"Don't I know it," Colleen said. "Back until about ten years ago, I rode horses every day. Now I find after the occasional ride that I'm sore for days. It's not fair—I so love to ride."

"That's the trade-off," Morty said. "You get to live, but you don't get to do all the things you love anymore. You have to do what you can at this age. How old were you when you started riding?"

"Six. I thought I was Elizabeth Taylor in 'National Velvet' and that I'd be a champion rider. When I was 13, my mother died, and my father sent me to a convent boarding school for girls. I only got to ride on holidays and school breaks."

"How did you feel about being with the nuns?" Morty asked. They were traversing a switchback trail that climbed higher and higher into the forest.

"I thought it was a raw deal," Colleen said. "I rebelled against a lot of their ways, sneaked out with boys, drank and had sex. I was probably the only Catholic girl in the school who managed to get birth control. But everything came to a head when I slept with a parish priest. They kicked me out, but he stayed on. I always wondered if he had a thing going with the Mother Superior, but I'm sure I'll never know."

"You must have scandalized them."

"You could say that," Colleen's green eyes glittered as she grinned. "My father wanted to lock me up, but he settled for paying for nursing school instead."

"We didn't have nearly as much excitement in the Temple I went to, but we did love seeing the Catholic girls at St. Agnes' School in Flatbush. Those plaid skirts were like a siren call for all the Jewish boys."

Morty pictured the groups of girls in saddle shoes and bobby socks, giggling and walking together with a swivel of their hips. He watched them like a wild species on the African veldt. But he'd only had eyes for Miriam, who had long black hair, dimples and a smile that melted his heart. He had called her his soul mate during their long marriage, so when she died he felt that a big part of him had died. But he'd gone on, as she'd wished, doing what good he could until it was his time to reunite with her.

"Sometimes I wonder whether I could have been a champion," Colleen said. "I have a daughter, Courtney, but she wasn't interested in horses, so I'll never know if she had it in her. Life takes you into the strangest places. She wound up becoming an attorney and works in Manhattan for a big firm. That's my baby, you know? She's a real doer. I miss her so much, but I have to wait for her to come here. She's too busy for me there."

"What happened to your husband?" Morty asked.

"Divorced many years ago. He's somewhere in Duluth, I've been told, on his third marriage."

"That's too bad," Morty said, wondering if it was or wasn't.

"I'd never been so lonely in my life as when I was with him," Colleen said with a bitter smile.

They hiked in silence for the next hour. Morty usually got energized about halfway through the hike, but he had to stop to eat an orange and regain his strength. He sat on a log near the stream. Colleen sat next to him. "Just can't seem to hit my stride today," he confided.

"Yes, well, I'm still waiting to hit mine. This is my fourth hike and I find it just as hard as the first three. Is that ever going to change?"

"Sure," Morty said. "The fifth hike is the charm."

"I don't know why I do it. I could just walk in my neighborhood or play pickleball, but something makes me come back."

"It's the beauty, right?" Morty said. A mule deer appeared several yards away and bent down to drink. He and Colleen watched. The quiet was punctuated by birdcalls and water sounds. A few minutes later, the deer bounded away.

"That does make it worth the trouble," Colleen admitted. "I'll tell you a secret: the first time I did one of these hikes, I was thinking about killing myself. It was on Granite Mountain. I thought when I got to the top, I'd throw myself off. Then at least there'd be people there so my body wouldn't rot in the sun forever. That wasn't long after Courtney left."

Morty was about to pop an orange segment into his mouth, then lowered it. "But you didn't."

"No. I saw an eagle at the top of a tree and I decided that I wasn't ready yet. Still am not. Maybe I won't. The eagle changed my mind and I haven't changed it back."

"Why?"

"I'm not sure. Maybe it was a sign. It seemed to be watching me." She laughed and shook her head. "Then it flew right over me, flew so close I could feel the whoosh of air on my face."

Morty smiled, unsure of how to respond. After he finished his orange, he washed his hands in the creek and they headed up the trail. Pain in his knee made him grunt, but it went away after a few minutes.

As they climbed the mountain, two more hours passed. Morty told her all about Miriam, her paintings, the way they'd dance on weekends until Miriam broke her hip. Then he spoke of how the cancer had killed her. A tear slipped out as he talked about the last days. "She was worried about me the whole time because she knew it would be hard for me. But she'd be proud of how well I've done," he said, sniffing.

"I'm sure she would be." Colleen said. Morty nodded.

"You should find someone who appreciates you, Colleen, it's never too late."

She started to say something flippant but stopped herself. Morty was sincere, so he deserved kindness. "Thanks for thinking that," she told him.

He gave her a tightlipped, grasped her hand and squeezed it as they stared into each other's eyes.

Morty hiked slower than usual, his breathing labored.

"I don't remember it being this hard to reach the top," he panted. They'd fallen behind the group, which up ahead had reached the top of the mountain and disappeared from view.

Colleen, ahead, turned around and waited for him. Suddenly, about 30 feet to the right, across from her, a shadow of a cat spring out of the brush. In a burst of adrenaline, he ran yelling "NOOOOOO!" toward Colleen, reaching her in time to turn and block the cat's lunge with his backpack. As it fell to the ground with a scream, Morty pulled the buck knife out of its holder on his hip and turned toward the cat, ready to do battle. The mountain lion got up and ran away.

"Jesus, Morty, you stopped it!" Colleen gripped his arm in terror. Morty nodded as he panted. "Let's get away, go to the top," Colleen said, grabbing his hand and pulling him up the trail. The other five hikers had heard the commotion and met them as they reached the summit.

"What happened?" Ed pushed in front.

"Morty fought off a mountain lion!"

Morty tried to speak, but he couldn't catch his breath. He saw the spectacular view of the valley ahead of them, its trees tiny, like the fake pine trees on the model train tracks his father had in the cellar of their Brooklyn brownstone. How odd that the image suddenly came to his mind after 50 years. He wondered what happened to that model train. He pictured his father, younger with dark hair, laughing. When his view spun toward the sky, he admired the deep sapphire blue that spread out above him. Blurry faces hovered over him, but the voices seemed to come from far away, then fade out as his consciousness dimmed.

Ed began CPR, while Colleen punched in 911 on her cell phone.

"C'mon Morty!" Ed yelled as he did chest compressions. Morty's face had no color, his arms lay still, his skin turning a pallid gray.

Several minutes passed, but to Colleen, they seemed like hours. Morty wasn't breathing, he wasn't moving. Finally, Ed stopped. He listened to Morty's chest.

"He's gone," Ed said, tears mingling with beads of sweat running down his face.

As they waited for the paramedics to arrive, Colleen sank down beside Morty's body and took his hand in hers. "Thanks, Morty," she said in a low voice. She thought she heard a whisper in her ear, "You're welcome."

Jibe
By Tony Reynolds

HE WAS REASONABLY SURE that his look of concern and husbandly demeanor was convincing. Her doctor was going on about the test they were running, and he hung on the doctor's every word, nodding at this suggestion, pursing his lips at this medical conclusion. But he already knew the outcome or the hoped-for one.

A quarter tablet every three days he was told. The poison would build up doing its damage slowly inexorably. Any greater dose and she would still be dead, but the molecules would pool in her organs and be detected. He had been assured, promised that it would be undetectable, untraceable but more importantly effective. And it seemingly was, he still had two tablets left.

The doctor went on. The liver, the kidneys, both were failing. Time was short, treatment options exhausted. Needed to find a cause. But the faithful husband knew there would be no discovery, couldn't be any discovery; ever.

It was late. She was sedated. He told the nurse he needed to go home for a few hours but would return to his wife's bedside that night. Would someone be here to let him into the hospital? Yes, the guard in the emergency lobby would let him in. Gratitude exuded from the obviously exhausted husband.

He showered and pulled on a pair of slacks and a tee-shirt. He had skipped lunch and dinner to make a showing at his wife's bedside; his stomach rumbled a bit. He could grab something out of the fridge before returning his vigil, unless, of course, they called.

He was particular in what he ate: she was not. It showed. She had let herself go, at least to his standards. He was still trim at sixty-seven, an enviable physique, a well-maintained body. She was 'relaxed' she would say.

He thought of the kitchen as two camps in a war zone; his was a Spartan's field, hers was a Bacchus' trough. He opened the refrigerator door and pulled a glass carafe of power drink. He closed the door and gulped down the whole container, almost greedily, eyes closed. When he opened his eyes to watch the last drops slip from its lip to his, he noticed a small note stuck to the bottom.

Her handwriting, 'Sorry dear.' A moment's pause. A cramp, a churning and nausea. His eyes opened wide. He dropped the carafe and spun through to the living room, then to his office at the further end of the house. He yanked open the desk drawer, and an empty bottle rattled around like the tail of a snake. And another note, 'Sorry dear.

The Chaplain
By Pat Fogarty

I ALWAYS TOOK MASS FOR GRANTED. It was something the family did every Sunday morning until dad's heart exploded. After that, mom could hardly get me and my little brother to attend school on a regular basis, never mind getting us to Sunday Mass. God knows she tried but as far as I was concerned, Mass was for sissies. The last time mom got me inside a church, I made such a ruckus talking and teasing my kid brother that Father Puglio stopped his sermon and gave me one of those looks; like he might come down from the pulpit and kick my ass if I didn't shut up. I buttoned my lip but after the way he stared at me, I wouldn't be caught dead in a church. Besides, as a teenager, I had more important things to do. Staying out all night and partying with my buddies Charlie and Dave took center stage.

Mom made excuses for my behavior— poor attendance and bad grades got me an academic diploma from Riverside High. I think half my teachers felt sorry for me, with dad dying during my junior year, and the other half didn't want me back the next year. After graduation, hanging out in Charlie's basement got to be a drag. NAFTA made sure there weren't any jobs in town; all the factories moved somewhere else in the nineties.

My pal Dave got arrested for breaking into a house. He caught a Judge with a bad temper. Dave got three to five for his first adult offense. I think the judge may have peeked at his juvenile record. About a week after Dave got sentenced my Uncle Joe popped in. I mean out of thin air like some magic genie, there he is in Charlie's basement sitting in Charlie's chair. He starts telling us how things were when he was our age and how bad he had it in Nam and all the bullshit he had to put up with. He goes on and on, I was getting embarrassed. Then he says we should do something with our lives, he tells us to go join the Marines.

I know it sounds crazy but that's exactly what Charlie and I did. Uncle Joe drove us to the recruiting station and the rest is history.

Today I'm a Marine stationed in a little sweatbox of a town called Jordan Junction. After boot camp, Charlie and I got separated. Last I heard, his battalion got hit hard up north near Irbil.

This Jordan Junction place is a smuggling funnel for the bad guys. Al Qaida uses this road to bring all sorts of contraband in from Syria. During the day hours it's not too bad, but at night this place is like Times Square on New Year's Eve. A huge caravan, three to four hundred Syrian cleared trucks come through every night. Big deal so they got papers that say they were inspected by the Syrian border patrol, they're as bad as their towel head brothers. Every once in a while, a rogue truck will join the caravan. Last week one blew up, killed six Marines at an inspection point and made five others invalids. Me, I'd rather be dead, saw a guy get both legs and some other stuff blown off in Nasiriyah. One minute he's riding in the truck ahead of us, next thing you know he's flying through the air like a scarecrow with no legs. Hit one of those I·E·D's, poor bastard. A medical chopper flew him out, we heard he lived. Damn, if we were going a little faster that could have been me.

That's when I found Jesus, not that he was lost but you know what I mean. I started going to services, made no difference who we had as a field Chaplain. If we had a Baptist Chaplain, I prayed with the Baptist. If we had a Methodist, Lutheran, Mormon, Born Again or whatever; that's who I prayed with. Today I pray when I wake up and I pray when I go to sleep. I pray when I walk over to inspect a truck and when I walk away from one. Yesterday they flew in a Priest to say mass and I couldn't believe my eyes, standing before me in camouflage gear was Father Puglio. He said Mass right in the middle of camp, my entire platoon formed a half circle around him. After mass, he said he wanted to have a little chat with me. I figured I was in for a sermon about being a jerk a few years earlier, but it took several minutes for his words to sink in when he said,

"Charlie is in a better place. His remains are being transported to Dover Air Force Base for embalming."

In the Spring of 2005 while sitting with my wife Susan in a Veterans Hospital waiting room in Arizona. A young Marine who had recently returned from Iraq began telling us about his buddy Charlie and how he and Charlie, two childhood friends, wound up in Iraq. Susan, a Viet Nam era U.S. Army Veteran and a retired nurse from the VA Hospital system listened to every word the young soldier had to say. When the Marine finished telling us about Charlie, I asked him if it would be ok with him if I wrote about him and Charlie.

This is his story and it's dedicated in memory of his buddy Charlie, and to all the men and women who gave all that there was to give.

Get it down. Take chances. It may be bad, but it's the only way you can do anything really good
—William Faulkner

Fog in a Trunk
By Gretchen Brinks

Letter to Claire Gireaux from inmate Joe Madera
9/4/2004,
County Jail, Santa Cruz, California

Hey Claire,

Wasn't I your Old Reliable all these years? Always there to help with the heavy work in your redwood forest acreage and that big ol' vegetable garden? And remember the 5 a.ms when I picked you up at your sweet-smelling home bakery in the damn fog to deliver your organic muffins to those New-Age-as-hell coffee shops? Good old Joe Madera, slow-moving, big hands and what you call "apple cheeks and clown hair," a guy living in jeans and flannel shirts.

Now I'm stuck in a crotch-grabbing orange jumpsuit.

We're both 32, but you're young and I was born old. You admired the boxes and trunks I built. You loved how I carved their lids "intricately." Making trunks was my labor, carving them my art, getting big bucks for them at craft fairs.

You loved the rare Brazilian wood one I gave you.

Now you hate it, right? Because detectives matched the sawdust on its floor to traces of it on little Manny's body and linked his murder to me.

I wish you didn't know any of this. You accepted me ever since we met at that 1989 Eel River Jerry Garcia concert. You told me, "You're a shy guy and a true original."

A damn loner is more like it; a soul who walked dark roads and deer trails to escape nightmares. All these years, you acted like I was the brother you never had. How could you never see that your good ol' doofus buddy was only a closed trunk of fog?

I'll never again walk your peaceful acres of redwoods or your red cabin filled with batik wall hangings, artsy photos, stained glass, pottery, painted silk, my trunks—all gifts from us craftspeople because we love you and the cabins you let us occupy for free.

You call us family.

I was safe living on your land, away from streets and crowds until you made me sell trunks at craft fairs instead of you doing that for me.

If you hadn't forced me into crowds, some kids would be alive instead of buried in carved trunks in a forest.

I can't stop seeing your wide-eyed, weepy shock when the Sheriffs hustled me in handcuffs to the patrol car on your dirt road. Now I guess you see me on the news. The serial child killer.

Claire, I never hurt those kids. I never put them through what I went through. I committed mercy killings.

Did you really not have a clue? You never asked about my past. "Only when you're ready to tell me," you said. You should've gotten me drunk and stoned, but no. You had to be tactful!

I owe you big time for giving me safe haven before your fatal mistake pushed me back into the world.

I'm going to show you what big old Wooden Joe's been hiding under his invisible lid.

Have you caught on to my fake name yet? Madera: Spanish for wood. I invented it the day I met you and was selling my carved pieces in that parking lot outside the Jerry Garcia show.

Who was Joe Madera before that day? A lot of him is still buried in fog.

My first real memory is a man with a red-brown mustache. He lifted me from a cold concrete floor and held me tight against him. His palm cupped my head and his other arm supported my bottom. "Bring a blanket!" he shouted. "This kid's freezing!" His voice was scratchy like his mustache. Something soft fell over my shoulders and he tucked it around me, soft and then warmed by his gentle arms around it.

I traced the letters on his badge. I started crying.

"You're safe now," he said, but my tears didn't come from fear. I knew he was different and wouldn't hurt me. I cried because I couldn't read his badge and learn his name, and I couldn't tell him mine because I didn't know it anymore.

My whole life until then had gone out of my head. All I had was a remembered image of a woman with a long black braid. She stood at a gas stove, barefooted and wearing a patched dress. She turned toward me and called, "Joselin!" Jose-*leen*, a nickname that means Little Jose.

Little Joe.

Was it me she was calling or one of the other kids I sense in that memory's shadows?

No matter. It's all I know from that life, so I kept the name. Jose. Joselin. Joe.

When my rescuer told me he was Sgt. Gary Mark, the name branded itself onto my brain.

I'll skip the foster home years, one the same as the next. all bad. No surprise: I couldn't make it in those pretty, clean places with rules and bedtimes and nicey-nicey smiles. Didn't know how to act. Threw fits without knowing why. Was baffled when foster parents acted shocked or sad or angry when I play-acted stuff I'd learned in the cold concrete place, though I remembered little of it except in bad dreams.

I ran away, ran away, ran away. At 10, I ran away for good. Social workers and cops couldn't find me anymore or didn't care to. I'll let you fill in the blanks about my life as a San Francisco street kid. You used to be a social worker there, you know how those kids survive. During those years, I didn't think about my lost younger life. I simply hustled and concentrated on staying safe and not getting caught for stealing or for crashing in abandoned houses.

Sometimes the fog inside me cleared, and I'd glimpse the woman with the long braid calling, "Joselin!" And I'd remember Sgt. Gary Mark's scratchy voice and mustache.

I guess I was around 16 when Max Levinsky stepped out of a low-down bar in San Francisco's Tenderloin district. He was an older guy, greasy ponytail, hands beat up and big-knuckled, scuffed work boots. Took one look at me with my hungry eyes and tight pants and said, "Son, you don't need to be selling your damn self. I'll put you to work and pay you and give you a room and no funny stuff"

Yeah, right, I thought; a john is a john. But I climbed into his pickup and damn if he didn't drive way the hell out to a ranch and olive orchard near Fresno! He taught me how to handle horses, work in his orchard and vegetable gardens and do scut-work chores. And damn if he didn't pay me decent money with no "funny business."

And Claire, the best part was, the old coot was a master wood carver. I loved watching him, so he taught me everything he knew.

Max turned me into a hardworking, honest-to-God human being. I felt so good, being busy and doing good work, that my thick, cold fog stayed locked deep down, almost forgotten.

Until the night when I was I think 18 or 19. Max and I were drinking beer and carving. I don't know why, but he lifted his thick eyebrows and growled, "Hey, you really believe you have six damn years of that so-called repressed memory shit?"

I'd confided that to him the first week I lived there. I couldn't believe he'd throw it back at me in such mean, ignorant words. I jumped up screaming like I was possessed, "I don't KNOW."

Then my knife was quivering in the wall next to his head. I ran to the barn and bolted myself inside, so I wouldn't kill him. Loved him. Hated him. Didn't know. He'd been like a father, so why did he turn on me with those mean words? I stayed in the barn for days, seems like, crying and wondering what the hell that fog inside me was hiding but at the same time scared shitless that maybe I'd find out.

Never talked to Max again. When I finally went back to the house, he was dead. I didn't kill him, Claire, honest, unless I caused his massive heart attack.

Did I?

In his will, he left me his land and house and tools. I found a realtor and sold the property. Then I filled the back of Max's battered pickup with his tools, carvings, slabs of wood and blankets, and I peeled out to San Francisco on a quest. "I'm a man now, Max, OK?" Like that, I promised the old guy, my old coot father-type, that I'd figure out how to open the box of fog he'd put me down for having.

It wasn't hard to find Gary Mark. He was still a San Francisco cop, only he'd become a plainclothes detective. No more blue uniform or big badge on his chest.

He almost cried when I told him who I was. He'd never forgotten me or my case. Since I was around 19 them, 1984, and acted like I was sane, he decided I was a strong survivor and had the right to know the truth.

What would I be like if he hadn't given it to me? Maybe just the same, I don't know. After all, what he told me already existed under my thick fog.

My memory still hasn't released clear images or the smells or the feel of the men Gary and his team arrested, but when he showed me photos of the abandoned oceanside warehouse where I'd been kept, I understood where my nightmares of cold floors and wet fog came from. All my life I've felt like gray, cold walls surrounded me. Sometimes I'd get flashes of sitting on a cold, gritty floor with a small window up high, framing fog so damp it dripped down the grimy glass. And that bit of memory or bad dream was linked to something bright that blinded me.

When Gary Mark told me my own story, I understood that damn light, all right.

The men confessed that when I was around 3 or 4, they'd bought me from my mother for a handful of hundred-dollar bills. "She was dirt poor, Joe," said Mark. "She and 10 kids lived in a cab-over camper in someone's backyard in Eastside San Jose. She hustled but she was sick. I got that information from your old neighborhood, but she and the kids were gone, and I couldn't find her. Neighbors thought she and the kids left the country."

He figured I was about 6 when he rescued me. "Maybe I shouldn't do this," he said, bringing a worn folder to his desk. "Really think you can handle seeing some rough stuff?"

"I have to know," I growled, and he slid the photos across the desk. They showed me that the warehouse was a small, junky place, not the vast universe of my cement-and-fog nightmares. Movie cameras lay on a table near a film projector aimed at a white wall. At one side was a single bed with a crumpled blanket.

"And these." Mark pulled out photos of a naked, beautiful, small boy: huge brown eyes flecked with green, bowl-cut dark hair streaked with copper, olive-pale skin.

Little Joselin. Little Joe.

Little me.

I felt tears I hadn't known were falling. "I have to know all of it," I said.

"You sure?"

"I have to know what's real and what's dreams."

He brought in creamy coffee for us. Then he ran a video the investigators had compiled from the films they found. "The prosecutor needed this for the trial," Mark explained. "It worked. The jury convicted the bastards and the judge threw the book at them big time."

There stood Little Joe, up close, beautiful body, huge eyes, face blank because he'd sent his mind far away. Then a man entered the scene.

I didn't watch long. I jumped up and slammed my fist into the wall.

"Joe," said Mark, "you know guys like them don't live long in prison. Both those pricks are dead."

Back outside in that 1984 July, confused and raging and crying, I drove hundreds of miles up the California coast, blind to everything but the road and what I'd seen in that video. When I reached the Eel River in Humboldt County, famous for pot and counter-culture, I saw a huge dirt and gravel parking lot. It was crawling with latter-day hippie kids selling jewelry, pottery, beads, food, tie-dye. Giant posters of Jerry Garcia hung against a backdrop of psychedelic colors. It was 100 degrees in the shade, but in the meadow beyond the parking lot, Jerry Garcia was performing.

So, I parked and began selling the carved boxes and beads old Max and I made at the ranch. When I was on my 3rd beer, I got into a conversation with a short young woman named Claire with amazing blue-green eyes, wild Orphan Annie hair and skimpy boobs. With her was her lover, a 19-year-old potter named Jimmy Medallion, and their friends Stan, a stained-glass artist, and his woman Nell, a weaver.

I had no idea then that you and I and the others would become friends who ebbed and flowed through each other's lives until we ended up years later living and working on our crafts in cabins on your inherited acreage near Santa Cruz.

But Claire, even on that day we met, it was too late.

A few hours before, I was alone in masses of people in tie-dye and selling carved wood while my mind endlessly replayed Gary's video of those men and little Joselin in the cold warehouse.

And then, across the crowded parking lot, I saw Joselin in the flesh.

I swear the kid was my 4-year-old twin: the mirror image of myself in the photos and video. The kid was barefoot in prickly dry weeds while his drugged-out, spotty-skinned mother ignored him, so she could keep selling quesadillas and beer from her rusty van's tailgate. Everyone around her was stoned and partying. No one cared about the hot, thirsty, dirty kid whose feet and ankles were bleeding from prickly weeds and broken glass.

Rage clogged my throat. Fog clouded my eyes.

No one was protecting the boy.

Bastards like the ones who took me would take him too. They'd destroy him, destroy his whole self. They'd leave him with nothing, but a lid nailed over a box of nightmares and fog.

Later, on the posters people put up everywhere, I learned his name was Onilo.

He was the first little Joselin I rescued from becoming me.

Justin
By Bruce D. Sparks

I FIRST MET WAYNE at Don's place through my brother Billy. Billy, being a member of the Junior Chamber of Commerce Mounted Posse, owned a horse by the name of Duke that he boarded at Don's place. Duke was a small horse for Billy, who was 6-foot-4 and well over 250 pounds. Duke was a curiosity to me 'cause he only had one testicle. Now why and how this fact came to be known to a 10-year-old boy in the first place is still a mystery to me some 60 years later.

Wayne was a man who had been around horses all his life. His knowledge of horse problems and their cures were always reliable and sound. But he was a drinking man and when on the juice, which happened from time to time, he was mean both to people and to animals.

Wayne owned a horse named Justin, a sorrel gelding with a lot of red in his mane and tail which seemed to be on fire. Justin was the largest horse I had ever seen in my life. He stood tall even for Wayne, who was 6-foot-5. Wayne had to reach up to grab the horn on the saddle to mount him. I was told Justin was a fine roping horse 'cause he was strong and quick from a jump.

The first time I got close to Justin he locked me over real good and wanted me to touch him. He sniffed around my head and neck as I rubbed his nose and stroked his neck. I felt like we would be together till the bitter end, he and I. Funny how those thoughts can come back to haunt you later. I liked Justin and I sensed that he liked me, too.

Don had several head of horses and was always looking for an extra hand to help feed, water, ride, and clean up after them. I would ride my bicycle down to Don's place to work with the horses. I didn't know a thing about these animals, but I was willing to learn and not afraid of hard work.

Wayne and Don worked together in the horse business and made it a practice of meeting often to work the horses and discuss buying and selling. Don, as president of the Yuma Jaycees, Junior Chamber of Commerce, was in charge of several of the other members of the Jaycees' horses that boarded at his place.

Soon I was introduced to an eight-year-old chestnut mare named Zona. I thought, because of being in Arizona, that was a fitting name for her. She was beautiful with a light-colored mane and tail, and very gentle to be around, especially for a kid who knew nothing about horses.

Contrary to popular opinion, a horse will intentionally step on a person and think it's the thing to do. I learned this right away with Zona and soon it became a ritual for her to try to step on me, and for me to avoid getting stepped on. I learned to wash, curry, and brush her, even to clean her hooves. I learned first and foremost how to clean out stalls and change water and feed. Zona was very tolerant of me and I of her. On her, I learned how to sit in a saddle, and how to control a horse and ride. It took months for me to gather this all in and understand the why of it all.

Zona was fun to ride but she had a game she liked to play. When nearing a fence or post of any kind, she would intentionally walk close so as to drag my leg against the object. I thought for some time that she couldn't see well. Once I figured it out, I would just rein her straight into the fence or post. She would give it a wide berth rather than bang her head. She could see just fine. I learned in that short time that horses don't forget things, and they can sense meanness in a person. I was not a mean person with animals, and I didn't know enough about horses to show fear.

Don had a stallion there named Patch who was said to be very mean to everyone--just because he could be. He never seemed to bother me while I was mucking out his stall. Then someone told me that males don't like to stay in a stall with their own droppings, unlike females who will stand in poop all day long and think nothing of it. So, if I didn't keep the stall clean, Patch would kick his droppings out all over the place and act mean. I guess because of my age and the fact that I posed no threat to Patch, he let me do almost anything with him and to him. I could water him down on a hot day, brush him, comb him, clean his hooves, and walk him around.

The one thing Don told me *not* to do is to try and ride him. He said that might be the end of me as a human being if I tried. I hadn't thought much about being a human being prior to that and I took the 'no ride Patch' thing as a challenge. I mean, he was my friend and I did things for him that he seemed to like, right?

One day when I was feeling particularly full of spit and vinegar and bored with the chores I was doing, I walked Patch out to the pasture. While hanging on to the hackamore he wore, I swung myself aboard and expected the worst from him. Patch didn't do a thing, so I gave him some heel. All he did was walk around with me on him like it was nothing. I leaned right, he'd go right. I leaned left, he'd go left. I leaned back, he'd stop.

This was not the excitement I thought I was getting into when I jumped up on his back. I got off and walked around in front of him. He looked at me while shaking his head up and down, with a look that I can only describe as "You are my friend." I had made a connection with an animal and I didn't even know how or why. I did love that horse. From then on wherever I went Patch would follow me. I could ride him anytime I wanted with no problem at all.

Then one day Patch wasn't there anymore. Don had sold him, and my friend was gone. Something I wanted with all my heart, in my short life, was taken away from me and it wasn't even mine to have. I couldn't even say "No, you can't do that." I was devastated over the loss and my two years of working with horses came to a stop. I put Zona and the others out of my mind and moved on with my life without even slowing down. Billy and I talked it over, and he came up with an idea. In Little Britches Rodeo, I would ride horses that I didn't know for eight seconds at a time, and then walk away from them if I could. Rodeo was my way of putting distance between me and the animals I loved.

I think about that black horse and the bond we made more and more these days. Maybe it's my age or maybe it's the need to remember pure, sweet days with a true friend. A friend that knows you for the person you are and responds with all they have. Every boy needs to have a friend that is true. Then he will know for sure those who aren't and give them as little of his time as possible. Don said the sale of the black horse was strictly business and I shouldn't concern myself with it. I have lived my life with people who have said that to me. It's business and not personal, you need to learn that.

Then there was the day that put a lid on my time with horses for the rest of my life. My brother Billy and I went over to see Wayne for some reason or another. I can't even remember now the reason for our visit. When we got to Wayne's place we saw Justin on the passenger side of Wayne's truck, kicking the crap out of the side of the truck with both back legs. I could clearly see a pitchfork sticking out of Justin's right hip. It was in pretty deep and bleeding a lot. The handle had been broken off and only the metal was visible, but it had to have been in his hip about five to six inches and was very painful for him.

Justin was on fire about the deal and had snot flowing out of his mouth and nose, and his back hooves were bleeding from kicking the truck. I could tell this ordeal had been going on for some time as Justin seemed to be getting weaker as he went. Then we heard Wayne yelling from under the truck for help.

Billy told me to try and get Justin away from the truck if I could and he would see about Wayne from the other side. Justin took an interest in us and came for us hell-bent on making us aware of his situation. Billy threw up his hands and started waving his arms and yelling at Justin to stop. But when that horse reared up on his bloody back legs and hooves, he appeared to reach for the sky. I swear he looked 20-feet tall. I know he didn't recognize us. That's when Billy and I ran for cover. I don't know why Justin came my way as I was running, but I knew I had to get on something or under something fast. I went under the rail fence beside the pasture.

Justin stopped at that point and just snorted in my direction. I could see he was bleeding from the mouth pretty badly and had several scrapes and gouges down both sides of his neck and shoulders, which were also bleeding. Justin stood there for what seemed like the longest time just looking at me, the same way he had looked at me the first time I met him. He seemed to say, "Who are you and what do you want?" Billy, by that time, had gotten to Wayne and dragged him out from under the truck. The next thing I knew, Billy was driving Wayne's truck out onto the highway as fast as he could with Wayne in the truck with him. Justin was almost tuckered out from all the excitement and loss of blood, no doubt.

I walked down the fence line toward the house and Justin walked slowly with me on the other side of the fence. I could see where he had gone through the fence, apparently on his way to go after Wayne, and I suspected the pitchfork in his hip was not an accident. I wanted to help him, but I also knew he was hurt. Did your Daddy ever tell you not to get to close to a hurt animal? I sure wasn't about to reach out for Justin right now. Even if I meant him no harm, I wasn't so sure he felt that way about me or anybody.

I worked my way into Wayne's house and called my Dad. He said he'd be there soon as he could. I gave him directions and of course told him about Justin and Wayne. Justin was over by the corral, just standing there breathing hard and bleeding. I kept out of sight from him and waited for Dad to get there. Dad drove into the drive very slowly and came up to the house. I met him outside the front door and showed him where Justin was.

He could see the horse was in serious trouble. So, he went in and phoned a veterinarian he had known for years. It wasn't long 'til the vet got there and looked the situation over. A Sheriff's Deputy was also on the scene as the vet had called them about being there to care for an injured animal without the owner being present. Things were getting complicated, but no help for Justin had been given yet. The Deputy had a Winchester with him and said he'd put the animal down if he got out of control. I didn't want to tell him the war was over, and Justin won. The vet then approached Justin with two syringes full of horse tranquilizer.

Justin seemed played out 'cause he just stood there and let the vet stick him with both needles. Maybe his pain was so great he didn't feel them. Soon he was down, and vet and the deputy pulled the fork out of his hip, with considerable effort I might add. Both rear hooves were split and busted, his shoulders and neck were cut pretty deep, and cuts around his mouth were pretty bad. All in all, Justin had taken a lot of injuries to get at Wayne for what we all knew was pure drunken meanness.

It turns out Wayne had been drinking and, as usual, was feeling mean and hateful. I guess he had gotten into it a bit with Justin over something in the corral. One thing led to another, and Justin got the pitchfork in the hip. Then Wayne got Justin's mouth over his right shoulder. Justin had bitten Wayne deep and hard. Justin's front teeth came down the front of Wayne's chest while Justin's lower teeth went down Wayne's back. The bite was deep and long, tore a lot of muscle and pulled bones out of place, breaking a few.

Wayne had lost a lot of blood by the time Billy got him to the hospital, but they saved him for a short while. Wayne's wounds became septic and within about three days he died. He didn't have much of a liver anyway from hitting the bottle so often and long, so old Justin really did him in.

The County Sheriff by court order went a step further with the situation. The death certificate for Wayne listed the cause of death as injuries and accompanying trauma sustained by an animal attack. Seems when an animal causes the death of a human, no matter what the provocation, the animal is doomed.

Billy and I were at Wayne's place cleaning up after the animals and caring for them as best we could when the Sheriff came to take Justin away. They brought a horse trailer and wanted to load him up and take him on his final ride. They were very clear that they had all the court documents and legal papers with them to do what they were about to do.

Billy and I were amazed that they would even talk about how right they were when that horse had done only what he could do, go after the man that had hurt him. Justin, being all banged up and bruised, was in no condition to fight a normal fight, but he wasn't going without giving them all he had in protest. He knew those men meant to do him harm and he wanted no part of their paper serving, nor any ride anywhere.

As long as I live I will never understand the ending of a life for spite. Wayne died because he was cruel to Justin. Now Justin must die because he defended himself against cruelty. I watched those men shoot Justin and kill him. The bitter end had indeed come, and I was there with him till then.

Just before they shot Justin he walked over to me and looked into my very soul. I touched him and rubbed his nose while he sniffed all around my face. I felt small, I felt hurt, I felt pain, and most of all I felt a kinship from him that only he and I could feel. Billy said it was the strangest thing he had ever seen Justin do.

Some say horses are really smart and act a lot like humans from being around humans for so long. I say they will steal your heart and your dreams about life faster than any woman I have ever known. Broken hearts about women will mend. Broken dreams about horses live forever.

I still remember Justin and his way of dealing with what he was given as his lot in life. Through him, I learned a very valuable lesson about doing the right thing, even at the cost of your life. He had taken all he was going to take from a cruel person, he did what he felt he had to do yet he remembered me and showed me his gentleness and friendship. Justin will live in my heart forever.

Narrative Essay:

Better Than Sex
Elaine Greensmith Jordan

I SAT ALONE in my office one morning, enjoying the view outside my window—a desert scene of manzanita brush and wildflowers—thinking of my Sunday sermon about the *New Testament* story when Jesus transformed water into wine at a wedding in Cana.

Startled at the sound of a knock at the church door, I opened it to a small man in grimy clothes.

"Where's the preacher?" he asked. "I got these troubles. Need money." He scratched his shaded chin, looking like a grizzled character in a western movie.

"I'm the minister here," I said, smiling and feeling pleased to help out a man of the Wild West. "I can offer you some—"

He took a step back, as if confronted by the evil eye. "You ain't no minister! I wanna see the *real* minister!"

"I assure you—"

"You're a *woman*, for Christ's sake!" he shouted and stepped back further.

I held on to the doorjamb, trying to look clerical. "Well, yes, but I'm the minister of this church, and—"

"I know why this church is going to hell, *lady,*" he shouted from his safe distance. "It's because of people like *you*!" His weathered face watched me as if waiting for me to levitate. We stood unmoving until he wandered away.

Sitting at my desk, I felt a dark pain press against my forehead. People like that poor tired cowboy, I thought, take me to be a sorceress. How could he? I'm a plain schoolteacher type, brown eyes behind glasses.

I took a long gulp of cold coffee, restoring my dented courage. What in God's name am I doing in ministry? Water into wine is harder than I thought. I sighed and heard another knock. Feeling some misgivings, I opened the door to Charlotte, a church member who stood holding a chocolate cake. She was smiling. The contrast with my former visitor made me smile too.

"They say it's a 'Better than Sex' cake," she said.

"Did you bring any wine?" I asked, enjoying the look on her face.

Did We Remember to Buy the Rings?
By Steve Healey

I WAS NEVER what you would call a handyman.

At a relatively young age, I experienced an epiphany. I realized I was the reason God had created plumbers, painters, and electricians. If the screwdriver or wrench wasn't working, I would grab my favorite tool the hammer and make fast work of whatever the project was. If there were parts left after I assembled something, I would put them away in case I ever found out what they were for. If the object I built didn't teeter or fall apart right away, then, in my mind, there was no need to worry about the leftover parts. Two or three years later I would come across the parts and still have no idea what they were for. Of course, I still couldn't throw them away, you never knew when you might need them in case something did fall apart. So, I would add them to an ever-growing stash of unidentifiable leftover parts.

Normally the most valuable and expensive player in my lineup of admired handy people was the auto mechanic. He was indispensable. If a washing machine broke, there was always the laundromat. If the wiring needed to be replaced in the house, it could wait as long as the house didn't burn down. But when the car wasn't running? That was a major catastrophe requiring immediate addressing. Even though a visit to the mechanic always seemed like highway robbery, whatever was wrong with a car had to be fixed. Period. No matter what the cost.

Though my step-dad was pretty handy with tools, for the most part, he didn't mess with cars and auto shop was not an elective in my high school. So, I learned nothing about cars except how to drive them. Auto mechanics continued to be wizards in my book.

My lack of mechanical knowledge came to light in a big way when I was in the Army. While in Viet Nam, I was assigned to perform preventive maintenance on our radio repair shop's truck. A much better preventive maintenance plan would have been to keep me from performing preventive maintenance on *any* truck. I was assigned to do a minor maintenance that included an oil change. I thought I'd done an ok job. I replaced the oil filter and checked the tires to make sure the pressures were correct. The lights and communications radio were working fine, all connections were made, and everything was in good working order. I drained the old oil, replaced the drain plug and put the new oil in. Everything on the checklist was checked and I was headed back to the radio shop feeling good that I had actually done an oil change and light maintenance on a small truck for the first time.

As I drove the truck back from the motor pool, it suddenly stopped running. The engine refused to turn over when I tried to restart it. After the truck was towed and checked out, it was determined that I had refilled the engine with a solvent instead of oil. There were barrels of each sitting right next to each other in the motor pool. I must have grabbed the wrong hose when I went to refill the engine. My minor preventive maintenance had turned into a major engine replacement. For the rest of my army career, I was never again assigned preventive maintenance on any vehicle.

Five years later, I'm back in civilian life and no more knowledgeable about auto repairs. I had a '68 VW that developed a severe oil leak. It was bad enough that it could have seriously damaged the engine. Young and relatively poor at the time, I had no idea how I could find the money to fix the engine. I had a good friend at the time named Wayne who was an active duty Air Force pilot and had actually taken auto shop in high school. He said he and I could rebuild the engine and save me a lot of money. Who was I to disagree? The price was right.

"VW motors are like glorified lawnmower engines. There's nothing to them," Wayne assured me. "We'll break that puppy down and rebuild it in no time. It'll run better than new when we're done with it."

"Neither of us has a garage. Where do you plan to do this?" was my question.

"On the dining room floor in my apartment, of course. The engine is small and light enough that we can pull it, put it on a dolly and wheel it into the apartment." And that's just what we did.

So, after buying a copy of *HOW TO KEEP YOUR VOLKSWAGEN ALIVE—A MANUAL OF STEP BY STEP PROCEDURES FOR THE COMPLETE IDIOT*—which I still own today, we proceeded with the resurrection of my car. According to the manual, there was actually a cassette recording available allowing you to compare what a normal VW engine sounds like versus engines with various problems. Even though it sold for only $6.50, Wayne believed we didn't need it.

Wayne flew C-141's out of McGuire Air Force base and was gone much of the time. During his trips, my deconstructed engine sat on his dining room floor, staining the carpet through the newspapers and blankets we had put down. When he returned from his trips, our "engine sessions" would start well enough. But then, as the partying began, we would veer off the intended flight path and end up crash landing after a couple six packs of beer and whatever else we happened to be indulging in at the time. As a result, it took almost two months to finish rebuilding the engine. Of course, other interruptions like realizing on a Sunday evening you forgot to buy the new rings, having to have the bearings pressed onto the crankshaft three times after bending them out of shape twice, and purchasing the wrong gaskets a couple times also tended to slow things down and give rise to the "Oh well. The hell with it. Let's just party" attitude.

Slowly, but surely, the engine went back together and finally, the day came to reinstall it. Amazingly, it went back in with a minimum of problems. It matched up perfectly with the motor mounts and everything reattached easily. We had installed new wiring, spark plugs, filters, even a new battery. We added the oil and checked and double checked to make sure we had done everything correctly. It took a bit of coaxing, but the engine finally fired up after 4 or 5 tries. It sounded so sweet that I thought about recording the sound on a cassette, so I could send it to the manual's author. I wanted him to know he had nothing on Wayne and me. I drove the car home the five miles from Wayne's place to mine.

The next day my friend, Donna, came over to my place. All proud and excited about rebuilding my car, I suggested that we go for a ride. I wanted her to hear how good the rebuilt engine sounded. Driving down a street just a few miles from home, I lost power. The VW just conked out. All of a sudden, I "flashed back," thought about the truck in Viet Nam and had a bad feeling.

I coasted to the curb in front of a house where a man was watering his lawn. I got out, walked around to the back of the car where VW engines were located and lifted the hood. The engine was on fire.

"Donna, you may want to get out of the car," I announced. "It's on fire." Needless to say, Donna, who would eventually become my wife in spite of that day's heated activities, was not nearly as calm about the situation as I seemed.

Turning to the man watering his lawn, who by that time had a rather panicked look on his face, I asked for help. He said sure. He responded by running into his house, coming back out with his keys, pulling his car which was in his driveway into his garage and disappearing back into his house. Evidently, he finally called for help because a few minutes later a police car came racing down the street, lights flashing and sirens wailing. The officer jumped out, opened his trunk, pulled out a fire extinguisher and instantly put the fire out. The new wiring, belts and plugs and all the work we had put in was just a pile of melted plastic, burnt rubber, and nasty smelling smoke.

About 10 minutes later, the local volunteer fire department finally arrived on the scene. One of the firemen, dejected because he missed the fire, grabbed a pair of bolt cutters and proceeded to sever the battery cable that ran through the firewall and into the battery compartment under the back seat. Even more major damage.

"You can never be too sure," was the fireman's self-satisfied justification.

Eventually, I did find out what caused the fire. There was a tiny hose between the carburetor and the fuel pump that we had forgotten to replace when we put the engine back together. It was old and frayed. It had worked itself loose and started leaking gasoline all over the engine which then caught fire. For the sake of a two-inch, fifty cent hose, the greatest mechanical accomplishment of my life had crashed and burned.

That day I learned to live by the axiom that it's cheaper to call someone who knows what they're doing right away instead of having to call them after you've totally screwed things up.

don't refurbish bathrooms. I don't build birdhouses or remodel kitchens. I don't even put oil in my car. I open the hood, look around, instantly get lost and close the hood again. The only thing I know for sure is where to put the window washer fluid. After that old VW motor, I don't mess with anything under any hood anymore.

So, thank you, God. Thank you for making all those carpenters, computer techs, and shoemakers. For the tailors, the bricklayers, and the refrigerator repairmen, who were the original pioneers of baggy pants. And most especially, for the auto mechanics.

And thank you to Wayne, wherever you are, for teaching me the value of earning enough money to be able to pay other people to fix my things right the first time.

Writers are always selling somebody out.
—Joan Didion

The River of Life
By Bruce Paul

Kayaking: I like the word. Unlike Tolkien's reputed fondness for *cellar door*—not because of the intrinsic beauty—but nonetheless, I like it.

Despite my experience.

It was autumn. Linda and I were on vacation in the Ozarks, in the remote woods of Missouri, looking forward to a week of relaxation. We rented a treehouse overlooking the river—literally overlooking the North Fork of the White River. From our deck, we could look down into water as clear as snowmelt in the Rockies. The river is spring-fed (Rainbow Spring alone pumps almost 140 million gallons a day into the flow) and provides some of the best trout fishing in the country.

And there is the whitewater.

I am not a fisherman, nor had I ever been kayaking.

Occasionally, a group of two or three kayaks would float by our treehouse—people merrily making their way toward Arkansas. I'm sure beer was involved. They would wave to us, and we would wave to them.

Early in our stay, I asked the proprietor of this little retreat community how he came to have the property, and he explained: After his father drowned in the river, he went to live in Arizona with his mother. Eventually, by inheritance, the land was his, and he began building treehouses and renting kayaks.

Drowned in the river?

On the third day, we decided to try kayaking ourselves.

The arrangements were simple enough: In the morning, be at the office at the appointed hour. A van would take us north to the drop-off point. From there we would float downstream at our leisure, back to our community in the woods.

In the shop, at the office, I saw the display of water shoes, but it meant nothing to me. I had never heard of water shoes. I also noted several signs informing me that—by law—the proprietor who rented equipment to me had no responsibility for my death.

OK. Fair enough.

In sight from the office, rapids roiled the river. We had a few questions. Clearly, on our return, we would have to navigate through this turbulence.

Paul, one of the staff, happily instructed us. "See that little channel on this side of that big rock? That's where you want to go."

"OK."

Sensing my concern, he added, "People do it all the time."

"And there are more of these along the way?"

"Oh, yeah. But it's mostly just an easy float."

"OK."

"Don't worry. If anything happens, just stand up. The river is shallow. Just stand up."

It wasn't the depth that concerned me. It was the rocks.

We headed north in the van.

The owner and another man, a guest at the retreat, sat in the front. Linda and I, and the other man's wife, were in the back. The road was unpaved for miles, until we got to the highway. The van bounced and rattled, and it was hard to hear any conversation, but I could make out some of what the owner was saying. Clearly a religious man, he was explaining how he wanted to provide opportunities for ex-convicts upon their release from prison. I think he was planning to set up a repair shop of some kind. The men could live on the property somewhere, work in the shop, and eventually return to the larger world with some skills and a new view of life. This was of some interest to me, because many years ago, I was a counselor in a maximum-security prison, and I wasn't sure about ex-cons living at a vacation retreat.

At the drop-off point, the sand and gravel ran smoothly down to a still cove. Easily, we were in the water, ready to go. We had rented sit-on-top kayaks—the kind you climb onto, not into (more like flip-flops than moccasins). Linda, being 80 pounds lighter than I am, took the cooler. I had only what I was wearing: swim trunks, a T-shirt, flip-flops, sunglasses, and a baseball cap. In my pockets, I had a camera, some cash, and a key to our treehouse.

Surprisingly cold, the river was as clear as vodka.

Photos were taken.

The adventure began.

Sometimes paddling, and sometimes just floating, we went with the flow.

Learning to steer was fun. Occasionally, we just floated backward, enjoying the view of where we had been. We would pass one another, taking turns being the lead. We took photos of everything: each other, a rock formation, an eagle's nest, the eagle majestically soaring . . . . Sometimes, in places where the river barely seemed to flow, we would paddle back upstream to get a second look. At other times, the flow quickened, and we would just float. Every now and then, we pulled alongside each other and passed the camera.

Eventually, we came to our first rapids.

No problem.

There is nothing like the first time—except maybe the last.

Now we were cruising. Occasionally, amid the rapids, one of us would hit a gravel bar, but it was always easy enough to push off with a paddle and return to the flow. I had fewer incidents than Linda, and I was becoming quite confident.

In time, at a sharp bend in the river, we decided to stop for lunch. We dragged our kayaks onto the shore, took the cooler to a shaded spot, found some rocks to sit on, and enjoyed a sandwich and a beer.

Then, it was time to move on. I removed my T-shirt. Linda took it and stowed it with the cooler. She passed the camera back to me, and I put it in my pocket. We were on our way.

I was in the lead as we floated lazily downstream. The sunlight was warm on my shoulders, and I was relaxed.

Rapids ahead.

The foam was to the right. There appeared to be a smooth course straight ahead. Here we go!

The next thing I knew, I was grounded on a gravel bar.

Not a problem. I had been here before.

But try as I might, I couldn't push off. I tried rocking *and* pushing with the paddle. Nothing. I tried to push off with my foot, but the rocks were slippery and sharp, not what I expected. This was not going to work.

I found my flip-flops and put them on.

I climbed off the kayak, so it would lift.

Immediately, it was ripped from my grip—taken by the current—and I was knocked down. My flip-flops were gone.

Stand up.

I tried to stand, but the current knocked me down and dashed me into the rocks.

Again, I struggled to stand, but the river was mighty. Whenever I tried to gain my footing, the current overwhelmed me. My feet hammered the rocks.

Tried again. Knocked down. For a moment, it was comic. Then, it became cosmic: Accept the pain, and try again. Only to be overwhelmed, swept away, and bashed.

A gallon of water weighs 8.3 pounds. A rushing river is incomprehensible.

By now, I had no idea where Linda was. I didn't know if she had passed me. Maybe she was still behind me, floating backward, admiring the scenery. Or maybe she was horrified, watching me crash through the rocks. Not that it made any difference. There was nothing she could do.

I am no stranger to chaos and drama in the water. In college, in the summers, I was a lifeguard. We saved people almost daily. There was even a time back then, in the flooding of early spring, when I took a life raft over a dam—just for the adventure.

Fifty years ago.

Now, on the North Fork of the White River, I was thinking: Flow with the current. Work toward the bank. As I was battered against the rocks.

I grabbed for a tree limb that reached out over the water.

But I was swept away.

I grabbed for another limb and was swept away again.

And again.

I clearly remember thinking: THIS IS SERIOUS.

Suddenly, miraculously, the paddle I was gripping in my left hand caught in something—limbs or roots—I don't know—and I slammed into the turnpike it made. The current pounded me against it.

Now, I was able to cling to a limb.

And I was not about to let go.

With my left hand, I was trying to protect my ribs from beating against the paddle. With my right arm, I was clinging to the tree.

Never in my life had I called for help.

Although futile, this was not completely foolish. There were summer homes and cabins nearby.

"Help!"

Was this like a car alarm in the city? Or maybe everyone was inside on the Internet?

"Help!"

The current ripped off my trunks.

Now I'm naked, clinging to a tree, banging against a paddle handle, calling for help.

Time slowed, and my thoughts raced, but I had no solution to my predicament.

Out of nowhere, to the rescue, Linda arrived.

Thank God.

She maneuvered her kayak near me, and I managed to pull myself across the bow—my cold white cheeks rising from the water.

Linda shouted, "Get off!"

"What!"

"Get off!"

"I'm not getting off!"

"Get off! I can't steer!"

"I just got on. I'm not getting off. I'm not getting back in the water."

Later, I learned Linda—my loving companion of 25 years—was contemplating knocking me off the bow with her paddle.

Eventually, we worked as a team. I climbed off—although still clinging to the kayak—and we made our way downstream to a spot where we could land.

I scrambled up the bank.

There I stood: naked, shaken, cold, withered, trembling.

"Put this on," she said, tossing my T-shirt to me. "Stay here."

Where was I going?

Linda hiked away through the trees, making her way upstream.

Cold as I was, I put the T-shirt on like I always do.

She recovered my kayak and paddle and returned to where I was standing, shivering. She pulled the kayak out of the water and stared at me in disbelief. "Not like that!"

"What? I'm cold."

"On the bottom. Put your legs through the arms."

So, I did, and there I stood in my T-shirt trunks.

Eventually, each in our own kayak, we continued, and soon we were in sight of the office. Well before those rapids we had seen in the morning, we pulled our kayaks out of the water.

"I'll be back with clothes." And Linda hiked off.

Standing alone, waiting, with large bruises from my shoulders to my broken toenails, I looked like an old Holstein bull—in a diaper.

At last, Linda arrived in her SUV. With clothes. Wonderfully warm clothes.

Amazingly, we had returned with all the equipment we had rented.

It has been months now. The bruises are gone, but my ribs still hurt, and kayaking memories remain.

I wish I could show you some photos, but of course, the camera is in the pocket of my trunks, in the North Fork of the White River, heading for Arkansas.

I now own a pair of water shoes—just in case—although I have no kayaking plans anytime soon.

Maybe next summer.

No Escape
By S. Resler Nelson

SHE DIED INSTANTLY, but I didn't mean to kill her. She fell, and I ran over her. It was an accident, a horrific one. Two others were injured, and I can barely walk. Now I'm in "the pen," scheduled to die. I suppose I'm here because of her death and my own ineptness. That's how we're treated in the end. No one comes to our defense once we're this far down the line.

The facility is packed with others—old and broken, young and unwanted, thin and starving. You name it, we're here. A pretty one with red hair gives me a quick glance. I'd limp over to her, but she looks angry and aggressive.

We mill around in the yard, baking in the hot sun, no food or water to fight over. Not that much oversight either, but there's no escape. A scuffle breaks out, and I avoid it. I'm crippled enough without getting knocked around. A long, jarring trip awaits us, and if I fall I'll be incapacitated. But then why should I care what shape I'm in when they put a bullet in my head?

Enough negatives. I think of my youth and my once promising career as an athlete. They said I was "handsome, a distance runner, highly gifted." I was their rising star, bringing in the big bucks. But the wear and tear on my body took its toll, and as I spiraled down the ranks, so did my favor. Eventually, I was just one of many cranking out measly earnings, another liability.

I'm half asleep, shifting my weight off my bum leg when the main boss saunters in and walks straight towards me. I figure I'll be the first one loaded in the transport. The guy's burly and strong, but there's no satisfaction in his eyes. He leads me out of the enclosure, into the open, and I see freedom. A field stretches before me, and I want to run again, just for the sheer joy of the wind in my face and my body soaring weightlessly over the ground.

Then I see her. She's tall and older, with a kind face. She approaches me, speaks a few words, and gently runs her hand down my aching neck and shoulder and leg. I don't flinch.

"He's got some heat in the leg that needs attention," she says.

"Sure, you want him? We've got younger, healthier ones."

"No, I want *him*. I remember when he was in his prime, and I watched him compete."

She hands the guy cash, and he counts it out.

"He's earned over half a million dollars. Shouldn't that have bought his retirement? Instead, he's slated for Mexico and a slaughterhouse," she scoffs. "He deserves better."

She eyes me again and walks me to her horse trailer. I stumble in without hesitating. As we drive away, I look back at the horses left behind and wish I could take them with me.

Finding Karen
By Dennis Royalty

Karen Stotts, you were just 17. I was 24. In the 43 years since our paths crossed at tornado-ravaged Monticello, I've wondered about your life. You endured so much.

IT WAS APRIL 3, 1974. I was a rookie news reporter based in West Lafayette, Indiana.

Notice I said "news" reporter. When *The Indianapolis Star* hired me that January, my hard news experience was minimal. I'd spent most of the previous three years covering sports for a paper that folded.

The Star assigned me to a one-person bureau, churning out news of northern Indiana. Short items mostly. Things like faculty raises granted at Purdue University, traffic fatalities and so forth. Break-in stuff. But April 3 seemed different. Ominous. Not a day for routine reporting.

It was raining hard, faucet-raining hard. Tornado warnings, too. So I phoned my boss in downtown Indianapolis, State Editor Ernie Wilkinson.

"Denny, this looks real bad. Better get to the state police post."

Understandable. The West Lafayette State Police Post was the emergency nerve center for a dozen-county area.

I got drenched scrambling from my Chevelle to the door of the post. Roaring winds made an umbrella useless. Not only that, it was dark outside, twilight-like. Odd for 3:30 p.m.

Inside, activity swirled. Police radios chattered and pointed troopers to calls for help. This was no drill. I found a phone and called Ernie.

He was about to send me to one of the most jarring experiences of my life.

Ernest A. Wilkinson was a devoted, passionate newsman. By the time I began reporting to him in '74, he was 49 and had been State editor for Indiana's largest newspaper for 14 years. On the way up, he'd chased hundreds if not thousands of deadline stories.

Breaking news was Ernie's lifeblood. Now on his desk were reports of a potentially massive tornado outbreak.

Ernie knew that Rainsville, a tiny community near the state's western border, was being torn apart. That tornado originated in Illinois and was rampaging through his territory.

Ernie also realized that from his experience, most tornadoes travel from southwest to northeast. And 65 miles from where he was sitting, he had a reporter not far from the likely path. Me.

Ernie guessed where this powerful storm was headed. He laid a ruler across the state map he knew almost by heart. He was searching for the most heavily populated area on the frightening route.

"Denny, head for Monticello. Call from there."

I remember no other conversation at the state police post, where troopers were overwhelmed by an overworked switchboard. So it was back to my Chevelle, back to chase a tornado, an excited 24-year-old suddenly handed a major story.

Danger didn't occur to me. It was sometime around 4:30 p.m.

Monticello, Indiana, population 5,000-plus, is the White County seat, hugging the Tippecanoe River. A 40-50-minute drive should get me there. Emerging from the furious rainstorm, I learned through radio static that this looked to be a major outbreak. So be alert, be ready to take cover.

Still, I saw little evidence of tornado-like weather. Neck-craning toward a brighter sky, I saw only clouds sailing at a rapid clip.

Maybe halfway there, the sky turned an eerie green. And yet it was calm as I approached Monticello. The time was about 5:30 p.m.

On the outskirts, a curiosity. A few cars were parked where the highway became a city street, right in the traffic lane. They'd stopped without regard for anyone behind. There were no drivers or passengers in sight.

I soon found out why. Parking off the pavement at the edge of Monticello, I walked into a nightmare.

Huge trees were uprooted, many resting on top of roofs or ripped through them. Debris littered neighborhood yards and streets, including downed power lines.

Now I knew why it was impossible to drive further into the city.

I saw cars overturned and others shoved into front yards, where they plowed deep gashes into lawns. The few people I saw wore dazed, ashen looks. They were emerging from cover, discovering what had happened to their Monticello.

A widespread power outage froze electric clocks at 5:17 p.m. I grasped the chilling reality that the storm had hit fewer than 15 minutes before I arrived.

Ernie's directive had placed me moments away from the midst of one of the most destructive tornadoes in the 20th century.

Instead, I was about to chronicle its aftermath.

I captured all that I could in my notebook as I made my way to the center of the city.

Each block seemed more devastated than the last. Weaving through rubble, I was dumbstruck to find the 10-block business area looking like a war zone.

The county courthouse, a tall limestone and steel structure that dominated the local square for 80 years, was crushed inward. A direct hit ruined in one horrifying blow an architectural gem and symbol of rock-hard strength. Its clock tower was toppled, and roof destroyed.

My training taught me to keep focused. "Get the who, what, when, where, why, and how," I thought. Surely dozens had been killed and hundreds hurt.

I needed a voice of authority and found it in a makeshift state police command center. I was told there were many injured. Worst cases were rushed to a local hospital that thankfully wasn't obliterated.

After a couple of hours of gathering facts and quotes, I realized I must call Ernie by deadline. But this was long before cell phones. Phone lines were down for miles.

Racing to the Chevelle, I drove for a good half-hour before I spotted lights in a rural residence. Figuring there would be a working phone, I pleaded my way to its use and called in my notes.

I spent the much of the next week in Monticello, filing news stories and using a tiny Instamatic camera to take the first front-page photo of my newspaper career.

My reporting focused on Monticello's portion of a much larger disaster. The combined storms eventually were characterized as a Super Tornado Outbreak.

Monticello, with approximately 350 injured and more than $100 million in damages (1974 dollars) had been struck by a tornado classified F4--winds reaching 200 mph--according to the National Weather Service. The big picture was 148 tornadoes affecting 13 states in an 18-hour period, the largest number of tornadoes recorded in a single event.

The Super Tornado outbreak resulted in 159 deaths (34 in Xenia, Ohio) and more than 6,000 injuries. Thirty of the 148 tornadoes rated the highest classifications, F4 or F5.

Somehow, there were only eight deaths in Monticello, despite being struck by a tornado that lay waste to an area of more than half-a-mile wide. The path of this particular tornado covered an incredible 121 miles in all, from Illinois to Rainsville to Monticello and beyond, although expert Ted Fujita later determined there were actually two tornadoes on the path (one dissipated, quickly replaced by another).

Forty-three years later, numerous memories remain for me. One came from touring damage with a local official. Amid rubble on the courthouse lawn, I spotted a heavy block cornerstone. Noting its date, I assumed it was from the courthouse.

Not so. The official recognized the cornerstone from another smashed building, a few blocks away.

Two days after the storm, April 5, was the day I met Karen Stotts.

Once again, Ernie Wilkinson triggered the story. "Denny, you need to interview the girl who survived in the river. Get over to St. Elizabeth Hospital."

St. Elizabeth was not far from my office, in next-door Lafayette. Seventeen-year-old Karen had been taken there for treatment of a concussion.

State Police had told me about Karen's incredible—and heartbreaking—story in time for my coverage in that morning's newspaper. Initial facts were sketchy and inaccurate (including the spelling of her name. That happens in a breaking story of this magnitude). But the most tragic elements were accurate: Karen was a passenger in a van that happened to be passing through Monticello, crossing a bridge over the Tippecanoe River. The tornado snatched the van from the bridge and tossed it into the water, a drop of more than 50 feet.

Everyone else in the van, the driver and four other teenage girls, were killed. But Karen, seated in the rear, managed to swim out of the vehicle. Despite the fall and swift current, she struggled through the water to safety. A woman near the river bank answered her cries for help.

The day after the tornado struck, April 4, was when I used my inexpensive Instamatic to photograph the van as it was removed from the river by a large crane. I later learned that one of the young girls' bodies was still inside.

By the next morning, April 5, Ernie heard that Karen had been taken to St. Elizabeth. I would interview her there.

"I think it's a miracle that I'm alive," she told me, and that quote became the lead of my page one article on April 6. It was my first front-page story as a full-time news reporter.

Karen was propped in a seated position in her hospital bed. She looked small and delicate. And, she was calm. Surprisingly so, I thought.

As we spoke, divers were still searching for all of her fellow passengers except the young woman whose body was in the van pulled from the river.

Donald Richards, their seminary teacher, was driving Karen and the other teens back to Fort Wayne, where she was a senior at North High School. The group had participated in an educational tour at Nauvoo, Illinois.

"The weather was calm, but black outside," she said. "We turned right onto the bridge and the wind started blowing. At first, I thought it was hail that started hitting us (the van). But it must have been sticks and stones."

At that point, Richards told his students to get on the floor. But wind rolled the vehicle over and over and off the bridge.

She remembered hitting the water, nose down, the rear window exploding, feeling someone else under the water, and then "we were swept away in different directions."

The van landed about 10 feet from concrete bridge supports, but Karen was unable to reach the structures as she thrashed to stay afloat.

She reached a point "when I felt I was going to die and was ready to die, but something clicked in my mind and I knew I wouldn't." Rolling on her back helped. Karen saw houses and tried to make it toward them. Finally, her head bumped a branch. She grabbed it and pulled herself to shore.

Reviewing my yellowed news clipping from 1974, I wondered if our roles had been reversed, would I have been as composed as the brown-haired teen I interviewed—only two days after it happened.

I closed my '74 article as it had begun—by letting Karen speak.

"I love each and every one of them very much," she said. "They are with the Lord. When He calls people, that's the way it is. He just didn't want me to go now.

"Someday, I'll be with them again."

Retirement brings the gift of time. This is what ended my decades-long excuse for not contacting Karen.

In June 2017, I Googled "Karen Stotts and tornado." There I found "In the Path of the Tornado," an article written by Karen Stotts Myatt and published in 2008 by *Ensign*, a magazine for The Church of Jesus Christ of Latter-Day Saints (LDS).

We connected on Facebook and spoke by phone several days before she turned 61. She called from her car, stronger of voice but with the same calm, straightforward manner.

After 43 years, we had another interview.

I learned that the young woman who converted to the LDS faith just eight months before her fateful trip went on to do missionary work and has been an LDS educator for 21 years. Karen teaches courses including college level. Donald Richards would no doubt be proud.

Karen lives in Sandy, Utah, about 20 miles south of Salt Lake City. She married Ronald Myatt a little more than five years after Monticello. Their "three beautiful kids" are 35, 33, and 31.

Are you OK, Karen?

"I have my moments," she said. "I still have some PTSD—getting worse, actually. I suspect that's because of my age. But I've never put this subject in the 'don't want to talk about it' category.

"It was difficult to stay in Fort Wayne," she said. "All the families (of victims) cried when they saw me." So she moved first to Salt Lake, then California, then back to Utah. But she keeps in touch with two of the families.

Karen recalls initially being taken to the hospital in Monticello. There, she was released because so many people had cuts and broken bones, while she had no readily apparent serious injuries. But the next morning, good Samaritans she stayed with noticed Karen forking a countertop instead of her scrambled eggs. That's how she wound up at St. Elizabeth, treated for a concussion.

Turns out she also pulled back muscles, an injury that still bothers her. "But I've led a productive life. I decided long ago you don't get over anything like this. It's always going to be with me. God helps you get through it."

She's never returned to Monticello. She was invited, but it didn't work out timewise. She did return to Illinois with her family in 2002 for the dedication of the new Nauvoo Temple, which has great significance for the LDS church and its members.

The original temple was destroyed in the 1800s, most of it by fire and the rest, ironically, by a tornado. The church bought land in Nauvoo in

1937, determined to continue its presence in the land where Joseph Smith and Brigham Young played key roles in the origins of Mormonism.

Karen wrote in the magazine that she carried an unnecessary burden of guilt for many years "because I was spared from death while four talented and lovely young women and our seminary teacher were not. Now, I felt healed. I knew I had been meant to remain on earth to finish my course."

I asked whether I had caused her further pain with our interview on April 5, 1974.

No. In fact, it took a while for Karen to remember me in our initial Facebook conversations.

As someone who lived through unspeakable tragedy, she had this advice for professionals like me:

"Sensitivity," she urged. "I cringe when I see how victims are interviewed on TV…questions get asked that reach the point of being crass."

That's not me, Karen, or at least not the journalist I've tried to be. I wish you the best, and I so appreciate the opportunity to speak with you. Again.

There is no greater agony than bearing an untold story inside you.
—Maya Angelou

Angel Fish, Guppies & Tetras, Oh My!
By John Maher

THE OLD MAN OPPOSED GIVING weekly allowances to his three sons. He regarded the practice as anathema, an absolute mortal sin, the product of misguided followers of the Dr. Spock spare-the-rod school of parenting. He believed in the tenet that nobody gave you anything. If you wanted or needed something, then you worked for it through hard labor. You earned your keep. He based this conviction on the hardships of his childhood as the oldest of four siblings of Irish immigrant parents. His father died at 39 years of age, leaving The Old Man the designated head of the house and chief breadwinner at age ten

With this as a fixed parental principle, my older brother Tom and I made money by mowing neighbors' lawns and shoveling snow from their driveways. I was six and Tom ten when we started doing this. Tom also had a newspaper route delivering Newsday, the leading daily Long Island rag. At nine, I took over his route. I had my own "walking around money," as my father called it. Most of what I made I saved to buy Christmas and birthday presents for my family. In hindsight, making my own money gave me a sense of independence and accomplishment at an early age. But, at the time I detested it and felt different from my friends and classmates who mostly got everything they wanted.

At some point, I decided I wanted to spend some of my cash on a tropical fish aquarium. Thinking about it now, I can't recall my motivation. My brothers and I weren't into nature or science; we focused on sports. It might have been that one of my friends had an aquarium and having one represented an acceptance thing. At any rate, when I told my mother, she was thrilled, which surprised me, because I expected significant pushback on the idea. Over the years, we had had about a half dozen goldfish swimming in little glass bowls. Added to this were many baby chicks and little bunnies in cardboard boxes, all of them acquired as Easter presents. The Old Man assigned my brother and me personal care for these poor creatures. Like kids our age, we paid attention to our duties for, oh, I don't know, 15 or 20 minutes. Then sometime later the animals croaked and promptly departed for God's Big Pet Cemetery in the sky. Mom cleaned up the mess and performed the burial services on our pet boot hill in the backyard.

So, my mother's positive reaction to my announced entrance into the study of marine biology came as a shock. She was overjoyed with the notion which was out of character. Mom could be a Pollyanna, but she reserved most of her excitement for her daily 4 o'clock silver bullet cocktails, martinis ("It's time. The sun is over the yardarm.") and dinner parties. Mom saw herself as a cross between Auntie Mame and the Unsinkable Molly Brown. And she loved Ethel Merman, baby.

Riding this wave of enthusiasm, we drove to the local pet store. I bought a 10-gallon tank. To make it an aquarium, I added rocks, underwater plastic plants and multicolored gravel to spread along the bottom. A miniature deep-sea diver attached to a filter to keep it clean. And a partially submerged glass heating tube, which contained heating coils to maintain the correct temperature. I also bought a fluorescent light that sat on the tank top and a long-handled wire fishnet to catch the four guppies I purchased, the cheapest fish available.

We put the tank, its components, and the four prized inhabitants on the kitchen counter between the breadbox and the three round ceramic canisters filled with flour, sugar and tea bags. That way Mom could look at the fish. It lasted there a week until she banished it to the den because of the filter's annoying hum and fishy odors. Moving the tank was no simple task. Filled with 10 gallons of water, it weighed over eighty pounds, but my older brother, Mom and I repositioned it without incident.

The den, also known as the TV room but never called that, was my brothers' and my special domain. At one time, it had been a screened-in porch on the side of the house connected by a single French door to the living room. After the birth of my younger brother Patrick, my parents converted the porch into a place where they could park three young boys. With the door closed, we'd be practically unheard during those infrequent times we were allowed in the house, which was in keeping with my Mother's principle that "children should be seen and not heard." (And the seeing part should be limited.) If we weren't outside playing or upstairs in our rooms either doing homework or sleeping, we were in the den watching TV with the door closed.

The den was a 12' x 15' room with windows on three sides, pine-paneled walls, a low white acoustic tile ceiling and a dark speckled linoleum floor. Built-in shelves along one wall held books and my parent's record collection of 1940s 78s and the newer 1950s 33⅓ LPs.

Mom decorated with an uncomfortable, torturous-to-sleep on gray Castro Convertible couch and two bent rattan armchairs and matching ottoman featuring ugly flowered cushions.

We placed the tropical fish tank along the den's long wall under the two windows that faced the side lawn. It sat on a black metal coffee cart that Mom had picked up at E. J. Korvettes, a new discount store on the Manhasset's Miracle Mile. Like much of Korvettes' merchandise, the coffee cart, a splendid example of Japan's 1950s industrial recovery, was seemingly produced from old Budweiser beer cans, unused Zero airplane rivets, and wobbly white plastic casters. It was bargain-basement and flimsy beyond description, but it conformed to my mother's economic doctrine of squeezing a buck until the eagle shit. She hated buying anything from Japan, those sneaky Oriental bastards had attacked Pearl Harbor, but she couldn't resist the price.

While Mom was untutored about interior design, she had even less knowledge about metal fabrication, manufacturing tolerances, and gravity. She had an associate degree in home economics from Pratt Institute that taught her to cook for 300 hospital patients but not for a family of five. Unfortunately, her course of study did not cover structural engineering or metallurgy. Although the black metal coffee cart appeared stable enough to bear a load of cups, saucers, plates, flatware, and cookies, it wasn't designed to support a tropical fish tank with 80+ pounds of water. But it proved an adequate platform for the tank so long as it remained stationary.

Over the course of the next few months, I added to the four-guppy fish community. I invested my newspaper route earnings in zebras, red mollies, silver tetras, blue bettas, striped angelfish, and a bottom feeder that looked like a little catfish. I bought two of each fish because I assumed they'd want company and anyway Noah had two of each on the Ark. I didn't get a second small catfish. It was too ugly.

A curious development took place. The more fish I brought home, the more enthusiastic my mother became about the fish tank. As her interest and involvement grew, mine faded, not because she was butting into my hobby, but because I was a 10-year-old kid with a limited attention span.

As I moved on to buying my first boat, Mom took over the care and feeding of the fish. Almost every day, she would appear in the den, turn on the fluorescent light, and sprinkle fish flakes on the surface of the water. Then she'd gaze on the different pairs of fish as they bobbed and weaved for the floating food and speak to them because she had named them. At one point, the guppies had babies. Mom was over the moon...

until a day later when she noticed that most of the fry had disappeared and realized someone in the tank was a cannibal. Crestfallen, this provided reason enough to have an early martini.

Disaster struck one Sunday afternoon. The Old Man was out of town on business and Mom was visiting neighbors two houses down the street. Tom, Patrick and I were in the den engrossed in the NFL football contest between our team, the New York Giants and the hated Cleveland Browns. As the game wore on, we reenacted plays from the game. Patrick would try to run the ball like Cleveland's famed running back Jim Brown. Tom would tackle him like Sam Huff, the Giants all-pro middle linebacker. And I would jump on top of both like Andy Robustelli, the Giants star defensive end.

This activity meant our bodies were flying around. The Castro convertible got most of the abuse and the bent rattan chairs, and its ugly cushions were strewn about in various directions. Then, it happened. The ottoman was pushed violently with a dull thud against the black metal coffee cart holding the fish tank. We stopped and watched transfixed. It drifted shakily along the wall on its spindly plastic caster wheels. Then it wobbled in slow motion back and forth, the to and fro movement speeding up as the wave action increased in the tank. The tank swayed like a metronome until the cart collapsed to the linoleum floor with a loud, wet thunk.

In seconds the three of us were standing there speechless, wild-eyed, mouths agape, our feet submerged in a three-inch pond of fish tank water that covered the linoleum floor. The flood was up to the doorsill leading into the living room. But there was no seepage out. Fish wiggled everywhere.

Maggie our pit bull barked once at the flopping fish and bolted from the room. As Patrick giggled at the sight, I intoned in a paralyzed state the proper invocation of "Ohmygod! Ohmygod!" Ohmygod! Ohmygod!" Then my older brother Tom, the family's designated manager-in-waiting and most cool-headed of the three of us, yelled, "STOP! Get the buckets out in the garage and grab the mop and sponges in the kitchen! GO!" Then he turned around and threw open the two windows along the wall that faced the side lawn.

Patrick and I returned to the den with the buckets, sponges, and mop and stood there dumbfounded with our mouths opened. Tom snatched a bucket out of my semi-paralyzed hand and scooped up water with abandon, tossing it out the windows onto the rose bushes and the side lawn. Recognizing a brilliant idea, Patrick and I joined in, bailing the fish tank water out the window like desperate men trying to save a sinking boat.

At some point in the operation, I said to Tom, "What about the fish?" My fish tank was still flopping on the floor albeit with declining vigor. "Johnny, they're goners. Scoop 'em up and put 'em in the bucket." I took the long wire-handled fishnet, and downhearted picked up my bettas and tetras and guppies and mollies and the lovely elegant striped angelfish. I placed them lovingly in a bucket. Then Tom and I gave them a burial at sea. We flushed them down the toilet.

We dried the floor with rolls of paper towels and put the furniture back in its exact place. We found the coffee cart hadn't broken. It had collapsed under the shifting weight of the water, which caused its shelves to rotate on the rivets that held them to the frame. Once pulled back upright, it looked fine, except for bent metal on the corners. We were even luckier to find that the glass on three of the four sides intact, except on the back side. It had cracked and given way when the tank hit the floor. We set it back on the cart, gathered up and put the multicolored gravel, rocks, and underwater plants back on the bottom of the tank, rearranged the filter and heater unit, and put the fluorescent light back on the top. Then we sited the tank and cart as it had looked. Once accomplished, we went back to watching what remained of the football game. When Mom came home, we were all smiles.

Tuesday night, two evenings later I was upstairs in "the boy's room," pretending to do my homework when I heard my mother's muffled scream from the den. I knew what was coming. Ten seconds later, she screeched up the stairs, "John!" What's interesting, she didn't call for her cherubic younger son Patrick the comedian of the family, or her older son Tommy, the paragon of virtue, the golden child. Oh no, it was the middle one, the one who was always causing trouble. She was beside herself. "How could you?"

I was uncertain about her being upset. Was it because we broke the tank? Or was it because when she went to feed the fish, the fish flakes didn't float on the surface of the water, but instead. they fluttered down to the tank bottom like snowflakes. At any rate, after trying to explain what happened without success, she gave me the ultimate rebuke, "Wait 'til your father gets home."

When The Old Man returned from his business trip, and I had to face the consequences, rather than taking my head off figuratively and literally, he was reserved. I chalked it up to fatigue from the trip. I was word-whipped for my stupidity and for upsetting my mother. But since I had wasted my own money, he concluded I was just a nitwit. The fish tank, its accessories, and the black metal coffee cart got parked out in the garage to gather dust.

Thirty years later, my brothers and I were having an infrequent dinner with The Old Man. He and Mom separated twenty years previously, their divorce lasting longer than the Vietnam War and bloodier. Tom reminisced about the fish tank episode, which by this time had become a featured and hilarious recollection for the three of us. Much to our surprise, The Old Man laughed and said, "God damn, that was funny what you did to your mother. I had a lot of trouble keeping it together when I had to scold you for it. That was really funny."

Mom, of course, never saw anything funny about the event.

The beginning is the word and the end is silence. And in between are all the stories.
—Kate Atkinson

Maynard Franklin's Passing
By Roger Antony

I RECEIVED A TELEPHONE CALL this past Monday from a man named Edward Cushing, who introduced himself as Uncle Maynard's attorney. He called to tell me that my uncle had passed away on Saturday at his home and that I should attend the reading of his Will in his Phoenix office on Thursday at 11:00 a.m.

Edward said that Uncle Maynard had written in the latest amendment to his Will that only his two nephews and niece should be present.

Maynard was one of my mother's two brothers. Her brother Tobias, seven years younger than Maynard, has been in declining health for several years. The last time I saw Tobias was at a family gathering at Maynard's house on Camelback Mountain six years ago. Tobias came with his wife Margaret, son Tom, and daughter Lucy.

On Thursday morning, I took the express elevator to the attorney's office on the eighteenth floor of the North Tower Plaza in central Phoenix. In less than a minute, I stood facing the Killingworth, Cushing and Roberts law firm receptionist, an attractive blond-haired woman who welcomed me to their offices, asked my name then gestured to their waiting area where Tom and Lucy Franklin were sitting.

Tom, an accountant with a local concrete supplier, rose and greeted me. He was tall, thin and wore glasses like his father. His sister Lucy, an eighth grade English teacher in the Glendale school system, sitting opposite him on a leather sofa also stood. She wore her auburn hair tied in a bun making her look older and more uptight than her brother. We shook hands as if we were business acquaintances, not family, and offered apologies for failing to keep in touch. Tom relayed that their father was in a nursing home in Sun City and their mother was living nearby in an apartment.

A few minutes after eleven o'clock a woman in her mid-thirties wearing low heels, a pinned striped black business suit with a red ascot approached us, told us her name was Marian and asked that we accompany her. We walked past several rooms with etched glass doors before she opened the door to a spacious corner conference room with floor to ceiling windows providing unobstructed views to the west and north. Before leaving us, she asked if we would like something to drink. In unison, we replied, "coffee."

While we waited for Marian to return, we stood shoulder to shoulder and stared out the north facing windows. It was another cloudless fall day and we could almost see Uncle Maynard's house on Camelback Mountain through a faint brown haze of smog.

Marian returned to the room a few minutes later with a silver tray containing a carafe of coffee and five glass mugs. She laid the tray down then left the room, returning a minute later with a second silver tray. This tray contained an assortment of pastries and bagels. From a small refrigerator built into the maple credenza that matched the south and east paneled walls, she retrieved a container of butter, a small carton of cream and a container of strawberry cream cheese.

Before leaving us she said, "Mr. Cushing is on the phone. He will be with you in a few minutes. Call if there is anything you need. My extension is 53."

My bagel was warm and delicious with a light coating of strawberry cream cheese. The coffee tasted like Starbuck's French Roast. I was standing by the carafe refilling my cup when the etched glass door opened and a man in his early forties with neatly trimmed jet-black hair stepped in. He wore horned rim glasses and a nicely tailored suit that did a good job of concealing his weight.

He introduced himself as Edward Cushing and quickly shook hands with Lucy, Tom and me. I was the furthest from the door, so I was last to receive his proffered hand.

In his left hand, he held a thick manila folder bound with a rubber band. Placing the folder down at the end of the table, he stepped to the refreshments on the credenza, drained the carafe, and added two packets of sugar before picking up the telephone. He pushed several buttons then spoke into the mouthpiece. "Marian, would you bring us a coffee refill?"

On his way back to the folder, he glanced appreciatively out the expansive floor to ceiling windows and said, "What a view."

He placed his coffee mug next to the folder, sat down and slid off the rubber band removing four sets of stapled papers. He handed one set of papers to each of us. At the top of the first sheet in big scrolled letters were the words, Last Will and Testament. Beneath the heading, the first line began with, "I, Maynard Franklin, being of sound mind."

I began reading and was on the third line when Edward Cushing cleared his throat and said, "Each of you has a copy of Maynard Franklin's Last Will and Testament. Mr. Franklin revisited his Will several times in the past year. The copy before you is his last recorded Will. He amended it on October sixteenth, ten days ago."

"Do you have any questions before I proceed?" asked Edward.

I looked to Lucy and Tom seated across from me. Neither appeared prepared to ask a question, so I did. "Mr. Cushing, will there be a funeral service for my uncle?"

"Per his instructions, there will be no funeral service."

"Do you know why?" I asked.

"Mr. Franklin did not want a funeral. His instructions are found on the last page of the stapled document before you."

I turned to the last page. Sure enough, my uncle had stated that he did not want an announcement in the newspaper or a funeral. He further stated that he wanted his body cremated and his ashes scattered in the Superstition Mountains. When I finished reading my uncle's latest codicil, I looked up to find that Tom and Lucy were still reading. I turned to Edward, who was trying to judge whether to start talking or to wait for Tom and Lucy to finish. A few moments later they both looked up.

Tom and Lucy stared at me as if I might be able to offer some insight into our uncle's actions. I gave a slight shrug then turned to Edward, who cleared his throat.

"Any questions?" he asked.

Tom and I shook our heads. Lucy said, "No."

Edward began reading the Will, "I, Maynard..."

According to my mother, Maynard had been the student in their family and the most ambitious. Her brother, Tobias, tried but never could match Maynard either as a student or in his career. She said that Tobias being the youngest in the family had suffered from the birth order syndrome. He was the least bright, the least ambitious and the least athletic in the family. In contrast, Maynard excelled at everything.

After graduating as valedictorian from college, Uncle Maynard played professional football with the Oakland Raiders for seven years before retiring from the NFL, returning to Phoenix and purchasing a small automobile dealership. He later bought three more dealerships and at the age of fifty was owner and CEO of four automobile dealerships in the Phoenix area. When he turned sixty-nine, he sold them to AutoNation, the automobile conglomerate.

My father worked as a lineman for Arizona Public Service, the local electric utility, and my mother worked as a nurse at Baptist Hospital. After a drunk driver killed my father, Uncle Maynard offered to pay for my college education. It took a big burden off my mother's shoulders, but she insisted that I could not accept my uncle's offer unless I worked for the money. As a result, I worked at one of his dealerships during the summers and on weekends throughout high school and college.

Maynard and his wife had no children. My mother always suspected that her older brother was too busy to raise kids and was content to lavish gifts on his nephews and niece.

Edward's baritone voice faded into the background as I reminisced. Moments later, I looked up to find Tom staring at me and realized that Edward was reading from page two of the Will, so I quickly turned the page. Just as quickly, another memory of Maynard and his wife appeared.

My parents rented an eight-person houseboat at Lake Powell for four days when I was in middle school. They made the reservation in early February for the first week in August and invited Uncle Maynard and his wife, Tobias and his family.

It was only the second time I had been to Lake Powell. After that, I visited the Lake at least once a summer. Ultimately, the Lake and the area were too inviting and when Elsie and I married, we decided to make Page our home.

On the houseboat trip, Tom and I were responsible for carrying the boxes of food and supplies from our cars to the houseboat. Just before we departed, Uncle Maynard told my father that we needed to stop at the marina. Unbeknownst to my parents, Uncle Maynard had rented two powerboats for the four-day outing so we could explore the small canyons inaccessible to the houseboat.

I spent much of my time during the trip in a powerboat. Once again, my uncle surprised us and made a great vacation even better.

When my mother and father were planning the trip, they considered a powerboat but decided against it because of cost. Cost never seemed to be an issue with Uncle Maynard. He was always intent on making the most of his time. He certainly made my vacation and I thanked him profusely when we landed back at Wahweap Lodge. As usual, he just smiled and said he was glad I enjoyed it.

The next moment I found myself back in the conference room with Tom and Lucy staring wide-eyed at me with a look of disbelief. Lucy's normally erect posture had crumbled, and her mouth sagged.

I looked to my left and saw Edward staring at me. I blinked a couple of times then shifted my gaze back to Tom whose hands now covered his eyes, his head bowed forward. Immediately, I knew that I had missed something terribly important in the reading, so I looked to the attorney.

Edward looked at me then asked, "Do you want me to continue?"

Nearly ten seconds passed before Tom looked up and, in a voice barely audible said, "Give me a minute, please."

Edward said, "Take as much time as you need. I'll let you talk among yourselves." He stood up and opened the door. Before leaving he said, "When you're are ready, call Marian or stop at the receptionist's desk."

Tom nodded then lowered his head while Lucy and I watched Edward depart. The room was silent for several minutes before Tom raised his head, cleared his throat and spoke. "I can't believe Uncle Maynard would do that."

Lucy added her tone seething with contempt, "He was manipulated."

"What?" I said.

"Weren't you listening? He gave his entire fortune to his arts foundation. We get nothing, nothing at all," Lucy said.

"Oh," I said. It was evident that Tom and Lucy expected to receive a portion of Uncle Maynard's wealth upon his death. Apparently, his decision to establish and fund an arts foundation precluded any inheritance.

My uncle's actions did not surprise me since he had been a benefactor for various arts groups and charitable organizations throughout his working years. Several times, he headed the Phoenix Chapter of the United Way and was one of their largest contributors.

Elsie and I had talked about my uncle on Monday evening. I explained to her that he had been a very special person to me: helping my mother after my father died, helping me financially to go to college and always giving meaningful gifts. It sometimes upset my parents knowing that my childless uncle's presents were always more sensible and insightful than theirs. As a result, I opened up his birthday and Christmas presents last, having learned that you always saved the best for last.

Uncle Maynard's practice of giving thoughtful gifts continued with our son who looked forward to his great uncle's gifts. Somehow Uncle Maynard knew exactly what a child wanted at every age and somehow always found that special gift. My uncle had been much like Ebenezer Scrooge helping Tiny Tim after the visitation by the third spirit in Charles Dickens' *Christmas Carol*.

"He gave his whole damn estate to charity," said Tom, "his whole fortune."

I responded, "It was his money. It was his choice."

"Don't you understand," said Lucy. "We are family. We should have inherited the money."

"Lucy, Uncle Maynard was very generous to us during his lifetime. We should be thankful," I said.

"Thankful for what?" said Lucy. "He was a senile old man. The lawyer probably convinced him to give away his money." Turning to her brother, she said, "We should contest the Will. He obviously wasn't of sound mind."

Tom looked at me and asked, "Todd, do you agree?"

"Tom, it was Uncle Maynard's choice. The money will help many people in the Phoenix area. I think he wanted to leave a legacy of goodwill."

"So, you think he was sane?" he asked.

"I think he wanted to give back to the community where he made his money. We all have jobs. We can get along without his money," I said. "You're an editor of an obscure newspaper in Page. Don't you want a new house, a new car, a boat, a vacation home and do some traveling?" asked Lucy.

"No," I said.

"You're a fool," said Tom. "We should have gotten something."

"We did. He gave us his love and his generosity while he was alive. That should be enough. Why should we expect more?"

Turning to his sister Tom said, "I've had it. I'm going to get a lawyer and fight this."

"I agree," said Lucy.

They rose from the table in unison and without saying goodbye left the room. A few minutes later Edward Cushing opened the door. His face did not reveal any surprise or concern given that two of the three people called to the reading of Maynard Franklin's Will had left in a huff and were contemplating legal action against his law firm and their uncle's Will.

Still standing Edward asked, "Are you comfortable with your uncle's decision to leave his entire estate to the Franklin Arts Foundation?"

"If that's what my uncle wanted, then I see no reason to dispute his actions," I said.

"Are you sure? Your cousins don't share your opinion," he said.

"I know. They expected to benefit from our uncle's passing."

"Todd aren't you a bit disappointed?"

I said, "My uncle was very generous to me growing up and has been generous to my son. He was an extraordinary man. I am going to miss him. I am comfortable with his Will."

"Good. I'm glad to hear that."

A moment later, there was a soft knock on the etched glass door. Marian opened it just enough to see Edward. When Edward nodded his head, Marian opened the door letting Uncle Maynard enter. I stared at my uncle in disbelief. He smiled back.

Since Monday when Edward Cushing called to tell me that my uncle had died, I had been thinking about him. I planned to write an article in *The Northern Sentinel* about him sharing with all my readers what a wonderful man he had been.

My uncle rounded the table, shook my hand and we embraced. Tears welled up in his eyes and mine. "Todd, it's good to see you. I'm sorry for the charade."

We looked at each other. I was about to ask why when he said, "It's not often one gets to see the future." He paused then solemnly added, "I was diagnosed with inoperable brain cancer two weeks ago. The doctors at Mayo give me two months on the outside. Before I check out I wanted to see how my family would react to my passing."

I looked to Edward Cushing then back at my uncle.

My uncle said, "Edward was following my instructions. He did a very credible job, don't you think?"

"I called my mother on Monday immediately after Edward called. She was terribly upset."

"I called your mother this morning while you were here with Tom and Lucy. I told her about the cancer."

"And," I said.

"She wants me to stop by tomorrow, so we can talk. Yesterday, I stopped at Tobias' nursing home and said goodbye to him. He did not recognize me; it's so sad." Maynard paused then said solemnly, "I wanted to find out when I die whether or not my family would contest my Will. I also wanted to find out if I could count on one of my nephews or my niece to head my foundation."

Maynard looked at his attorney. Edward nodded, "I agree."

I looked from one to the other, "Agree with what?"

"Who will head my foundation," said my uncle. "Todd, I'd like you to head it."

"Me?"

"Isn't it obvious," said my uncle. "Todd, we need to sign some papers today."

"Are you sure?"

"Of course, I'm sure. Ever since you worked in my first dealership, I thought you would one day take over for me. I just wanted to make sure, that's all."

"But I don't have any experience running a foundation."

"Don't worry, if Bill Gates' father can do it, so can you. You have discipline, character and people skills, all of which you will need."

Turning to Edward, my uncle said, "Can you have lunch brought in? Todd and I need to talk about the future."

Personal Essay:

More Eggs & Tomatoes
By Darlis Sailors

AS A CHILD I USED TO think being kind was not fighting with my brothers, not being selfish with my toys or not grabbing the last cookie on the plate. But as I grew older, my understanding broadened.

To be kind meant to be concerned about others, not as one big *do-all* but in *little seeds of kindness* every day.

Positive seeds/deeds can be scattered about, unnoticed by anyone but those who need them. Kindness might be an encouraging word to the weary, or a cup of coffee and a listening ear. It could be a card that says *Thinking of You,* or anything done to meet a specific need that won't let go of your heart.

Kindness can turn up in an act so small that you don't even remember doing it. Some people call it "doing a good turn."

In our early-married years, we began full-time ministry in a small church with a growing congregation. My husband was their first associate pastor. His salary was small, but housing was also provided.

The budget was tight, and utilities were high. We shut off two of the bedrooms to create more efficient use of the living room wall heater. Living near the church eased car expenses, but parishioner kindness had a great impact on the budget, too.

One of the founding families started bringing us homegrown tomatoes and a flat of eggs. We received them joyfully. One time as I was thanking them, the husband said, "We drive to an egg ranch up in the hills and it's just as easy to buy two flats as one." They continued their kindness for several years.

We left that church and moved out of state; however, ten years later they called asking us to return for further ministry. By then the church had really grown, but it was nice to see the family that had been so kind to us in our early years.

We were excited to tell them how their constant supply of eggs and tomatoes had blessed us. But much to our surprise, they said they did not remember doing that.

There may be no reason for you to remember your good deeds; however, they may remain forever in the mind of those who experience them.

We have never forgotten those eggs and tomatoes. In fact, those *seeds of kindness* have born much fruit over the years because we have tried to repay them by *paying it forward*.

Everybody walks past a thousand story ideas every day. The good writers are the ones who see five or six of them. Most people don't see any.
—Orson Scott Card

Fire and Snow
By Don Martin

THE DAY HAD BEEN GOOD. Lots of new snow, lots of sun, and a good friend made the day exhilarating and enjoyable. George and I had caught the first lift, had stopped for lunch on top, and had finished the day just cruising on the intermediate runs. Our faces were burnt in spots, and brown in others from the sun off the snow. Our legs were tired from skiing and were made heavier by our ski boots. Now it was time to relax, to sit and drink beer, to talk and joke, and to predict the conditions of tomorrow. We sat simply enjoying that feeling that the end of a day of skiing brings.

We sat there in old stiff wooden chairs in front of a huge fireplace crackling and spitting from the wood brought in from the snowbank outside the back door of the bar. This fireplace was large enough to garage my car, and it consumed enough wood in one year to build a football dome. We sat before this roaring dragon of a fire hunched forward staring into the flames with a pitcher and her offspring of two mugs sitting before us on a long low wooden table—a table scarred from decades of abuse from skier's boots and tired legs.

My friend George, and I were avid skiers. George would excuse himself as much as possible from his Volvo dealership in Bellevue to ski. A veteran of well over thirty years of skiing, he could handle any run under any condition. George loved to ski. He was always willing to try a new run or make that extra run at the end of a day. Red and brown from the sun and beer, his bright blue eyes danced beneath his bushy, salt and pepper eyebrows. We sat and relived the day, gesturing with our hands certain turns and jumps that we had made.

The Snorting Elk was filling with the day's skiers and the beer and conversation began to flow. The clomp, clomp, clomp on the wood floor added to the growing din in the "Elk". Soon the tables were all full of skiers; sweaters and jackets hastily discarded and spilling over the backs of the wooden chairs, some on the floor neglected for conversation and beer. It was 1983, and as the volume of skiers increased, so did the smoke from all the cigarettes, hanging a foot or so below the yellowed ceilings that, I swear, had not been cleaned since the day the Elk was built. Not the atmosphere one would find in downtown Seattle. No stress here from lawyers whining about a motion lost, or a deal gone awry.

A crowd had formed around the small bar waiting for their turn for beer, occasionally a skier would turn away from the bar, and clomp, clomp back to his friends, his hands full of mugs and another pitcher of beer, a smile on his face. Today was not any different from any other day on Crystal Mountain, and that full feeling of satisfaction and the glow from the beer began to settle on the crowd.

George and I soon had others flanking us in our perches before the fire. Sharing our long table with other mugs and pitchers, conversations with total strangers began. First a few comments about the day, then a continuous dialogue. This peculiar atmosphere would often lend itself to the sharing of the darkest of secrets with complete strangers. Stories of dark confessions could sometimes be heard at the Elk, however, this day secrets were not the order of the day, quite the contrary, today tall tales soon dominated the conversation, which brings me now to my story.

I had noticed, from early on in the evening, a man sitting next to me on my left, an older heavier fellow. He had sat down earlier with a mug and a grunt. He simply sat and stared into the fire, apparently relaxing and letting conversations float by. Sometimes he would grunt and shift his great bulk in the stiff chair which he sat, and at the same time reach to his mug, take a long swallow, and return the mug to the table. His mug, or what would be left, would land with a thump on the wood table, and his ham of a hand would then disgorge the mug and return to his giant face to wipe away the flecks of foam clinging to his mustache and beard. He was, as I mentioned, a very large fellow, and I noticed that his every movement was followed by a grunt or a snort of sorts. Apparently, any movement required a great expulsion of energy on his part, and I must admit, I wondered how such an individual would ever make it down a ski slope. George had taken absolutely no notice of this great fellow next to me and recited a ski story I'd heard several times before.

Nonetheless, I was delighted at the proportions that this latest version had grown. George was expounding about how changing snow conditions and the effects that sun, at certain times of the day, had on snow. George said, "The effects of morning sun on fresh snow is entirely different from the afternoon sun on old snow. And, as you know, a skier must adapt, not only with the proper wax but also with technique!"

At last, the great fellow sitting to my left began to add to this conversation. "I think, ahem, conditions of this morning, specifically on top, were comparable to conditions at Colorado, or the French Alps." Needless to say, I could not imagine this giant anywhere near the top of Crystal Mountain, not to mention the Colorado, or the "French" Alps.

"Certainly" George replied, "However, we here at Crystal, may only enjoy those conditions for only a few scant hours in a given day, and then perhaps, only for a day or two for an entire season."

George leaned back, the chair creaked, and he shot me a quick glance. He looked at the man next to him and studied him for a moment. The man continued to stare at the fire unmoved by George's inspection.

George asked me, "Carl, would you please pass me the pitcher?".

I handed George the pitcher, handle-first, and he poured beer into the man's mug then into his own. George set the pitcher down and sat back in his chair. The three of us sat and stared into the fire.

"Thank you, my name is David." George said, "You're welcome David. My name is George"

I then offered my hand and said, "My name is Carl, pleased to meet you, David."

"Same here Carl," said David as he shook my hand a couple of times with a firm grip.

And after a few seconds of silence, David said, "Ah yes, the Pacific Northwest, I suppose that we all must suffer for the beauty here that surrounds us. A minor thing really, when you add together all that this part of the world has to offer."

George and I looked at each other like 'What is this guy talking about?'

"You're probably wondering what it is that I am talking about," David said. Both George and I were a little afraid to nod our heads in agreement.

"I suppose," David said, "it is the changing conditions here that keeps my attention. What the snow is in the mornings is not what it is in the afternoons. Typically, by afternoon, no matter how perfect the snow may have been that morning, it will become heavy and difficult by afternoon. In fact, the snow can become so heavy by the sun that avalanche conditions can be created in a matter of minutes depending on the angle of the sun, the slope of the mountain, and of course the temperature."

George and I nodded our heads in agreement, like two young executives listening to a CEO's unsolicited bit of wisdom.

The Elk had become very dark by this time as the sun had gone down outside. The fire began to provide light as well as heat to the three of us sitting there. The rest of the skiers in the Elk had begun to quiet down and conversations became muted. Some people had left for home and the dark drive home down the mountain. Others were standing and putting on their cold wet ski gear. A few shuddered as their outstretched arms slid down the sleeves of their damp jackets. As usual, by this time of the early evening, the tables closest to the great wooden front door sat vacant. The Elk was warmer at other tables away from the yawning door. The Elk was certainly far warmer sitting in front of the fire.

In the flickering light of the fire, I watched as Big Dave reached over and helped himself to another mug from our pitcher. George reached down and poured the dregs into his mug. I reached down to the empty pitcher and went to the bar. I sat back down and set the pitcher on the table.

David renewed his conversations on avalanches. "Yes, the avalanche, the bane of all skiers. I have seen men snuffed out like fleas in its white fury." He turned his great head and looked at me, then looked at George. The light of the fire on his face and beard made him look weathered and beaten, his appearance gave his last statement legitimacy. He slowly turned back to the fire.

I could tell that George was affected. Normally George would have either called David's statement bullshit or would have come up with some equally sounding momentous statement. Instead, George stared intently into the fire.

At last George broke our silence. "I was in Europe, it was January, and I was skiing the French and Italian Alps for two weeks with my fiancé and some friends of ours." George sounded pretty serious all of a sudden.

"We were skiing at St. San Marin. The conditions were perfect. It would snow every night, then sunshine during the day. We took advantage of this and tried to helicopter ski whenever possible. We were having an absolutely wonderful, wonderful, time; endless days of untracked powder, sun, good friends, our youth."

"The hotel packed these huge lunches in big backpacks for us each morning, and at noon we'd find some vista and eat, drink a little wine, it really was great."

"On the fifth morning of this paradise, we were dropped at the top of this one ridge that I can't remember the name of and skied down to the ridge below. We stopped to rest and look around. It was cold and clear, I remember that. We were just standing there chatting when I heard a rumble. I looked over the shoulder of my wife to be and saw that the entire face of snow behind us had started to slide towards us in some weird slow motion."

"There wasn't any time, we all realized that immediately, we were doomed. No one spoke a word, we all turned away and began to ski literally for our lives. I never looked back and I doubt anyone else did either. I'll never know. But, the noise was terrifying, and the wind tremendous. I think that wind, the wind forced ahead of an avalanche, probably bought precious seconds of life for my fiancé and our friends. I think that it contributed to saving my life."

George stopped to drink some beer.

I must admit, I was a little shocked. I'd never heard this story from George before, and I've heard a ton of George's stories. But, I never knew that George had been engaged before Beth, and I'd known the both of them for over fourteen years. There you go, just when you think you know someone.

Big Dave seemed unaffected by George's story. He hadn't stopped looking in the fire since George began. However, he still had some of our beer in his mug. I took a couple hits from my mug. George continued with a guilty lilt to his speech. "I really wasn't the best skier that day, in fact, all the others were better skiers. I was just a little faster."

"I must have reached around 65 to 70 miles per hour, I swear. I've never skied that fast before or since. But I was so scared, not from the speed, all I could hear was this tremendous rumble, my skis felt like brakes, I couldn't ski any faster."

"I didn't notice the cliff until I was right on top of it, not that it really mattered anyway. I just went on over this 50 or 60-foot cliff, only I didn't sail like you see in a James Bond movie, I basically dropped 50 or 60 feet and landed in some deep snow. The base of the cliff was very steep, so I just basically sank into the heavy snow and stopped at the base of this cliff. I immediately got up and climbed back towards the rock face. Just as I reached the rock face the avalanche began to spill over the top of the cliff. I just became one with the rock in hopes that the cliff would offer some protection, kind of like walking behind a waterfall. It didn't take more than a second before I became completely sealed in my snow tomb. I had probably about 18 inches of space between the rock and the edge of the snow and I had ducked underneath a ledge about 2 feet high, so I had enough room to crawl back in forth about six to seven feet at the base of this cliff. I guess I was lucky. I was alive. I'll never know what happened to Ann. They never found a trace of anything."

"But I was as alone as anyone could ever be, and god it was dark."

At this point, George visibly shuttered, and I wished that I could turn on all the lights at the Elk, to help George finish his white nightmare. I was convinced that this story was for real, as never before had George sounded so convincingly honest.

George forged on. "I must have sat there in the dark, in the snow for over an hour collecting my wits before I even moved. Funny how your instinct of survival can kick in and really save your butt. During the whole deal, I still cannot remember ever consciously thinking ' If I am to live.... then, I must do this, then this...' Anyway, I took my pack off and inventoried what I had. I figured I had enough cheese, crackers, apples, and sandwiches to last about three days. Fortunately, or unfortunately, the wine was in one of the other packs."

"You know, I've always believed that if I ever got caught in an avalanche, all I'd have to do is free my arms, dig out enough room to breathe, then dig myself on out.

Simple. But that notion is fantasy, the reality inside an avalanche is very different. What really happens is that once the snow starts to avalanche it almost liquefies due to the heat generated by all the friction and the energy that's released. It kinda turns into a big Slurpee. But when it stops moving, for whatever reason, that Slurpee instantly solidifies, it turns to ice, rock-hard ice. So, I felt around inside my dark ice prison and discovered that exact fact, I was unable to locate any soft spots in the ice."

"I figured that I had two choices. Wait for help to come find me and dig me out. Help was unlikely as the helicopter had set us down miles from nowhere, it would be several hours before anyone noticed that we were missing, and if a rescue party was formed they would wait until light, finally if they waited until light they probably wouldn't come anyway because they'd figure we'd all be dead anyway. Therefore, any rescue effort would not be rushed, they'd take their time looking for our bodies."

"I had to figure out how to survive, number one. Number two, how to survive long enough to dig myself out. As I mentioned before, I figured I had enough food to survive. I was dressed for subzero temps, but not for days at a stretch, but I had nothing to chip the ice with. So,

I rummaged around in the dark and discovered that even though I didn't have the wine, I had the wine opener."

"Bravo." said Dave, "But what is a spoon against a mountain?"

George turned to David and said simply "True, but, as they say, I'm here to tell 'ya."

David chuckled, shrugged, and helped himself to yet another slug of our beer.

"As I began to chip at the ice my biggest concern was the spoils from the ice that I'd chipped. I was worried that if the walls of the cavern that I was in were too thick, I'd fill up my little space with ice. Another concern I had was air. With no source of fresh air, I'd likely suffocate. But air was the last of my worries, so I kept on chipping."

"So, I chipped and chipped and chipped and chipped and chipped. I'd chip for about four hours at a whack, then try and sleep or rest for about four hours. At first, every time I'd stop to rest or sleep, I was afraid that I'd never wake up. But I did. I rationed my food in such a manner that I'd only eat once every waking cycle, and then only a few bites. I had no idea how many tons of ice surrounded me, or how long it would take to tunnel to the outside. After what was about two days, I began to weaken, but not fatigue. I was surprised that I was able to survive and at that time I realized that if my food held out, I'd probably make it. By that time I'd probably chipped about ten feet into the ice wall. The cavity that I'd first found myself in had long been filled with the ice tailings. What I was doing was chipping a tunnel moving it along my side with my hands, then kicking the ice behind me with my feet."

"After a time, the tunnel behind me filled with the ice, so I had a space to work in that was about six or seven feet long and barely large enough in circumference for me to work in."

"I can't remember exactly when, but one time when I was chipping I struck something that was not ice. At first, I thought it might be a tree that had gotten caught in the avalanche, but I rapidly realized, to my absolute horror, that I had uncovered a frozen leg of one my companions. I never dug far enough to discover if there was a person attached to that leg, or whose leg it may have been."

"I started to go mad. I'd been in darkness for what seemed an eternity, and then to uncover that leg, well, it was too much. I started to scream. I screamed in desperation, in terrible dark loneliness. I felt totally helpless, that I'd been abandoned by the world and forsaken by God, ignored by Him, left to die in a frozen tomb with the frozen remains of my companions who I began to resent. I resented their fortune at having died so quickly and painlessly while I was forced to suffer in this ice tomb, digging for nothing, digging until I died from exhaustion, or worse, starvation."

"I figured that I'd never get out. So, I stopped and slept. I woke up and just lay there, I decided that if I was to die, I wanted to die asleep, not digging ice, digging, digging, digging. I was not going to die trying to claw my way to a freedom that did not exist. For all I knew, I had hundreds of feet yet to dig before I got out. I guess I just flat gave up. The hell with it, I thought, I'll just die. So, I went back to sleep, confirmed in my defiance against a pointless death. Comforted against a death that would only come from pointless digging, digging, digging. Assured in knowing that when death came, it would be on my terms, at my choosing, at my time. I was not going to die digging one more inch. So, I slept."

"When I woke up, guess what, I saw light. Not a bright light beckoning me to join my dead relatives and friends in some cosmic group hug, but a faint kind of glow. I knew immediately what it meant, the sun was out, that daylight was out there and that I was close to my freedom. With a renewed strength I attacked the ice. I chipped and clawed and dug and clawed, I took my mittens off and clawed with my fingers and nails, all the while chipping. I was still mad, I started to laugh, first giggling, then laughing outright like the demented. It seemed as if someone else was making all the racket like someone else was in that hole laughing in my face, but it was only me. I was going mad."

"Finally, I punched through. Shafts of the most beautiful golden sunlight began to pop through the hole I was making to the outside. God, it was bright and so beautiful. I stopped once just to let the sun's rays spill on my face. It felt so good. It felt like life was running into my hole giving me strength and energy. The madness left. The laughter had stopped, I was myself again. I finally had a hole large enough to get my arms out of, and I just pulled myself out. I flopped out onto the snow and sunlight. I laid on my back and opened my eyes to the sun burning over my head and stared into the white heat."

George stopped talking and looked into the fire. I looked down at my feet and shuffled my boots around, feeling a little awkward, but really feeling amazed and a little confused that my friend sitting next to me had kept this incredible story inside for so long, and then to let it out in front of a dying fire, and to a total stranger. I felt as if I were the stranger to George, I felt as if I really did not know this friend of so many years, and I wondered why he'd never told me.

Before I said a word, David, the beer bogart decided it was his turn to speak. "That was truly an amazing story my friend. I think that I've never heard another quite like it; however, I have one of my own, that pales in comparison, but I feel compelled to share it with you now." David licked his lips and looked at the empty pitcher of beer, the light from the fire dancing inside. I got the hint and went and got another. When I returned it was obvious that nothing had been said as the two sat staring into the fire. At last David began to speak.

"I have only told this terrible story once or twice since it all happened. It still pains me to think about it, much less relate it to two complete strangers that I'll likely never see again in my life. Yet, what better setting than this to share it, especially following the incredible trial you endured George. Mine is different in many ways, but, death is still the constant, and survival the end."

"I was in France. I was born in France in 1933 and lived there until shortly after the war. I had relatives in England that raised me after the war was over as there was no one left in my immediate family to carry out that responsibility. My family lived in the mountains, in a small village called Vincinces, and had for generations. My father was a carpenter. Anyway, the war came, and we remained relatively untouched by hostilities. Oh, occasionally we'd see airplanes fly over, and the Germans had a small garrison in the valley, but we remained relatively unscathed by the war. At least that was the way it appeared. My father and uncle as I discovered were leaders in the underground, but I never knew that or to what extent until years later. It was their involvement and activities that brought the Germans one day to our house."

"There was a train tunnel at the far end of the valley. It was not a busy train line because the rail line ended on the other side of the mountain in an isolated valley that had even a village smaller than our own. For some reason, the Germans had built something in that valley. Trains began to run with a frequency that was very unusual. The train cars were always closed, sometimes large flat cars would go by with large machinery hidden under great tarps. One day the train entered the tunnel and the tunnel blew up destroying the train. The Germans came in force that day and ransacked our village, several houses were put to the torch, the former inhabitants forced to watch. Of course, the

Germans were looking for whomever it was that destroyed their precious train in the tunnel. The violence escalated, several were beaten and tortured in the attempt to discover who was responsible. No one knew who it did, but that did not stop the Germans from their violence. The less the villagers spoke, the more frustrated became the Germans, and the more violent they became. Some men were beaten to death. Two days after the tunnel blew up, a Colonel from the SS arrived to expedite the investigation. He took twenty-five villagers to the town square, tied them all together, doused them in gasoline, and burned them all to death. He announced that twenty-five more would die in the same manner the next day if those responsible did not come forward."

"I'll never know how the Germans discovered that my father and uncle blew the tunnel, but they did. I believe that it may well have been my father, or my uncle, or both that somehow got a message to the Germans that they'd done the tunnel. They could not let more die for their own lives. The Germans came to our house in full force three days after the tunnel to capture my father and uncle. My mother, aunt, and my sisters had left months before to work in factories near Paris. Besides myself, there was only my father, my uncle, and my brother at the farm. The Germans roared up in big trucks. Soldiers spilled from the backs of the trucks running to each side to form a line. The line approached. My father yelled at my brother and me to run to the mountains and not come back until it was safe. We ran to the barn behind the house. We heard gunfire. We ran into the barn and grabbed our skis. The gunfire got louder. We took our skis and ran into the forest behind our farm. The Germans were too busy shooting up the house to notice our escape. There was a trail through the woods that led up to the mountain. I was so scared. I never looked back, I just followed my brother. We started climbing up the mountain and out of the forest. We looked down and saw that our house was on fire and that the Germans had the house surrounded. By the looks of their movements, it was obvious to us that it was over for my father and uncle. My brother urged me to keep moving as it was likely that the Germans would discover our tracks and come after us. I was crying, and my brother told me to stop, that there was time for that later, but that now we had to keep climbing to escape the Germans that were sure to follow."

"We were above the tree line out in open rocks and snow when the Germans spotted us from below. It was a long way down and a few shots were fired in our direction, but none came close. The whistling bullets made us climb faster. We climbed for our lives, our only hope of escape was to reach the top ridgeline and ski down the other side to safety in the forest below. I was confident that given a slight advantage, we could lose the Germans in the large forest on the other side. This forest we both knew very well as we had both spent hours and hours exploring and playing games beneath the green cover."

"Suddenly, the snow around us began to erupt. Small fans of snow jumped around us. Somehow the Germans had caught up to us. I saw my brother throw his arms open wide and he flung his skis into the snow. He fell face down. I saw tiny holes in his jacket. But I could not stop running, I was so scared. The Germans were so close that I could hear the muffled thumps of their boots pushing through the deep snow."

"I finally reached the ridgeline and threw my skis on my feet. Understand, that skis, bindings, and boots were primitive compared to that of today, so it took only a few seconds. Just as I turned to ski down the other side I saw the helmets of two Germans bobbing behind the snow ridge after me. I turned the other way and looked down the other side. To my horror, I realized that I stood over a cliff of some twenty meters and below that the snow started in a very, very steep descent to the edge of the forest. The snowfield from the bottom of the cliff to the edge of the forest was about 1000 meters."

"I looked around trying to figure out another way down when the Germans finally popped up over the ridge and began shooting at me. I had no choice, so I jumped off the cliff, tips down determined to die at the mountain's hand, not by a German bullet."

"I soared down past the face of the cliff about a meter off. All I could see was the snowfield rushing up to meet me. I could hear the popping of the German weapons, but they missed, I guess that I was falling too fast for them to hit me. I knew that once I met the bottom, fell into the snow, that it would be all over, if I managed to survive the fall, in whatever condition it was likely that the Germans would finish me off."

"But the strangest thing happened to me. The snow at the bottom of the cliff was very fresh and very, very light. The wind had blown up the valley all night, so several meters of the absolute lightest snow had piled up at the base of the cliff. It was still very early in the morning and very cold, but the sun was shining. The snow was as light as dust and several meters thick, sucha condition is very rare. I dropped in this white fog and kept on going, almost tunneling beneath the surface. I cannot remember for how long, it seemed forever, but I continued my descent through this air light snow. I could not see a thing and I choked and coughed, but I continued on down the hill under a fog-like mist of powdered snow. The Germans could see nothing."

"Finally, I popped through this white dust, this layer of very unique snow, several hundred meters from the base of the cliff, but I dared not stop. The shooting renewed and several bullets came near but not close. I was too far away. I made some turns to throw off their aim and disappeared into the forest and escaped the Germans."

"Incredible!" stammered George. I thought a little too quickly, given the story that I'd just heard from George.

That's when David slowly turned his great head in our direction, his eyes were slightly closed, and he said, "But true."

Swordtail
By Elizabeth Allbright

ANDY SLUNG THE KAKAI STRAP of her gas mask over her left shoulder, placed her sandals on top of her school books and walked barefoot down the cement walk to Haena Drive. The lei-hua was blooming after the early morning rain on the slope beside the bomb shelter door. As she leaned forward to check for buds, her gas mask swung forward and banged against the tender stalk. The flower shook. Sandy whispered, "It's okay. It's okay."

Sandy looked around the corner toward the Hammaker's yard. Mynahs had set up a scolding chorus. A mynah shot out of a tall avocado tree and dived, pecking her on the head. Sandy felt the top of her head. What have I forgotten? She looked down at her books and shoes. My lunch! She ran up the walk and into her house, slamming the screen door. The lunch box was on the kitchen counter where her mother had put it before she went to work at American Factors in Honolulu that morning. It was the same lunch every day, but Sandy checked to make sure. She felt warm, comfortable anticipation in her stomach. "My favorites," she murmured, thinking of her mom and the homey dessert of oatmeal animal cookies.

On her way down the steep asphalt slope to Atherton Street where she could walk on soft Chinese grass for a while, Sandy thought about her Saturday plans. A fishing expedition to the jungle behind Manoa Valley with Billy. They would ride their bikes to that special place where the strawberry guavas grew, then carry their jars to the stream. She pictured the guppies opening and closing their mouths in the rushing water. Their heads would be pointed in the same direction as they sunned in the shallow, sandy places. But they were almost too easy to catch. Maybe some swordtails would swim into the little new net Daddy had made. Sandy imagined her hand on the coat-hanger-wire handle, dipping deftly in to catch the wily, inch-long fish who wore rainbow shimmers on their silver bodies. To catch one of them would be exciting.

The only interesting thing at school that day was weighing and measuring. Sandy felt good about seeing how much she had gained over the summer vacation. Her old weight when she was nine at the beginning of the year had been sixty-five pounds. Now, a year later in 1944, she weighed seventy-nine pounds. That was a big gain, considering she had been one of the smallest in the class last year. A boy in sixth grade called her fatso when he passed her in the hall that morning. She looked down at her body as she walked home that afternoon to see what he meant. After having Mom and Daddy worry about how thin and small she was for so long, it was really strange to be called fat. The only fat place she could see was in front where the gas mask strap crossed her chest. It hurt there and itched most of the time.

She had been told that the gas masks had been issued to the civilians and military of Oahu when a gas attack by the Japanese became an imminent possibility. The threat of mustard gas scared everybody. The government announced that there was little that could be done to prevent the gas from burning the skin, but it was hoped that the masks would protect the lungs. Sandy listened in horror as her teacher explained that tubs of water would be readied for the children to climb into naked, except for the monster-faced masks, of course. Sandy privately felt that it wouldn't work, besides the school didn't own any tubs. She had decided that being naked in a tub of water with her classmates was worse than getting burned.

She shifted her books to her other hand. Today the class had had a warning from the school nurse to watch out for mosquitos. It seemed funny that a little thing like a mosquito could put its teeny, pointy mouth into your skin to suck your blood, and then leave behind germs to make you sick. Maybe weak, half-sick people were the only ones to get it. "Not me," she said.

Every puddle got a thorough inspection. She zig-zagged home checking for signs of stagnant water. She took a shortcut across a ditch choked with sticky blue plumbago and spied a rusty can filled with rainwater. Two worm-like mosquito larvae wriggled menacingly in it. With a shout, she tipped the can out onto the ground. "There, you boogers! You can't get anybody sick now because you will never grow up!" She stared at the larvae, small as thin rice grains moving feebly on the wet earth.

When she climbed to the top of Haena Drive, Sandy saw Taffy, the next-doors' golden retriever, sniffing at the croton bushes near her front door. Taffy had a habit of growling and chasing her. Sandy had followed her dad's suggestion that she not let out any fear. She kept it locked behind her skin. She advanced steadily toward the dog. By walking briskly past him, she was able to open the front door of her house and slip out of his reach.

"Darn this war," she said to her panda puppet. "I wish I could go swimming. We used to live down near the beach, but ever since Pearl Harbor, we've lived in this house. Now I have to take two buses to get to Waikiki. Besides, I don't like it down there much anymore. So much barbed wire, so many soldiers and sailors. Sometimes they look at me in a funny way. One time I was wearing my bathing suit and stopped walking on the street to fix my sandal strap. A jeep full of men came by. One man holding a camera took my picture. The men all hooted and whistled." She waited to see how the panda took that information. His embroidered mouth seemed to turn down. Sandy sighed. Another hour before either Mom or Daddy would be home. She got a pencil out of her desk drawer and started to do her math homework.

The next day, a piece of cardboard clipped to the spokes of her bike's front wheel played ticking music. It went with the feeling that Sandy always felt when she was starting out on an adventure – a kind of tickling just under her ribs and on the soles of her feet. She pedaled hard up a rise, then coasted down toward Lanihuli Drive where Billy lived. She parked her bike by the front steps of his house and then walked around the house until she was under his bedroom window. "BILLY...BILLY...CAN YOU COME OUT AND PLAY?" Sandy was just gathering breath for another round of calling when Billy himself came alongside wheeling his bike. His bike basket was full of glass jars, just like hers was.

"Here I am. All ready. My mom put some seemoy and some avocado sandwiches in a bag for us to eat while we're fishing." Billy's blond hair stuck up in back. His mom called it a cowlick. On his tan face was a sprinkling of eager freckles. Sandy could tell he was excited because his eyes behind their thick glasses were blinking rapidly. The hated gas mask was left behind under her bed. Sandy laughed. It was going to be a good day. "C'mon, Billy, what are you waiting for?" They pushed off, giggling as the jars clinked in rhythm to their churning feet.

With an asthmatic wheeze, the Woodlawn bus pulled up to its last stop at the end of Manoa Valley. The driver stood to turn his sign around. The thin Marine got out of his seat. "I'll get off here." He was wearing a perfectly pressed regulation uniform with gleaming spit-polished shoes. The bus driver shifted his belly behind the wheel and grinned. "Pupuli," he said. Some of the kamaainas onboard snickered. The Marine patted the gun at his waist. "Going to do some target practice," he said. He knew that respect for his non-regulation gun, for his shiny metal buttons and bars kept their voices friendly, but their fingers made circles in the air next to their ears. They laughed, wiggling in their seats as if he was in on the joke too. "Pupuli haoli," the bus driver said again. "You're not gonna look so pretty when you walk back to town."

"It's okay," said the Marine. "I can hitch back before black-out." He stepped onto the damp, reddish soil of the jungle that sprawled in ancient disorder at the foot of the mountains. He waited until the bus had turned around, rolling up a rise and out of sight, then he turned to the tangle of trees and vines. He thought about hitching a ride back to the rehab center and shook his head. "Not if I can help it," he said aloud.

The jungle's shade lay only a few feet away, but he hesitated. He needed to clear his mind for what he wanted to do. He went back to last night. He had been resting on a rattan lounge out on the beach front, long after all the other men had gone into the blackout-sealed billet. He knew they would read, play cards or just stare, anticipating the dreams that made them scream in the night. Turning in his hospital issue cot, he'd awakened many times to his own crying. The shrapnel wounds in his legs were healed now. But his brain was hot with memories of the Battle of Midway. Like a radio without a knob to turn it off, it played on and on. Staring up at the paling sky, he had planned to buy a black-market pistol. He knew what he wanted to do on his first pass. Now here he was. The pistol rode on his hip. He fondled it. Dreamily, he pushed aside some branches and entered. He did not notice the small ripe fruit that stained his blouse with its juice.

Something waited for him in the jungle. The scars on his legs felt it. Something in that dark moistness would be a kind of going away present. It would lead him on if his nerve failed.

A metallic blue dragonfly buzzed past his left ear, dipped, then disappeared into a bank of glimmering, dark green shadows. To his left, ginger perfume hung in the air. Like white spiders, the flowers clung to the plants. He turned away toward a sunnier, open area where he could breathe the simpler, wild green smells. Vegetation caressed his ankles, hips, and shoulders. Humming insects lulled the battle noises in his head. Warmth and fecundity saturated the air. He leaned against a tree to rest.

The bus passed Sandy and Billy as they puffed along on their bikes, going in the opposite direction. The driver gave a friendly honk of his horn. Sandy waved absently. Far down the road, she could see the curved space where the guavas grew. She pointed, smiling significantly. Billy nodded. When they arrived, they got off without speaking and pushed their bicycles into the undergrowth.

Some time was spent picking fruit. It went into their mouths and into their lunch bag for later. Eating guavas was an important part of the fishing trip. But there was a peculiar sharp taste to the guava seeds, or maybe it was the skin. Sandy held a guava in the palm of her hand and waited a moment in case there was a message from the Menehune. None came.

Billy pushed on ahead into the leafy thicket bordering the deeper jungle. "I hope we can find the stream in this direction," he said. Sandy hurried to catch up. Once past the thick small bushes, they could walk more freely. Tall trees, koa, poinciana, here and there a banyan, or a sandalwood, trailing lianas, full of quiet birds and whirring insects shaded the stunted undergrowth. The earth was soft and moldy, a comfort to Sandy's sore bare feet already turning orange from the volcanic iron.

"A dragonfly, a huge one!" whispered Billy. "It will lead us to the water." He leaned his bike against a tree and ran after the dragonfly. Sandy propped her bike next to his, picked up a jar, and then followed slowly. It was too hot to run. She wanted to feel the trees, to peer into the shadow. Maybe this would be the day when she would see a Menehune. She wasn't sure she would like one if she did see it. The Hawaiians said they were small men, very strong, with much mana power. They didn't like people to see them. They didn't build fish ponds or gardens anymore. Maybe they had gone to another island.

Her mind was so busy that she wasn't paying attention to where she was going. A sharp kuykui thorn caught on the thick cotton of her shorts. As she twisted around to free herself, she saw a tall man standing in the shadow of an old banyan. He was very still, but his eyes were looking her way.

Sandy wanted to run, but she knew from her experience with Taffy that she must not show fear. She stood holding her jar tightly and looked at him directly. He took a step forward. "Hi," he said in a quivery voice. "What are you doing here?"

Angry now, Sandy said, "I'm looking for fish for my aquarium ... my friend and me. This is our jungle. What are *you* doing here? I've never seen a soldier around here before." Then she noticed the black holster at his belt and the bulge of the gun inside it.

"I'm not a soldier. I'm a marine. I'm on leave, just looking around." His smile was a thin line.

Sandy dug her toes into the loam. The gun is all wrong, she thought. She felt her muscles tense. Wary now, she said, "My friend is waiting for me."

The Marine took a few self-conscious steps toward her. He took off his hat and waved it at some gnats buzzing in his face. "I'll just go along … maybe watch you … fish." His hand went down to the holster, resting there.

Sandy's heart was knocking her breath around. She managed, "Okay," then began walking purposefully in the direction that Billy had taken. The Marine was close behind. She could feel the heat of his body. It seemed to reach out to her. She hurried, ducking and scooting around trees, almost crawling through tightly packed vegetation, feeling sleek, like a mongoose. She moved instinctively, knowing that if she were quick enough, agile enough, she could lose the Marine. But she did not dare to run.

The stream appeared in a leafy channel. Billy. Where was he? Her head swung left and right. She almost called his name, but that would tell the Marine too much. Instead, she squatted at the edge of the water, pretending to study it.

Awkwardly, he crouched beside her, looked at her for a moment, and then put his hand on her shoulder. "Don't be afraid," he said. His hand slid around her shoulder, around the side of her halter top, where it rested on a new, round breast. He cupped it gently, smiling dreamily at something behind his eyes.

Scalded by embarrassment, forgetting her fear, she pushed his hand away. "Don't," she said. Angry tears pricked her eyes. "If you are going to be in our jungle, you have to act right."

He blew out a sigh as if he were just waking up. He seemed to think for a long time about what she had just said. He sighed again, "What do you mean *our* jungle? I don't see anybody here but you and me.

Sandy gripped her glass jar. "It belongs to me and Billy … and the Menehune." Suddenly the need to feel a nearness to the ancient Hawaiian nature spirits that lived in the stones and woods pushed her to boldness. "I see them all the time," she said. "There are some, right over there behind the ginger plants, watching everything you do."

"Oh, little girl, the war's made me too old to believe in your Menehune, much as I'd like to," he said.

"They are not just *my* Menehune. They belong to the old Hawaiians. They even dug this streambed," Sandy said loudly so that if there were any listening, they would feel proud of themselves.

Something crashed through the undergrowth downstream. An insect nearby clicked. A breeze whiffled the trees. A few leaves blew into the shallow water at their feet. A startled school of guppies burst into a flower pattern and then regrouped when a lonely, proud swordtail swam into the shallows.

Sandy whispered, "Look." The Marine had a hard time seeing it at first. "There," said Sandy. "Here, you can hold the jar while I try to catch him in the net." He took the jar with both hands. A tickling lightness filled her calves with strength. She pushed herself up in one quick movement, pulling the little wire-handled net from her pocket.

He nodded, rising unsteadily on his long legs. He looked at the child's flushed face, beaded around the hairline with bright drops of sweat. Her face was turned expectantly toward his. The whites of her eyes were so clean that he felt like smiling. There was something he had forgotten. He felt it wither in the blaze of her steady gaze.

"Well?" she said.

"Spunky," he thought. She brandished the net. He said, "Okay, let's get him."

The lightness had gathered in Sandy's throat. She glanced out the corner of her eye at the Marine. He held the jar as if he had forgotten the gun. She swallowed carefully. He stared into the moving water and then pointed to the fish. It was half hidden, now, under a submerged plant. Only its tail was visible, wavering back and forth in the current. "There," he said.

Sandy was poised to dip her net in at the second when the fish would emerge when something pushed its way out of the ginger clump. She jumped, turning anxiously. Billy stumbled out of a thicket of wild ginger, his glasses were perched crookedly on his nose, one bow missing. He wiped his face with his shirt tail. Mud covered one whole side of his body from knee to shoulder.

"Billy, where have you been?" Sandy cried.

He stood there blinking. His chin stuck out. He looked at the marine who kneeled by the stream to fill the jar with water. "I fell in the mud and lost my glasses. Looked for 'em for a long time," he said as his hands made knuckles. "Is he fishing too?"

Yes," said Sandy. "He's helping us."

Billy glared. He marched over to the Marine and started to say something when the Marine yelled, "Quick!"

Sandy gave a mighty scoop with her net, and then deftly released the contents into the jar. The Marine held the jar up to the light. The swordtail glinted in the water, circling curiously. Both Sandy and the Marine whooped and laughed, pointing and saying, "See, see!" to Billy.

"Okay, okay," said Billy. You don't have to get so excited. After all, it's only a fish."

"Only a fish!" Sandy wailed. "Oh, Billy, you don't know how hard …" The words stopped in her throat.

The Marine saw the exciting light fade from the girl's face, leaving instead an odd greenish expression. She glanced at the gun at his waist, then at the boy. Sudden rage raised the Marine's arm to throw the jar at the boy named Billy, but the noise in his head crashed through the moment, tightening his grip on the jar. He began to sob, backing away from the children, hugging the jar to his chest. "Get out of here," he cried loudly over the din of the battle which roared in his head. Weapons rattled on his left! He saw leaves and branches quivering – a sure sign that Japanese soldiers were surrounding him. His voice rose to a scream. "Go find a hole! Dig in! Hide! It's too dangerous here for you kids. Get out of here, get out!"

They ran. As they crashed through the jungle, branches whipped their faces. Rocks seemed to rise up to bruise their toes. Sandy floundered, feeling that she had never really seen the jungle before. Finally, Billy yelled that he'd found the bikes. Sandy had just gripped her handlebars when she heard the Marine's hoarse shout, a bang and breaking glass.

Narrative Essay:

A Visit to the Tarlton Cross Mound
By Mark Wenden

ON A WARM DAY IN September 2009, I drove with my wife Kim along Route 159 in southern Ohio toward the small town of Tarlton. We had spent a long weekend in the area visiting historical sites. I have lived most of my life in Ohio, but my wife is from out of state, and I wanted her to become familiar with the history that had given me an unshakeable bond with Ohio since childhood. We had visited the Hopewell Cultural Center and Mound City Group, Adena House, Ohio's first governor's mansion, grilled hamburgers at the Seip Mound and read the somber monuments at the Logan Elm State Memorial. Now, as a last stop before returning to our home in the Columbus area, I wanted to show her the Tarlton Cross Mound. To our disappointment, we found that the park was shut down, not for the season, but permanently, and entrance was prohibited. But when we stopped in a small carryout in Tarlton to buy cold soft drinks for the ride home, we asked about the park, and the locals told us that people visit the mound all the time, and we should not worry about the chains and Keep Out sign.

So, we went back up the road and parked outside the gate, and walked through the parking lot with its cracked asphalt overgrown with weeds, and through an old entry arch leading us to the path up to the mound. It was a short walk. The mound was small, as Indian mounds go, about 30 yards from the end of one arm of its cross shape to the other, with a circular depression at the center. A small metal Park Service plaque still stood next to it, pointing out that the orientation of the arms of the cross (the northern arm points directly north) gave evidence that its builders had some notion of astronomy and that no one knows which ancient culture actually built it. Other than that, the mound and its immediate vicinity showed no signs that anyone had cared for it for years. The trees nearby showed decades of unpruned growth, and vegetation threatened to overwhelm the mound itself in its dark and humid embrace. The appearance of the site had changed so radically, that it was only as we were turning to leave that

I realized that I had been here before and remembered how it had looked the last time I saw it.

The woods around the mound had been trimmed back and cleaned up then, and the grass on the mound itself was neatly mown. It was a crisp autumn day in 1961, and the late afternoon sun grazed the mound with cheerful rays, dappled by the swaying of branches dancing in the light breeze.

I was seven years old then, and as I stood at the end of the southern arm of the cross, my heart was in my mouth. As my mother fed the baby and looked after my four-year-old sister in the old Ford station wagon, my father had brought my older brother, older sister and me up the hill to the mound. We each had taken a position at the end of one of the arms of the cross and had been instructed in how to stand gravely at attention and in what to say as our turns came up. Our father began:

"I am Father North Wind. As my icy breath shakes the naked branches of the winter trees, children huddle in the lodges. The women go out only to gather firewood, and the men to set traps for beaver and mink, whose fur grows long with the cold, the better to keep the people warm."

Then my older sister recited her part, "I am Older Sister East Wind. My warm spring kiss brings blossoms and new birth to the land. The women plant corn and begin to gather berries as the mother bear leaves the den with her new cubs."

Next, it was my turn. I stammered and had to be reminded of my lines in the "solemn ceremony." "I am Younger Brother South Wind. I bring the white haze of summer, pierced by the cry of the cicada. The ears hang heavy on the cornstalks, and the braves set out on raiding parties to fight against our enemies!"

Finally, my older brother, though perhaps feeling too old to participate in this silliness, nonetheless spoke his lines well. "I am Older Brother West Wind. My clean and chilly breezes turn the fall leaves red and yellow, and tell the deer to put on fat for the coming winter. The men hunt them and the women and children dry and smoke the meat, and gather fruit and nuts for the hungry times to come."

As I walked with my wife down the hillside path away from the mound back out to our car by the road, some thoughts went through my mind. It had never occurred to me as a little boy that my father must have composed the contents of the "solemn Indian ceremony" in a matter of seconds as we arrived at the mound all those years ago. "Show an Irishman three things, and he'll spin you a tale," I thought to myself with a smile. My father had also been a teacher, one much-loved and respected by his students. Now, almost fifty years later, though the made-up ceremony seemed, in our more cross-culturally sensitive times, to be a somewhat condescending example of cultural appropriation, I realized at the same time how many significant ideas had been introduced or reinforced in that short, impromptu family activity at the mound: the importance of the cycle of the seasons to pre-industrial people, respect for the ideas of simpler societies, and how their beliefs and ceremonial lives may have meshed with the way they made their living, not to mention the value of learning your lines quickly and not being afraid to speak in front of a critical audience.

"How sad," I thought, "that the park is closed, and no other father will be able to enrich his children's lives in a similar way, giving them the sense that people long-forgotten, who were different from us, still matter somehow. At least, he won't be able to do it here."

My wife and I agreed that it was one of the best weekend trips we had ever taken together. The memory of the visits, nearly fifty years apart, still floats up into my consciousness now and then.

"Storytelling is the most powerful way to put ideas into the world today." --Robert McKee

Respecting Bees
By Mark Wenden

I WAS KNEELING IN THE DRIVEWAY in front of my parent's garage putting clean grease on the chain of my 3-speed Schwinn Racer, when the tedium of the lazy Midwestern summer afternoon was broken by shouts in loud, angry Russian. I looked up in surprise to see our next-door neighbor shirtless in his backyard, dancing about and slapping himself, and barking out phrases. "...tvoyu mat'! Chornyi blyad! Chort vozmi!" which had to be horrible curses. His lawnmower, still running, stood abandoned. As I gaped at him uselessly, he eventually stopped the swatting, killed the engine of his mower, and approached the fence. He had lived next door for about a year, and I did not know him well. To me, he looked old, though he probably was only in his fifties. He was quiet and seemed to always move in a deliberate way, wasting no motions. He always had a weary look about him. Resting a hand on the fence he asked me, in his slow, accented English, whether we had any baking soda in our kitchen, and if so, could he use some to make a plaster, as he had just been stung by yellow jackets (which he called bees) whose underground nest had been disturbed by his lawnmower. I told him I would look, and he asked me to bring whatever I found over to his kitchen.

As I rummaged through my mother's cabinets, it struck me how odd it was that this man had crossed half the world to be stung by yellow jackets in a backyard in Ohio. The word in the neighborhood was that he had served in the Red Army during World War II and survived heavy fighting during the German invasion. Then, as a reward for his heroism, he was convicted on trumped-up charges of collaboration with the enemy and thrown into a labor camp for ten years. Surviving even that, after his release, he defected from the Soviet Union by swimming to Finland where it borders Russia on the Baltic Sea. He applied to be permitted to immigrate to the US. Before the war, he had worked as a civil engineer. Possessing such useful skills, and with Cold War sentiments being on his side as well, permission was granted. He arrived in the US in the late fifties and worked menial jobs until his English was good enough to apply for work in his profession. He lived alone, and no one knew what had become of his family.

Having found a box of baking soda, I trotted over to his back door and he waved me into his kitchen. He carefully mixed the soda with water in a bowl and dabbed the paste onto the angry-looking stings with the back of a spoon. He was mostly silent, occasionally sucking some air through his teeth and muttering. He did not seem to mind that I stayed and watched. Perhaps he didn't want me to leave with the baking soda in case he needed more.

When he had applied plaster to all the stings, and I counted more than ten, he went to his garage, where I heard things being knocked about on a shelf. He then emerged into the yard with a can of insect spray. He thoroughly doused the opening of the yellow jackets' nest and sent a good long stream of insecticide down the hole. He came back inside and threw the empty can in the trash.

"I hate bees too!" I said, wishing to show that I sympathized with him for the pain the stings must be causing him.

"Who said I hate bees?" he answered in his carefully enunciated way (Khu sayt I hett biss?). He sat down at the kitchen table opposite me and gave me a look that meant, I knew immediately, that he wanted to say something he considered important.

"Actually, I respect bees. The bees which sting-ged me were only defending their home. I feel they have every right to do this, and I admire their self-sacrifice and the singleness of their purpose. They did not hesitate to fly out and attack me, though I am many times larger than they, and my lawnmower must have been terrifying as it passed over their nest."

He raised a finger. "Where I grew up, in addition to many kinds of bees, there are other animals such as bears and wolves, which can easily kill men. I never hated them for this ability, but learned to respect them, to stay out of their way and not disturb them." I felt puzzled by this short talk of his. It was the longest I had ever heard him speak at one time, and replied, "But didn't you just walk out there and wipe out their nest with bug spray?"

"Yes!" he exclaimed. Then he leaned toward me and fixed me with an intense look. "This is what you must understand, boy. I do not hate them for being what they are. And I even admire some of their finer qualities. But if they attack me, they are making a tragic mistake. I will kill every last god damn one." I saw the gleam of a gold tooth as a tight smile slowly cracked his face. His expression relaxed, and his eyes crinkled slightly in amusement as he registered my surprise, both at his language and at what seemed to me, at my age, to be self-contradictory thinking. He patted me on the shoulder and thanked me for the baking soda.

It wasn't until years later, in a world history course at Ohio State University, that something reminded me of this conversation, and I realized he had been talking about much more than bees.

My Brother
By Georgia Sparks

I DON'T REALLY REMEMBER the last time I saw him. It had to be on one of his many trips back home after being on the racing circuit. I have an old family photo that was taken in front of my sister's house. That may have been the last time he came to see us—the last time I saw him or spoke to him.

He was seven years older than I, but thanks to home movies, I have memories of him as a boy. I watched as that skinny, fair-haired boy pulled weeds in our backyard. I watched as he walked us to and from school. I watched as he hula hooped at my birthday party. He could hula hoop better than anyone I knew.

As a child he was asthmatic, and while I don't remember him ever having an asthma attack, I do remember him tying a handkerchief over his mouth and nose, like a cowboy bandit, to keep from breathing dust. Our home was in Phoenix, so there was plenty of dust around. When he was called for the draft, he smoked cigarettes to trigger his asthma. It worked--he was 4-F and avoided the military and Vietnam.

My memories are scattered when I think of my childhood years. Actual memories are intermingled with stories of my brother's adventures. Times were tough then, so my crafty Mom made earrings out of rick-rack and sent my brother out to sell them in the neighborhood. The few extra dollars from earring sales helped buy milk. A boy could go out and sell door-to-door in those days without being abducted or threatened by gangs or drugs.

I vividly remember the time he asked to have his hair cut in a mohawk. My parents, though less than enthused about the idea, gave in to his request. The mohawk was not at all attractive, and his hair was soon buzzed to the scalp to remedy the mistake. Even a bald head was better than that haircut.

Because of our age difference, he was in his last year at elementary school when I was in first grade. I saw him at school only if he was working as a patrol boy or cafeteria helper. Whether he was the crossing guard walking us younger kids across the street after school or wiping off tables in the cafeteria during lunch hour, it always felt special being around him.

He moved away from home when he was 16 and went to live on a ranch in Prescott. Because of his small stature, he was encouraged during his childhood to become a jockey. That seed of an idea grew and motivated him to go to work on a horse ranch. He lived in a tack room, mucked stalls, and learned everything he could about horses.

Eventually, he became a jockey. He was good at it and did very well for himself right out of the gate. In a short while, he earned enough to pay cash for a brand new 1965 Ford Fairlane 500. I still recall the day he drove it to our house where he painstakingly installed clear vinyl seat covers over the white leather seats. He also painted the whitewalls on the tires black--though I never really understood why.

During racing season, he traveled to various cities in the United States and Canada. We were excited when racing season opened in our city because we would have his company for a while. And as an added bonus, since he had limited space in his travel trailer, he downsized his music collection and gave us the record albums he was tired of listening to.

I wrote letters to him in those early days. It was a geography lesson just keeping up with his travels: Spokane, Washington; Wilkes-Barre, Pennsylvania; Toronto, Ontario; Calgary, Alberta; Saskatoon, Saskatchewan. I remember receiving letters from him, too. I'm sure he knew how much he was missed.

My dad was extremely proud and really came alive when my brother was back in Phoenix to race. Dad would go to the racetrack in the wee hours on Sunday mornings to watch him gallop horses. My sister and I would sometimes go along on those cold, dark mornings, but we spent more time sitting in the coffee shop drinking hot chocolate than actually watching my brother ride.

Today he would be in his seventies. I sometimes wonder what he would have done with his life had he lived. Jockeys have a short window of time for their career before they are too old to race. I don't know if he had learned any other skills. Jockeying and horses were his whole life.

I guess it should be no surprise that his life ended on a racetrack. The story goes that he was riding a horse, as he had done no doubt thousands of times before, when the horse veered into the guardrail. My brother was thrown from the horse. He was only 34 years old, but he died doing what he loved.

The funeral was held in another state and set for the very day that I was scheduled to have a C-section delivery. Needless to say, I couldn't attend my brother's funeral. But as my wonderful brother whom I dearly loved was being laid to rest, another young man whom I dearly love entered this life. There was this gift in my arms; my firstborn son. I felt somehow that my brother was replaced, and the loss didn't seem nearly so great. Maybe that's the cycle of life. In my experience, it's more than just a cliché.

Unexpected Grace
Joanne Sandlin

HURRIEDLY GRABBING A CARTON of rocky road ice cream, I almost ran into a young woman and an older couple turning into the frozen food aisle. I paused to avoid a collision. The man clutched his wife tightly to provide a steadying arm.

I saw the familiar face of someone with the blank stare of dementia as well as her choppy gait. I smiled at the trio as they nodded appreciating the opportunity to pass easily. The man dropped behind as the younger woman gripped the older lady picking up the pace to move her along.

He said to me, "My wife needs to get quickly to the restroom."

I asked if she was well. He dropped his eyes replying, "She has dementia."

I told him I experienced that in my family and understood the difficulties it brings daily.

He then stood upright proudly stating, "My name is Lester and I am 91 years old."

His smile reflected his joy in that accomplishment.

"Lester, I am so glad to meet you. I wish I had a big button you could wear saying how young you are."

His even bigger smile affirmed his obvious delight in my interest.

Sensing he might, I asked him if he happened to know the Lord. Looking at me seriously, he related, "If I didn't know Him, I couldn't have made it all these years as well as not being able to carry on with my dear wife's illness."

"God's grace is truly sufficient for us just as He promises in his word, isn't it?"

"Yes, from the day we accept Him into our life through all the peaks and valleys we experience on the journey, He is right there with the grace we need for each circumstance."

"Amen, Lester, what a great testimony."

His easy smile again lit up his face.

The women appeared, and Lester turned quickly with a wave of his hand and joined them.

Moving my cart to the checkout stall I felt blessed to have shared Lester's reminder of God's grace that he carried into every day as he lovingly cared for his wife having experienced it from the day he asked the Lord into his life.

Placing my items on the belt I smiled as I picked up the ice cream pausing to silently thank the Lord for my encounter in the frozen food aisle.

Truth is so rare that it is delightful to tell it.
—Emily Dickinson

The Spelling Test
By Sue Favia

BY THE THIRD GRADE, I was getting to know the reputations and unique characteristics of some the nuns at St. Katharine's Elementary School, at least at the lower grade levels, which was the entire first floor. Sister Norton stood out among them all as the most feared. After only two years of schooling, my reputation seemed to precede me as well. I was the third Favia, following my two older sisters.

After our combined six years of delinquent tuition and book bills, the nuns were not happy to see one more Favia on their roster who couldn't pay her way. So, I was marked before I even walked through the door.

The nuns were on a short fuse most of the time, and any spark could set them off. It seemed that I short-circuited them more than most, and Sister Norton was one of the worst nuns for impulsive, unpredictable, and very strange behaviors. She would roll up taffy into little bite-sized balls and keep them in her top desk drawer. Eating was not allowed in the classroom, other than lunch, and our candy break. Despite this, Sister Norton would sometimes slip a piece of taffy into her mouth when she thought no one was looking. But I was looking. She must have rolled them each morning before class.

One morning, after a particularly violent disciplinary confrontation, she tried to bribe me with one of her taffy balls. It disgusted me as she cautiously leaned over my desk, nudged one into my hand, and whispered,

"Susan, your mother doesn't need to know about this morning."

I put my hand up to my mouth, mimicking a chewing motion as I pretended to eat it. As if her sweaty, smelly taffy ball was a fair exchange for my secrecy. I never talked to anyone about the abuses anyway. Not even to my friends who were present in class, the ones who saw the terror on my face and the tears in my eyes as I stood in the middle of seventy classmates. I wanted to be someone else with my friends. I didn't want to be the person they saw being belittled and humiliated.

It was late afternoon, and our class was taking a candy break after lunch. It was one of those rare occasions where I joined in the line of the candy privileged. But I knew how to save money when I wanted to. When I found a penny, I'd put it away until I found another penny, or I'd find a pop bottle to exchange for two pennies. I had a keen eye and a good ear for copper hitting pavement, and I could see the reflection of a pop bottle a block away. And on the home front, the back of the couch, after my father was done with his nap, was where treasures were found.

I knew what I wanted well before I got to the front of the line—the biggest chocolate bar there was. I paid my five cents and took it to my desk as if it were a badge of honor, making a point not to rip it open too quickly. Savoring the pleasure, I propped it up on the front of my desk, letting it sit for a few minutes, proud of my constraint. I also wanted my classmates to see that I could afford to buy candy, too.

We had a fifteen-minute bathroom or candy break, or both if we were fast enough. The class was still silently walking back and forth, each row of students taking their turn in the hall to purchase their sweets, on the long fold-up table, when Linda Musgrave tapped me on my shoulder.

"I'll trade your candy bar for my Cinderella wallet," she said.

Huh, was she crazy? A Cinderella wallet for a candy bar? I'd have traded my shoes for that.

Okay," I said, tempering my excitement. I was exploding inside at the prospect of owning a Cinderella wallet. Other than a Cinderella watch, nothing could have surpassed this exchange, and Linda Musgrave was offering me this treasure for one Snickers bar.

I barely took a breath before grabbing the candy bar off my desk and agreeing to the swap. I held on firmly to the bar as I handed it back to her, holding out my other hand for the wallet. When I was certain I had a secure grip on the wallet, I let go of my candy. I flipped around in my seat, gazing at my new wallet for a moment, touching and tracing Cinderella with my fingers before opening it to inspect all the features inside. The wallet was pale blue, with a white inlaid center and Cinderella wearing her blue and white dress, with her golden-yellow hair pulled high on her head, tied with a blue ribbon. Inside were clear plastic inserts for photos with another slot for my identification. My name. I couldn't wait to see it in my best cursive writing. On the other side of the wallet was a little pouch for change, with a flap to keep my money from falling out and a strap that snapped the wallet closed for safety.

While I was examining the photo insert, it slipped out of the slot. It seemed like a simple thing to fix, but I fumbled for a while and couldn't put it back in its place. I was becoming frustrated and certain that I'd broken the wallet before I even got to show it off. Linda had already consumed the entire candy bar and was licking the melted chocolate off her thumb when I turned around and told her I thought I broke it. I asked her how to put the photo insert back in place.

"Oh sure, that's easy. Let me show you," she said, and I handed it back to her. I was thrilled to see how quickly she replaced the tab, relieved that I hadn't broken it. As I reached back to retrieve my wallet, she pulled her hand away to keep it out of my reach.

"What are you doing? Give it back!" I demanded, reaching over her desk and trying to grab her arm. Our desks were catty-corner to each other and butted up together, as was every other row to allow more space in the room. This arrangement made it easier for us to talk and reach back and forth.

"I changed my mind," she snapped, pushing my arm away. Now she slid the wallet into her desk. I couldn't believe what was happening.

"That's my wallet! We made a deal, and you ate my candy bar. Now give it back to me." Now my squeal caught Sister Norton's attention.

"What's going on over there, Miss Favia?" she said with her usual irritation when she spoke to me.

"Linda took my wallet, s'ter, and won't give it back to me," I said.

"Do you have her wallet, Miss Musgrave?"

"No, Sister, I only let her see it, and then she tried taking it from me. It's mine, Sister. My mother bought it for me last week," Linda replied with a smirk.

"That's a lie, sister, I traded it for my Snickers bar and she ate th—"

"Turn around, Miss Favia," she said, discounting my response and cutting me off. "Class get your paper out for your spelling test."

The conversation was over. I knew not to persist. Arguing with Sister Norton would prove to be far worse than losing a wallet. I was crushed by the loss of what had almost been mine, even if for just a moment. I felt cheated and betrayed, and I was angry that I let it happen.

Linda and I had never been friends, though we weren't really enemies either. We just never played together, and we never walked to or from school together, even though we only lived a few blocks away. If we were ten feet from one another on the same sidewalk, we would have stayed that way all the way to school. She had a way of looking at me that let me know she wasn't interested in being friends. Linda was the tomboy type and had a tough nature about her. She never actually did anything to me, but I always had a sense that at the slightest provocation, she could—and would. She was much taller and heavier than I, so, there was no way I could intimidate or force her to return the wallet after school.

Gone were my nickel, my candy bar, and my Cinderella wallet. I tried to hold back my tears and anger as I prepared for our spelling test. Everything had to be taken off our desks, so we were not tempted to cheat and look at our books. We had to spell twenty words that were taken directly from our spelling workbook, and Sister Norton always recited them in the exact same order as the text. But for extra precaution, Sister Norton had spelling guards that walked up and down each aisle, watching to see that no one peeked into their desks to look at the words or try any other methods of cheating.

We had those old wooden oak desks with black scrolled wrought iron frames and legs. We could slide our books and papers in and out of the opening, making easy access for slipping the workbook out of the desk just enough to peek at the words as the spelling guard moved down the aisle. Sister Norton always chose the smart students as spelling guards during the test because she knew they could spell any word that was in the book. The smart ones were always chosen to help the nuns: washing the blackboards, distributing worksheets, handing out tests, passing out holy cards for outstanding work, or guarding the bathrooms to see that there was no talking there either. Next up in rank to the spelling guards were the patrol boys, and only second in line of importance to the altar boys, who were supreme among them all.

Before and after school, the patrol boys stood between the two single-file lines with their white straps around their waists and crossed diagonally over their chests. Their job was to make sure no one talked or stepped out of place. It must have been that diagonal strap that made them feel like little soldiers or maybe cadets. Our lines formed at the threshold of the classroom door, threading through the long hallway, down the stairs to the main floor, and out of the school grounds for an entire block before we could fall out of line, and silence.

Sister Norton began reciting the spelling words one at a time, allowing a moment before moving on to the next word. At every opportunity after each word, I turned around to give Linda another look of contempt and disapproval in hope that she would change her mind and offer the wallet back to me. Her head didn't budge as she hovered over her paper. Again, after the next spelling word, I tried to get her attention, hoping to find a shred of remorse or shame. But her physical demeanor didn't change, and she never diverted her eyes from her paper. She held her head low, letting her straight sandy-brown hair hang over her paper as if she were afraid someone might copy her spelling words.

As the next word was recited, I looked back again and caught sight of something very strange. I waited for the next word to be called, and then more carefully turned around to be certain of my observation. What I saw was the slightest offset of a second piece of paper, carefully placed underneath Linda's spelling sheet. On my next glance, I knew she had written the entire twenty words on the second sheet. While spelling each word on her test paper, she had the bottom sheet with the correct words already written. Linda would then, I surmised, slip the top sheet back into her desk when the test was over, leaving the correctly spelled words ready to hand in.

Now, had I been smart—and I wasn't—I would have blackmailed her into giving me the wallet back. But, I didn't realize that I had leverage, so instead, I did what any scorned eight-year-old girl would do. Rat on her! Squeal! Sing like a canary! I doubt Linda even realized that I saw what she was doing before I raised my hand to even the score. It was a rare occasion that I raised my hand for anything, other than to go to the lavatory, so when my arm went up, particularly during a test, Sister Norton seemed surprised—or was it annoyance?

"Yes, Susan—what is it?"

"Sister, Linda Musgrave is cheating on her spelling test," I said with the triumph of the victor.

You could almost feel the air sucked from the room as everyone simultaneously gasped and inhaled. All that was left was a frightening silence as the spelling guard swiftly moved in on his prey and stood at her side like a proud centurion waiting for Sister Norton to take action. Then, that terrifying and oh-so-familiar swooshing of her habit and the clicking of her beads as she entered the narrow aisle with a swift stride. Only this time she wasn't coming after me. You could feel the pounding of her feet on the wooden floor as everyone sat motionless in their own self-preservation. Now I knew what it was like being on the "other side;" they were scared too. As Sister Norton reached Linda's desk, she grabbed her spelling papers in a rage. Seeing what Linda had done, she crumpled them up in her pasty white fist.

"Stand up, Miss Musgrave—stand up!" she screamed.

Now, Linda was in group two, which was the average-level students. I don't remember her ever getting into trouble. I assumed she would have to stay after class for at least a week, not be allowed to go outside for recess after lunch and would very likely have to write on the blackboard a hundred times one of the Ten Commandments that best represented her offense. That's usually what happened to the 'good kids' gone bad. It all happened so fast...

"Open your mouth," Sister Norton shouted. Linda had a confused look on her face, as did I and the rest of the class.

"Did you hear what I said? Open your mouth!" Linda parted her lips slightly as if to speak, and the next thing I saw was Sister Norton stuffing the wad of papers into Linda's mouth, forcing it open wider—the entire spelling test.

"Open, I said!" she screamed over and over, stuffing and twisting, making sure it wouldn't fall out. There Linda stood, tears streaming down her face and her mouth wide open, stuffed with her spelling test—both sheets. And in the next moment, Sister Norton spun around and rattled and swooshed back to her desk, continuing with the next spelling word as if nothing had happened. Linda stood in unimaginable humiliation next to her desk, crying and drooling through the wads of paper.

Oh no, what have I done? I felt my face go hot and my heart beat at an alarming speed while I struggled to complete my test, never turning my head or even my eyes in Linda's direction.

The rest of the day was a blur. I couldn't concentrate on anything. My mind was racing, and I couldn't formulate a full thought. This was not what was supposed to happen. I only remember thinking; *How I will I get home*? I never had the foresight to consider what the consequences could be, for either one of us.

My short life flashed before me. I envisioned Linda's chubby fist traveling toward my face as she sat on top of me just out of the vision of the patrol boys—or worse, me running for my life every day after school, wondering when and where she would catch up with me and wreak her revenge. I was already strategizing on how I would get home, how many yards or alleys I could cut through before she would spring on me. I was counting on Norton keeping her after class, at least the first day. That was the normal procedure after any violation of rules. But this was by no means a normal day, and Linda left school, as usual, in front of me in line.

As the line split up a block away from school, I slowed down and pulled back as far as possible, walking as close to other kids as I could. I knew she wouldn't hurt me if I was in a crowd. But one by one, with each passing block, the kids thinned out. And then I was walking alone, holding back almost a full block behind Linda, darting behind parked cars and bushes until she turned two blocks before my house. I was safe for now, but then there was tomorrow and there would always be another tomorrow.

This routine went on for weeks; I would walk a block behind Linda and then duck off into a backyard to take another way home. My wandering nature certainly paid off. I must have known a dozen or more ways of getting home: across prairies and fields, over fences, and through backyards and alleys.

Linda must have been so traumatized that she was afraid to even look at me, much less speak to me or treat me badly. But I still kept my distance from her, never losing sight of that day and always wondering when she would snap and retaliate. As the months passed, I became less cautious, and the space between us grew shorter, but never too close to inflame an old wound. And for the next five years at St. Katharine's School, we never spoke another word, nor any time thereafter.

Another Story
By E. S. Oleson

IN THE BED NEXT TO his father's lay a man of similar age, ancient, the features equally pale, the gaze equally vacant.

"Hello," he said to the unfocused eyes, "I'm Emilio's son."

The man turned barely at all in his direction and began to mumble. Ed leaned over to catch the words as they spilled out of the toothless mouth. He strained to hear and eventually made out that the patient was reciting a litany of the cars he had owned in his life. The first was a Ford followed by another Ford. That was followed by others, a Pontiac, a Buick, then a Studebaker. The list went on . . . a Dodge, another Ford. The man became visibly excited by this life's inventory, and from time to time he would back up in his list to correct the year or the model name. With trembling fingers, he counted off their succession until sleep overtook him and the hands dropped to his chest. His eyes closed, and the mouth dropped open, a bit of spittle on the lips.

Ed looked over at his father in his own sleep. He knew his father would regard this man's close company as yet another affliction even though he, too, had his own list of cars. Sleep was his only blessing.

"The debris we leave in our wake and stuff in our pockets," Ed thought. "Damned, worthless lists."

That evening Emilio sat and watched the sun set across the lake. As sunsets went it was a good one, but hard to distinguish from so many others. A mix of cumulus in the distance turning brilliant gold underneath, a smudged mauve over that, still and windless. Another sunset, he thought. He remembered the sun setting in the haze of Delhi, and the abrupt setting into the Patagonia at Bariloche, and how the Caribbean's humid heat between Miami and Havana dissolved the sun and the ocean into one dazzling brilliance.

And then Emilio added that evening's sunset to his own list.

I can't write five words but that I change seven.
—Dorothy Parker

Memory Loss: Aid to Physical Fitness
By Shirley Willis

EVER NOTICE, WHILE ELDERING GRACEFULLY that you've acquired, along with stray nose hairs and fragile bones, a bit of difficulty with remembering where you put that, um, comb? And the cute flowered sneakers? And the pink fuzzy sweater? Or what you were going to do with them? That happens to all of us, right? So, this morning, rather than pulling a frowny face, I ran the reel of ageless pep talks about turning challenges into strengths—while still in bed, of course. That put me back to sleep faster than a fistful of Ambien.

Seventeen minutes later, I awoke all motivated and self-directed. While stretching I plotted how I'd repurpose my misfiring memory as the catalyst for calorie burning. Today, if I lost something, I'd slap on my Fitbit and rack up the steps. It went like this.

I searched the bedside table for my eyeglasses and knocked over a stack of books. I rearranged the books, searched under the bed for the glasses and found my long-lost slippers, two mismatched socks, and enough dust to form half a person—a hundred calories, I calculated. I put on the slippers and stumbled out of the bedroom to locate the dust mop. On my way, I stopped by the coffee pot for a wake-up jolt and promptly spilled coffee on my newly retrieved slippers because I can't see as far as my feet without glasses.

I visualized. "If I were a pair of glasses, where would I be?" This works every time, right? Not really.

One of those funky light-bulb moments struck. My glasses must be on the couch where I nearly wet my pants—another challenge— watching Betty White in reruns of "Hot in Cleveland" last night. Man, what I'd give to have her writers directing my script.

I straggled into the great room. Searched the couch. Searched under the couch. Located the remaining half of dust to create a person. Remembered when creating a person was way more fun and burned oodles more calories. Remembered the dust mop for under the bed. And now the couch. Headed to the laundry room on the opposite side of the house. Got halfway there and remembered my glasses. Went back to the couch. Searched some more. Gave up. Remembered the coffee. Headed back to the kitchen counter. Groped for the cup. Slipped on spill. Checked for broken bones. Thought, "This is how it all ends." Racked up another hundred calories. Remembered my glasses again.

A mental image blinked, showing glasses perched on the bathroom counter where I was reading a prescription bottle before bed last night. Was that only last night? I headed back through the bedroom and tripped on the dust from my earlier—I think it was earlier today—under-bed search. Checked again for broken bones. Not yet. Shook half person off my pajamas. Sneezed. Sneezed two more times. Blessed myself. At least another hundred calories. Headed to the bathroom for my glasses—more calories.

Eureka. Glasses found. I slammed them on my face, adjusted them while checking the mirror and decided it must be a fake mirror. Nobody looks like that, not even in the morning. Back in the kitchen, I rewarded myself with a double-chocolate, frosted, applesauce and raisin muffin for all the calories I'd burned.

Total Benefits:

Walking, bending, reaching, sneezing and growling. Chewing, well more like sucking. I calculated the calories adding brain activity which also burns major calories. I checked the clock. I'd only been up for seven minutes and burned three hundred calories. Well, maybe it was three hundred calories. My math was never that good. I traded the coffee for chocolate milk with a morning scoop of ice cream and forgot the calories. Chocolate fix on board, I had enough strength to find my Fitbit. Tomorrow, I'd tackle addition and subtraction. Now. Just where was the Fitbit? And the dust mop. And . . .

Bob Matthews
By Roger Antony

BOB SAT ALONE in the dimly lit movie theater with what looked like a nearly full bag of popcorn propped up in his lap.

In a few moments, the cleaning crew would come in and sweep the aisles removing any discarded bags, boxes and drink cups before the next showing. Bob had watched the movie twice already. After each show, he would leave, duck into the men's room then return just as the lights were dimming and the preview of coming attractions were starting.

The bag of popcorn was just a prop. He had eaten all but a few popped kernels during the first show. What few kernels he hadn't eaten he spilled out into a napkin after everyone had exited the first show. He used napkins and stuffed them into the bottom of the popcorn bag, then put the popcorn back in the bag. One would think he had a nearly full bag of popcorn. This was what he wanted people to think as he sat through the second and third shows.

He spent most Saturdays away from home, as far away from home as he could get without a car. Some Saturdays he spent at the library, some he would walk through the woods to the Army base nearby where his father worked and watch the soldiers march. When he had the money, he'd go to the movies.

Bob's father was a captain on the base. He was in charge of the drill sergeants and had more than two hundred fifty men beneath him. Bob's father was a mean man like all the drill sergeants. At home, he seldom spoke to Bob or Bob's mother with compassion or understanding. It was always an order: do this, do that.

On weekends it was particularly bad since his father got drunk every Friday night after leaving the base and barely sobered up by Monday morning. Those were the hours that Bob stayed away from home. Sometimes he stayed away until Sunday evening, leaving his mother home alone with his father.

From past experience, Bob knew that if his father got drunk before dinner on Friday night, the weekend would be bad. Bob either made arrangements to sleep over a friend's house on Saturday night or took his sleeping bag, which he kept in the garage alongside a small duffel bag, to the local park to sleep.

The park contained four ballfields fanning out from a small clubhouse containing a concession stand and a public restroom, which was kept unlocked year-round.

Tall pine trees surrounded the park on two sides. Running through the pines on the east-side was Silver Creek, a tributary of the Argyle River.

Five years ago, when Bob was only nine he spent a lot of time in the park along the creek. The water was teaming with life, from spiders gliding on the surface of the water, to guppies in the pooled areas, to frogs and snakes at the water's edge.

Bob no longer spent time capturing guppies to take home and show his mother. Now he used the park as a weekend retreat from his father's abuse. He tolerated his father during the week when he was sober. During the week, his father would have a couple of beers after dinner. On weekends his father would get drunk and mean. That's when Bob made sure that he was away from home.

The theater manager signaled the start of the next show by dimming the lights. A few seconds later the speakers came alive and the screen displayed brilliant colors and the coming attractions. Coming attraction previews lasted ten minutes. Bob had timed the two earlier showings. He waited until it was a few minutes before the end of the coming attractions before he flushed the toilet, washed his hands and left the restroom carrying what appeared to be a full bag of popcorn.

He found a seat in the back of the theater this time. For the first showing, he sat near the front of the theater. During the second showing, he sat in the center of the middle aisle halfway back from the screen. It was his favorite location. For the third showing, he found a seat in the back row adjacent to the wall.

Bob loved movies and when he was old enough he wanted to move to California and write for the movies. He was certain of that. In fact, he had started writing a movie script based upon his life.

For now, he kept the names of the real people in his story. He had already selected who would play the parts in his movie. Ernst Borgnine would play his father, Eugene Matthews. Donna Reed would play his mother, Margaret. A new young actor needed to play him. Bob was thinking of James Dean or Vince Edwards. Either would do, but he favored James Dean because he felt that he looked a lot like James Dean.

The third show let out just after six-thirty. He waited until everybody had left before leaving his seat. He left the phony bag of popcorn on the floor, then walked to the front of the theater and exited. He normally left through one of the exits near the screen rather than exit back into the theater lobby where he might be seen by the theater manager or friends.

Bob squinted as he opened the door, the sun still bright in the sky on this early June evening. He pulled his ball cap down across his forehead keeping his eyes shaded from the sun. He had several choices: go home and eat with his parents or buy a hamburger at the Dairy Queen two blocks away. Either way, he'd have to go home to pick up his sleeping bag.

His father had gotten drunk early on Friday night, a bad omen. Bob was certain that he'd be meaner than hell if he showed up for dinner.

He jingled the three-quarters in his pocket, enough for a drink and a hamburger. He made his decision to eat at the Dairy Queen then sneak into the garage and get his sleeping bag. He was about to cross the street when a large hand was planted firmly on his shoulder.

Before he had a chance to turn around he heard his father's slurred voice, "Son, where you been?"

Bob turned to face his father, a tall, lean forty-two-year-old man with short cropped blond hair, wearing a green Army tee shirt, khaki pants, and black highly polished military boots and devoid of a smile.

"I've been at the movies, sir."

"Your mother's been wondering where you've been," he said.

"I told her I'd be gone all day."

Eugene Matthews' eyes were partially glazed from too much Jack Daniels. His father usually started with beer. If he wanted to get drunk, which was his standard operating procedure on Friday night, he'd switch to Jack Daniels. A few shots of Jack and he was buzzing. A few more shots, he'd get abusive. A few more and he'd get meaner than hell.

Margaret would go upstairs to the bedroom and get in bed and try to go to sleep. Even if she wasn't asleep when Eugene came in she would fake it. He could be really abusive if he found her awake.

Sometimes in a drunken stupor, he would stare down at her in bed and cuss at her. Sometimes he would turn around and go back downstairs and fall asleep in front of the television. However, most nights he would shake her until she woke and then tell her how old she looked, or how she couldn't fix a good meal or whatever negative thought came into his inebriated mind. He might even slap her.

Bob could hear his father's voice through the walls of the upstairs bedroom. He often heard his mother pleading with his father to stop hurting her. At times he felt he should go into his parent's room and protect his mother, but he never did. His father was a big man. When he was drunk, he seemed to get stronger and more fearless.

Bob used to lock his door to escape his father's tyranny, but his father had busted his door lock more than six months ago to get in and spread disapproval and discontent with his son. The lock didn't keep his father out that night and now that the casing around the strike had been damaged; it would no longer lock.

Bob spent most Friday and Saturday nights away from home, but his mother had no choice. She had to stay at home. She endured his father's invectives and diatribes.

Eugene grabbed his son's upper arm and said, "Son, let's go home."

"I don't want to go, sir."

"What do you mean you don't want to go?" His father's slurred voice taking on a hard edge as he held on to his son's arm.

"Let go. You're hurting me," Bob said.

"I'm going to hurt you more if you don't come along," he said.

At fourteen and six feet three inches tall, Bob was three inches taller than his father, but forty pounds lighter. Without realizing it he pulled his arm free from his father's grasp and said, "No, I'm not coming home."

"You're coming with me, you little piece of shit," said Eugene reaching for his son's arm only to find air. Bob had turned and was running down the street.

Eugene gave chase for fifty or sixty feet then stopped, put his head down and puked on the sidewalk. People nearby looked at the hunched over man as vomit splattered on his polished boots and pant legs.

Bob knew he was well ahead of his father, so he stopped and looked back. He saw his father bent over discharging food and bile onto the sidewalk while others stared at his father wondering whether or not to call for help.

Eugene rose unsteadily and looked at his only son. "You son of a bitch," he yelled, then with his left-hand wiped vomit from his lower lip and repeated, "you son of a bitch."

Bob watched his father turn and slowly saunter away. At that pace, it would take his father at least fifteen minutes to get to their house. Bob turned the corner and started jogging. He could be home in less than five minutes. He needed to check on his mother before his father got home.

Mrs. Matthews turned from washing dishes in the sink as her son entered the back door. "You okay?" She asked.

Bob waited a moment to catch his breath. "Dad tried to drag me home."

"What?"

"He met me in front of the movie theater and grabbed me. He wanted me to come home."

"I'm sorry Bob. Your father's drunk again. He's not himself."

"He's always drunk and he's coming home. He's mean tonight," Bob said looking at a reddish blue bruise forming on the right side of his mother's cheek. "Did he do that to you?"

"It's not bad," she said.

"It's not bad? You say that every time. He shouldn't hit you. He's your husband, not your master."

"Don't worry son."

"Mom, I do worry. He's going to be home in a few minutes. I'm not going to be here. We ought to call the police. He needs help."

"Don't Bob. It'll ruin his military career."

"So, we have to accept his drinking because of his career. How about our lives? Aren't we supposed to have lives without fear or abuse? My friends have fathers in the military and they don't get drunk and hurt their family."

"Bob, your father has a problem."

"I know he has a problem. He needs help." Bob looked at his watch. It was nearly fifteen minutes since he had left his father. "What are you going to do, Mom?"

"Nothing," she said while drying the last plate with a towel.

"Well, that's great. I'm leaving."

"Bob don't go. I need you here."

"So, he can hit me like he hit you?"

"He won't do that to you. He loves you."

"He loves me. Yeah, right. He loves me so much that he gets drunk." He paused then added, "Is that right? Am I missing something? Dad needs help."

"He knows that."

"Then why doesn't he get it?"

As Margaret said, "I don't know," the front door opened. A few moments later Eugene walked through from the dining room.

He stared at his wife and son. "I see you've come home," Eugene said with a menacing tone.

"That's right. I wanted to make sure Mom was okay."

"Your mother's fine," said Eugene.

"Yeah, if you forget about the big bruise on her face," said Bob.

"Yeah, your mother deserved it."

"Really, I guess beating up on little women shows your strength. Is that it?" Bob said taunting his father.

"You smart ass," said Eugene.

"Why don't you pick on someone your own size?"

"You mean like you," Eugene said looking up at his son.

"Yeah, that's right. Me. I'm fourteen years old. I'm a real threat, right dad? I'm your enemy?"

Eugene stepped forward prepared to strike his son. Margaret turned to face her husband. "Eugene stop it. He's your son. You're drunk."

"Yeah, he's my son: smart ass fourteen-year-old."

"So, you intend to hurt me?"

"You're goddamn right, you smart ass."

"Eugene, don't you dare touch your son. Eugene, you hear me?"

Spitting out the words, he said, "I hear you, you old bitch."

As he lunged toward his son, Margaret grabbed a frying pan from the counter and swung it catching Eugene on the back of his head forcing him forward toward her son. Eugene collapsed into his son. Bob held him for a second before lowering him to the floor.

Margaret, shocked by her actions, stared down at her unconscious husband. She let the frying pan drop from her hands and stooped to her prostrate husband. Bob stood motionless, aware that his mother had protected him from his father and that she was now in mortal danger.

While she bent down and stroked her husband's head, Bob picked up the kitchen wall phone and dialed the Townsend City police. His mother looked at him as he spoke into the telephone and described to the dispatcher the circumstances.

Fifteen minutes later four policemen in two patrol cars arrived. Bob and his mother were sitting at the dining room table when the officers arrived. The screen door was unlocked, and Margaret told them to enter. The officers came through the door single file.

Two officers went into the kitchen where Eugene lay. One bent down and felt his pulse and put his ear adjacent to Eugene's mouth and nose and listened for any sound of breathing. The second policeman using a radio contacted dispatch and relayed the need for an ambulance.

Two of the four officers left before the ambulance arrived, the other two remained and interviewed Bob and his mother. Margaret had tears in her eyes as she answered the officer's questions including how she came by that bruise on her face. She knew that her statements would be used by the military to demote or discharge her husband. When the officers had completed the questioning of his mother, they turned to Bob and asked him whether he wanted to add anything to what his mother had said.

"No, sir."

"Ma'am, your husband needs help."

"I know," she said.

"Unless he gets help, there could be a repeat," said the officer doing most of the questioning.

Mrs. Matthews affirmed her understanding by shaking her head.

"Are you going to press charges, ma'am?"

"What do you mean?"

"Your husband has committed assault and battery. He can go to jail."

"Oh no, not jail."

"If you file charges, he'll serve some time, usually thirty days. It may make a difference."

"What difference would that be?" Margaret asked the officer.

"Your husband will know that he can't treat you that way without repercussions."

"But you don't have to live with him," she said, her face damp with tears.

"That's right, I don't. You and your son might want to move out at least for a while."

"Move where?"

"Ma'am, it's just a thought. It's entirely your decision. Just keep in mind that most abusers do not stop abusing until they're stopped."

Mrs. Matthews looked at her son then at the officers. "What does that mean?"

"Jail time," said an officer.

Bob turned to the officers. "I want to press charges. I want him to serve jail time. He deserves it."

"Are you sure?" The taller of the officers asked.

"Yes," said Bob. "I'm sure. Mom, it's for the good. Dad's been getting more violent every weekend."

After the ambulance carrying Eugene Matthews and the two officers left, Margaret and Bob sat in the dining room wondering whether or not they had done the right thing. Before departing, a police officer said that Eugene would probably be sober enough to be released on Sunday. "Being a military officer, he'd get bail without a hitch."

"I think we should move out tonight," said Bob.

"Move where?"

"What about Aunt Mary? She'll take us in. She's got room in her house."

"But she lives in Colorado. That's nearly four hundred miles away."

"Dad's going to be mad when he gets home."

"I can't leave your father."

"Do you love him? I mean really love him? He certainly can't love you, to hit you around like he's done for years."

"I'm not sure," she said. "How are we going to live?"

"We'll find a way."

"Are you sure?"

"I'm sure that Dad will be meaner than ever when he gets home. I don't think we want to be here."

Bob and his mother packed the family car with clothing and personal items. As a military family, they had moved a half-dozen times. This station was the longest for Eugene Matthews, five years next month.

It was nearly midnight by the time they finished packing. Bob locked the back door and checked throughout the house to make sure they had everything they needed. He had even crawled up into the attic to get their winter clothes. His mother grabbed all the pictures and the address and telephone directories. She was certain that when her husband found the house vacant, he would presume that she and Bob had taken off to be with a relative. He'd find their telephone numbers, but why make it easy for him.

Margaret took some cooking utensils and silverware, leaving Eugene enough to get along.

On the way out of town, she stopped at an ATM and took out the maximum amount. She'd do it again when they were in New Mexico and again in Colorado. There wasn't much in the account, but she'd get as much as she could.

Margaret's sister, Mary Anne, a seventh-grade teacher, lived alone in a three-bedroom townhome in Castle Rock, a town midway between Colorado Springs and Denver. Mary Anne, six years older than Margaret, had moved into the townhome almost four years ago with a boyfriend who left shortly afterward opting for a job in California.

His mother stopped at an exit along I-25 north of Santa Fe. Margaret debated whether or not to call her sister. They were five hours away. After debating the pros and cons, she dialed her sister.

The six o'clock call on Sunday morning woke Mary Anne from a sound sleep. Bob overheard his mother's side of the conversation and when she hung up she had a smile on her face.

"What did your sister say?" Bob asked.

"I woke her up. She wants us to come."

"Is that why you're smiling?"

"No. Mary Anne said that Eugene called her a half hour ago. She told him she hadn't heard from me in more than two weeks and if she did he'd be the last person she'd tell. He said he wanted me to come home. Mary Anne told him it was about time I left him. He called her a bitch, but she had the last word. She told him to go to hell and then hung up."

Bob was watching his mother intently, fearing she would start to cry, except she didn't cry. Instead, she wrapped her arms around her son's waist and smiled up at him. "If he'd left you alone I would've stayed."

"Mom, you shouldn't have put up with him."

"What was I supposed to do? You don't marry for better. You marry for better or worse."

"Mom, it couldn't get much worse. We made the right decision."

"You're probably right," said Mrs. Matthews.

"Mom, I am right," said Bob.

If you write one story, it may be bad; if you write a hundred, you have the odds in your favor.
—Edgar Rice Burroughs

Red Leather Boots
By Diane Phelps Budden

RED LEATHER BOOTS! How I wanted a pair. Bright red, flat soled, fitted below the knees, these red boots were made for dancing—folk dancing. They added excitement and energy to the traditional Hungarian national costume: white tulle blouse with full sleeves and pleated skirt encircled with red and green velvet ribbons; white apron; red velvet vest and "parta" or headdress encrusted with gold braid and decorations. Red, green, and white ribbons, the national colors of Hungary, fluttered down the back of the headdress like birds in flight.

The costumes were worn by the children's folk dance troop at the annual Hungarian Grape Festival. This was back in the days when Cleveland, Ohio, was home to the largest Hungarian community outside of Budapest. The festival was held throughout September and October in Hungarian social clubs and churches in the city. Brought to Cleveland by immigrants around the turn of the century, the festival was held wherever Hungarians settled, much as it was in the "old country." Its peasant roots in Hungary were a celebration of a successful harvest season. Each year, before the traditional folk dancing and soulful violin music began at the festival, and following a custom hundreds of years old, men attached clusters of grapes to wires strung high in the hall's side yard: a veritable cloud of red and purple overhead. Children, and even some mischievous adults, would try and "steal" the grapes without being caught by the "judge," who fined the thieves and embarrassed them as loudly as possible. The money was donated to the church. I remember my tiny grandma Lila, usually quiet and reserved, plucking down grapes that were out of my reach, and barely within hers, as fast as possible. As we made off with our grapes, she would yell encouragement to other would-be thieves, obviously enjoying her role as rogue robber.

My sister and I had willingly agreed to learn the children's folk dances. We would have participated even without my mother's insistence just to have the red leather boots. In the characteristic way of the older child, my sis perfected the energetic steps and twists and turns yelled out by our instructor, while I followed along as best I could. I loved dancing, but I was easily distracted.

I found a photograph of our dance troop among my mother's mementos when she passed away, maybe thirty-five young girls and a smattering of boys. (As usual, the boys chose not to folk dance.) My sister and I are both sitting in the front row of the photo with our hands and ankles crossed like the other girls, very ladylike. My hair is cut short, a rite of passage at our home upon graduation from elementary school after a childhood of braids. My sister smiles happily, not me so much. I suddenly remember I had a spectacular case of poison ivy, especially on the fingers of both hands, slathered with calamine lotion by my mother. I had locked my hands and fingers together as if in prayer and rubbed them back and forth fiercely to alleviate the itching. "You'll only make it worse," my mother pointed out. She was right, of course.

As I study the photo a second time, I muse about my upbringing compared to my own children, influenced as I was by a strong immigrant background. Can only second-or third-generation children experience an ethnic upbringing from the old country?

In her book *The Italian Americans: A History"* author Maria Lautrino presents her view of the immigrant experience: "….an isolated first generation dedicates itself to finding work and raising a family; a more secure second generation, recognizing the chasm between its parents and the culture, seeks to eliminate ethnic traits; and the third and fourth generations set about reclaiming ancestral roots to better define the self…."

The elusive old country—I had no idea at the time it meant my grandma's family farm where she had been born and her family struggled to make a living. She had emigrated 40 years earlier when she was 21 years old with $ 26.00 in her pocket and a trunk-full of belongings. She also brought Hungarian customs and traditions that would help shape me as I grew. Like other immigrants, she was looking for a better life in the golden land of America.

It seems like my grandma always lived with us, upstairs in our two-family house in the city, then in the suburbs where she left her Hungarian community and customs behind. She had a knack for giving the perfect back rub as we talked about the day's events in her room. She used broken English and added Hungarian words for emphasis. She also "read" the comics to me, making up stories to match the images; cooked traditional Hungarian dishes (I've never had authentic strudel since she died); and lectured me on the dangers in the world that she read about in her Hungarian-language newspaper.

My second-generation mother worked hard at distancing us from our heritage. She had spent her childhood looking in from the outside, trying to be as American as possible. She wanted her family to have the American dream she saw around her. When my sister started school and had pronunciation issues with English, we were banned from speaking Hungarian at home. My sister and I never did speak it again after that—a loss for both of us—but my parents continued to converse in Hungarian with each other when they didn't want us to know what they were saying. (Oftentimes, we could figure it out anyway.)

In the late '50s my parents built a house using the GI bill and moved out of the city to a middle class, very white suburb, as many families did. I ended up chasing my version of the American dream. In our new suburban life, there was no place for grape festivals and folk dances.

My kids experienced a very American, very middle-class upbringing, so I didn't think it was important to share much of the family's immigrant heritage with them. I was wrong about that. I fell into the same trap as my mother and avoided emphasizing my differentness as I was growing up and raising children. Yet, there it was, part of childhood memories that I have come to embrace as I age, as is the wont of the third generation. I think I sensed it wasn't "cool" to be Eastern European in my hometown at that time. Celebrating your roots wasn't in vogue as it is today. I was fully assimilated into white, suburban America and wouldn't have done anything to rock the boat. (Although, I remember when I ran for president of the student council, I used my last name in my campaign posters: "Vote Vajda." *Catchy*, I thought at the time.)

I have many Hungarian treasures passed down through the family: my grandma's beautifully crocheted doilies and dresser scarves; my mother's expert embroidered linens; dishware with folk motifs; Hungarian playing cards; lots of photos of people from the old country that intrigue me. Who were these very serious-looking people in the stark black and white photos? Nobody seemed to know, or I have forgotten what I was told. In one family shot, the man wears an ill-fitting suit, the mother has covered her head with a babushka, and an array of adults and children encircles them. Is this my grandmother's family? On closer examination, the babushka woman could be her mother, and the man her brother—I see a family resemblance.

I wonder if my mom came to miss the Hungarian traditions her mother instilled in her as she grew up. She was always proud to be Hungarian.

She did continue some Hungarian traditions. At Christmas, we opened gifts at 12 midnight—timed to miss Santa Clause. She bought us Madame Alexander dolls dressed in the national Hungarian dance costume when we were teens. We were more interested in our high school friends, so the dolls were sold along the way. When she began collecting buttons later in life, she prized the Hungarian buttons she was able to find. She became upset when the meaning and pronunciation of Hungarian words she had used when younger eluded her.

Touring Russia a few years ago with my daughter, I stood in a Moscow subway station, viewing the lovely, elaborate murals and sculptures placed in the stations for the enjoyment of the rush of commuters passing through. At one station, I saw a very colorful, wall-sized mosaic mural of a harvest festival in Ukraine. There were a few folk dancers, easy to pick out in their costumes complete with, yes, red leather boots. I studied the boots closely. One dancer was giving a little kick. I snapped photos of this seemingly happy celebration—you never can tell for sure in Russia—focusing on the red boots that were evidently an important accessory for many Eastern European folk costumes. It was amazing that I had traveled so far from home and the memories of the red boots only to reunite with them once again in Russia.

My red leather boots? I never got a pair. Neither did my sister. My mother couldn't afford to buy them, I guess. I'm sure we made her feel guilty about that. We sure wanted those red leather boots. Funny thing? As I study the dancers in the Hungarian Grape Festival photo, none of the girls are wearing boots, red or otherwise, not even the instructor. They're wearing loafers or Mary Janes, just like me.

The Traveler
By Greg Picard and Wendy Picard Gorham

SHE REMAINED SEATED, silent and unmoving, as Chris Becker slowly edged the State Park green pickup into the worn pavement spur of campsite 107 and shoved the gear-shift into park. The crunch of his tires made her turn and look, gray strands of hair dangling across her eyes. Inevitably, on camp checks, someone didn't want to pay, and it never worked out well. Even though law enforcement was part of his job description as a Ranger, it wasn't why he had joined California State Parks. He loved nature and wanted to encourage others to love it too. This was especially easy to do in a place like Humboldt Redwoods with its 300-foot-tall trees, their fluted red columns of shaggy bark fading into the moist morning fog above. Making first contact with a camper over a money dispute, however, was never a good way to start the relationship.

"Good morning!" she said. At least it was a pleasant start to the encounter. Sometimes people became eerily silent when 'the Man' came by to collect the $10 fee. They would turn away or make an effort not to be in camp when staff might come by. This friendly opener was far more encouraging to Chris, yet he was perplexed, upon his cursory examination of the campsite, to realize that she was camping with the bare minimum: a beaten and dented aluminum coffee pot and one small well-worn cast iron skillet sat on the grate above the remains of a slowly smoldering fire. A tarp draped over the picnic table as a makeshift tent barely sheltered a tattered and patched military issue sleeping bag beneath it, and at the far end of the bag, a faded blue rucksack had apparently doubled as a pillow.

His feet sank into the moist duff and needles as he moved off the pavement. "Kind of cold this time of year for just sleeping on the ground with a bag. We get a lot of rain here in the redwoods, too. Don't you have a tent?"

"I don't need a tent. If the picnic table won't shelter me, I can always use your laundry room for the night." She leveled her eyes on his, not really baiting him, but not really innocent either. "'Sides, I got plenty of garbage bags to put on if the rain comes down too hard...stay just as dry as can be." She grabbed her sack from under the table with a weather-reddened hand and shifted from her place on the ground. With much effort, she finally got her leg up and under her enough to rise and grab the edge of the picnic table. Hoisting herself up, Becker could see she was straining and her pale color was not a good sign.

"You okay, ma'am?" His medical training was nagging at him now, and he wondered if he should just abandon the issue of the fee and consider her a patient. Becker was at least supremely glad she hadn't sought refuge from the weather in the laundry. At this late point in the season only a handful of campers were in the park at any given moment, and truly most of them weren't up in the woods to do their wash. If she had gone in there and had some sort of medical problem, he might not have found her for hours. It wouldn't be the first time some homeless person sought shelter in the laundry. Sometimes he wondered if he should replace the 'Laundry' sign with one that said, 'Social Services'.

"I'm fine; nothing a good cup of coffee won't cure…that and maybe being 30 years younger." She took a few slow steps toward the dwindling fire. She appeared to be testing her legs. It reminded him of a newly born deer he had stumbled upon years ago. Its mother had been killed by hunters, poachers actually, and it was taking lonely and tentative steps into a bleak and unfeeling world.

Stepping a foot or two forward, into the spot she'd just vacated, he smelled the distinct odor of alcohol…and onions from where she had stood.

"You traveling far?" he asked as she hobbled stiffly back to the table and lowered herself onto the scarred and cracked bench seat. He made a mental note that it needed to be refinished before the weather got too wet; with close to 80 inches of rain a year, nothing dried out in winter. It also brought into stark relief the level of multi-tasking this job required. He was really struggling with which hat he should be wearing at the moment: medical responder, law enforcer, nature protector, or facilities maintenance.

"Traveled far all my life. But travel implies you have a place to be going and a place to be from…now I've got neither. So maybe wandered is a better word." She pulled out a well-worn tin coffee cup from the pack at her side, "You want some coffee? I got another cup for company."

"You're traveling alone and homeless?" The realization began to dawn on him that perhaps he was going to have to channel a skill set that wasn't really part of the job description according to the State of California, and yet was something he found use for out here in the back of beyond more often than one would expect. He was going to need to listen. He was going to need to care.

"Homeless is such a dirty word, son. I'm not homeless. The world is my home." She made a sort of expansive gesture with her hand that was simultaneously profound and yet also kind of comical, like some down and out game show hostess still trying to point out the potential prizes to be won. Only in this case, at this moment, perhaps the beauty of this place was somehow the prize.

Chris hated to bring it up, but he figured it was time. "You know there is a $10 fee to camp here? I didn't find a pay envelope for this site in the Iron Ranger pay deposit."

"Yes, I know." Something in the timbre of her voice changed almost imperceptibly and some of the folksy slang element seemed to dissipate…almost as though she had been play-acting, and yet not really. Maybe more like another version of herself was emerging from inside the rumpled woman before him. It was strange and subtle, and Chris wasn't sure. He thought that he might just be imagining it. But when she spoke again, there was a definite shift. "I've got a Ph.D, so I did learn how to read. Unfortunately, I am cash strapped until my disability check arrives next week."

This was not what he had expected her to say. She was novel, and Becker was curious and decided to stall. "What's your Ph.D. in?"

"Philosophy. Most useless degree in the world, but I loved it."

Becker stifled the urge to chuckle. He knew it was misplaced and inappropriate, but he couldn't help but think of a few philosophy majors that he had known in college. The image he held of them in his mind seemed to support the possibility that they could have all ended up homeless…it seemed like a cerebral pursuit with little actual boots on the ground application. He was practical and pragmatic—perhaps to a fault sometimes—and he was skeptical of some of the things people chose to study in the hope of making a career out of them.

"Really? Wow…what did you do with it?" He assumed she hadn't graduated from a doctoral program and then immediately become homeless, and so suddenly he was keenly interested in connecting the dots.

"The only thing you can do with a degree like that…teach other poor unsuspecting students the useless art." She chuckled wryly and took a sip of the steaming black coffee. "Ah, nothing like a good cup of Joe." The colloquial vernacular seeped back in at unexpected moments, punctuating the juxtaposition of her circumstance. "I was at Duke for fifteen years. I loved that place. I loved that job. Thought I'd die still lecturing in those venerable halls."

"What happened?"

"Life happened, son—it always does."

They were both silent for a moment in the crisp autumnal air, as each digested that little bit of bitter truth. For Chris' part, his mind wandered to Lori and the baby. The last two years since Allie's birth had been a whirlwind, but not so much that he hadn't clearly felt the disconnect between himself and his wife. He wondered if that was just a natural part of life. Did children bring some couples together and somehow cast the distance of others into high relief? He couldn't shake the feeling that he was standing on a cliff with a tidal wave rushing down on him. It made him wonder if she had family out there somewhere.

"Ever get married? Any kids?" he asked.

The pause was so long Becker began to wonder if she was going to answer. "You never believe it until it happens to you." Her words had a faraway quality to them like she was talking to herself more than to him. He somehow knew he shouldn't interrupt, not even to encourage her, so he waited.

"She had been a beautiful baby, my girl Charlotte. She grew into a fine young woman. She was the kind who would take in every stray cat she saw; stray humans, too. She actually started a non-profit for orphans when she was sixteen. I think she was always looking for the father she never had in every man she knew. Unmarried, I had considered an abortion. I can't even wrap my mind around how empty life would have been without having known her. When she married that man, I cried like any mother would—watching her baby girl in white with a cluster of roses and a face full of hope. Not a year passed before I was crying again—only this time the bouquet was for her grave."

Chris sat in silence, transported through the raw power of her grief. He imagined attending his own daughter's funeral, and he couldn't even complete the thought without his chest tightening and his heart racing. He wanted to ask what had happened, but he couldn't make the words come. She must have read the question in his eyes.

"He wasn't a good man." She didn't say more, and he didn't pry, and yet a million scenarios played in his head while he waited for her to continue. "Foucault and Derrida couldn't explain how a man could strangle a woman with his bare hands and not be sorry. Suddenly I didn't have much use for philosophers. I didn't have much use for anyone."

They sat a few minutes more, letting the morning sun penetrate the foggy wooded coolness and warm them from the outside as the coffee did its magic on the inside. She stirred and began packing up her things.

"Can I give you a ride somewhere? I was thinking of getting a burger down in Garberville if you are headed south. There is room in the truck if you are thinking of going that way."

"A burger, at 8:00 in the morning?" She looked at him quizzically and Chris looked at his boots trying to hide from her gaze. Perhaps he should have instead been trying to figure out how to explain transporting a civilian in his Park truck without proper permission, but at the moment that didn't seem to matter.

"Ok, Garberville sounds as good as anywhere." She smiled and extended out the weather-reddened hand. "The name's Mae Redfield."

"Nice to meet you." He reached out and solidly gripped the woman's hand and then hesitated for a beat, considering how to address this ragged study in contradictions, then decided there was really only one choice, "Dr. Redfield. I'm Chris."

The ride through the southern half of the park's 55,000-acre ownership always gave Becker a lift. Massive coast redwoods lined the highway as it paralleled the river. Today it was within its banks. This winter, if the predictions were right, it likely would flood, perhaps leaving this same highway a dozen feet under water in places.

"So, you mentioned you are on disability, what happened?"

"During the murder trial," there was a pause and she breathed deeply, "I tried to kill the guy." She was so mattered of fact in her tone that Chris coughed and shifted uncomfortably. "The bailiffs who tackled me broke my pelvis in six places. I'm lucky I'm alive and can still walk at all. The head injury from being knocked around left me with epileptic attacks."

Chris was left speechless but managed a weak, "So where are you headed. Any place special?" He felt tension rising in the pit of his stomach and he was hoping to change the subject.

"Folsom Prison."

"Whoa," he reflexively took his foot off the gas for a second, then, slowly depressed the pedal again, "that sounds pretty serious." He knew some of California's worst felons were housed there.

"Yeah, it is serious. I have to meet someone. And it has to be Wednesday."

The small hairs on his neck rose up, "You have a meeting with someone at the prison?"

"Yes, we have unfinished business."

~~~~~~

The sun was shining brightly in Folsom as she waited along the front walkway. She sat on a bench with the .38 concealed under her backpack, just another homeless person loitering and looking for a handout. She watched as the door opened and thought *what goes around comes around* and fingered the trigger in her lap. Her eyes were fixed, unwavering, on the discharge door. She waited. There was a calm about her that belied the churning of her thoughts. She imagined lifting the gun slowly, taking aim, and feeling the cool metal of the trigger smooth against her finger. She imagined the glint of the sun on the barrel and the glint of fear in his eye the instant before the bullet found a home in his heart. She imagined....

From the corner of her eye, she caught movement. An attendant was pushing a man in a wheelchair out the side door. Visiting hours were over, so she wondered what this person was doing here this late in the afternoon. She was annoyed at the momentary break in focus this distraction had caused. She was determined not to miss her chance. But as the two approached, she could see the one pushing was a prison employee...and the realization dawned on her that the man in the chair was her daughter's killer.

Only fifty-three years old, but fifteen years of prison had taken a toll she had not expected. He was slumped and drooled from the corner of his mouth. Stroke. The vacant look in his eyes bespoke the lack of stimulation he could receive. It was as if the world around him didn't exist, and some inner dialogue was all he had. Perhaps he was out of one prison, but it seemed he would forever remain in another. She slowly watched as the attendant struggled and shoved to get him in the city's disability transit van.

She watched the van pull away from the curb and head out the long drive toward the main road, then put the revolver back into her pack, took a deep breath and slowly rose and walked toward the Folsom Lake campground.

"What goes around, comes around," she whispered, "one way or the other." *A philosophy of sorts*, she thought to herself.

"Who's to say that dreams and nightmares aren't as real as the here and now?"
—*John Lennon*

Egyptian Nightmare
By S. Resler Nelson

HE WAS GONE. Just like that. Only moments ago, my friend, Alex, had been beside me, guiding me as we shopped in the souks of Old Cairo. He was leading me through crowds in streets too narrow for cars. We were talking and laughing, and then he disappeared.

At first, I thought little of it. Surely, he'd just been sidetracked and had taken a quick detour into a shop to look at something that intrigued him. Any minute he would resurface, and we would continue sightseeing. But he didn't return.

Ten minutes passed, and it felt like an hour. I hadn't moved, remembering my father's advice when I was a child. "If you get lost or we get separated, stay put. It's easier to find one person than two."

Looking down the street in both directions, I tried to peer into each alcove. I didn't see Alex or anything else that looked familiar. I hadn't a clue as to where I was. Why should I? I had just arrived in Egypt today, and I was relying on Alex, who knew Cairo well.

Suddenly, I realized that I was a blonde female and a curiosity among the throng of dark faces. Egyptians passed by me—women with black, kohl-lined eyes lowered, and men in cotton full-length galabeya robes, with bold, almost seductive stares. I started to feel uneasy.

The street was dim, even with a hot, noonday sun overhead. The walkway was shadowed by balconies and overhanging canopies. Skeins of fabric, cotton robes and carpets hung from shop awnings. The smells of spices and urine, fruit, and perfumes mixed in the stifling air. And always the crowd, pushing in two directions like two streams running counter, moving in a singular sea, making me slightly dizzy.

A Muslim call to prayer echoed from a minaret, *"Allah Akbar,"* followed by melodious chants that drifted across the city.

Still, I waited, glimpsing at everyone, yet no one, trying to be inconspicuous, yet knowing I was obviously out of place.

A young Egyptian boy about thirteen appeared before me.

"Are you English, madam?" he asked softly.

"Yes," I lied, not wanting to divulge I was American.

"You need a guide? I can show you for a small price. Many things to see and buy. I show you," he said and reached out his hand toward mine.

Instinctively, I withdrew.

"I'm waiting for my fri . . . husband. He is showing me around," I answered quickly.

He looked knowingly at my ringless hand.

"I will be over there if you need a guide," he said and pointed to a café down the street. I watched him as he walked away and sat down among the men who were sipping coffee, talking, and smoking from free-standing water pipes.

Thirty minutes passed, and it was now clear that something was terribly wrong. I began plotting what to do next. It would be best to take a taxi back to my hotel and wait for Alex to contact me. If he didn't, I could notify the authorities. It seemed useless to continue standing in the middle of the souk.

The boy appeared before me again.

"Is madam still lost?" he asked.

"Of course not. But my husband has been detained. I will need a taxi."

"Yes, madam. Taxi no problem," he smiled.

He was a handsome boy, tall, thin, and unkempt. His curly black hair was scruffy, and his striped galabeya was stained and unraveling around the hem. He wore no shoes and his feet were calloused and dirty from walking the streets. But his smile was bright, and his brown eyes shone.

"Follow me," he said confidently, and I did. We continued in the direction Alex and I had been walking. He turned off the busy street into a dark, narrow alley. My heart quickened a beat, but I was in no position to argue.

Two emaciated cats hissed and growled at one another in the recesses of a closed doorway. They stopped, watching us approach. The boy stomped his foot, and the black one yowled and rushed behind me, causing me to gasp.

"I don't like cats," he muttered. "They are bad luck."

To my relief, the dismal backstreet opened into a slightly wider one. But it soon tightened and curved into another deserted alleyway that looked as though it would dead-end. Arabic music drifted from inside a dark opening. I failed to see how this was leading us to a taxi, and a sudden panic overcame me.

"Are you sure you know your way," I asked faintly.

"Do you know yours, madam?" he answered, and his voice sounded deeper.

I glanced behind me, hoping to see someone on the street, but it was still bare. How could one street be so crowded and another devoid of life?

"Perhaps we should be going the other direction," I suggested gingerly, still looking away.

When I turned to the boy again, a man was facing me. He was older, much older. One eye had been blinded and only a pale, whitish orb stared from the socket. A large scar crossed from his cheekbone to the corner of his mouth, causing his lip to droop. A long dark-handled dagger flashed in his hand. I wanted to scream, but no sound would come. Fear was choking me. Something cold and wet touched my hand.

I screamed so loud that I startled myself awake and bolted upright in bed. My collie whined anxiously and nudged my hand with his cold, wet nose. I recoiled, a leftover reflex from my nightmare.

"Oh, Laddie," I smiled and hugged his soft, sable coat, happy to find myself only dreaming. He looked at me curiously, with head cocked, and bounded from the room. I could hear my mother singing off-key in the kitchen, clinking dishes and silverware.

"Are you awake, Liz?" she shouted.

"Yes, Mother."

"Well, you'd better start moving. I'm fixing you a good breakfast for your big adventure. Your flight leaves for Cairo today, you know."

≈≈≈

After twenty-one hours of flights, the jumbo jet landed at Cairo International Airport. Alex was waiting and ushered me through customs and the crowds until we were outside hailing a taxi. After my nightmare, I planned to stick to him like pitch on a pine tree.

He was tall, dark, and handsome. Sorry to use the cliché, but he was, and I wondered why I broke up with him—other than the fact that when he moved to Cairo for an American Embassy job, I wasn't carefree enough to go with him. Seeing him now for the first time since he'd left the States, I might have to rethink that decision.

It was midday and hot. Alex said, "I thought we'd drop by the Hilton. You can check in, and then I'll show you around."

That's what we did, plus have lunch at the hotel. Afternoon and we were back in a taxi, headed for Old Cairo and the famous Khan al-Khalili souk.

"You'll love the shopping and the people. Such an international mix," he said, but flashes of my eerie dream emerged.

Once there, I have to admit the marketplace was colorful, expansive, and unique—wall to wall tourists from many countries and walks of life mingling with the Egyptians. We explored the souvenir shops, seeing everything from spices and curios to artwork and clothes, amidst lively Arabic music. I never left Alex's side. He probably thought I was clingy, and he was right.

As we moved with the flow of people, two busloads of Japanese tourists swept through, and I was carried along with them. When I tried to stop, I felt like a rock protruding in the middle of a river, so I kept moving with the current. Finally, they thinned out enough that I could anchor myself.

It was then I realized that Alex was nowhere in sight. I told myself not to panic; we just got separated. Stay put and he'll reappear. He'd be looking for me, too. Any moment he'd resurface, and we would continue exploring. But he didn't. Long minutes passed, seeming like half an hour, and his tall frame failed to crest above the crowd.

An Egyptian boy emerged before me. He was a striking child, lean and ragged, maybe ten or eleven years old. His wavy black hair was disheveled and his soiled, white galabeya robe was tattered around the hem. He wore no shoes, exposing youthful feet that were soiled and toughened from walking the streets. But his smile was genuine, and his dark eyes sparkled.

"Is madam lost?" he asked.

"No. My fri . . . uh . . . husband has been detained, and I'm waiting for him."

He glanced at my ringless hand and grinned. *Did he believe me?* He must know many tourists leave their jewelry locked in hotel safes.

"You come to my grandfather's shop and wait," he suggested. "You sit until you see your friend come by."

His offer was inviting. The overhangs offered little shade, and I wasn't used to the heat. Besides, I felt conspicuous standing alone as others wandered by. I imagined they were from all over the world, but they were *with* someone or in a group.

"Follow me," the boy said confidently, and for some reason I did. We continued in the direction Alex and I had been walking, and I thought if we walked much farther without seeing him, I would refuse to go on. My dream kept haunting me.

At this point in my story, you're thinking *take out your cell phone and call Alex. Cut the drama.* But I forgot to mention, the year was 1990 and cell phones were relatively new. In fact, the first portable cell phone emerged on the market in the 1980s, and the cost was prohibitive. The world was so different then.

I was about to ask the boy his name when he stopped near a dark, narrow alley. My heart quickened a beat. Two cats, mangy and scrawny, hissed and scowled at one another in a darkened doorway. They stopped quarreling, wary of us. The boy stomped his foot, and the black one yowled and scurried behind me, causing me to jump aside.

"I don't like cats," he muttered. "They are bad luck."

My eyes stayed on the cats, and when I turned back to the boy, a man was facing me. He was old and so hunched over that his galabeya touched the ground in front of him. One eye was covered with a well-worn patch. A large, jagged scar crossed from his cheekbone to the corner of his mouth, causing his lip to gape slightly. I almost gasped at the similarities between the old man and the one in my dream.

The boy frowned, not amused by my rude stare.

"This is my grandfather, Gamil. And I am Assad. Here is our shop," the boy said, with a sweep of his arms, gesturing at a small alcove, crammed with touristy items—oriental rugs, t-shirts, glass bottles of perfumed oils, handmade sandals, and much more.

Assad asked my name.

"Elizabeth," I said, still holding back.

"My name means lion," he said with pride. "What does your name mean?"

"I have no idea," I answered, and he gave me a quizzical look.

His grandfather turned away and went about showing his wares to a couple of Middle Easterners. The shop was marginal, and I figured the old man and Assad struggled to earn a meager living.

I sat long enough to rest and reassess the situation, and then I rose to leave. At once, the boy was at my side, looking up at me with those deep brown eyes, and saying, "For a dollah I will help you find your friend. I know my way, and you don't."

I'd abandoned my "husband" references, as the boy didn't seem to be buying it.

Rather than meander alone, I agreed. "Okay, but we must go back the way we came."

Assad swept a dark lock of hair from his forehead and smiled, "Yes, madam."

I offered him the dollar, and he quickly took it from my hand. Then he motioned with a nod of his head, "Come . . ."

Alex and I had taken several detours as we walked, and I wasn't sure where I was anymore. I glanced back at the grandfather's shop. The old man didn't seem to notice or care that Assad was leaving with me, and that made me wonder about their relationship.

"We find him, madam. Not to worry," the boy said and moved out with a self-assurance that both amazed and concerned me. *Was I being foolish to follow him?* How many times had he "guided" a stray tourist for a fee?

But I kept stride with Assad—until I lost him, too. He slithered through a bunch of young men and vanished. The men were Egyptian, and they seemed rough. Most were bearded and muscular, wearing modern European clothes, and arguing among themselves.

Again, I was alone and distraught. Only this time, I decided to take charge. Surely a police officer would pass by, or I'd encounter someone fluent in English—maybe even an American tour group.

I stood still, considering my options, when Assad reappeared, pushing through the group of men with Alex close behind him. The boy seemed quite proud of himself when he realized that the man he led was the one I'd been searching for.

Alex gave me a hug and said, "This young man saw me standing alone, looking through the crowds for someone. We connected, and here I am. Clever boy."

He smiled at Assad, and the young boy beamed. "Sorry I lost you, madam, but I found your friend."

"You certainly did, Assad," I said, hugging him, not even considering if that was orthodox.

Alex relaxed his shoulders. "Assad says he's been watching over you."

"That's true," I said, a rush of relief enveloping me.

Looking down at the boy, Alex said, "This is for you." He slipped Assad a twenty-dollar bill. It would go a long way in his daily struggles.

Assad grinned and turned to me. "I have something for you, madam."

He held a small replica of a lion in his outstretched palm. It was handcrafted in reddish clay, and the lion's mane had been etched into shaggy strands. The likeness was crude which made me cherish it all the more. I knew he'd made it.

A thank you seemed inadequate, but I said it anyway. "Thank you very much. I will keep it always."

He smiled one last time at us and skipped through a throng of people before he disappeared.

We have the clay lion to this day—a reminder of Egypt and Assad and kindness.

Give Me Another Drink
By Cordell Compton

"I'LL ASK YOU THAT ONCE AGAIN, Officer Parker. How many drinks did you have that night, the night of April 14?"

"A couple, maybe. I don't believe it was more than that."

"Are you sure? Can you be absolutely positive about that statement?"

Officer John Frederick Parker slumped in the chair on the witness stand. He shuffled his feet, clasped his hands and looked at them with focused intensity.

"The Tribunal is waiting, Officer Parker. What is your answer?"

Although he was just barely thirty-five years old, it seemed to the members of the Military Tribunal that the witness had aged visibly before their eyes in recent days. Finally, Parker sat up in the hard, uncomfortable witness chair. Even though the windows were open, the room was stuffy with little cross breeze in the humid and dank air. Cigar smoke drifted around the room and formed a blue haze near the ceiling.

Parker looked up at Assistant Judge Advocate General John A. Bingham who stood less than three feet away. Bingham leaned on the railing of the witness box that separated the two men.

"I'm sorry, Sir, I cannot be exactly sure how many drinks I had that night. But I don't think I was drunk."

Bingham spun around and glared at the Tribunal's exalted members who were sitting high on the bench in their formal uniforms, medals and battle ribbons hanging on their respective chests like so much wallpaper. He slammed his fist down on the witness box railing with an echoing SMACK that bounced off the walls.

"Don't think you were drunk! What kind of answer is that? What kind of officer are you? Matter of fact, what kind of *man* are you? The biggest responsibility in the world was yours that night. And do you know what?" Bingham's face now was no more than a foot from Parker's. "You failed miserably in those duties, Officer Parker. Dereliction of duty is too kind a phrase to use in your case. Propriety and the high standards of this Tribunal prohibit me from voicing what I really think of you and your actions on the night of April 14. Or should I say your inactions?"

Officer Parker slumped again in the chair. His chest heaved as he groaned and gasped for air. Assistant JAG Bingham continued to glare at his witness. Perhaps "victim" would be more appropriate.

Major General David Hunter, the Military Tribunal's president, puffed himself up in his chair on the bench. His fellow general and brevet general officers flanked him on either side. Brevet Colonel Horace Porter was the only officer serving on the Tribunal below the rank of general officer.

General Hunter coughed and cleared his throat. "Does the Government have any more questions for this witness?"

Bingham, at last, stepped away from the witness box that encapsulated the demolished form of Officer John F. Parker.

"A closing comment, Sir. Officer Parker, while you are not on trial during these proceedings, if the Government determines there was any dereliction of duty or malfeasance in the performance of your duties, you may, in fact, be subject to a trial to answer for your actions. Do you understand, Officer Parker?" asked Bingham.

Parker slowly nodded his head. Bingham looked down at his witness and for a brief moment, a thin shred of compassion welled within him.

"Let the record reflect that the witness nodded his head in acknowledgment of my statement," said Bingham. "The Government has no further questions."

"Very well, the witness is excused. You may step down," pronounced General Hunter.

Parked reached down and collected his duty cap that earlier had clattered to the floor of the witness box. He nearly tripped getting out of the box and had to quickly grab onto the railing that had separated him from his tormentor during the day's examination. Parker half shuffled, half dragged himself down the aisle and disappeared through the door at the rear of the makeshift courtroom at the Old Capitol Prison. A husky pair of army sergeants acting as bailiffs for the Tribunal closed the door behind Parker.

Major General Hunter rapped his gavel on the bench. "The Tribunal is adjourned for the day. The Tribunal will reconvene tomorrow at 10 a.m."

"All rise," barked another army sergeant standing to the left of the bench. General Hunter and his fellow officers stepped down from the bench and filed out through a side door. As soon as Col. Porter's coattail disappeared through the door, the courtroom cleared instantly.

The Military Tribunal Clerk, George Graham, glanced at the clock over the rear entrance. It was exactly 6:37 p.m. General Hunter had gaveled the session to order that morning promptly at 10:00 a.m. The Clerk noted the time in the Tribunal's Record of Proceedings log book.

He tucked the book under his arm and delivered it into the custody of the Master at Arms.

Graham's work for the day was completed. It was long and grinding for him as well as for the rest of those persons in the tight confines of the courtroom. Even so, the day was relatively short compared to other days during the Tribunal's sessions. The testimony was fascinating, dull, insightful and contradictory—often at the same time. Tomorrow was Friday and he eagerly awaited the weekend's respite when the Tribunal was not in session.

During brief breaks in the proceedings during the day, Graham kept thinking to himself: if only Officer Parker had been in the theater that night and had done his duty, the world would surely be different now and this Military Tribunal would not be in session. What if Officer Parker had not weakened in his desire for a drink at that critical moment? What if Parker had stayed at his post? And would he have been able to stop the horrible deed? And what if Charles Forbes, the president's valet, and messenger, had not allowed Booth into the presidential box?

Graham noticed the room had darkened since it was nearly dusk. The day's session ended before the gas jets had to be lit. The approaching darkness matched George Graham's mood as he trudged from the courtroom.

~~~~~

Officer John F. Parker gave many hours of testimony that hot June day in 1865 along with several other persons. Parker was not on trial himself but under the withering examination by Bingham, he felt as if he were on trial for his life. In a way, he was.

If someone chose to study Parker's appearance, the person would have difficulty describing him afterward. With a sturdy build and standing several inches over five feet in height, Parker had few distinguishing characteristics. He kept his beard closely trimmed. His dark brown hair did not touch his shirt collar and he always wore a beret regardless of weather. This hypothetical witness would have been forced to describe John Parker with the bland and unhelpful word as; average. Only when he dressed for duty did he assume any outstanding demeanor. The revolver strapped around his waist gave this ordinary man a level of authority.

Parker had a job with the Washington, D. C. Metropolitan Police Department and was assigned as a guard at the White House during the closing days of the Civil War. He accompanied President Abraham Lincoln to Ford's Theater the night of April 14, 1865, when Lincoln was assassinated by John Wilkes Booth. Parker was not an official bodyguard of the president. In fact, Lincoln had no official bodyguards during his presidency in the true sense of the word. At the time, more emphasis was placed on protecting the White House rather than the president himself. Although troops were quartered at the White House during the war, the safety and protection of the president was, at best, casual.

Frequently, Mr. Lincoln rode his horse to the Old Soldiers Home that was near the White House. He enjoyed getting away from the pressures of directing the war efforts for a few hours' respite. He rode at a leisurely gait that allowed him to tip his tall stovepipe hat to well-wishers along the route. During his excursions by carriage when guests or Cabinet officials accompanied him, seldom was there a semblance of any kind of protection save the carriage driver.

After Lincoln was escorted to and seated in his box at the theater on the night of April 14, 1865, Parker left the theater for the Star Saloon next door on 10th Street, N.W., for a drink. He may have had several drinks, but no one really knows for certain. In another tragic oversight Lincoln's valet and messenger, Charles Forbes, allowed Booth into the presidential box. Booth was well known at the theater and had no trouble gaining entrance. Forbes mistakenly assumed that Booth merely wanted to greet the president. Had that event not occurred or if Parker or anyone else had been nearby, Booth might have been stopped or at least hampered in his effort to kill the president.

Along with the other three hundred sixty-five witnesses, Parker was called to testify in the trial of the eight accused conspirators. In the days and weeks after the assassination leading up to the Military Tribunal's proceedings, he began to feel that many persons pointed fingers at him regarding his actions – or "non-actions" as Bingham spat out during his testimony – on the night of the president's murder.

John F. Parker thought he knew his job's duties and believed he had performed them well and yet . . . .?

~~~~~

The background of John F. Parker, as we say, was mostly normal – which is to say it was troubled, erratic, unsettled and unguided. John was born May 14, 1830, to Elias and Mary Parker at their farm in Hagerstown, Maryland. Their farm was modest in size and unpretentious in keeping with other farms in the area. Elias often swelled with pride and false modesty as he swapped stories and yarns at the Hagerstown General Store. "Yes," he would say as he leaned back against Fred Johnson's counter, "my place is just about the right size. Twenty-five acres is big enough to support my family but not too big to handle." Of course, John Parker had a contrary opinion had he been allowed to voice it. To him, the farm was too large especially when he was dragooned into helping with the field chores such as plowing and weeding their corn, beans and tobacco crops.

John's family was about average for the era. He was the youngest of his three brothers and four sisters. His mother died giving birth to the youngest daughter when he was eight. His oldest brother Donald had little interaction with John who instead chose other diversions such as finding ways to escape the farm while chasing after the neighboring farm girls. John's oldest sister Margaret likewise had little interaction with him. After the death of their mother, Margaret became the *de facto* mother to the younger sisters and brothers. She did not care for the "assignment" but handled the job with as much energy, grace, and dedication as possible.

To be fair, John Parker did not have much interaction with his brothers and sisters except the normal family squabbles that occasionally erupted. John always raced them to the family table making sure he got his share of the meals and more if possible.

After his mother died, John quit school in the fourth grade. Had he voiced an opinion of his actions, he probably would have noted it had not been a great sacrifice for him. He was a poor student; his reading and writing skills were barely adequate to keep him from being classified as illiterate. Math was a great mystery to John, but he clung desperately to any money he might gain from the outside jobs he performed on rare occasions.

Around the time when John was fifteen (1845), he was introduced to another John – Mr. John Barleycorn. At first young Mr. Parker was revolted by the taste of the other John. The amber liquid felt like molten lead as it singed his tongue and attacked his throat on its way to his stomach. He remarked Mr. Barleycorn burned his "innards" for hours afterward.

As events sometimes tend to work themselves out, Parker grew more tolerant of the amber fire he consumed. His older brother and other lads from the area would sneak a bottle to his care from time to time. John developed a taste or immunity to Mr. Barleycorn's side effects. In fact, he became quite fond of his new friend's acquaintance that stayed with him throughout his life.

~~~~

John F. Parker was not charged with any crime or dereliction of duty during the investigation of the president's assassination. The Military Tribunal determined that he had discharged his official duties adequately on the night of April 14, 1865. He and other members of the Metropolitan Police Force had accompanied President Lincoln from the White House to Ford's Theater as prescribed which was the extent of their duties.

As a result of the publicity from the Military Tribunal's investigation, the public inferred that Parker had, in fact, failed in his duties to protect the president even if that were technically not true. Parker was only one person affected by the president's death. Among his police force colleagues and superiors, he was considered merely "adequate" as an officer. Parker's life-long affair with Mr. Barleycorn began to affect his work duties. In 1868 he was discharged from the Metropolitan Police Force for "violation of rules." The circumstances were hazy but whispered talk indicated Parker was increasingly too fond of the liquid fire he consumed.

From his discharge in 1868 to his death in 1890, Parker bounced among a series of menial jobs none of which he retained for any length of time. He died a poor man carrying an invisible and undeserved but real shroud of guilt with him.

≈≈≈

"Did you hear about John Parker?

"No, what happened?"

"He died last month from heart failure, I think, and was buried in the Pauper's Field outside town," replied Fred Johnson, a casual acquaintance of Parker's.

"Well, I hadn't seen him for months," said Richard Swensen, "he never seemed to shake the guilt that he drug around."

"Yeah, that was too bad," said Johnson, "I wonder how things would have turned out if Lincoln had lived?"

The Leader of the Band
By John Maher

ENERGIZED AND FIT, I trudged up "Heartbreak Hill #1" on my daily 3½-mile morning trek around Prescott Canyon Estates. I had The Rolling Stones on my iPod, the sun strong, the sky cloudless and brilliant Arizona blue, the air crisp and cool. All was right in my world.

My daily walks include a regular internal dialog. Random thoughts breeze into my consciousness, and I kick them around until another surfaces. I enjoyed listening to my music and quiet reflection, my style of meditation. Sometimes a song will trigger a long-buried memory, a tender reminiscence. And I give myself to contemplating

On this day, as I strode along breathing in the bracing air, I examined the productive actions I was taking for my health, steps I hadn't adhered to when I was working full-time. After retiring eight years ago, I put being healthy at the top of my to-do list. I work out daily, starting with my jaunt around the hillsides where I live. I stretch, I lift weights, I do cardio exercises.

As I was reviewing this litany of steps and giving myself a high five, I said, "I know I'm gonna die, just not any time soon" … and the instant this thought occurred, I realized it was a favorite maxim of The Old Man. My next thoughts flashed to that hospital room in San Jose, California on that dismal day in early November 1990.

Tom, my older brother and the family's designated administrator-in-chief, called me at my job in New York City with the news. "The Old Man's cancer's back. He's in the hospital. It's inoperable. They're discharging him Saturday. You'd better come out." Unsaid but understood, The Old Man was terminal, and they were shipping him home to die. I needed to fly to California to say my goodbyes. Two days later, I was on an American Airlines non-stop from New York to San Jose.

Tom and my younger brother Patrick met me at the San Jose airport. When the three of us got together, laughter and comedy ensued, leading to total bedlam. Because both brothers lived in Los Angeles and I lived in New York, our get-togethers were annual events. The airport welcoming's tended to be even more raucous from pent-up anticipation.

This time it was small hellos, brief hugs, and limited conversation. The ride to the hospital was quiet and solemn.

When we turned and got off the elevator on the third floor of the hospital, I peered down the short bright cream-painted corridor into my father's dimly lit room. He was sitting in profile on the edge of his lowered hospital bed. His elbows were on his knees, his head hung over, the silhouette of the beaten contender on his stool in the corner.

I came in the door first and rested my palm on The Old Man's shoulder in greeting. It was bone, no muscle. I was stunned. My father was always well-built, muscular, 190 pounds, with deltoid shoulders like small boulders. A gifted natural athlete with God-given talent, as a young man he earned money as a pro football player and as a light heavyweight prizefighter. When he retired from the book publishing business in his late sixties, he bought a condo next to a golf course. He played 18 holes every day, Monday through Friday and 36 holes on Saturday and Sunday. Vanity kept him doing his Canadian Air Force exercise routine every morning until cancer lodged in his colon at age 78. Now he was that detested object, a veritable bag of bones. I felt heartsick.

I gritted my teeth and said, "Hey Pop."

He swung his head and peered at me, his ice-blue eyes glazed and used up, the fire gone. He replied in a labored voice, "Hey John-o." He noticed my hand lingering on his bony shoulder as if waiting for a miraculous change, and he said with faint recognition, "No meat left there."

"Ah, what the hell, Pop," I said. I pulled up a chair and mimicked his elbows-on-knees posture. Tom and Patrick came in the room, murmured hellos, and stood behind me their arms folded in anticipation. We tried to exchange banal pleasantries... how was your flight, how are the kids, how's your job... but the four of us knew these were an air-filling delay. Then Tom asked, "So what's the deal Pop?"

"It's like the old Myron Cohen joke about Morris the spy and The Big Black Dog." Tom, Patrick and I gazed at each other puzzled. Myron Cohen was one of The Old Man's favorite 1950s comics, a regular on The Ed Sullivan Show, a master at telling his jokes using a Yiddish accent. But we were baffled about the reference, given the circumstances. The Old Man, perceiving our bewilderment, launched into the tale.

"Israel intelligence sees that the Arabs are fitting to launch another war. So, they call in their best spy, Morris, to turn up out what's going on. They send Morris secretly into the various Arab states neighboring

Israel to dig up information. About six weeks later Morris returns with his report and meets with the Israeli leaders. They say, "So Morris, vat's going on?" "Oy" say's Morris, "It's terrible, just terrible. In the north, the Syrians have 150,000 men, 1,000 tanks, and 300 planes. In the east, the Jordanians have 100,000 men, 500 tanks, and 200 planes, and in the south, the Egyptians have 200,000 men, 1,500 tanks, and 500 planes." "Oy vey, this is very bad," said the leaders. "But Morris, what about in the vest, vat's in the vest?" "Oh, mien gott, dis is da vourst! This is very scary" says Morris. "In the vest, they gotta big black dog!"

Tom, Patrick and I chuckled politely, uncertain how this story fit The Old Man's situation. We said nothing. The Old Man lifted his head, studied us, and sensing our confusion said, "What I've got is the big black dog." The baseboard heater hummed, and we waited. He sat back, considered us again, and said, "I have to tell you, it's given me many dark nights of the soul." Now our understanding was complete. The three of us exhaled in unison. We were looking at the inevitable. The Old Man was going to die. We said nothing, just tight-lipped, jaws clenched. I held down my despair.

Then, The Old Man brought us back to the real world. He barked, "Hey, help me over to that thing… I gotta go" while pointing at a porta-potty on four aluminum legs sitting by the room's washbasin. I positioned myself on one side of The Old Man, Tom on the other, and we hoisted him from his place on the edge of the bed by putting our hands under his upper arms. I was shocked at how light and frail he was, this skeleton that'd been a super-being. We helped him shuffle over to the toilet; he opened the back of his hospital gown, spread his feet and sat. Again, Tom, Patrick and I glanced at each other, shocked speechless by the image of our once commanding father sitting there going to the bathroom in front of us. Heartsick and afflicted by this public humiliation, I turned my head.

The Old Man was never the nurturing, avuncular, pipe smoking, Robert Young Father-Knows-Best parent. He was a hard-nosed individual, a first generation, ass-out-of-the-pants, Irish-American kid whose intelligence and drive made him a success in book publishing. He once said to my mother, in response to her criticism of how tough he was with his three sons, "I'm not raising boys. I'm making men." The U.S. Marine Corps was perfect for The Old Man's personality and a template for his parenting skills. We paid heed to his commands and followed his orders without question or comment. We referred to him behind his back as "The Old Man," because that's what he called himself to stress a point:

"Your Old Man knows what he's talking about." His use of the "Old Man" moniker came from his time in the Corps; it's a term of grudging respect enlisted men and subordinates use the term covertly when referring to commanding officers. We used it as well because it fit.

As I stood in front of The Old Man perched there on the portable toilet, I looked at the ceiling, I looked at my feet, I looked at the wall. Then, out of the corner of my eye, I glanced at him. He had assumed the elbows-on-knees pose, but this time he juggled a roll of toilet paper from one had to the other. He caught my eye, turned his face up to mine as I focused on him. Then he flipped the roll of toilet paper, and I grabbed it with both hands.

"You gotta help me here," he said.

My mind reeled. This wasn't happening. I was paralyzed. My father, a man I held in awe, a man whose physicality and his willingness to bring it red-hot kept me fearful most of my life, a man I knew as all-powerful, of towering strength… he wanted me to wipe his butt. I stood there dumbfounded my mouth open, my eyes lasering from Tom's eyes to Patrick's and back again, wordlessly begging for help, desperate and panicked.

With conviction, The Old Man said, "Hey, I wiped your ass when you were a baby. Now it's your turn to wipe mine."

Then a resolution hit me. Tom had always held the favored position as the eldest son in the family. For me, Tom had been coach, cheerleader, confidant, and consigliere, the responsible one. So, I flipped the roll of toilet paper to him and said, "You're the oldest. You do it." His eyes went full with a startled expression, and I let out a laugh. Once again, the onus was on the golden child. Then the laughter started from the four of us, and Tom did what he had to do.

Three weeks later, The Old Man awoke at 2 AM with a terrible ache in his chest. He was in a rented hospital bed in the second bedroom of his condominium. The doctors had said as the cancer advanced, there'd be growing heart discomfort. They prescribed liquid nitroglycerin and morphine mixed with juice to relieve the pain. My brother Patrick stayed with The Old Man, kept him company, and slept next to him on a cot. The three of us decided that one of us had to stay with him. We wouldn't leave him alone. Marion, The Old Man's second wife, hearing raised voices from his sick room, entered from her bedroom. When she understood The Old Man was in pain, she said she'd go to the kitchen to get his medicine and juice. As she turned to go, The Old Man, a 40-year dedicated Alcoholics Anonymous member and a rigorous follower of

Bill W's steps, laughed and said, "Better make mine a double," an ironic reference to a double shot of booze. As Patrick held his hand, he laughed again, closed his eyes, and went to The Big Cocktail Party in the Sky.

"The leader of the band
Is tired and his eyes are growing old
But his blood runs thru' my instrument
And his song is in my soul
My life has been a poor attempt to imitate the man
I'm just a living legacy
To the leader of the band."
—Dan Fogelberg, 1981

Literary Genre: Steampunk

Up the River
Bill Lynam

TWELVE OF US signed on to navigate the Demerara River in the heart of British Guiana, South America. We stopped at intervals to map the river along the traversable portions where streams or other rivers intersected. We expected to take our findings back to the Royal Geographical Society (RGS) in London for likely sugar cane plantation sites that could be established along the river. On board, we had a full complement of engineers, botanists, geographers, cartographers, porters, and several militias-for protection.

In Georgetown, the capital on the coast, we'd hired a guide, Jirol, who said he spoke most of the tongues of the indigenes. Unfortunately, it soon became apparent he was not up to the task and only wanted our money. During our first encounter with the natives, he made a show of talking their lingo, then the natives tried to kill him. We rescued him and ourselves and kept continued. We immediately became uncomfortable with this dust-up and the savagery of the natives. Henceforth, we would be less friendly as we adventured upriver.

Our RGS expedition started hilariously at headquarters, where after too many brandies in early 1876, we ginned up this new adventure. Now, six months later, after a seven-week crossing by sailing vessel, and a riverboat steamer from Georgetown, we worked our way up the Demerara.

Another local interpreter told us that no one should journey farther than Palemon up-river, as only death and destruction for white men could be found there. The locals in Georgetown suggested all the natives were hostile to outsiders and cannibalistic. When we tried to hire bearers, most of them left after they found out our destination. Finally, we engaged some coastal mulattoes as bearers, at an inflated price.

We brought trade goods: hatchets, knives, rifles, gunpowder, beads, bolts of bright cloth yardage and bags of colorful buttons. Regardless of the admonitions to not go, we expected the natives to welcome us with our trade goods and help us out with our mission. Governor Young, the Crown representative, told us the natives did not like visitors. He explained that they had a deadly, poisonous powder they would sprinkle on interlopers. To overcome this threat, we made a huge steam-operated bellows connected to a rubberized airbag with hoses and a spigot gun. If anyone tried to powder us, one or more of us would man the high pressurized steam gun and fire hot salvos of steam against the invaders to repel the deadly toxin. Meanwhile, the rest of the party would start shooting to defend us from the hostiles.

Of course, the natives are only one of the threats if you considered the other dangers found in the jungle from exotic animals and plants; for example: jaguars, black caiman, electric eels, red-bellied piranhas, green anacondas, bull sharks, pit vipers, assassin bugs, giant centipedes, common vampire bats, and a host of other creatures and insects. Depending on which you encountered, you could be eaten, crushed, stung, bit, weakened and certainly, make you wish you'd stayed home.

The plants our naturalist suggested we watch out for: angel trumpet, white snakeroot, belladonna, strychnine trees, wolfsbane, castor plants, crab's eye and many more. Just brushing against or ingesting one of these plant parts would ensure you'd never go home.

After traveling about 120 miles up the Demerara, we came under attack by poisoned arrows. Four of our members were killed outright. Arrows put holes in our bellows bag and all the steam fizzled away harmlessly. This attack sent the rest of us scattering for cover. Some hid on the boat, others jumped into the river and others ran into the jungle. Lord Harold Bloomingdale, our engineer, began to swim away from this hostile reception, then started screaming. Piranhas ate him alive. Nobody jumped in to save him, not even his valet who scurried below deck.

The natives' attack came so fast and furious and so unexpectedly, we hardly had a chance to put our steam–gun into action. On top of which, it wasn't powder they sprinkled on us, but rather, an avalanche of spears and arrows that surprised us. Surrounded and captured, resistance seemed futile given the number of the war party. The fierce-looking natives had bamboo skewers through their eyelids and noses. Clad only in loin-cloths, they carried bows, arrow quivers, and lances, and menaced us with their weapons while taking us prisoner. I didn't know what my captors were up to when they stuck several of us with their spear tips. Maybe, they wanted to see if we bled. We did—profusely after several holes were punched in me and my fellow prisoners. Our bleeding appeared to be great fun according to their reaction. They giggled and shouted to one another like they had just captured some nice fat boars and verified blood pulsed through them. After that, I fainted. When I came around, I found myself depending from a bamboo pole, lashed hand and foot, and being carried. They'd bound me with jungle vines and hoisted me into the air for the trip like I was one of the local marsh deer.

I found out why my back felt raw and stinging. When my bearers traversed over a hump, my back was dragged along the ground on the little hillocks before the ground leveled out again.

In the village, they threw me into a hut and took all my clothes. Now, I was as naked as they were, except I felt ever more so. They'd taken my Saville Row boxers with little hearts on them my wife had given me. In any other environment, I would have felt extremely embarrassed —being nude, but here, it was sheer terror. For two days I lay bound in the dark— no food, no drink and no clue what was coming next. I dreamed of my wife and children so far away and wondered whether I would ever see them again. Delirium set in with a fever. I passed out, awakening with chills, moving in and out of consciousness. The downriver boys had it right—death for sure to intruders. Where was my courage now?

In lucid moments on the third night, I looked through the loose thatch of the hut and could see the tribe gathering around a fire. It was a huge bonfire in the middle of the compound flaming up as logs thrown on it created a cinder of spectacular fireflies dancing up from the impact. Tar torches lit the compound, and the natives were moving in rhythm to drums that pounded out a beat sounding like a tattoo from my old regiment, but much weirder. The music was a call and response and it echoed out into the surrounding forest. Other beats followed, sounding more like a xylophone with drum intervals. During the musical interludes, I heard the natives jabbering away. I wondered what they were up to besides getting ready for dinner. The aroma from the fire reached into my hut and reminded me of roast beef or pork with an acrid odor of burnt hair and a coppery metallic malodor. I looked closer at the fire and saw a vision of my future or that night's meal.

Our guide, Jirol, or his remains, dangled on a spit. Gutted, a pastiche of leaves covered his feet and chest. A pole stuck through his axis and bindings of liana held him tight to the pole. The ends of the pole rested on two "Y" stakes on either side of the fire. Women at each end turned the spit like a rotisserie rotating and basting him periodically with some liquid. Every once in a while, it looked like one of the ladies would also throw some kind of powder on him, because the fire, a coal bed now, would sparkle and glow when the substance scattered and hit the embers.

Looking away, I felt sorry for Jirol but not too much. After all, he almost got us all killed during our first encounter with the natives. Being isolated in the hut, I had no idea how many others of our party remained or held captive, if any. If I was the only one left, would I be next on the menu after they digested our guide? I didn't want to think about it and immediately started making plans for my escape.

I'd sweated so much when I had the fever, the moisture eventually loosened the ties on my wrists and I easily tore the bindings off. Late that night I scrambled to make an opening in the back of the hut. Listening for sounds in the compound, I heard no noise and thought everyone was sleeping after their festivities. Squirming through my homemade back door, I crept to the river's edge, chose a pirogue beached there, gathered extra paddles and slipped into the river, lying flat in the bottom of the craft should anyone be watching. I Quietly moved out into the downstream current.

Under better circumstances, I would have looked for my companions if I could have. That thought didn't occur to me. It was either every man for himself or for dinner.

It took days of canoeing and portaging, but I made it back to Georgetown, living off the land, finding fruit along the way. There was also fishing gear in the canoe I purloined, and I put it to good use. To avoid traffic on the river, I holed up during the day to avoid any unfriendly encounters and paddled downriver at night.

When I reached Georgetown, Governor Young kindly put me up in a spare room at Governor's House. I idled my time on the beach, regained my strength and recovered from my wounds. It was three months before the next relief ship arrived and I was able to book passage for home.

One day at the market by the waterfront, I came across a native peddling his wares—shrunken human heads for sale. One looked familiar. It had golden blond hair, a full beard, and a dimpled chin. Inspecting it closer, I decided I had to have it. It was my expedition companion, Sir Ronald Babcock, our group's geographer. I'd bring him home to his wife.

This is a true personal account of my travails on the expedition to discover and map the origins of the Demerara River in British Guiana. And, to seek and map potential plantation sites up to the river's headwaters for the Crown and the Royal Geographical Society expedition of August 1876.

Attest, Viscount Reginald Plimpton.

From the Annals of the Royal Geographical Society 1876

James Gardener 2.0
By D. August Baertlein

The old man hobbled to the receptionist's desk, knees crackling. "I got this free Neo-Physician coupon slipped under my door," he said.

The woman cocked her perfect face to one side and aimed kaleidoscope eyes at him, then turned to read words suspended in midair. Words he couldn't see.

"James Gardner, ninety-four." She turned back. "You've been avoiding us, James."

"Yeah, well. Last time…" James pushed his glasses up the sweaty slope of his nose. "I was having trouble typing on those mini-keyboards and you sharpened my damned fingertips!" He waggled ten pencil-point digits at her. "Bloody things ache when it rains."

"That was ten years ago. Finger-Points are old technology." She laughed. "So is typing. Now we can interface you directly to the InterWeb's, brain to Artificial Intelligence, better known to most as A-I."

James sighed. "Just the knees, please." He wasn't getting burned again.

The receptionist read on. "Oh, James." She tsked. "You should have come sooner. We can do so much more than knees. Eyes." She nodded at his glasses. "Hair. Skin." She cringed at his sagging jawline.

James clicked his fingertips together. "Just make my knees stop hurting."

"We can make everything stop hurting," she said. "Eliminate pain forever."

"That sounds…"

"Great?"

"Too good to be true," he said.

"Oh, it is!" she said. "So good. Our complete neural system transplant replaces your congenital wetware with brand new, silicon-fiber neurons, eliminating all pain."

James shifted his weight from left knee to right.

"Congenital wetware?" he said. "You make it sound like it was diseased from birth?"

"Exactly." She pushed a Hover-Chair up behind him. "Sit." (He had little choice.) She handed him a drink in a cut crystal glass.

The juice was sweet and cold, so tasty he drank it all in one swig. The Hover-Chair nestled softly around him and he began to dose, his eyelids fluttering shut, his thoughts dissolving to fuzz. He was almost asleep.

"James, we meet at last." A man's voice boomed in front of him, but James couldn't open his eyes to locate the source.

"Coupon," the receptionist gloated. "Under his door. He never saw the CyberMail we sent all these years. Probably didn't know he had an account."

"Ha!" said the doctor. "Well, we'll upgrade the old boy now. He's been an unsightly, bumbling drain on society long enough." He paused. "Eyes, hair, skin, neural system…"

'Just knees!' James tried to scream.

"Oh, wait!" said the doctor, and for a moment James was relieved, but only for a moment. "We can upload his consciousness directly into one of those new robo-bodies."

The receptionist clapped. "Yes. And we'll upgrade his mental acuity while we're at it."

When you read a short story, you come out a little more aware and a little more in love with the world around you.
—George Saunders

The Burial
By Greg Picard

IT WAS DINNERTIME. I and Ranger Chris Becker were hungry. It had been one of those no lunch days. As the leftover stew from yesterday warmed on the stove, he absentmindedly looked out his kitchen window. The view of the pines and the meadow always soothed him after a long day of struggling with the bureaucracy of being a government employee trying to just do his job. It seemed like more rules came down from headquarters every day. Most weren't thought out well from his perspective.

As the beefy aroma of the warming stew reached him, it set his stomach to grumbling, and with that symphonic backdrop, his kitchen window raised the curtain on a play he hadn't planned on watching.

He watched as two men and a small child walked up the knoll just 30 yards from his cabin. He didn't normally see many folks enjoying the park near his house since there were no trails there. But, that would not have been particularly curious except that one man carried a shovel and the other a large white canvas sack that sagged heavily under the weight of its contents.

"Crap!" He clicked off the burner under the pot and reached for his gun belt that he had laid on the dining room table. He hadn't bothered to take off his entire uniform, only his shirt since he was hungry and, in a hurry, to eat first. He dressed quickly and rather than mess with driving to where they had parked their vehicle, he just stomped out his back door and crossed into the woods just above where they had headed. By the time he got there, the hole they were digging was already a foot deep and two feet across.

"Good grief, you guys dig faster than a hungry badger."

Both men looked up in surprise, and Chris was taken aback to see tears on the one man who was on his knees next to the hole. Becker rarely had that effect on people until he put handcuffs on them.

"What are you guys..." Becker stopped mid-sentence when the kneeling man moved his leg, and Chris saw the limp Cocker Spaniel laying still on the ground on top of the canvas sack.

"We just came to bury Jack here. He always liked to come to the park, and it is so beautiful here," the standing man said as he stared down at the hole.

"Well guys, that's a bit of a problem. I'm sorry you lost Jack, I really am. You see, we don't allow burials in State Parks and especially in an area where we have sensitive Native American cultural artifacts and rare natural resources that we are trying to protect.

Great sobs were escaping the one man by now, and Chris noticed the little girl was starting to cry as well. He knew that if parks allowed this kind of thing to go on, people would be burying pets everywhere. The integrity of the resources was at stake, and it just wasn't consistent with the park mission.

Becker looked at the hole. The damage was already done. Nothing essential had been destroyed or unearthed that he could readily see in the late afternoon light. The chill of late fall surrounded them under the pine trees. The forest was in a mood to surrender to the little death of winter only to be reborn next spring as it had for millennia.

No one spoke, and Chris waited a full ten seconds.

"Look, guys, don't ever do this again. Don't tell anyone you did it. It just can't be allowed. I'm going home now, and I'm gonna pretend I never saw you. Don't put up any marker. He reached out and stroked the little girl's hair. She reminded him of when his daughter, Allie, was that age, and her first cat had died from a rattlesnake bite. Some lessons are learned hard. No reason to make them harder now, he thought. It was more than just making "park friends" in the political maelstrom that was California budget allotments. It was more than enforcing the abundance of regulations when people's desires outweighed their good sense brain cells. It was about him being human when he could get away with it.

He turned and walked back to his pot of cold stew. Tomorrow he would make sure the spot was covered with pine needles. Maybe he would dig it up first. Maybe not.

Details makes stories human and the more human a story can be the better.
—Ernest Hemingway

One Bronx Saturday
By Pat Fogarty

I WAS ELEVEN WHEN 'West Side Story' hit the silver screen. I did not know it, but I was growing up smack in the middle of a melting pot. In the early 1960's my South Bronx neighborhood consisted mostly of Irish and Italian Catholics, but we had a fair share of Finnish, German and Swedish Lutherans. They stuck together like a herd of moose. On the nicer neighborhood streets, a wealth of Jews lived in newer buildings and employed a smattering of Blacks as 'supers' and janitors.

So, when Ernesto Delgado moved into a nearby building, he was more of an oddity than a threat. Ernesto was the first live Puerto Rican I had ever seen. Living a block away in the Bronx meant he was in a different crowd than mine. We never called it a gang, because all we really did was hang out together and make sure kids from other crowds didn't pick on or bully one of us. On my street alone, there were a dozen small apartment buildings with about twenty kids in each one. With so many youngsters' running around, a firm rule voiced by our parents was to "Stay on the block, so I can see you." This edict was strictly enforced— the busybodies, yentas, and our mothers could look out a window and see exactly who was doing what. Some of the older women would place a pillow or cushion on their windowsill or fire escape and watch the street all day and into the night. If we stepped out of line, our mom might get a phone call and we'd be in for it.

Ernesto became friends with Jimmy Stanton, a kid I knew from school. They lived in the same building two blocks from me. Jimmy introduced me to Ernesto. And, even though they were in the 164th Street crowd and I was in the 162nd street crowd, we all became friends. We loved to play baseball and we were Yankee fans.

During the summer my parents would let me leave the block on Saturdays to play baseball on one of the fields near Yankee Stadium. There were six grass diamonds outside the famous ballpark and we always mustered up enough neighborhood players for a game. In the mornings before I left, mom would make cheese and mustard sandwiches, wrap them in wax paper and put them in a small brown paper bag. When I got thirsty, the public water fountain at the park was the best water in the world. With everyone using it, the water was always nice and cool.

On those summer days, we'd play ball from eight in the morning until late afternoon. Sometimes on a hot Saturday after a game, we'd head a few blocks over to the Harlem River where some of the guys would dive off an abandoned dock for a swim. I never went in. A few years earlier my mom had laid down the law about going in the river. As an eight-year-old, I had ventured to the river with some friends, collected blue crabs at low tide and brought them home. I got a beating and to this day, although more than a half-century has disappeared, I can still hear her words, "Young man, don't you ever go in that river again."

Well, that Saturday at the river we built a raft from pieces of scrap wood and broken pallets. It floated. Most of the guys jumped into the river and started to play "King of the Raft." Ernesto was holding onto a corner of the raft as the current started to drag it towards deeper waters. Jimmy was "King." I stood on the dock having as much fun watching, as they were having pushing each other on and off the raft. Ernesto managed to climb onto the raft. Jimmy pushed him off the raft. Caught up in the moment, with everyone hollering, splashing, and trying to dethrone Jimmy, no one noticed Ernesto sinking.

The cops took us in and questioned us individually. I was twelve at the time. For the next three days parents, police and just about the whole neighborhood gathered at the river. My mother was standing with Ernesto's mom when a police boat dragging the river found the body. As her son was being pulled from the river Mrs. Delgado let out the most horrific scream I had ever heard. I couldn't even look at her.

No one was blamed for Ernesto's drowning, but something ate away at my soul. Jimmy Stanton and I stayed friends but we both grew up drinking a lot. One night in a bar when we were in our twenties Jimmy told me he knew Ernesto couldn't swim. I asked him, "If you knew, why'd you push him off?"

He looked at me, started crying and said, "I don't know. I swear to God, I just don't know."

Dad Knew Mickey Mantle
By Tom Spirito

My Father was not a fountain of parental advice. I have often noted that the only bit of useful knowledge he passed on to me was, "Son, be true to your teeth or they'll be false to you." He would expound on this gem of wisdom with a solemn look and a slight whirl of his right-hand index finger skyward as if these words had been inspired by the almighty and passed personally down to him, and on to me. He would then look down at me, smile, laugh and give me a big hug. After decades of infections, cavities, pulled teeth, and gum surgery, I have got to admit, he got that one right. But who knew that would be the one and only bit of advice to me that he would get right? I could have saved myself a lot of pain, and money, if I had only paid heed to that pearl of wisdom; that one pearl.

Actually, I do remember a day when Dad got it unbelievably, almost mystically right. Mom had passed away sixteen months before and I was slowly realizing our lives were increasingly ' going off the rails." I was feeling insecure and in total denial of the many ways my life was changing. Our future seemed uncertain and frightening to this coddled and spoiled only child. Mom's death had replaced me as the center of our universe and left us with a black hole in our lives.

It was Saturday, October 10th, 1964, a classic Fall day in New York. Dad and I were attending the third game of The World Series at Yankee Stadium between our Yanks and the Saint Louis Cardinals. Yankee Stadium, that high temple of America's favorite pastime, the holy house of my boyhood heroes, was bathed in sunshine in all its hallowed majesty. It even smelled glorious. We were seated in the mezzanine seats along the third base line. It was late in the game, and Dad and I had managed to cover the floor under our seats with peanut shells, Dixie cups, and hotdog holders. The Yankees and Saint Louis were tied at the bottom of the ninth one to one and the fans were loudly buzzing in anticipation as the Yankees left the field. The air became electric when it was announced that Mickey Mantle would be the first batter for The Yankees. The crowd bellowed its approval. I stopped eating and sat fixed at the edge of my seat in anticipation. Mickey, my hero, the guy on the pedestal, at the center of the altar I worshiped at was coming up to bat.

Out of the blue, Dad stands up, grabs my hand and says, "Let's go. Mantle's going to hit a home-run, and we can beat the traffic outta the Bronx." I stared up at him in astonishment and blurted, "What, go now?" Dad grabbed my hand and pulled me up off my seat. We rushed to the stairs. Down we hustled to the ground floor and stood in the alley right behind home plate. Mickey was in the batter's box by this time taking a few practice swings. To this day, burned into my retinas, is the image of that large, black number 7 centered beneath those broad shoulders. And then they were in motion, rotating quickly. It was the first pitch to Mickey and the last of the game. A loud crack of the bat reverberated back to Dad and me. The ball lofted high towards the right-field bleachers and was gone in the upper deck. The entire stadium was on its feet yelling, howling, whistling in one cataclysmic roar. My Father jerked me backwards and we sprinted for the exit leaving Yankee Stadium with 67,000 screaming fans and Mickey's triumph behind. My brain was swimming. As we dashed to our car, I kept looking in awe at my Father, and repeating, "How did you know, how did you know?" Dad just smiled and pointed that swirling index finger skyward.

We certainly did beat the traffic out of the Bronx that day. I'm sure most folks would say it was just a lucky hunch inspired by the fear of getting stuck in one more colossal traffic jam on The Cross Bronx Expressway. I could never see it that way. For me, a vulnerable 14-year-old, it was one of the most wonderful and amazing days I ever spent with my Father.

After Mom died, Dad struggled with the loss of, in his words, "The love of my life." He remained single to the day he died, thirty-three years later. As a single father trying to raise a son, he got so many things wrong. But on that Fall day in Yankee Stadium, my Dad knew Mickey Mantle and what he was about to do. It was a day that all Fathers should pray to have with their child. It helps me to forgive, but not to forget.

Pirates of Jungle Gym Isle
By D. August Baertlein

MY BROTHER AND I GUARD our treasure from the pirates of Jungle Gym Isle. Today it's two gold medallions given to us by a serving wench in the kitchen.

"Take your cookies outside, boys," she says. "I don't want crumbs on the floor."

"But Mom," my brother says. "Those buccaneers out there will plunder our booty."

"Rival pirates, eh?" Mom looks thoughtful, then digs into her pantry. "Stow your cookies in this fine treasure chest." She hands us an old tin box with roosters painted on it.

"Roosters?" I say. "That ain't piratey!"

My brother shakes his head, "It's got no lock."

"Outside!" Mama points out the door to the realm of those thieving scallywags, the Pirates of Jungle Gym Isle. "Dad worked hard on that play structure," she says. "Now play, ye wee brigands. Play!"

I stash the gold medallions in that dumb rooster tin and tuck it under my vest. We unsheathe our swords, adjust our eye patches, and swagger out the door. Mom shuts it behind us. Haaaarrrrd.

Our boots have barely touched sand when my brother yells, "Pirates!" and sure enough, two scourges of the sea are sailing at us, fast.

Sally Longnose tries to distract us with her fancy zig-zag tacking, while Blackbeard takes a swipe at the treasure chest under my vest. I hold it close and show him the cold steel of my sword.

"ERRRR!" Blackbeard growls as he whooshes past, but I can see by his toothy smile he's just playing with me.

"To the ship!" I order (because I'm the captain today), and we scramble aboard our fine vessel, the *Lady Oak Tree*. "Ow!" A dangling acorn smacks my good eye. I switch my patch.

"I'll climb up to the crow's nest and keep watch on those brigands," my brother shouts.

"Aye! Good plan!" I say. "I'll stay behind and guard the treasure." But my belly growls and gives me away.

"Oh, no ye' don't, ye' scurvy rat." My brother snatches the treasure chest from my hand and starts to climb.

He makes it halfway up the rigging with our loot under his arm. Then a slip of his elbow sends it plummeting.

It bounces off the ship's mainmast.

"Arrgh!" he cries. It smacks the yardarm with a mighty whack.

"Curses!" I shout.

The treasure chest lands downside up under the hungry eyes of those pirate dogs. Painted roosters stare blindly up from the box, making no effort to defend our booty. I wish they could at least squawk a warning cry.

Blackbeard leaps on our treasure in a flash. But Sally pokes her long nose in and snags the box from under Blackbeard's stubby snout. She's off across the grassy sea, our booty clamped in her teeth, Blackbeard hot on her heels.

Round and round, they go, tail-flags flapping in the wind. Up and over Jungle Gym Isle they romp, then they splash through Blue Lagoon wading pool.

"After them!" my brother yells.

We leap from our ship, the *Lady Oak Tree*, draw our swords, and advance upon those thieving pirates.

"Avast, ye' mangy curs!" I shout. Sally slows to a trot.

"Sit!" I say in my deepest tough-pirate voice.

Sally stops. Her brown eyes roll to the left, then right. She sits back on her haunches. Blackbeard watches from the shadows.

I walk real slow right up to Sally Longnose. "Drop it," I say, "or it's the plank for ye'."

Sally drops the slobbery treasure into my hand, then stands at attention, tongue flopping out the side of her muzzle.

"Good lass." I scratch her behind the ears until she wags her big white flag of a tail.

"She surrenders!" my brother shouts, and we dance a pirate jig. Together we board the *Lady Oak Tree*, Sally Longnose, Blackbeard, my brother, and me. We sit in a circle on deck, just above the steep, steep plank that slides down to the grassy sea.

I open the treasure chest. My brother gasps.

"Our cookies!" he cries.

The two gold medallions are gone. In their place are a pile of gold dust and a scattering of golden nuggets.

Plenty to share.

My brother and I divvy up our treasure, leaving a few crumbs for the pirates of Jungle Gym Isle.

It's possible, in a poem or short story, to write about commonplace things and objects using commonplace but precise language, and to endow those things—a chair, a window curtain, a fork, a stone, a woman's earring—with immense, even startling power.
—Raymond Carver

The Ugly Ones
By Mark Wenden

I SQUAT HUNCHED BY THE FIRE, looking out from under our rock shelter at the wide valley below the bluff. I am old now; I no longer count the winters of my life, and my bones, broken and healed times beyond memory, ache from the chill wind that rustles and swirls the brown and yellow leaves along the ground. Low grey clouds drive the wind through the valley and give the air a sharp crispness in the nostrils. Biting cold will soon grip the valley, and I move closer to the fire. At times like this, I recall my younger sister Speaks-Little and often I weep.

Speaks-Little was born when I was a sapling but not yet a man. She was a healthy baby, and our mother was filled with joy. Before long, however, my sister began to act in odd ways. As an infant, when our mother would smile tenderly and coo at her while offering the breast, she would sometimes stare past her mother or begin to cry. And as she grew into a toddler, there were times when our mother would show her annoyance with Speaks-Little for some childish misbehavior, but the baby would run laughing to her mother as though unaware of any tension between them.

When Speaks-Little reached the age where most children begin to chatter and pester their siblings and mothers with endless questions and begging for bits of food, she remained almost entirely silent, uttering words only sparingly, thus earning her name. This continued even after five or six summers had passed, and just as when she was a toddler, she often seemed unable to grasp the feelings of people or the general mood among a group of the People. She had a hard time catching on to the right way to act at times. One of the great hunters among the People, my cousin Smash-skull, was the keeper of a sacred flute, made of bird bone. Smash-skull, who had earned his name at a very young age by leaping from rocks higher than a man's head onto the back of a bull aurochs driven past by fellow hunters and smashing its head with a stone, was also a shaman. His powerful connection with the spirits of prey animals helped greatly to improve the hunting success of the People, beyond even his strength and bravery. One day, Speaks-Little was rummaging among the personal things he kept in his sleeping robe and found the bone flute. She put it to her mouth and began to tootle merrily. Smash-skull, who was outside our shelter working on straightening a lance shaft for the next hunt, heard the sound and leaped up and ran in, his eyes wide with shock and fear. "Girl!" he shouted. "Put that down! It is for speaking to the deer, the bear, and the wolf! It is not music for pleasure, like our singing by the fire at night!" Fearless hunter as he was, Smash-Skull was terrified that idle playing with the sacred bird-bone flute could confuse or even anger the animals we relied on for food and spoil the hunt.

Another time, after the death of one of the oldest and beloved mothers among our clan, Speaks-Little ran about laughing and trying to catch a butterfly while everyone else sat solemnly in a circle, telling tales from the life of our elder while red ochre, the color of blood and life, was applied to her body. By that time, everyone knew she was not like the rest of the People, and no one paid her any mind or tried to correct her.

At about the same age that these things happened, we began to notice that Speaks-Little had some unusual abilities. She could sing like a bird. After a successful hunt, the members of our clan would stoke the fires and heat flat rocks to cook meat. Before long, our shelter would fill with the smell of wood smoke and sizzling fat. The women would sprinkle dried herbs on the meat to add flavor. Soon the only sounds would be the crackling of the fires and the munching, chewing, and grunts of satisfaction. Bellies full and hearts full of joy and contentment, we would then begin the drumming and singing. Awkward and shy in normal speech, Speaks-Little would blossom in song. Her voice would rise clear and strong as she sang of the courage and cleverness of the hunters, of the beauty and swiftness of the animals and our gratitude toward them. She would sing old songs about the People's love of our valley and hills, and how the changing seasons mirror our own lives. Her singing caused people to experience strong and sentimental emotions, and when the fires had burned down to glowing embers, men and women would retreat to the sleeping robes together. Much coupling always occurred following a successful hunt, but as Point-Flaker, known for his humor, once joked, "Speaks-Little's singing is probably responsible for the birth of many babies!"

As one summer followed another and Speaks-Little began to mature into an attractive young woman, red-haired and fair-skinned, she began to impress the People with another rare skill she had developed. Because she found it difficult to understand people and converse with them, she spent a lot of time alone, wandering through woods and meadows, following game trails along streams and rivers, learning the ways of all the animals, from the martens along the streams up to the mighty wisent and mammoth that roam the grassy valley. Her spirit bond with the game animals was powerful, for she seemed to know what drew them, what frightened them, and where they would go. She began to guide our hunting parties, and their success in finding game increased wonderfully. The respect of the People for my younger sister grew, and many of us, including her own older brother, felt shame for the way years earlier we had mocked her with childish cruelty.

One autumn, as the days were growing grey and chilly, a party of five men of our clan set out on a hunt. Speaks-Little had told us that a grove of chestnut trees not far from the main river that flowed through the valley was beginning to drop its fruit, and the red deer that the People love so dearly would be heading there to fatten up for the coming winter on the nutritious nuts. We knew of a narrow gorge through which the deer would have to pass to reach the chestnut grove, and we headed that way to set up an ambush. Three of us, were positioned ahead on the path the deer would have to follow, and two hid ourselves, on the flanks with our stout stabbing lances, ready to rush the confused animals as they saw the men ahead and tried to turn and find a way out. Our trap worked as well as my sister had predicted, and we killed two sleek bucks. We quartered them and slung them over our shoulders, ready for the trek back to camp. We were a happy band, laughing and joking about the feast we had to look forward to, and the tender attentions of the women that would follow. As we followed a game trail through the lightly wooded slopes above the river, we heard the sounds of walking that rustled the leaves, walking like that of the two-legged, not four, and we heard the murmur of voices. Wondering who it might be, from which clan, we rounded a rocky promontory and gaped in amazement as we found ourselves face to face with a group of Ugly Ones.

The Ugly Ones. Never had I seen any this close up; I had only seen them a few times in my life, always from cover and at a distance. There were six in this group, all men, no doubt a hunting party like ourselves. They were startled at our approach, for we had moved silently after first hearing them, and both groups raised spears and took an attack-ready stance. After a few moments of staring and tension, Smash-Skull held out his left hand in a supplicating gesture and slowly began to lower his spear. The Ugly Ones slowly lowered theirs, and it was clear they had no real desire to risk death or injury in a skirmish. None of our party spoke their language, and none of them spoke ours. By hand gestures and pantomiming, however, they let us know that indeed they had been hunting but meeting with no luck finding game. That explained why they had strayed so far into the territory of the People.

These hunters were clearly hungry and tired, so we offered to share some of the still-warm remains of livers and hearts of the deer we carried. These organs are delicacies, and normally the reward of the hunters who make the kill, but we had each eaten our fill before setting out for home, and our curiosity about these strange and different beings prompted our generosity. The Ugly Ones seemed to appreciate that they were being given special treatment and offered us some of the shells that they wore around their necks, which we accepted with pleasure. Again, through gestures, we told them that they would be welcome to come with us back to our camp and join our feast. They agreed gratefully, and we began the two-day walk back to our rock shelter on the bluff. During our journey, both groups managed to pick up some of the words of each other's language, though not much.

The party of Ugly Ones seemed to enjoy our feast, smiling and laughing as they murmured among themselves between mouthfuls of delicious red deer meat. They joined in the drumming that followed, and we began to feel that perhaps they were not so different from us in many ways. And they were spellbound by the singing of Speaks-Little. Their eyes were fixed on her, almost hungrily, as her voice rose, fell, and trilled in time with the rhythm of the drums, though they could understand nothing of what she sang. They spread their furs to spend the night with us, and though I was tired from carrying deer for two days and went to sleep early, as I nodded off, I am sure I saw one of our women beckon to one of the less repulsive ones to join her on her wisent robe.

The next morning, the Ugly Ones joined us to eat again, and through a combination of gestures and basic words, told us that they needed to resume their hunt, as they had clan members of their own waiting for meat at their camp in a neighboring valley. We had sympathy for their lack of luck finding game, for the hearts of the animals are fickle, and we ourselves were no strangers to hunger. Smash-Skull turned to me as Speaks-Little sat next to me at the fire, and made this suggestion; "Tale-Teller, Speaks-Little, how would you two feel about accompanying these Ugly Ones on their hunt? You might learn more of their language, which could prove useful in the future, and if you help them find game, I think they would be thankful to us and think kindly of us. It would be better for the People if the Ugly Ones were not a threat since now they know the location of our camp."

"They make me uneasy," said Speaks-Little. "But I will go with them if it helps the People."

"I share your feelings, sister," I said. "There is something about the way they talk among themselves that makes me think they are ridiculing us. They may be treacherous. But like you, I will agree to go if they want us to. Learning their true nature and forming some kind of bond with them is worth the risk if it makes our clan safer."

This being said, Smash-Skull related our suggestion the best he could to the Ugly Ones. Their eyes flickered to one another as soon as they understood what was being proposed, and they agreed immediately.

And so, the two of us, sister and brother, set out with the hunting party of the Ugly Ones. Speaks-Little performed pantomimes, mimicking various game animals, asking the hunters what they would prefer to stalk. They answered, as best we could make out, that their favorite was the giant wooly mammoth, but this was not the best season for hunting them, and in any case, they had too few in their party. Taking down a mammoth took a large number of men, all brave and with plenty of experience. We suggested that going after red deer might be good, as we had been successful a few days ago, and the Ugly Ones agreed the meat was tender and sweet. So, we set off again toward the gorge where our previous ambush had been so effective. It would be another two-day walk.

As we walked through a wooded area that required us to walk single file, I noticed idly, that up ahead on me on the trail, an Ugly One seemed to be missing. The People only count to ten; above that number, we just say "many," and even for numbers less than ten, we usually have little need for precision. How I wish now that I had paid more attention.

Without warning, I felt a slamming blow to the side of my head. I heard a rushing, ringing sound, and everything went black as I fell sideways to the ground.

When I awoke, it was almost dark. I looked around, confused, with my head throbbing and my vision blurred. There was no sign of the Ugly Ones. I got up and stumbled along the trail. As I neared the narrow gorge where the ambush was planned, I nearly tripped over something large on the path. I looked down and saw the bloodied body of my sister. I stared in shock for a few moments, and then I vomited, continuing to retch and heave even after my stomach was empty. Then I began to sob. I had seen hunters gored and crushed by game animals and many who had died of disease, hunger or old age. But this was a murder, something almost unknown among the People. Speaks-Little had not been killed by an animal; her body clearly bore the marks of spear wounds, several of them. And more horrifying yet, her robe was pulled up, and the insides of her thighs were smeared with blood and seed of men. The Ugly Ones had raped and killed my precious sister, who had never yet coupled with a man in joy. There is no doubt they had planned it; one of them had sneaked off the trail and around behind me to try to kill me, so they would be able to attack my sister without anyone to defend her. Yes, that day we learned the true nature of the Ugly Ones.

Now after many winters, the rage and grief rise up in me still. They had left Speaks-Little on the path, as though she were nothing more than rubbish. If they had succeeded in killing me, it might have been months or years before our remains were discovered, decayed without ceremony, without the story-telling, without red ochre to give us blood and life in the afterworld. As it was, I had to bring Speaks-Little back to camp by myself, sometimes carrying her, sometimes dragging her when my shoulders grew too weary. If I had gone back to get help retrieving her, animals would have certainly consumed her and scattered her remains, leaving us nothing for our rituals.

The Ugly Ones. We see more and more of them. They have no respect for our territory. Some of the People have learned their speech, but never well, for their language, like them, is tricky and full of deceit, and we cannot master it. Their language allows them to talk about things that may have happened but have not. It makes it easy for them to lie. A young boy asked Smash-Skull, the summer before he was trampled to death by a wisent, "If you can play the bird-bone flute to attract the game animals, could you play a different tune to make the Ugly Ones go away?"

As Smash-Skull pondered how to answer the boy, Point-Flaker, always the witty one, told the boy "If we could do that, we would have tunes to send away mosquitoes, fleas, ticks and lice as well!"

The old ones always said that in the time of the Long-Ago Mothers, back in time before memory, there were no Ugly Ones in the valleys and plains of the People, but it seems to me that like other pests, they have always been here and always will be. They seem to grow closer all the time, killing more of the game that the People depend upon, and sometimes the People themselves. With their tall slim-waisted bodies, brown skin and blue eyes, their small noses and jutting chins, their high foreheads and baby-like flat brows, they are the Ugly Ones. With the spear-throwing sticks that enable them to kill game from a distance, their deceit, and treachery, their violence, and contempt for anyone different from themselves, they surely are the Ugly Ones.

And so, I weep for Speaks-Little when the growing chill of autumn reminds me of her death, and I weep for the People, for with dread I feel that we will share her fate.

Expository Essay:

The American Rattlesnake
By Pat Fogarty

Yogi Berra, a man noted for his sagacious quips, once said, "There are some people, who if they don't already know, you can't tell them." Yogi's tidbit of worldly advice is especially true when it comes to rattlesnakes.

The rattlesnake is the most feared animal in the western hemisphere. The distinctive sound made by the rattle of its tail is an eloquent warning that few misinterpret.

Most sane people, who come across a rattlesnake have the genetically inherited common sense to cease all forward motion and back away from the creature. Unfortunately, every year approximately seven thousand people receive a venomous bite from this cold-blooded carnivorous reptile. And interestingly, it should not surprise the intelligent reader that seventy percent of the people bit by a rattlesnake are males between the ages of sixteen and twenty-seven. Most of us know the type—they are the self-imagined invincible ones who believe they know it all. It's usually not a good practice to cast blame on a dimwitted victim. But let's be honest; being a show-off and messing with a rattlesnake is just plain dumb.

The powerful hollow fangs of the rattlesnake can pierce the thick hide of a buffalo. They function like natural hypodermic needles and are capable of injecting a lethal dose of poison when the snake senses a threat.

Toxic compounds in the venom destroy tissue and kill blood cells. This wreaks havoc with the circulatory system. It also causes internal bleeding and respiratory failure. Besides the acute pain from the toxins, survivors often lose fingers, toes, feet, and hands. So, even if you are wearing gloves and high leather boots, you should give a rattlesnake a wide berth if you ever encounter one.

Native American cultures held conflicting opinions of the rattlesnake. Some pre-Columbian tribes considered the snake to be a good omen because of its power to kill. And, other tribes perceived the snake's ability to kill as a sign of evil and destruction. But, regardless of how a tribe viewed the creature—the rattlesnake was an important part of their culture. Totems of the serpent were used in their sacred rituals. And, the canyons of the arid American southwest are riddled with prehistoric rock art depicting the rattlesnake and other indigenous animals.

On the other side of the North American continent, in the State of Ohio, hundreds of earthen mounds built by Native Americans dot the landscape. Many are over three thousand years old. The most striking mound created by Native Americans is in the shape of a snake. Stretching more than 400 meters "Serpent Mound" is the largest surviving example of a prehistoric effigy mound in the world. The beautifully preserved ancient earthwork depicts the form of a slithering serpent with an oval shaped head.

In Mesoamerica, an area we now call Central America, the Aztec civilization worshiped a Plumed Serpent they named Quetzalcoatl—a god that took the combined form of a bird and rattlesnake. Throughout Central and South America images of the snake are a common find at archeological sites.

In modern times, the habitat of this venomous pit viper extends from the mountains of southwestern Canada, to the grassy plains of northern Argentina.

There are thirty-six known species of rattlesnakes with about seventy subspecies. Make no mistake, they are all dangerous. But, by far the deadliest rattlesnake in the world is the Mohave rattlesnake. In its natural desert environment; camouflage, speed, and aggressiveness enhance its ability to kill small rodents and birds. However, those attributes in the viper increases the danger of a hiker or camper being bit. The snake is greenish brown in color, and when fully grown it's about thirty inches long. But, don't let its size deceive you. The venom of the Mohave rattlesnake is conservatively estimated to be ten times more lethal than any other rattlesnake. So obviously, if you are hiking in an area where these creatures reside; be extremely careful where you step. Very few people survive a nip in the leg from this serpent.

A few years ago, an Arizona woman living in the small town of Paulden was bit by a Mohave rattlesnake when she stepped out of her home to walk to her car. The neurotoxins in a Mohave's venom are very deceiving and the bite did not seem serious to her. The woman's first instinct was to strike back at the snake. She picked up a garden rake and unknowingly wasted precious time trying to kill the elusive reptile. Within minutes she was writhing in pain and gasping for air. Her husband rushed from the house, realized what had happened and called for an ambulance. The emergency dispatcher understood the seriousness of the situation and sent a helicopter to airlift the woman to a hospital in Flagstaff. She died on the way.

So, if you happen to hear the unique sound made by the flickering of a rattlesnake's tail—stop moving, try to assess the location of the snake, and by all means retreat.

However, if you ever visit the Catalina Islands, beware of the oxymoronic Catalina rattlesnake. Over the centuries the rattlesnakes isolated on the Catalina Islands in the Gulf of California have evolved, and these deadly creatures no longer have the ability to grow a rattle.

We tell ourselves stories in order to live.
—Joan Didion

The World According to Arnie
By Greg Picard and Wendy Picard Gorham

NONE OF THEM ARE 'blacks and whites' anymore," Arnie Blusten spit out around his cigar. He stood to peer at the vehicle through the only dirt-encrusted pane that was not replaced by plywood in the window frame. Mavis Blusten sat in a vinyl settee looking more like an overfull sack of potatoes than a woman in her early forties. When she rose to cross the bare wooden floor, the lumps of cellulite at the hem of her shift showed imprints of the buttons used to tuck the Naugahyde to the padded chair frame. Sulfurous bruises, tinged the same color of the chair's black vinyl, sagged beneath her left eye.

"What do you suppose they want way out here at this hour?" Mavis' voice was a thin and reedy squawk. Together they both watched as two men in khaki climbed out of the white with green four-wheel drive GMC. A stripe slashed boldly across its door with a government seal centered on the decal of a six-pointed star. The setting sun off to the west cast shadows across the narrow track of Boulder Creek Road."Whatever it is, you can bet it isn't something you need to bother yourself with!"

Arnie eyed the fading bruise on his wife's cheek. "Now get in the kitchen and make dinner. I'll take care of this."

Yellowed Sycamore leaves swirled and began to dust the earth with a warning of impending winter. The San Diego County deputy's companion had a different park service patch and badge. They were just stepping onto the aged and creaking wooden deck when Blusten yanked open the door. "This here's private property! You'd best be moving on down the road! You got no cause to be messin' with me!"

"Mr. Blusten, we hate to bother you, but we need to talk to you about your son, Jack." The tall deputy put on his friendliest smile. "It seems he was involved in some trouble down in Cuyamaca." Here the smile faltered, "We have him in custody on a warrant for murder charges. Could we come in?" In response, a gust of late fall wind caught the screen door, and it yawned open. The return spring "twanged" to its limit and the peeling wood frame cracked against the siding. Blusten shuffled back a half stride.

Arnie and Mavis Blusten had lived in the hills behind North Peak for 16 years. At sixteen, Mavis had their first and only child, Jack. Arnie spent most of his time at the Julian Hotel as their part-time handyman and at the Wrong Branch as the town drunk. Mavis was ill-equipped to give Jack the proper upbringing he needed, but she tried to give him some love and attention. Mostly, it was too little and too late. He grew up a lonely child, spending his first five years in the very same cabin in the woods the deputy and the park ranger now stood. Their nearest neighbor was eight miles away. All that changed when he started school.

He approached kindergarten with the same intensity that he approached his Teddy bear. Deprived of the contact with others his age by life in the virtual wilderness, he literally assaulted other children in order to get their attention. The school bus was not a frightening new experience, but rather a wonder of new "toys" with which to play.

The deputy stood while the ranger sat on the vinyl settee. Arnie tried to make the wiring in his alcohol worn brain connect. "How could Jack have murdered anybody, why that's as silly as saying I done that!"

"Actually, Mr. Blusten, we're talking more than that." The ranger had deep creases in his forehead from time in the sun, and the tan was peeled raggedly along his hairline as he removed his Stetson hat. "My name is Chris Becker. I work in the park, and I needed to let you know that it would appear that from the evidence that Jack is responsible for the murder and sexual assault of one of the maids at the Lakeside Motel cabins...a young Hispanic lady just here in this country.

"My son don't know no Mex wetbacks. He wouldn't associate with that kinda trash!" By now, the cigar ash had collapsed on Blusten's yellowed undershirt.

The balding deputy leaned forward, and the leather from his Sam Browne Belt creaked. "We're pretty sure the semen swab samples will paint a different picture, I'm afraid, as will the tissue samples under three of the victim's fingernails. The witness statements put him there coming out of the room she was cleaning."

Ranger Becker broke in. "He asked that you be notified. I expect you'll want to talk to him at the County Jail."

Arnie rubbed his sausage-like fingers across the two-day growth of beard, not sure what to make of all this. He looked toward the kitchen and wondered vaguely what Mavis had started for dinner.

Mavis was a good cook, he thought to himself.

Mr. Bow Tie
By Dolores Everard-Comeaux

I'D BEEN SUFFERING FROM a dratted writer's block and ducking the muse that feeds creativity for some years. I always planned to return to writing once I reached retirement. Time yelled, "How in heavens can you work writing into your crazy schedule? What about the *block*?"

The ANTS (anxious negative thoughts) in my brain blared. Green toxic words slid between neurons and tickled my amygdala to form Nervous Nelly thoughts. Ageism touted, "Thinking's not sharp enough. Spelling sucks. Shorterm memory *kaput*! Long-term memory short."

"*Sha Bebe*, listen up!"

That got my attention. It appears my muse speaks Cajun French and has signed on to squash the ANTS. She whispered gently, "Don't pay attention to rules and regulations of writing for the draft. Remember what your editor at the newspaper said years ago: "Just write. Keep writing."

What a trip that was writing for my hometown daily rag. My incredible editor, Preston L. Pendergrass, whipped my dangling participles into shape, found my misplaced modifiers, and beat into my brain journalistic jargon. He actually forgave my grammatical goofs like "petro" for gasoline and "ladies" for women. He commented that not all women were ladies. In our hometown, he was considered a master grammarian.

What a character! He was as regular as a clock at his desk each morning, clad in a stiff, starched white shirt. It was punctuated by a bright bow tie clamped for dear life to his collar. Sometimes, I imagined the bow tie to be a red helicopter landing on that stiff collar. My desk faced his office door. Often, I sneaked a peek to see him pecking away with two fingers on an old manual typewriter at warp speed.

For as gruff as he sometimes seemed, he had a warm and squishy heart. I was a single mother of two and had put their Christmas on layaway early in the fall to penny-pinch and pay it out coin-by-coin. The day before Christmas Eve, I went on my lunch hour to the department store to retrieve their Santa. To my horror, I found that the store had put the tiny black and white TV, plus a couple of other small items, back on the shelf. I returned to the newsroom in tears. The song," A Hard Rock Candy Christmas," played in the back of my mind. I told the editor my tale of woe then scooted back to my desk. Tears trickled past my nose, as red as Rudolph's. Almost immediately, the department store called that they had replaced my meager presents. It occurred to me that my editor might have clout in the community and that tie stuck to his collar was really bright red angel wings.

As obit editor, one time I mucked up and buried a person in an opposite cemetery to where the burial was to be held (there were two cemeteries in our hometown). The family came storming in to kill me. The editor with the bright bow tie invited the couple into his office for a "crucial conversation." I had already started cleaning out my desk, certain of being fired and wondering how to make ends meet with little income. In fact, I had the boys on free meals at school, and the newspaper had given them bright red windbreakers with the name of the daily rag boldly stated on the back. These jackets saved me a few needed bucks in the coat department. They may have been an embarrassment to the boys, since no other kids wore bright red windbreakers with *The Baytown Sun* blazoned on the back.

A burial miracle! The upset couple left the editor's office with a promise of rerunning the obit correctly. I wasn't fired. However, I remained under the editor's scrutiny. His persistent and patient mentorship taught me the trade. More than journalism, I learned the power of forgiveness and that it's okay to mess up. After all, we humans are messy mortals at times.

I owe much to the newsroom and an editor who gave me a trade and encouragement to write. I learned much from this stern character, which could cause my knees to knock and heart to pound when corrected. But best of all, I received a valuable life's lesson from that editor, who donned a bright bow tie that sat a hand span above an incredible warm and forgiving heart.

A Christmas Test
By D.R. Roe

HER CHILD IS BORN the first of November, just three days after her twentieth birthday. A child herself, she's now responsible for the needs of her infant son.

Nearly a month later, her husband announces he has taken a new job. It's in the city almost one hundred miles away. A week later she finds herself in a new town far from family and all that she has known.

The Christmas holiday brings a blizzard with bitter temperatures, high winds, and heavy snowfall. Her husband has been gone for several days. The job has not turned out as he had hoped. He admitted that the responsibility of a family was more than he could bear. Now alone with her infant son in a strange and unfamiliar place.

She is not surprised by this turn of events. In the two years of marriage, he never did prove himself much of a husband. During her pregnancy, she often wondered of his capabilities as a father.

The stress is beginning to take its toll; having no money, and the meager food supply is nearly gone. The lack of proper nourishment has inhibited her body's ability to produce milk to feed her child. The last thing she wants to do is reach out to her parents for help. The thought of hearing the disappointment in their voice is discouraging.

After washing the cloth diapers by hand, she hangs them around the apartment to dry. She sterilizes the glass bottles in boiling water in order to fill them with sterilized water; her hope is that the water will help satisfy the baby's hunger. The Doctor had said that, if needed, the premixed formula could be used to supplement the baby's diet.

Formula is available at the drug store less than a half mile from the apartment—62 cents a can. "There must be some change around here somewhere," she declares. She searches under the cushions of the sofa, high on shelves, on top of the dresser, in all the drawers, and under every piece of furniture. She finds a total of fifty-nine cents. More is needed.

Although she doesn't know any of the neighbors in her building, from deep within she finds the nerve to knock on their apartment doors to ask for the needed three pennies. No one answers at the first few doors. At the next, the door opens. An elderly woman wearing a plush robe that drags on the floor stands in the doorway. "Yes dear. What is it?"

"Could you please help me? I need three cents. I will pay it back."

"Well, I think I can spare three pennies." The woman pulls the pennies from a bowl of change on a table by the door. "No need to worry about paying it back. Merry Christmas."

"Thank you so much." She pushes the pennies into her pocket.

Back in her apartment, she stuffs the fifty-nine cents in the pocket with the pennies. Outside, the heavy snow is whipping about in the high winds. She wonders if she can battle this monster.

"I'm not sure if I can do this," she mumbles.

It is now 6:30 p.m. The baby begins to cry again. The water worked for only a short time.

After putting on her meager remnant of a coat, she wraps the tiny baby in a warm blanket, and bundles him completely in a quilt, covering his face to protect him from breathing the cold air.

"Here we go, Little Bit. We'll get you something to eat real soon."

Approaching the outer door of the building, she swallows her fear and pushes it open. The wind snatches it, slamming the door against the outside wall of the building.

"You have to be kidding me!"

She tries to grab hold of the door with her one free arm, but the wind is so strong she can't move it. Grumbling in disgust while struggling with all of her body weight to close the door against the force of the wind.

On the descent down the icy steps, she grasps tightly to the railing to keep upright. In the parking lot she can more easily balance her weight. She presses her precious cargo snugly to her chest. Her only thought is to forge ahead in spite of the storm.

It is impossible to see more than a few feet because of the heavy snow. She has to squint her eyes, lean forward, and push headfirst through the pommeling conditions.

The bitter wind slices through her worn torn coat, burning her skin. She looks up with hopes of seeing the lights of the shopping plaza in the distance. But there is only darkness. The snowflakes sting as they hit her face.

Before long, her body feels weary and begins to ache. Every muscle beseeches her to give up. But there is no shelter. It is imperative to press on, although feeling like she's been walking forever. She then sees the lights above the drug store faintly peeking through the heavy snow.

"I can see the sign," she murmurs to her son. "It's kind of blurry, but we're getting closer."

A ray of hope shines, rousing every bit of strength within to step up the pace in anticipation of getting to the phone booth that stands at the outside corner of the parking lot.

Once inside, she closes the door between them and the unyielding tempest. Inside the booth is a small shelf, just the right size to set her bundle on.

"Wow! Check it out, Little Bit, it's just your size."

Arms weakened, they hang limp at her sides.

"Thank you, Lord, for this shelter where I can rest awhile. And thank you for this perfect spot to lay my baby on."

The only lights that shine throughout the shopping plaza are from inside the drug store. It is the only store open on this Christmas Eve. Approaching the store, she sees a few cars parked in front, proclaiming she is not the only one out on this night.

As she opens the door, a blast of heat from inside smacks her in the face. Upon stepping inside, the warmth engulfs her as if stepping into a cloud.

Once she finds the section where the formula is shelved, she sets her bundle on the floor and unwraps the blankets that envelope the child. He had not stirred since leaving the apartment. The young mother fears the worst. Has she smothered him by clutching him too tightly?

As she lifts the blanket that covers his face, the shock knocks her back from her squatted position onto her buttocks. These eyes looking back at her are not the eyes of her infant son. These are wise eyes that seem to hold all the knowledge of the universe. Mesmerized, she is unable to look away, for what seems to be several minutes. She has the feeling that he is inhabited by an angel traveling with them on their journey. And they seem to be totally aware of what she is experiencing.

Breaking away from the trance like state, she turns her attention to the task at hand. She looks for a can of premixed formula, but there are none to be seen. Frantically shifting about all the items on the shelf, she cries, "No! There must be one. Please!"

Then, obscurely placed in the back on the top shelf, hidden behind other items, she finds a can of premixed formula. It is a far stretch to reach the lone can.

"Thank you, Lord!"

Scooping up the baby she hurries to the cashier, pulls the change from her pocket, and places it on the counter next to the can. The clerk rings up the purchase.

"Exact change. Thank you and have a Merry Christmas."

Hating to leave the cozy warmth of the store, she wraps the baby and the can together in the blanket. While exiting, snow blows in the open doorway. Conditions outside seem worse than before.

After taking advantage of a short pause at the phone booth, she again sets out into the snow squall. Soon the lights from the shopping plaza are blotted out and darkness is the backdrop for the heavy snowstorm. The howling, blustering wind whirls the intense snowfall about her, yet she walks effortlessly as if she is surrounded by a protective bubble.

Upon entering the apartment, she catches the reflection of herself in the mirror hanging by the door. She is surprised to see there is not a single snowflake adorning her hair or coat. The blanket covering the baby is also dry.

"How can this be?" she utters in amazement.

Because she had no tree decorated with tinsel and lights, she lights a candle in celebration of Christmas Eve. Later nestled in the rocking chair feeding her baby, she gazes at the flickering flame with a smile of gratitude and affirms,

"You know, Little Bit, I think a Christmas Angel helped us tonight. I believe we are going to be just fine. Merry Christmas."

The Ballgame
By Bill Lynam

THE DRIVE TO CITI FIELD was slow. Traffic clogged 126th street as the cars crawled into the stadium lot. The parking attendants weren't helping as it seemed to take forever for them to make change for the drivers.

Sarah sighed, she felt like she had another migraine coming on. "Can't we go any faster? What's the holdup?"

"Just look at the traffic," Brad said. "You want me to run over these guys. If I pull out, I'll never get back in line. So, hang on. We're almost there."

Brad muscled the steering wheel over to avoid some jerk sleeping at the wheel ahead of him. "Get moving, damn it," he shouted to himself as the driver finally woke up and accelerated to close the gap between him and the car in front.

Parked and in the stadium, they took the elevator up to the Acela Club level in the seven–year old clubhouse. It featured indoor patio–dining with a premium view of the diamond and had a bar and restaurant noted for its ballpark cuisine.

Seated at their table a half–hour before the game, they looked down on the field. The groundskeepers were still doing some last minute clean–up along the baselines. One guy looked like he was dusting the second base sack, the number 4, the keystone position that's defended by the baser and the shortstop. Brad mused to himself, the guys lollygagging to get on TV as the camera crews pan the field before the game. He probably told his girlfriend, "Watch second base just before the game. When I dust the bag, it's a wave to you sweetie."

Looking over the menu, Sarah spied a local craft beer on the menu and thought it was just perfect for this event. When the waiter came, she ordered, "I'll have the Tribeca salad and a pint of *Evil Twin Double–Barrel Jesus*, please."

Brad followed with, "A cheese bratwurst and a pint of the *Warm Elephant* ale."

The TVs stationed around them were full of sportscasters making pre-game analysis and schmooze about the line–up for both team's players. Today it was the Mets versus the Cleveland Indians on the Met's home grounds in Queens.

"Sarah, are you feeling any better now that we're here?" Brad inquired.

"Somewhat," she said, though not too convincingly.

Sarah sighed, then looked at the TV screen and the commentators prattling on, then opened her purse and applied another layer of lip gloss. Baseball wasn't her thing. Anyway, this was going to be her last game, even if Brad has paid over two grand each for the ten game companion seats. She had other plans. Pushing back her chair, "I'm going to the lady's before they serve," she said, as she spun to go down the hallway.

Brad, watching the TV, nodded but didn't say anything. He loved the game. He wanted to shout, "Go Mets!" But thought better of it for all the fans around them at their tables. He liked the indoor Acela bar. Nice and warm, great view through the glass panels and the acoustics of the sound-system were perfect and they had a fine view of the play. Those poor schmucks outside in the seats down below were all bundled up, sitting in the cold trying to wring some warmth out of their hot dogs. For a mild April in Flushing, it was 50 degrees and clear. A good day if you were a fan. Lunch, a game, a brew and thou, he thought, what could be better.

The food showed, and Brad waited a while for Sarah to return. Then, it was another ten minutes. The brat was getting cold. *What was the hold up? Did they have a line at the lady's?*

Finally, he dug into his plate *No point it letting it get any colder. She'll come eventually.*

His cell rang when he had half a mouth full. It was Sarah.

He said, "What's up? Your foods getting cold."

"No, it isn't. It's a salad, Brad. This is hard to tell you in person. I'm getting a divorce. Also, I'd like to tell you, I hate baseball and some other things. We'll talk later. Stay there. You can have my salad and enjoy your game. I'm taking a cab home and packing. Goodbye Brad."

Writing is not necessarily something to be ashamed of; but do it in private and wash your hands afterwards.
—Robert A. Heinlein

Second Chance
By Melody Huttinger

ANNE STARED IN THE MIRROR one more time, fixed an imagined lipstick smudge and smoothed her hair. She huffed. For cripes sake, get over yourself. It's just coffee, not a date to the opera. She grabbed her purse and started for the door but couldn't resist one last look at her full-length image. Ugh, the trendy skinny jeans drew attention to her newly acquired muffin top. Damn the holidays!

She'd always been slim, but it was harder to keep the weight off now that she was officially an old person. Past sixty qualified for being old, didn't it? In spite of the hip sayings—forty is the new thirty and so on, she didn't truly believe sixty was the new fifty. At least her knees didn't believe it. Still, she looked pretty darn good for her age. At least that's what her friends told her. Of course, it was possible they were lying to make her feel good.

Now she had to change clothes, for the third time. With a grunt, she lifted one leg to tug off her tall spike-heeled boots (a recent purchase, along with the skinny jeans), ended up collapsed in a tangle onto the carpeted floor. The door opened, and her husband of twenty-nine years poked his head in.

Joe grinned. "Whataya doing down there? Trying out a new yoga pose?"

"Very funny. Now pull me up." When upright, Anne hobbled over to the bedroom chair with one boot half on, sat and held up her feet. "Can you help, please?"

"Sure thing." He grabbed the fashion footwear and eased them off. "Need anything else, Annie? I'm heading to the dock to help Jerry paint his boat."

"No, have fun." Typical Joe. He was always helping one of his many friends do something. He hadn't even asked what she was doing. And that was exactly why she was going on this rendezvous. Benign neglect. Most of their conversations included his beloved boat or what was on the menu for dinner.

As the door closed on her husband, Anne scurried across the room and rushed into the large walk-in closet. She unzipped the jeans and with difficulty, peeled them down, ending up breathless from the effort. Who came up with such a stupid thing as skinny-jean, anyhow? If you were past thirty, they made you look like a frog with pockets. She surveyed the row of hanging trousers and chose a black pair with and an elastic waistband. So much for trying to look young and cute.

Ignoring the stylish boots, Anne reached for sensible flats. Better than breaking an ankle for the sake of impressing an old flame with her youthfulness. Anne rechecked her lipstick and re-combed her blond bob. At least her hair looked good. No gray—only her hairdresser knew for sure and Miss Clairol wouldn't tell. She glanced at her watch. Got to get going. It was a good thing she'd started getting ready two hours early.

Stuck in traffic twenty minutes later, Anne wondered just when her smallish town had morphed into a nightmare of waiting through two or three light changes every day. Damn the tourists!

As the minutes slowly ticked by, Anne began doubting whether her escapade was ethical or even moral. Maybe she shouldn't go through with it. There was still time to turn the car around. No harm, no foul. After all, she hadn't seen Sean in thirty years, until the chance meeting when she'd been out with her girlfriend, Karen, last week.

She'd recognized him immediately, sitting across the room in the Coffee Clash Café. He hadn't changed much, still handsome and fit looking. His hair black as a raven's wing, just like she remembered. It was a little odd, but then some people didn't seem to age.

A tennis racquet lay on the seat next to him. He'd been a pro when she knew him, and throughout the years, articles in the paper would report his victories in exotic locales. Hometown boy makes good and all that. He probably wouldn't even remember her. But man did she remember him.

Anne was plotting how to casually run into Sean when he stood and headed for the exit. She leapt out of her chair, and sprinted for the door, 'accidentally' bumping into him.

"Sean!" she'd said like she'd just noticed him, and not been surreptitiously salivating for the last half hour. "Do you remember me? We dated way back when."

"Hey, Sugar! How could I forget you?" He gave her a peck on each cheek, European style. "I have a court reserved right now, but let's get together sometime. Give me your number."

She fumbled around in her purse for a pen, but he pulled out his cell phone. "What is it? I'll put it in right now."

Feeling stupid and hopelessly out of date, she muttered the digits to him. He flashed her a movie star smile and dashed out the door.

After he fled, Karen walked over and gave her a sly look. "Was that Sean O'Conner? You practically knocked him over with your exuberance." She smiled. "Don't blame you—he's still a total hunk."

Anne felt her cheeks inflame. "I just wanted to say hello."

Karen patted her arm. "It's okay by me. Frankly, I always was surprised you chose Joe over Mr. Wonderful."

Anne jumped to her husband's defense. "Joe's a good man, great father, and—."

Karen laughed. "And hopelessly predictable."

On the way home from that fateful meeting, Anne convinced herself Sean would never phone. And that was for the best. She was happily married, well, mostly happily married. Joe had a paunch, (not an all-out beer belly) and was losing his hair, (not as bald as a ping pong ball) and was way too settled into the retirement lifestyle, (besides his friends, and the boat, only interested in the game on weekends). When he remembered she was there at all, it was to order another beer or more chips. It turned out, their plans of traveling the world after they both retired was her dream, not his. Damn ESPN!

Back when they were both twenty-nine, Anne met Joe at a party. Tall, average looking, and kind of bookish. Not her type at all, but she was between boyfriends and they began doing things together. To her surprise, she fell for him, hard. They had one blissful summer, the best of her life. For the first time, Anne was in love and began making plans to tie the knot.

One-night Joe took her to a romantic bluff overlooking the city and she was positive he would pop the question. She wiggled close, and he said, as if he were continuing the conversation, "so I'll be leaving tomorrow for the city. The specialized training, they offer is essential for my career." He never mentioned marriage or even pursuing a long-distance relationship. Anne was too stunned for words.

That night her world crumbled and fell to dust at her feet, but dignity wouldn't allow her to cry and carry-on about it in front of him. She was a big girl, and relationships ended. That's the way it was. It was simply a summer romance and now it was over. Kaput.

After wallowing in self-pity for an entire week, Anne forced herself to go to happy hour with Karen. They were drinking and laughing, (a glass of wine or two makes everything better) when a meltingly handsome guy stopped by their table.

"Hi, I'm Sean," he said to Anne, ignoring Karen. "I haven't seen you here before. Would you like to go out sometime?"

Anne blinked and stammered, "I . . . I don't know." The abandonment by Joe was still raw, but then she thought, why not? She took a breath and said, "Yes, I would."

His fabulous smile lit up the dim room. "Great!" He wrote down her number, (that was before cell phones), and said he'd call her in a day or so.

The day or so turned out to be more than a week, and Anne had nearly forgotten the incident when her phone jingled, and it was Sean. They began dating. He was fun and attentive, and always dropped her a postcard when he was on tour. But he wasn't Joe.

Anne told Sean about Joe, but instead of putting him off, it seemed to make him more determined than ever to win her. She gradually felt her shattered heart mending, and Sean began looking better and better. He was getting pretty serious, and there was nothing not to like. He made great money, traveled to exciting places and kept in touch.

After a few months of a whirlwind courtship, he presented her with a one-carat diamond.

"Flawless, just like you, Sugar," he'd said.

It was the most beautiful thing she'd ever seen, but since her breakup with Joe, it was hard to contemplate marriage. She stalled. Sean was about to leave on another trip, and Anne promised to have an answer upon his return.

Then Joe showed up. Just like that, no phone call, no letter, no nothing, just showed up on her stoop. She opened the door and he was standing there, flowers in hand, grinning like he had all the numbers on the Powerball ticket. The old feeling rushed back, and Anne nearly fainted from light-headedness.

But he wasn't getting off that easy.

"It's been months! You can't just waltz in after all this time and expect me to fall all over myself." Anne began closing the door. "Besides, I have a new boyfriend."

Joe put his foot out, effective as a door jam. There was a long silence as they stared at each other through the crack. Finally, he said quietly, "I thought we had an understanding. I only took that training, so I could get a promotion into management. Now we'll have enough money to get married, Annie."

Her knees wobbled like Jell-O. "Married? You should have clued me in."

He swallowed. "I could've sworn we talked about this."

Typical Joe. He always thought they talked about things, but mostly it was in his head. Smart, funny, good-hearted, clueless. That was her Joe.

They were married the following weekend, and when Sean returned from his tennis tournament, Anne had the difficult task of telling him she was married. He took it well, considering. She heard that within a couple of months, he was engaged to someone else. Anne preferred to believe it was a rebound situation and not a character flaw.

Life was good during the intervening years of settling into family life and raising children. Not exciting, but good. Every once in a while, though, Anne couldn't help but wonder, what if? Especially when she saw the sports page with a picture of Sean trouncing his opponent by serving an ace ball. Or partying with the jet set. Or meeting the Prince of Monaco. She could've had a life of adventure, met famous people, gone to galas on the arm of a delicious guy to the envy of every other woman in the room. Instead, she had Joe.

So, when Anne ran into Sean that day, it almost seemed like a second chance. Not that she really expected him to phone. Thirty years was a long time. He was probably married, too. But the very next day, he did call and asked her out for lunch. She'd hesitated, then said, "How about coffee? We can meet at the Coffee Clash."

At last the traffic eased and Anne wheeled into the café lot. Shoot, it was full. She spotted a slot across the street and after several attempts, maneuvered her full-sized SUV into it, all the time wondering why she hadn't bought that Mini Cooper.

She was so near to the next car, Anne had to suck in her stomach to squeeze out. After the close encounter with the door, she straightened her clothes and walked to the cafe, glad she didn't have to negotiate the uneven pavement in her spike-heeled boots.

Sean, sitting at an outside table, stood and pulled out another chair when he saw her. "Hope this is okay. Reminds me a little of Paris."

Anne's heart hammered. What she wouldn't give to actually be in Paris. With him. She sat, and he helped her chair in. She sighed. Just as gentlemanly as she remembered. "It's good to see you, Sean."

"You, too, Sugar."

She smiled. His pet name for her.

A pretty, twenty-something waitress showed up with her pad and pencil ready. After ordering them both Non-fat Lattes with a double shot, Sean gave the girl a seductive smile and said, "Thanks, Sugar."

Anne almost choked on her sip of water. 'Sugar' was his special name for *her*, not some random barista. Did he even *remember* her real name? He hadn't used it even once. She swallowed her disappointment and said, "It's been a long time, you must be married by now."

"Not at the moment. In the middle of a messy divorce."

"That's too bad, after so long. Didn't you get married right after we broke up?"

Sean looked blank for a moment. "Oh, not *that* wife. There's, uh, been a few since then."

"A few?"

"Well, only four."

"You've been married *four* times?"

"Five, including the first one. But I don't usually include her because we were both so young, and it only lasted a couple of months." He began counting off on his fingers. "The second one didn't understand me, the third was a total bitch, the fourth was boring and this last one is completely crazy."

While Anne sat dumbfounded, Sean rattled on about the horrible women he'd been involved with. When she managed to ask about children, he went off about how his one son, at seventeen, had run away to Los Angeles to become a devoted Steampunk fan.

He complained about the loneliness of life on the road and then groused about returning to his hometown to teach tennis skills to old ladies. Sean had nothing good to say about anyone or anything. He never asked one question about her life, not even if she was married.

And throughout this non-stop tirade, Anne's eyes kept revisiting the part in his hair. Could it be? Yes, definitely. The telltale sign of gray roots.

Was this the same person from so long ago? When had he become so thoroughly self-absorbed or had he always been that way and she didn't recognize it? Anne felt trapped by his diatribe but couldn't find an excuse to exit without seeming rude. The boredom became complete after fifteen minutes, but she endured the harangue for another ten before she'd had enough. She stood abruptly and gathered her purse.

He put his hand on her arm. "I'll call you soon, and we can go play, like old times," he said, flashing bleached-white teeth.

She shook off his hand. "Sorry, better not. My husband wouldn't like it." Anne felt instant gratification at the stupefied stare he gave her and walked away without a backward glance.

Joe was home for lunch by the time she got there, fixing himself a grilled cheese sandwich. "Can I make you one, Annie?"

"Sounds good." She plopped down at the kitchen island and noticed a travel brochure. "What's this?" she asked, picking it up. The cover read *Paris and The Wine Country of France*.

"For our trip next month. I just picked up the tickets from the travel agent."

Anne's jaw nearly hit the floor. "What trip?"

Joe blinked. "We talked about it, right?"

She ran to him, laughing, and snuggled into his arms. "Typical Joe."

I'm Going to Hell
By Tom Spirito

IT WAS MY SECON SEASON working at The Roundup Ranch Resort located in the Catskill Mountains of New York. The dude ranch was nestled in a horseshoe-shaped valley, on three thousand acres of green pastures and forest. I had been promoted the previous Fall from "pilot" to dude wrangler. You may be wondering what does a "pilot" do at a dude ranch. "Pilot" was the slang term for the barn boy because his prime mission was to scoop up all the horse poop and "pile it" here and "pile it" there. Yup, I piled it here, there and everywhere for the entire previous season. But now, I was a "Catskill Cowboy." This was the fulfillment of my youthful fantasies, born out of a misspent childhood in front of the boob tube, jam-packed with rootin' tootin' Hollywood Western action, courtesy of Gene, Hoppy, The Ranger, and Roy. Cowboy was actually, pronounced "Kaboy" in New Yorkese. One of my favorite guests dubbed me with that moniker one day when he said, "Tom, you're a real Kaboy." I took this as a compliment, thought it sounded kind of catchy, and so "The Catskill Kaboy" was born.

The Summer season of 1968 didn't get busy until schools closed around the metropolitan New York, New Jersey area. But before the schools released their howling mobs, they took them on their class trips. Roundup Ranch was the day trip destination for one inner-city Catholic school that I called "Our Lady of Perpetual Saddle-sores." They would arrive in two school buses loaded with children, ranging in age from too young to not old enough, escorted by several nuns. Yes, NUNS! Now being a naive, young man of Italian descent and raised in the Roman Catholic faith, I had a great respect for nuns. Correction make that a great fear of NUNS! The sisters ran roughshod over these children of the asphalt jungle. After deconstructing much of the ranch facilities, the nuns assembled the little darlings into groups of about thirty and marched them down to our stable for their first experience on horseback. Well, I knew the drill for mounting dudes pretty thoroughly by this time and was confident that although a challenge, we could handle this "cast call for The Lord of the Flies" without a hitch.

What I wasn't prepared for was that the nuns would be accompanying the kids on the trail ride. Now, this was 1968. Nuns were still wearing the traditional attire from the top of their white mitered crown to the black veiled robes cinched at the waist with rosary beads and a crucifix, right down to their little black granny shoes. And just to make it interesting, we didn't have a mounting block. Now children were easy to mount up. You just put your hands under each armpit and up they went.

Adults of varying sizes were a bit more challenging. First, you'd help them put their left foot in the stirrup. Second, you hold the reins and brace the saddle with your left hand. Third, have the rider grab hold of whatever they could reach with their hands. This often included the wrangler. Fourth, gently cup your right arm under the prospective rider's butt. Fifth, lift them up and into the saddle. By the numbers, this was almost always a pretty slick and quick operation known as "dude launching." On this fateful day, I drew the plum assignment. My nun was about 4 feet tall and almost just as wide—not exactly equestrian friendly to put it kindly. Not that there aren't many talented and skilled riders in the plus weight range, I'm no lightweight myself. However, this was not a problem of physicality, but of culture and upbringing. I was going to have to TOUCH A NUN! Not just touch her but manhandle her. I tried to dig way down for courage, thinking of the examples of all those WWII and Western movie heroes. I smiled and said, "Howdy Sister." Her eyes bored through me just like an alien heat ray from a sci-fi movie and I knew I'd seen this horrible thing before. I felt that Nun's ruler come down on my psychological knuckles, just as it had so many years ago on my actual knuckles. My mind kneeled and prayed for a miracle or at least a little mercy. Why didn't we have a mounting block, a ladder, a forklift, something? Why hadn't we taught these horses to kneel?! Clearly, the under the armpit heave-ho wasn't going to work. The adult mounting procedure by the numbers would have to do. Lord knows how I got her foot, that little, black, granny shoed foot, into the stirrup. Inspired, I placed the reins in my teeth, a la John Wayne True Grit style. I knew I would need both hands to propel Sister to escape velocity. The Sister's reach enabled her to just barely grab the stirrup fender on either side. I could see she was going to be of marginal assistance during the launch procedure.

We had arrived at the moment of truth. I couldn't feel my right arm. It was moving as if a trained reflex had taken over, like the soldiers that jump up out of their foxholes and move forward into no-man's land and I was definitely in NO-MAN'S LAND! I cradled her butt in the crook of my right arm and gave a mighty upward boost with the help of my left hand on her left cheek. At this point, time seemed to stand still as my observable surroundings became a surreal, disorienting, blur of swirling, blinding, black veils circling my head. A jarring impact to my left temple jerked me back to the unfolding horror of my situation. Sisters' crucifix had just bounced off my noggin' with a slightly hollow "THUD!"

Suddenly I heard a new auditory sensation, akin to the crack of doom, the Sister "GIGGLED!" Oh God, I'd touched a NUN's butt and she GIGGLED! Oh Lord, let it be no more than a tickle. Desperately I thought that perhaps I could find salvation in the confessional. A voice deep inside me said, "Fat chance there "Kaboy." I had broken the Eleventh Commandment: "Thou Shalt Not Touch A Nun's Butt and Make Her Giggle." It was no use. I knew I was lost. For sure, I was goin' to hell. No ifs, ands, or BUTTS!

Fun at the DMV
By John Maher

Last week my wife told me we need to renew our driver's licenses this year. Because of our age, we're in that dreaded demographic designation, Senior Citizen. We're required to retake the written exam, which adds insult to the indignity. The thought fills me with venom. I hate the DMV. Hate isn't powerful enough. Detest, despise, abhor; there aren't enough words that describe my deep abiding animus for this torture palace.

My judgments about the DMV are long-standing. They first surfaced on a Monday 57 years ago, the day after my 16th birthday. Like all the teenagers I knew, I had to get my learner's permit precisely on my 16th birthday. Since September 18th, 1960 fell on a Sunday, going to the DMV had to take place the very next day without question. Getting your learners-permit on your 16th birthday was an inalienable rite of passage for every teenager living in New York State. On the appointed day, I insisted that my mother pick me up at school and whisk me post-haste to the DMV in Mineola six miles away from my hometown.

Although my older brother Tom had briefed me about getting my learner's permit, thinking about the process produced sweaty armpits and jangled my nerves. My anxiety increased when I entered the DMV with my mother in tow and saw the overflow crowd of people. A sea of sullen faces loitered in messy lines that snaked all over the place. Other unfortunates sat in endless rows of painful plastic chairs waiting to be summoned to the counter. As a point of reference, this was the lone New York State DMV office for all of Nassau County. The County's 1960 population was 1.3 million people. To say the place was crowded would be an understatement.

My first DMV experience introduced me to the two issues that colored every later visit. I cannot discount the pain caused by the long lines or endless waiting. They're bad enough. It's the misery of dealing with brain-dead DMV clerks and the insufferable eye exam that get my back teeth grinding with dread.

Over the years, I've endured visits to DMV offices in four states. In some, the crowds were smaller and the wait less. But the clerks and the eye exam seemed the same. I am convinced that all DMV clerks must attend the same training school that teaches the three S's: Slow, surly and stupid. It doesn't matter if the DMV office is in New York, South Carolina, Massachusetts, or California, they're all the same. They process the paperwork at sloth speed, they are doing you a favor by their existence, and they have IQ's three points lower than a stapler. These attributes varied by office and state. It's a matter of degrees. But for the eye exam, they were all the same.

I've been hypersensitive about being blind in my right eye since I was little. I've always felt different, not entirely whole. My mother abetted these feelings. Soon after the doctors removed the eye when I was nine, my mother stated that my having one eye was a family secret. I was not to tell friends or schoolmates of my condition. It wasn't until 1999 after moving to California to take care of my 86-year-old mother I learned the reason for this family secret. During an intense conversation one afternoon she told me the deep-seated guilt she'd carried for 50 years. My mother blamed herself for my congenital cataract and eye surgery. She didn't want people to know what she believed was her responsibility.

Anything that brought unwanted attention to my having one eye sent me around the bend. The eye chart at the Mineola DMV that day in 1960 mortified and humiliated me. I had to explain to the cretin behind the counter why I couldn't see line #3 with my right eye. The mob behind me in line looked on with impatience. Every DMV visit after this where I had to read an eye chart dredged up the old bugaboo. Except for one episode that put the quietus to my sensitivity.

Since I planned on staying in California after I moved there in 1999 to take care of my 85-year-old mother, I needed a California driver's license. I drove over to the DMV office in Fountain Valley, the town next to Huntington Beach. The office was a one-story red brick nondescript building that belied its vast interior. On entering, lines meandered everywhere. Row after row of hard fiberglass chairs held disconsolate people looking like they were awaiting execution. There were no directional signs or information counter. A low hum of English, Spanish, and Vietnamese murmured voices competed with counter clerks barking "Next!" and "Step up!" and the regular timpani *blam, blam, blam* of smashing self-inking office stampers. I had arrived at Dante's ninth circle of hell, the one dealing with treachery.

I asked people in two different lines what that line did and at the third found it dispensed blank forms completed at standup shelves along the walls. Luckily, I had brought a pen. There were unfortunate others left adrift without writing implements; they're probably still there.

After a wait of 15 minutes, the gargoyle behind the counter informed me that reciprocity did not exist between California and Massachusetts. I couldn't just exchange my license. I was required to undergo a written exam and an eye test. Then she pushed the application forms at me and instructed, "Go over there, fill these out, and then get in that line there." She used her thumb to suggest a general direction further along the long counter where other misfortunate victims were filling out forms. As the heat of aggravation mushroomed, I repeated the Serenity Prayer several times in my head.

After a 20-minute wait in the second line, I arrived at the next hurdle. The garden gnome with coke-bottle glasses behind this counter seized my completed forms and scanned them without a greeting or a word. Then she looked through them again. And again. I was bemused that she took that amount of effort to check a dozen filled-in spaces on two pages. Satisfied, she shoved the forms back at me with a "Go over there" coupled with a chin move directing me toward a line down the counter. Like all the other lines in the building, it wound around an array of lanes fenced in by black cloth barrier tape stretched between stanchions.

After another interminable wait in a line of shuffling feet, I made it to the next position. Since patience and a capacity to tolerate stupid people are not in my family's DNA, on arriving at the counter, my mood was on a slow simmer. I was just this side of seething… at which point the broad-hipped troll behind the counter barked, "Step to your right, cover your right eye, and read line #3 with your left eye." And, so it began. Since I had my right eye removed, I'd worn an artificial eye. The current one was custom made, and you couldn't tell I was wearing a "glass eye." It was so well made that even doctors mistook it for a real eye. So, I covered my right nonsighted eye as instructed. Why confuse the woman right off? That would take place soon enough.

After rattling off lie #3 and line #2 to the counter lady's satisfaction, she again barked, "Cover your left eye and read line #3 with your right eye." I looked at her and replied, "That's not going to happen. I'm blind in my right eye." She scrunched up her face, squinted her eyes and glared at me with annoyance. Apparently, I was screwing up the routine and lo she would deal with this breach of procedures.

She reached under the counter, shuffled some paper, withdrew a form, and slammed it on the countertop. With the power of a very important person and peering at me down her nose, she announced, "Take this to an eye doctor. He needs to complete it." My mood shifted from frustrated bubbling anger to confusion. I said, "Why? Why do I have to have this filled out?" She studied me as if I were mentally disabled and said, "You need to have a doctor confirm your condition." My confusion morphed into the fourth stage of anger. I blew right past bothered, mildly irritated and agitated to indignant.

I took a deep breath and said, "I need a specialist to tell you I have one eye? I've told you I have one eye. Why would I come in here and lie about having one eye? What would be the benefit?" She ignored this with a dismissive expression and, "It's the rule."

I reached up with my right hand and removed the artificial eye from its socket. It's only held in place by the eyelids. Cupping it in my fist, I smashed it onto the countertop and opened my hand to display the eye face up. It lay there on the bare Formica surface looking forlorn but pristine and alive. Pointing at it, I said, "That's a glass eye. I am blind in my right eye." Seething and raising my voice, I pointed to the empty socket which drew her attention to it. I said, "That's an empty eye socket. There's no eye in there. I am not paying a specialist $200, so he can peer in here and tell me I'm missing my right eye."

The counter woman's face looked like someone having a stroke. Her eyes were as big pie plates, the sides of her face drawn in tight, and her mouth a constricted rictus line. People tell me I'm a scary looking person when I'm angry. I guess my Irish mug is partly to blame. To compound this, I weighed over 300 pounds, so I suppose my angry visage and size could be intimidating. Without equivocation, I can report that having an enraged, large, one-eyed man who's just plucked out his eye affected this woman. While I couldn't see them, I sensed the people in line behind me retreating like unarmed combatants or remora fish searching for a place to hide. They wanted no part in this action.

With her face frozen in mid-seizure, the counter woman barely audible said, "Wait here." No one remaining in the line behind me voiced any objection to the delay. She scurried over to a single plain grey metal office desk anchored in the vast sea of emptiness that encompassed the area behind the counters. At this desk sat a dark-haired middle-aged, bespectacled man. He was Jabba the Hutt's 2nd cousin or a distant relative. He didn't merely sit in his high-backed leather office chair. It was more like he had been poured into it.

The harried counter lady leaned into Jabba across the desk. With her palms planted on the desktop, elbows locked, shoulders tight, she reported her recent interactions with the incensed behemoth at her station. She delivered her summation with furtive looks in my direction, which prompted matching nervous glances from Jabba. After about 30 seconds of back-and-forth, the counter lady moved to Jabba's side of the desk where he pulled out an enormous white covered loose-leaf binder from a desk drawer. This tome had to be a foot thick. It was the most massive loose-leaf binder I had seen. Ever.

The pair turned pages in rapid succession, jumping from section to section, ostensibly looking for a relevant DMV regulation or directive that would tell them how to deal with an angry one-eyed man. Then Jabba closed the tome with finality, and the counter woman hustled back to her station at the counter. With her head drawn back from her shoulders and her chin tucked, face tight with repressed panic and trying to maintain composure, she said, "Please go over there and take your written test. Then come back here." A slight head nod to the left suggested I move to the testing position down the counter.

My mood had changed. The anger dissipated, replaced by an internal smiling gratification. Regardless of the outcome, I had won. At least on this day, I had successfully explained to a DMV ninny why I can't read an eye chart with my right eye.

When I arrived at the testing area, I found the counter person there very accommodating. I surmised she had heard my bellowing and demonstrative explanation. I also figured she saw the other counter lady's reaction. Her expression told me she understood clearly that I had one eye, that I was not at all happy with the DMV, and her best interests would be met by quickly administering the written exam.

I passed the written test, had my mugshot taken, and got my license. I had won, proof of the adage, "The squeaky wheel gets the grease," especially if you have one eye and weight 300 pounds.

The Role of Trees in a World of Torture
By Dan Dražen Mazur

LIKE MOST PEOPLE, I also immensely dislike children. This uneasiness is primarily caused by not knowing if the little brat you are dealing with is to become a good-natured tree hugger with the beard and body volume Santa could be jealous of—or grow up into a menacing skinny person with tiny mustache, ridden by an inferiority complex, raging testosterone, and ruthless egocentric personality, known simply as baby Adolf. The early signs of future behavior are highly unreliable, and the following story might illustrate this.

It was one regular Sunday, the day after Saturday, when little Josef discovered a plot. He was a withdrawn child, quiet and immersed into his own fantasies, who never caused much trouble to his parents. His hair was strong and plentiful, and his eyes were radiating curiosity and intelligence.

The Dzhugashvili family would come to the city park every summer Sunday as usual, where his parents would spend some time enjoying the afternoon shade and talking nonsense. Joseph could filter out their yapping by watching birds and squirrels, and by trying to figure out their everyday doings, and guessing why they are alive.

That fateful Sunday Joseph noticed that the tree normally growing straight across the bench his family usually occupied, was no longer there. Naturally, one would think that the tree was cut down and removed for whatever reason. However, there was another, completely mature tree at the same place where the old tree was, which was odd. Josef remembered that the missing tree had one big branch growing horizontally out of its main trunk, high above the ground, and leaned directly over their bench, providing pleasant shade for the people underneath. The current tree was also quite big and tall, but its branches reached out at an angle, going straight upwards, nothing like the tree Joseph remembered.

Joseph kept this discovery to himself but made sure to remember what the tree which replaced the original tree looked like, hoping when they visit, the old tree would be neatly back in its place. Joseph thought maybe 'his' tree had been taken to be repaired, and another one was put temporarily in its place, not to cause disturbance, panic, or protests of sensitive park visitors. Typical thinking of a kid his age.

Next Sunday Joseph realized that the tree that was there replacing the original tree was also no longer there, but was replaced by another one, even skinnier and taller. The Sunday after there was another tree there, replacing the one that replaced the one which replaced the original one. Surprised and disturbed more than ever, Joseph began observing other trees in the park more carefully, and to his amazement discovered that his original tree didn't disappear, instead, it was relocated and now growing toward the edge of the park. Joseph was sure this was 'his' tree, recognizing the horizontal branch. The second replacement tree was also found but relocated on the other side of the park.

Although young for his age, Joseph realized that these trees were so huge that relocating them regularly around the park must have been a monumental task for which many people and heavy machinery had to be involved. Curious as he was, the Sunday after, Joseph brought with him crayons and marked the five trees around the bench with numbers, 1, 2, 3, 4, 5. His tactic was to mark the tree closest to their bench with number 1, next closest with number 2, and so forth.

Next Sunday, Joseph's suspicion was confirmed as he determined that the trees marked with 1, 2, 3, 4 and 5 were at their new locations, namely 3, 4, 5, 2, 1, using the same method of counting. The trees 5, 2, and 1 were moved completely outside of the original distances, while 3 and 4 were further away from their bench, and replaced with trees from different park areas, that Joseph didn't get to mark yet. To figure out if there was a pattern in these trees rotating was confusing and difficult, impossible.

One would think that frustrated Joseph would share his discovery with his parents, but he kept the revelation to himself. He was never compassionate about his parents, finding them boring and a nuisance. As much as it was irritating, his inability to figure out what was going on, he also felt triumphant - somebody was regularly rotating trees around the park, and nobody but him seemed to be noticing that.

As Joseph was growing up, he never forgot this, and years later, when his position allowed him, he ordered an investigation regarding the rotating trees. Unfortunately, it showed no results.

"Comrade Stalin, here is the investigation report. I am afraid we couldn't determine how it was possible to rotate the trees. We actually concluded this wasn't possible."

"Are you insinuating that I am a liar?!" Joseph yelled and jumped from his chair. He was upset because earlier that morning he discovered an unacceptable pimple on his forehead.

"Of course not, comrade Stalin. I'm just saying you were a boy then. Your imagination was vivid. We were simply unable to figure out what had happened," the man said, barely able to keep the contents of his intestines inside.

"We have determined that around that time a new town manager was hired, but we couldn't find any connection between this fact and the tree rotations."

"I want to see that man!" Joseph ordered, returning to the safety of his chair.

His order couldn't be fulfilled because the man had been dead for a decade, so Joseph never found a definitive answer to this mystery. Upset, Joseph ordered the disrespectful comrade who dared to question his honesty, be sentenced to the gulag. This bothered him quite a lot, but it also remains unknown how much this event contributed, if at all, to the world's history of tyranny.

When my mother told me this story I couldn't rest and find peace because of the mystery. Due to circumstances beyond my control, I was given the opportunity to go through the archives of the park and recreation department. I found out a simple answer to the mystery. That new director who took up the park manager position before the rotation of the trees had begun, had been the manager of a huge automobile tire shop where rotating of automobile tires was an everyday routine. He must have continued the practice out of the habit.

Now you know why I'm leery of being around children.

Genesis
By Gretchen Brinck

STARS FLARED OVERHEAD, then vanished like bright pebbles flung into a river. Jenna scooted deeper into her sleeping bag. It smelled of smoke, pitch, pine needles, clean dirt, sweat.

It smelled of Drake.

Here, where trees stopped growing and craggy slopes angled toward the mountain top, she could feel his ropy arms around her and his wispy beard against her neck. They'd always made love when they camped in the wilderness.

Directly above her, something else burst into flame, so close she could hear its small whoosh over the treetops. The ground shuddered when it hit beyond the fire pit. Multicolored flames darted out. Then darkness. Then a dull glow like an unquenched ember.

Jenna struggled into her jeans and boots. If the trees started burning, she'd have a dicey time escaping down the steep mountain trail.

But nothing caught fire. She huddled again in the sleeping bag and stared at the knot of shimmering heat.

Drake would have loved this experience. She'd done the right thing, climbing to this lonely, wild place for remembrance. The funeral had been nothing but a stage on which friends portrayed melodramatic grief. "Oh, Jenna," Drake's trekking buddy Ben had moaned to her turned back, "I was right beside him when ... there was nothing I could do. God!" He'd given a little sob. "At least let me return his backpack to you." He'd forced his card between her clenched fingers. "Call me when you're ready."

Ready for what? To learn how a skilled hiker like Drake could fall from a Himalayan trail and die?

"Look at that thing," she whispered to Drake in her mind. The fallen star throbbed redly till the moon sank toward morning.

When dawn woke her, she saw a small crater at the tree-line. The meteorite's flames had left glittery trails across the dirt.

Her boots crunched as she approached. Up close the burn lines glistened like mercury. A few feet below the crater's lip lay a black stone the size of a baseball.

Jenna's chunk of outer space, part shiny, part dull, glinting with crystal or mica, couldn't be less like a mega-ton, dinosaur-killing asteroid. It was just an ugly little rock.

Still, she used a roll of film on the scene when the sun rose higher, though Drake, not she, had been the expert at nature photography.

Sunday night Jenna made her long drive back to the overpopulated San Francisco Bay Area. At work on Monday, she robotically performed administrative tasks for computer nerds, but Drake and the meteorite crowded her attention. When she surfed the net that night, she learned that few human beings had ever witnessed an actual fall. She downloaded images of recovered meteorites. None matched hers. The known ones were "interplanetary." Was hers different because its origins were farther away -- intergalactic?

Scientists would go crazy over it.

"Yo!" Drake shouted in her head, and she saw the giant footprint they'd once come upon while cross-country skiing. Drake had raised his gloved fist. "Yo, Sasquatch! Head for the high country, Dude! Stay a mystery!"

Scientists would lock her meteorite into a chamber, chip it, zap it with x- and other rays, microscopically examine it, burn it with chemicals and argue over it in esoteric journals. Yo, Drake.

She told no one.

Saturday, she returned to the wilderness and struggled for hours up the deer trail to the tree-line.

Something had happened around the crater. Small mounds had erupted along the burn lines as if the mercury-like stuff had bubbled. Jenna came close. An inch high and an inch across, the gray-green lumps had smooth surfaces except for minute clefts across their tops. Jenna touched the bottom edge of the nearest one. The surface gave beneath her finger like firm flesh.

Of course. The things were just succulents. But how could they grow at this high altitude, in barely cooled intergalactic lava?

She couldn't stop gazing at hers, as she already considered the one she'd touched. Utterly minimalist, yet pregnant with possibilities, like the round end of a fertile egg. A cell about to divide. A mushroom cap concealing spores. A baby's bottom. A female mound.

The head of a male organ.

What? Tears burst from her eyes. This stupid nothing of a plant had struck her deepest wound. She and Drake had planned to have children soon.

Chilly drops hit her face. She stalked away to set up her rain tarp.

In the morning the succulents shone with raindrops. Jenna watched herself gently scoop hers up along with its soil and metallic particles. Drake had never taken anything from the wild nor left anything behind. He'd even packed out used Band-Aids and toilet paper.

But I just have to have this succulent, she told him, or his spirit, though she couldn't say why.

At home, she planted it in an artsy cappuccino mug and set it on the kitchen windowsill. Her orange cat, Muffin, sniffed it and then stepped over it, draping it with filaments of fur.

The following weekend Jenna boxed up the slim photo-essay nature books on which she and Drake had collaborated. She'd collect their royalties, but without Drake's beautiful photographs to inspire her, she doubted she'd write copy again. She paused over a studio portrait of his fascinating Asian-Polynesian face. Packed it with the books.

Then she watered the succulent. When she gave it a quarter turn, she noticed a lentil-sized, pale orange blemish on its lower edge.

Was the plant multiplying or did it have a fungus? She squinted. The bump seemed textured and no, this couldn't be. She rummaged through drawers for a magnifying glass and looked again.

The orange growth, wearing an expression of fat-cheeked contentment, was Muffin.

"Oh, God! Kitty kitty?"

Muffin bumped his forehead against her shin and rumbled.

Jenna picked the magnifying glass back up. Muffin's minute replica appeared solid and furry and three-dimensional. Was it moving? She couldn't tell.

"How did you do that?" she asked the plant, but as she spoke, she remembered Muffin draping fur across it. She plucked one of her own reddish-brown hairs and set it on the succulent's tiny cleft.

In the morning a dot had appeared next to Muffin's image. Jenna checked it morning and evening for days before it was large enough to be examined through the magnifying glass.

She saw herself: a lean, naked woman with reddish brown hair. "Oh, wow!" Jenna's delight bordered on love.

Could the succulent extrapolate images from sources other than hair? And would it accept flora as well as fauna? In her patio outside the window, pots and planter boxes burst with spring blooms. Jenna picked a purple petunia blossom and dropped it on the cleft. A pin-sized purple outcropping rewarded her in the morning. She tried the root of a cyclamen bulb. That worked too. When she gave the succulent an ant, the bug scuttled away instantly, yet next morning another tiny bump emerged.

Jenna squatted by the windowsill. "OK," she said. "You use lots of sources and you capture a being the second you touch it." Her eyes traveled over its round shape. A lot of space waited to be filled.

On her next free day, Jenna offered, in one hour, a chrysanthemum leaf, fresh tomato pulp, a feather, an orange peel, an onion skin, a garlic clove, a coffee bean and her favorite yellow petunia. In the morning she found a multitude of new bumps. She could hardly bear the long wait till she could capture them in the magnifying glass.

In addition to the plants, the succulent had replicated an aphid, a bird mite, a hummingbird, a ladybug, a tomato worm, whitefly, a fungus and weird things she didn't recognize but which must be microbes or mitochondria or bacteria or nematodes.

But she couldn't find the yellow petunia. "You don't take the same species twice?" Jenna returned to her patio and collected seventy-two more samples of plants, bugs, and worms.

On Monday she called in sick and foraged neighborhood flowerbeds and vegetable gardens, then gathered urban wildlife droppings from a shrubby vacant lot. It took hours to give the plant all the new offerings.

In the morning, when she'd seen the dozens of new outcroppings on the Mound, Jenna packed trail mix, juice, a thermos of coffee and her sleeping bag and headed for Golden Gate Park. She stepped from a sidewalk into the Park's dense, varied growth and plucked twigs, leaves, droppings, and insects. When darkness fell she switched on her flashlight and continued till she dropped asleep beneath a eucalyptus. She woke chilled with fog, ate a handful of trail mix, and kept going. She didn't go home till the trail mix had been gone awhile, didn't realize she'd been collecting for seven days till she checked the date on her computer.

When she finished giving Golden Gate Park to the plant, pinpoint dots completely covered its surface except the hairline cleft on top.

But if the Mound was full, why did Jenna still feel empty? "We've barely begun," she pleaded. "There's so much more I can give you." Something went wrong with her eyes. She squinted through the magnifying glass but could no longer see the dots. They had vanished into their gray-green landscape as she spoke.

The plant had made room for more.

"Why?" she asked, though till now the question hadn't occurred to her. "What will you do with them?" She set it on the floor, sat lotus style and gazed down at it till it blocked out the walls, the kitchen, the wind blowing through the window. Jenna did not know if it was day or night when she sank into sleep.

In her dreams, she glimpsed a gray-green planet through clouds. She descended to its surface, which held only dirt and lichen and pure, swift rivers. She and Drake plucked sparkling stones from a riverbed and threw them over their shoulders. From her first stone sprang a brilliant blue kingfisher, from Drake's a drooping willow. Jenna's second stone created a leaping trout and Drake's stone created a brown bear. Jenna opened her eyes to her moonlit kitchen. She understood.

The Mound was gathering life for a clean new planet and she'd been appointed its life-giving goddess.

At sunrise, she drove to work and packed her things. Her boss Arnold, sleeping beneath his desk as computer nerds are wont to do, woke and leaned in her doorway, running his fingers through his unwashed hair. "You look terrible," he told her between yawns. "You shouldn't make life-changing decisions while you're grieving."

"Grieving?" Pain over Drake had shrunk like the replicas on the plant.

She sublet her apartment to a desperate college student and dropped Muffin off with a cat-loving friend. Then she loaded Drake's old van with clothes, cameras, camping gear, credit cards and the plant and headed for the coast. She slept next to the highway above a rocky beach.

At dawn she tucked the succulent into a net shopping bag. She'd take it to the samples, not the samples to it. Dangling the bag from her wrist, she scrambled over slimy rocks to the tidal pools.

With every wave, fleshy plants opened and closed like mouths seeking the multitude of tiny life forms. Even the slime Jenna skidded over was vibrantly alive. "So amazing," she told the plant, dropping sample after sample into the bag on top of it. "You'll love this."

Cold water crashed over her head. She fell sideways. The wave tumbled her over barnacle-covered rocks, then dumped her on the beach and fled. Its rushing wake sucked the bag out with it. Moments later the bag reappeared in the rising curve of the next wave, crashed on the shore, rode away again with the undertow. Jenna plunged into the surf after it. Her mouth filled with gritty seawater. She dove through the next breaker and swam Filthy with seaweed and foam, the bag floated on the swells as if waiting for her. She kicked her way to it, tied it to her wrist and let the waves wash her to shore like driftwood.

The cappuccino cup and metallic dirt were gone, but the succulent lay tangled in the bottom of the bag. Its gray-green skin had gone blotchy and was streaked with sand and salt. It looked sick.

Jenna untangled it and held it gently. Tears ran down her cheeks. "Don't die," she pleaded. But how could the plant and the replicas survive a half hour in the salty ocean?

The plant nestled easily in her palm. Its flat underside had no roots. She faced the fact she'd been avoiding: the Mound was no more a succulent than the space rock was a meteorite. It was a womblike vessel incubating strings of DNA for the clean, pure planet she'd seen in her dream.

Jenna rinsed the mound in a drinking fountain by the parking lot. Then she set it in the van's window. The mottled surface slowly coarsened into pinpricks.

In the morning she bought a series of microscope lenses and a tweezer-like holder. Through one she examined the mound's surface. Sea life sprang into view: a seal, sea lion, fish, whale, dolphin, shrimp, plankton. The mound had taken full advantage of the sea water's animal excrement and sperm, plant spores, and all other traces of life. Far from destroying the Mound and its DNA, immersion had proved a shortcut.

She jotted a quick plan: she'd travel north during summer, and by late fall would head south, and in addition to here and now life forms, she would give some extinct species a chance for new life in her little world.

She taped the plan to the dashboard, started the ignition and lost track of time. Nothing mattered anymore except collecting life. She took the mound everywhere with her in its net bag. It plunged into rivers, lakes, swamps, was dragged through the underbrush of forests; it absorbed desert microbes, bone dust from long-extinct creatures, pollen from rare plants Jenna located on heritage farms, dung and guano from zoos. It dangled from her arm as she swam with seals in the Galapagos Islands and when she hiked in a protected Amazon rainforest rich with exotic and endangered species.

And every night when she was alone, she cupped the mound --by now swollen as if pregnant -- and, using ever stronger lenses, plunged into her created world. Its scenes endlessly fascinated her yet remained endlessly incomplete.

One evening she pulled up the van in Puerto Natales in Chile. In a day or two she'd take a bus to the spectacular national park, Torres del Paine. She lit her lamp, held the mound and picked up the strongest lens.

And saw only gray-green.

Where were her lovely forests and animals, her resurrected extinct species, her exotic crops? She ran her finger lightly over the mound's surface. It felt grainy. Through the lens she watched a green dot appear and resolve into a scraggy pine tree. Next to it a flesh-colored pinprick emerged: herself.

Terrible emptiness opened within her. "Not yet," she pleaded. Jenna turned tear-filled eyes to the calendar she'd taped to the van's wall. Yesterday must have been Sunday; locals had thronged the churches. She pulled an ATM receipt from her purse. March 27, it said. Three days ago.

She felt as if she were swimming up from murk into fresh air. Drake had died a year ago today. His funeral had been held two weeks later, April 14. That meant the space rock fell into her life on the 15th.

Could she make it to the California mountainside in two weeks? Battered by a year of rough travel and minimal maintenance, the van barely ran. She'd spent chunks of her dwindling funds on jury-rigged repairs.

She packed her few worthwhile possessions, sold the van to a pair of guides cheap, and used her last shred of credit for an airplane ticket.

On the way to the airport she made the cab driver stop twice so she could pick interesting roadside grasses for the mound.

During the all-night flight, she leaned her head against the cold window and clutched the net bag as her recurring dream came. She and Drake threw bright stones that became living beings as they hit the ground.

She woke gasping. How would the recreated life forms propagate if the mound collected only a single sample of each one?

She took the mound into her palm. The mushroom cap, a dividing cell, the female organ, the rounded half of a fertile egg. There had been at least thirty mounds at the crater. She visualized one merging with hers, each with its own load of DNA.

But hers carried richer treasure than the others. What could they collect up there at the tree-line except a pine tree, a few seeds dropped by passing birds, maybe a drift of pollen or feathers? No humanity.

When she arrived in the San Francisco airport, she hurried to a pay phone and dug out her long-forgotten address book. "Ben?"

"Jenna? God, where did you disappear to? Your boss said . . ."

"Come get me. Bring Drake's back pack."

"Well, sure, but are you all right? You sound . . ."

She forced herself to be patient. Months had passed since she'd spoken to a human being for any purpose other than achieving access to an offering for the mound. "I'm sorry, Ben, I'm weirded out from jet lag. I was in Patagonia."

She waited for him outside the terminal, shivering in fog. He pulled up in a vintage VW bus and jumped out. "Jenna?"

"Yeah."

"Is that all your luggage?"

"Luggage?" She hefted her backpack and Guatemalan shoulder purse, lifted the net bag on her wrist, then caught the expression on Ben's face. "What's wrong?" she asked.

"You look so different."

She leaned toward the VW's side mirror and saw weathered features and long, knotted hair.

Later she'd have time to care. Not now. "You brought Drake's pack?"

"It's at my place," said Ben. She'd forgotten how his eyes smiled through his wire-framed glasses.

He took her to an old Victorian house in San Francisco where he had a three-room apartment filled with color. For curtains and bedspread, he used brilliant Indian tapestries, and he'd covered the walls with his own travel photos, prayer flags and baskets. Incense burned in a metal holder.

He made her shower and work tangles out of her hair while he prepared rice, vegetable curry and a fruit and yogurt dessert. On the way to his kitchen, wearing his robe and dangling the net bag from her wrist, she gave the mound a thread from a wall hanging she suspected contained yak wool; then she added a bit of ash from the incense. She fell asleep over the fourth bite of rice and woke late the next morning beneath a patchwork quilt on the couch. "I'm at work," said the note on his refrigerator. "Back at 5:30."

In his closet she found Drake's back pack. State-of-the-art when he bought it, its light-weight, waterproof fabric was torn now and stained with ground- in mud. Himalayan mud? She scraped a bit and gave it to the mound before she opened the pack's clasps and buried herself in Drake's familiar possessions, baggy tan shorts loaded with pockets, his favorite old jersey, blue jeans worn soft with age, his battered down jacket and hiking boots, a crumpled shaving kit, though he'd seldom needed to shave.

The zipped inner pocket of the pack held what she was looking for: a plastic bag of used Band-Aids spotted with Drake's blood. She dropped them into a bowl of cold water, and when the water turned pink she dropped the mound into it. She was white, he was Asian and Polynesian. Would the mound consider him different enough from her to be a sample?

She cleaned everything up and climbed back under the quilt with the mound in its net bag. When Ben came home, she borrowed money from him. "Will you be back?" he asked, his eyes sad behind his glasses.

She leaned into him, slid her arms around him. More than a year had passed since she'd last embraced a human being. Warm and nice, yes, but still an intrusion. "See you later, I think."

She caught a Greyhound bus and made it up to the tree-line at dusk on April 14th.

Sticks, bits of fur and feathers, rotting meat, maggots and flies and other debris surrounded the crater. She had to scrape it away with sticks to get at the mounds. To the naked eye their surfaces seemed as smooth as the first time she'd seen them, but like hers, they had grown.

A fox trotted across the dirt as if she weren't there and dropped a small rodent onto one of the mounds. Then he lay down inches away with his chin on his paws and stared intently at his gray-green lump, nose twitching, ears lifting. She suspected the animal's rapt expression matched her own when she studied her mound through a microscope lens.

What fascinated the fox so much? Fox pheromones? Scents of the hunt? Jenna realized she wasn't a life-giving goddess, mother of all living things in a tiny world. Like the fox, she'd been seduced and enslaved. And for what?

Suppose instead of populating a new planet, the mounds' creators subjected earth's life forms to cruel experiments in some floating, alien lab?

Jenna strode to the fire pit, and when she forced the damp wood finally to catch, she studied the flames. Should she entrust the mound with the thousands and thousands of DNA strands she'd given it, or should she burn it?

Imagine giving these wondrous life forms a chance in a clean, pure place. If it existed.

She lit her lantern and pulled out her best lens. She trained it on the mound.

Against the gray-green backdrop, perfectly formed, stood Drake's replica. Her own emerged, its hand touching Drake's. Gradually flora and fauna came into view around them, not static but in motion. Trees and grasses swayed in invisible winds. Ancient and modern crops grew, animals browsed. She and Drake walked in a vivid rain forest swarming with life.

Let it be true.

Jenna took the mound to the crater and set it with the others. Then she climbed into her sleeping bag and waited.

Long into the night, the rock in the crater began to glow like an ember. It shimmered, then briefly shot out flaming arms. Their flash of light revealed the mounds flattening as they released their cargo to the rock. Jenna jumped when the tiny stars burst across the sky. Her rock shot up from the ground and streaked across the treetops. When it joined the others, she lost sight of which glittering speck was hers and she realized what a wealth of earth life the group must have gathered. They flared, then vanished like bright pebbles into a river flowing to a distant soil.

Pussy Cats
By Joe DiBuduo

Stealthy paws silently fall as felines strut onto my lawn of sand, a Siamese's drawn-out meow heralds, throughout the cat hood, telling all who hear, that my yard is the place to go, to show their glee, that they can pee for free on my turf. Cat trinkets are left for me, covered in tiny mountains of sand like miniature burial mounds.

"You're not welcome here," I shout and chase them away. But they soon return to use their outhouse made of sand, where they don't have to pay a damn thing, to do what nature demands. A dog is what I need. I go to the pound and put a kitten in my hand, to see which dog hates cats more than me. Pitiful pups crammed into stalls, unfit for a dog, or even a cat, they're all waiting to be gassed. Aroused by my human scent their adoption hopes rise. They beg to be saved, with made up yelps, and all forget about the feline in my hand. Except, Molly, a sixty-pound white Lab, she snaps, snarls, and tries with all her might to get her lunch at first sight of the cat I hold.

She's the one I want, I tell the keeper of these surplus pets. I'm happy to think that my home turf will be cat free, once Molly comes home with me. I stop at the store to get what she needs, a bone, a blanket, a bed, a bag of food. I brush and bathe her in my tub, getting her ready to show those cats, they no longer rule. Rough, ready and smelling sweet from doggy shampoo, we sit and wait until a Persian saunters into my yard and begins building a burial mound in the sand. My heart fills with glee as I point at the Persian and declare, "Get him, Molly."

She can't wait to get out the gate, barking, and snarling, her feet slip on the floor as she tries to push through the door. I fumble with the latch in my rush to free this horrible hound onto my monument strewn lawn. To show those cats, a beast now lives here. Finally, the door bursts open, a ball of white fur speeds in the direction of the cat lazily scratching through the sand. A hairy back balls up to the sky, claws extend, a screaming yawl that scares even me, stops Molly in her tracks. She turns around and heads back to the entry in fearful flight, with an apparition from every dog's nightmare in hot pursuit. Yelping in fear, she burst through the door that I barely close in time, to stop the demon cat from coming through. Shivering from fear Molly sits there, ashamed that as a dog, she is nothing but a pussy cat.

Skeletons & Spooks
By Greg Picard and Wendy Picard Gorham

IT WAS A FULL MOON NIGHT...and a blood moon at that. Ranger Chris Becker sat motionless in the front seat of his primer gray '72 GMC, in the gravel space next to his mobile home and contemplated his next move. The bloody hand on his windshield was motionless too. Clearly, it was rubber, but it looked real enough to get his attention. That someone would come all the way back to the staff residential compound at Olompali State Historic Park to leave such a 'gift' made little sense. He wondered if it had been a joke by one of the other park employees. He stepped out and pulled it from underneath the wiper blade. The culprit had even gone to the trouble of smearing ketchup all over it. After wrapping the mass of rubber and goopy tomato in an old Jack in the Box napkin he scrounged from the glove box, he resorted to wiping the mess off his own hands on the grass under the monstrous old Bay tree that fronted his porch. It brought to mind how the tree had split in the middle of the night—a year ago on this very night in fact. It had smashed the mover's van that was parked under it. They had been almost finished assembling the two halves of his doublewide. There was a lot of real blood that night on the two laborers who were sleeping in the van.

Since then, Becker never did like Halloween.

He looked around at the other four mobile homes in the small compound. The cars were all gone, and no lights were showing inside. He knew Mikey had taken his kids to town to raid one of the ritzy neighborhoods in Novato for candy. Elaine was on shift at Mt. Tamalpais State Park. Both the others had teenage kids, and he figured they were probably off at parties somewhere like his daughter, Allie. As he stood in the weakening twilight and watched the moonrise, he heard the phone ringing in his residence and ran, taking the porch steps two at a time and fumbling for his keys in his pocket as he went. By the time he got inside, it had gone to the message machine, and he recognized the caller as he grabbed the receiver off the hook.

"Hello," he huffed catching his breath, "what's up?"

Woody Call said, "now why does there always have to be something up. It could be something down...or something sideways." Becker could picture Woody sitting with his lopsided grin in his Batman mask that he had worn into headquarters earlier in the morning.

"Take that mask off!"

"What mask? I'm not wearing a mask."

"I know you, Woody. I know you're wearing it. You are sitting in the Pantoll Ranger Station and greeting visitors in that mask!"

"Jeez, what a Halloween killjoy. And just when I was needing my superpowers."

"I'm not liking the sound of this...." Becker said.

"Yeah, well boss, it appears we have a group of witches having some big ceremony at Alice Eastwood Group Camp. Huge bonfire and everything. They looked like such nice old blue-haired ladies when I checked them in this afternoon, but I think they are planning on roasting small children or something. They're all dressed in black, and they've got a huge cauldron boiling, and I'm pretty sure it ain't full of beans and franks. Elaine went through there on patrol a few minutes ago, and they were doing some kind of chant and ceremonial boogie stomp around the cauldron."

Only in Marin County, Becker thought.

"So, is Elaine still down there?"

"Yeah, I asked her to keep an eye on 'em, knowing as how you are still looking for a girlfriend." Faint chuckling was barely audible, "I figure maybe they'll all turn into playboy bunnies at the stroke of midnight and you might want to join us."

"Tell you what, keep me posted. I need to pick up Allie from a party. If things get any weirder, I'll join you guys up there. The main thing to remember is that under the constitution they can do their white witch thing, or black or polka dot witch for that matter, as long as they don't violate any laws. So, any frickaseed babies, feel free to go on a witch hunt, so to speak, but otherwise keep your distance."

"Did I tell you there are now about 50 of them up there?"

"Fifty? Jeez! They can't even fit that many cars in the parking lot up there. Any broomsticks?"

"Do we charge the same price for parking your broomstick?" Again the faint chuckle on the other end of the line, "Actually, 'Lainey says they brought several cars and a small bus in just before dark...hold on...wait a minute, she's on the radio and says they're getting pretty animated now...she's putting it through her mic. I'll put the phone closer to the speaker."

Becker could clearly hear the screeching and howling, even over the phone. The only word he could finally make out was "death" and then nothing but one lonely, blood-curdling scream...then sharp, sudden silence.

"Lainey's pretty creeped out. She says it looks like there's a body on the ground now."

"Okay, go back her up and find out what's going on. I'll get up there as soon as I can."

He slipped on his uniform shirt and gun-belt and got into his assigned patrol sedan that he kept parked in front of his mobile home. Allie's party was on the way to Mt. Tam, and since cauldron-crashing was an imprecise business, he figured he'd better pick her up early. There was no telling how this evening might go. Besides, Allie was 16 going on 30, but her friends weren't. He figured she'd be better off on a Halloween late night with him in a riot or a gunfight rather than with the other teens at a party in the wee hours. As he flew down the four-lane, he tried to raise dispatch to say that he was on duty but got no response. Then he tried Woody and Elaine with the same result.

"Damn crappy radio system," he muttered. The Department had been talking about upgrading it for years but still couldn't come up with the funds for the Northern California improvements.

Chris took the Freitas Pkwy exit off the 101. Fortunately, Allie's party was right off the freeway and would cause little delay. He took the front steps to the brightly lit stucco home two at a time and rapped on the big oak door loud enough to overcome the cacophony inside.

"Hi, can you get Allie Becker, I need to pick her up," he said to the teenage pirate wearing an eyepatch who answered the door.

"Allie, there's a guy dressed as a cop for Halloween here to arrest you."

A moment later Allie stepped to the door with a surprised look. "Dad, what are you doing here so early?"

"I've got an emergency, and I figured it might keep me too long, so I figured I'd pick you up early. Get your stuff and let's go."

"Okay," she eyed him hesitantly as she turned to get her purse and coat. She waited until the ignition had turned over and he was edging the nose of the sedan away from the curb before asking, "What kind of emergency?"

"The stupid kind. Typical Halloween. Most likely there's nothing to it, but I'd like to run up to Tam and see for myself."

"Okay...?"

"We're kinda going to another Halloween party," he said.

"Huh?"

"Woody has a bunch of witches causing a ruckus at the Alice Eastwood Group Camp on Tam. It may be nothing at all, but I thought I'd mosey on up there."

"This is a bit more than 'mosey' I think," she leaned over to look at the needle of the speedometer. "What's the big hurry?"

"I've tried to raise Woody and Elaine, and they are not answering their portable radios. Could just be they're in a dead spot, I don't know. But Elaine said there was a body on the ground, so…"

Becker backed off on the gas a bit. "Probably nothing. Actually, I was also concerned that there would be some inappropriate goings on with the crowd at your party." He gave her a surreptitious sidelong glance.

"It was pretty dull. A couple of the guys were really immature. When do they grow up, Dad?"

"Don't ask me, I'm not done yet, but I'll tell you when I am." He turned and gave her a quick grin. "They grow up soon enough…maybe twenty-five or so if they're average."

"Twenty-five! Sheesh!"

"Well, it's not going to be a problem for you anyway, because you're not going to be allowed to date until you are forty."

"You wish."

"Hey, I'm just lookin' out for my girl."

He tore through Mill Valley just barely above the speed limit and hit his emergency lights and pushed it harder uphill on the straight section of Panoramic Highway before turning at the Mountain Home Inn onto the park's Eastwood Road. Still, no radio traffic had come from Woody or Elaine, and that bothered Becker. *What could they be doing that would keep them out of radio contact for this long,* he wondered.

"When we get there, I want you to stay in the car. I'm going to park it back quite a ways and walk in. Lock the doors just in case."

"Okay, now you're scaring me."

"Hey, it's Halloween! It's what I'm supposed to do!"

"Dad, Jeez! Be serious!"

He held his finger to his lips and shot her his most stony look. Then he quietly snapped the car door shut and complete darkness enveloped them. His footsteps faded across the gravel toward the group camp. She could barely make out a campfire in the distance.

"Well, this is pretty boring," Allie muttered. She got out of the car and walked around it and hoisted herself up and sat on the hood and watched where her father's silhouette had disappeared in the trees. Allie strained to hear or see anything. After ten minutes of sitting in the stillness listening to the crickets, she gave in to the urge to head into the trees toward the faint light of the campfire. *How bad can it be...some old ladies having a party,* Allie encouraged herself while redwood branches dragged at her hair as she dodged limbs and bushes.

She fell once and stifled a scream as the branches poked and broke around her. She lay still for a moment and then rolled to her feet wondering if the noise could have carried to the group camp. *And you're walking in the woods in the dark without a flashlight because why?* She thought to herself. It wasn't long before she heard voices. High pitched, agitated women's voices mixed with what she was sure was her Dad's voice. She wondered where Woody and Elaine were, and she was still too far to get a good look at the group campsite yet. Another 100 feet and she'd be out in the open. She hesitated. She thought she might be able to move in the dark in the open area if she stayed out of range of the campfire, but she could also see a full moon just cresting the horizon over the hills. She decided she needed to act quickly.

As she moved she noted shapes moving in the light of the campfire. She could clearly hear her father's voice now.

"You really believe that?" he said.

"Yes, we do!" The woman's voice was husky and firm.

"Well, I don't know quite what to say, I'm afraid," Chris said as he turned to face the crowd of robed women and their leader. As he did, he noted movement out of the corner of his eye on the horizon. One of the women caught the movement in his gaze and turned, and seconds later she exclaimed, "Look!" and raised a long arm to point.

Becker could make out a fuzzy gossamer figure standing with a frond of leaves attached to her branch woven crown and overarching her head. More scattered vegetation decorated her silk and bejeweled robes. In the dark forest edge, she seemed half woman and half tree. A true wood wraith and all he could do was whisper breathlessly..."Oh, shit no."

"It's the woodland princess," one of the witches whispered. "She's come at last as we've asked so often!"

There was a breathless silence, and Chris wondered what the hell was going to happen next.

"Uh...yes...I've...come, what is it you wish of me, mortals?" The last was done somewhat hesitantly with arched eyebrows, and a flourish of her hands spread high and wide.

One thin older woman at the back of the group said: "how about impeaching that sleazeball womanizer pervert President, Bill Clinton."

"I don't interfere in mortal governments. He is your chosen leader. You voted him in. Who do you want now, Donald Trump, Mel Gibson, Whoopi Goldberg? Surely you have something of real importance that you seek on this night of all nights?"

"Could you make his thing rot off then instead," the woman muttered.

Becker stared in disbelief as his daughter held the rapt attention of the entire coven. He didn't know if Allie was just jerking their chain, but he knew these women were taking her seriously. With her Princess Leia costume from the party, in the moonglow, and newly adorned with some foliage from her walk from the car, she looked pretty convincing. She remained on the slight rise above them and warming to her role she repeated with impatience, "What is it you wish? My time is valuable. I haven't got all night!"

Becker spoke up quickly, "I think you might ask that she protect you from being arrested for illegal drug use because that's where this looks like it's headed." He had no actual proof of drugs in possession, but he hoped the hint might get them motivated to at least leave. Woody and Elaine had taken "the body" that had fallen faint during their chant, and all signs pointed to use of hallucinogens and downers with a little dehydration thrown in. The three of them were at the campground road entrance now waiting for the ambulance.

"The Reif of the Shire here," and at this, she glanced sidelong at her father, and he could swear he saw a mischievous smirk playing at the corners of her mouth, "says you dabble in potions! You know that is forbidden! White witches do no harm. That means no harm to yourselves as well!" Allie was beginning to seriously expand her impromptu part and it worried Becker. "You come to a sacred place like this to pollute yourselves? What makes you think you can desecrate the customs of the sacred people!"

"It's just a little pot."

"A pot? You mean a vessel of emptiness? Void? Meaningless? Is that what you smoke? Are your souls empty like the vessels of which you speak?"

"No, Princess, it's weed, you know, marijuana, a plant."

"You consume weeds like the asses of the field? Why have I wasted my time with you?"

Becker noticed a few in the crowd had drifted back toward the parking lot. He figured they were either scared of prosecution or had decided this was too weird for late night Halloween consumption. Either way, it was all good as far as he was concerned. Even their leader seemed a bit nervous.

"The Goddess demands we cause no harm! You polluted yourselves. I'm done with you!"

What happened next Chris couldn't fully explain, but it had an incredible effect. The untended bonfire had grown weary, and shadows lengthened. Headlights and red and blue strobes from the arriving ambulance flashed across the camp in the eyes of the gathered group. The heavy mist coming off the Pacific Ocean was returning, and fast-moving clouds were racing across the night sky. One suddenly covered the moon for a few seconds, and amidst the headlight glare in everyone's eyes and the black shadow suddenly cast across the camp, Allie simply…disappeared. One minute she was there and the next she wasn't. He wasn't sure how to explain it, and it caused him some level of unease, but the remaining witches actually screamed out. Even their leader seemed finally at a loss for words.

Becker waited a couple of heartbeats to compose himself and then said, "It's late…I think it's time for you folks to head on home, don't you think?" He hoped the calm encouragement would work. He really had very little to base an eviction upon. He noticed as he said it that the group had dwindled down to about a dozen now, and lights were coming on in cars in the lot. Two or three still there were casting nervous glances at each other and the departing members.

It became a traditional stare-down as classic as Main Street in Tombstone. He had the image of Wyatt Earp flash in his mind, and under the circumstances, it took all his concentration not to laugh at the thought and break the spell. Finally, their leader huffed and turned toward the parking lot.

The ambulance was pulling away as the last car left the lot, and Becker asked Woody and Elaine to stick around for a minute while he took care of something. He walked back to the dying bonfire and up the slight rise toward where Allie had been giving her performance.

"Okay, they're all gone. I sure hope you haven't really dematerialized. Otherwise I'm gonna have a hell of a time explaining this to your teachers…not to mention the pain in the ass report I'd have to write in the morning." He continued to carefully pick his way through the dense foliage. "Allie, where the heck are you?" This time his voice was a little louder and the slight edge to it hinted at the real concern welling in the pit of his stomach.

"I'm over here." The voice came wafting across the moonlit landscape, and there was a whining tonal quality to it. Becker followed the sound of the voice. "Be careful, there's a pretty deep culvert or drainage ditch or something over here, and you might break your ankle...like I think I did!"

He used his flashlight and saw what she had done. The drainage washout was a fairly sharp cut along the small ravine. "You broke it? What happened?"

"Well, I was clearly coming to the end of my daily B.S. allowance," he could barely see the roll of her eyes punctuate the slight pause in her story, "and I was wondering what the heck I had gotten myself into when the clouds suddenly rolled in and covered the moon. I figured it was time to 'exit stage right' as Shakespeare would say. I almost fell in that washout on the way in here, and I figured if I jumped just right I could maybe sort of vanish." She looked up sheepishly and shrugged her shoulders. "Don't look at me that way...I was improvising!"

Becker didn't know whether to laugh or be worried about her injuries. "I hate to tell you this, but that wash out was a pit toilet that failed, and we later removed it.

"Eeeeew...you had to tell me that!!!"

"We cleaned it up pretty well. Don't worry. Let me see your foot," he said as he slid down the washout, skittering dirt and debris across her already smudged costume. "Can you move it?"

"It hurts, but I guess I can move it okay."

He felt and probed the bones and didn't get much response. "Probably just a sprain or a strained tendon. We'll get you home and get some ice on it. I've got a cold pack in the car we can put on it for now. Sit tight, and I'll bring the car around here closer, so you don't have to walk far."

"Okay...but Dad," she looked sheepishly at him, "can I keep the flashlight? I don't want to be here alone in the dark."

"What? The Woodland Princess is afraid of spooks?" Chris hesitated only a brief moment before he hugged her and left her with his big black Maglite cradled in her lap.

Moving slowly, more by feel now than by sight, he made his way through the brush and trees toward his patrol car. The night air was cooling by what felt like ten-degree increments. He shivered involuntarily and wondered if Allie was freezing in that little gully. She might even be having a bit of a shock response depending on how bad her ankle really was. Concern for her and a general sense of urgency quickened his pace, but the logistics of the near black night held him back. He wished he had his flashlight now. Luckily, another minute and he could make out the outline of his vehicle in the weak cloud and tree filtered light of the moon. Chris got in and revved the cold engine. The sound broke the utter silence of the night and sent a welcoming and familiar rumble through his tired frame. He covered the 100 yards to the main camp in no time and saw Woody and Elaine waiting.

"I think you two have paid your dues for the day," Chris tried to be playful to offset the bizarre display they had dealt with.

"You sure?" Woody raised an eyebrow, "I thought maybe I would hang around and see what they had planned for an encore."

"Not me! I have a date with a hot bath," Elaine was already halfway to her truck as she spoke. She punctuated her statement with a quick wave of her hand as she opened the door and swung up into the driver's seat.

"Well, if that's how she's gonna be...spoilsport!" Woody was trying to be ever jovial, but Chris detected some relief below his bravado. "I guess I'll head out too. 'Night, boss."

When Woody's headlights were pointed toward the road home, Chris focused on getting Allie. He parked the car next to the now extinguished bonfire with his headlights aimed as best he could toward her location, and he jogged back over to her quickly now that he had light. Rather than trying to climb out of the drainage, they hobbled down the washout with Becker supporting most of her weight. Fortunately, it ended in the clearing not far from the now smoldering embers of the bonfire, and soon they were in the car.

"Just one thing I want to know. Whatever made you do that!"

"Do what?"

"You know darn well what. First, tramping down there in the dark, when I told you to stay in the car, and then playing the woodland nymph goddess thing."

"I was a princess, not the goddess. The Wiccans and White Witches have a Goddess and a God."

"And you know this how...?"

"It's all the rage at school. I have a green aura, in case you didn't know. At least Renee says that I do. She's into all that stuff, crystals and auras. She has an aunc that she wears and she says it gives her a presence or something..."

"I think your aura may have changed to brown tonight." Chris barely suppressed a laugh.

"Eeeew, stop reminding me! I'll have to scrub all over with bleach!"

"So, Renee is the one you went to the Renaissance Faire with?"

"Yeah, kinda fits, huh? In fact, she has worked the Faire a couple of summers. Boy, those are some interesting stories! She told one about the time these five teenage guys hogtied her and wouldn't let her go until she had kissed each of them." She glanced at him and paused when she realized the eyebrow raise he was leveling on her was more the angry dad than the amused adult. She stumbled a little to recover. "She's cool though, Dad, don't freak out. She's just...experimental, you know? But more than that she's a 16-year-old girl!" she said, playfully, "you know we are all a little bit nuts." She waited for a beat and continued. "Actually, her life is kinda surreal. Her mom and dad are divorced but they have dinner together every night at her house, and they are still friends and even talk about dates the other one is going on!" Allie shook her head in disbelief at the recollection of what Renee had described. "But the most definitive evidence that she hasn't quite grounded herself in reality, is what she told me last week after you picked us up from the movies..."

"Well...?" Chris was trying to be patient and let the story unfold without being a police interrogator, which he had to admit was a nagging tendency at the moment, but he was not having much success.

"She said, 'Allie, you may not realize this, but your dad is pretty hot...and he has a nice butt' to which I replied in the only words possible... 'oh God, kill me now.'"

Becker laughed out loud as he finally cranked up the Ford Interceptor and headed back out the park road.

"I always taught you to be polite Allie, so did you say something comparably nice about her Dad in response? Perhaps about his backside?"

"Well, her Dad looks like a turtle, so..." Allie glanced sidelong at him as they edged onto the main road and Becker choked back another laugh.

They traveled leisurely in silence for a few miles before he said, "Maybe I'll let you date when you're 30 instead. We'll see," he laughed.

Fifteen minutes later, they pulled into the space in front of their mobile home, and as the headlights played against the small front porch alcove, they could see a crude stick broom leaning against the front door.

"Well, look at that," he pointed, "do you suppose one of the ladies from tonight flew in here on the way home to her cave?" They got out and walked up to the steps.

"Well dad, nothing I've ever heard of said anything about witches living in caves, so I'm going to go with 'no'." She picked the broom up tentatively and let her hand run lightly down the length of the handle to the sparse and unruly fan of straw at the business end. "What is this made out of? Hay? Seriously Dad, where can you get a willow wand and hay broom these days? This looks like something Hester Prynne would have swept the floor with, not something you could pick up at Home Depot."

"I think it is straw, not hay." He knew it was a stupid distinction to make, but at the moment, he felt the need to be logical and intellectual in order to combat the little prickling hairs he felt beginning to stand at attention on the back of his neck.

"Oh, well that clears it up nicely, thank you." She rolled her eyes emphatically in his direction. She extended the broom toward him as though the item suddenly was somehow dangerous or poisonous. "Here, you look at it. Do your Native American tracking thing or dust it for prints or put it under a blacklight or something." It was clear she was rattled but was trying to maintain composure.

"Well, the first thing I notice with my significantly developed and highly honed investigative skills is that I saw something just about identical to this at Walmart a few days back."

Allie began to object, "Dad, no. That isn't from…"

"Second, there is actually a white note impaled on the finial of our porchlight waving to get our attention."

Allie jumped up and grabbed the slip of paper. "That's weird, it says *"Til next time! Be ready!"* She handed it back to him. "Now I'm getting really creeped out, Dad!"

"Let me see it." He held it and examined it carefully and turned the thin slip of paper over to inspect the back.

"Yes, but if you look at the other side, it also says Wal-Mart, one box baby wipes, two large tubs Similac."

"Huh?"

"And," Chris was really building up a head of steam, plowing forward with his newfound revelation, "there was a bloody rubber hand on my car earlier this evening. Allie, who do we know with a warped sense of humor, and a five-month-old, and who also knows where we live and has a scanner in his truck and his house to listen to the park frequency to keep tabs on his wife even when he's at work as a medic for Novato fire."

"You're kidding me. Oh, brother, that dufus had me creeped out."

"Look," he pointed to the mobile home across the compound, "his car is parked in the usual spot, and I would swear I just saw the drapes parted so he could laugh at us finding his joke. Well, let's give the medic a dose of his own medicine."

"You mean his own 'potion'!"

As he put the keys in his front door, Chris explained his plan. Ten minutes later he was on the phone in full 'panic mode.'

"Luke, I've got an emergency over here, and I noticed you are home. Allie's having some kind of seizure, I don't know what the heck's going on. Will you come take a look at her while I call the fire department!"

Sixty seconds later Elaine's husband, Luke, pounded up the porch steps as Chris held open the screen door.

"When did this start," Luke asked as he saw Allie's toothpaste foamed mouth and opened his first responder bag.

"About five minutes after we got here…We drove home from Tam, and she was fine all evening. All she did was come in and turn the TV on to the news for me and then handle this broom we found on the porch. I think she must have been allergic to it, or there is something it does to her for some reason."

Allie gave another stunning, choking, spitting, growling, twisting performance before bursting out in laughter and covering Luke with foamy Crest toothpaste as he knelt down to deal with her airway.

Becker fell back against the hall doorway literally holding his gut as he joined in. "Gotcha back…!"

Luke was stunned and speechless, staring first at Allie in her white and flowing gown, now all rumpled and covered in goopy streaks of saliva and toothpaste, then at Chris leaning heavily on the doorframe trying to catch his breath between bouts of laughter.

"Back?!" Luke stammered, unsure whether to laugh or be offended, "Back for what?"

"Oh, what? You can dish it out but you can't take it?" Allie was calming now and trying to smooth her wild hair back from her foam smeared face.

"Don't get me wrong. This was a great prank. Possibly illegal, but an absolute ten on the 'I need to change my pants' scale. But seriously, what's going on?" Luke said.

"Well man, I have to give you credit. You sure can play it out and keep a straight face for the long haul." Chris paused for a moment. "The broom, my man! The bloody hand on the windshield, the broom, the note…payback!" Chris was losing a bit of steam with the need to explain the situation, "the note, and the broom you put on the porch, and the hand…?"

Luke was facing them both now as they all absorbed the moment. They were waiting for a look of recognition or playful chagrined acknowledgment. Instead, a strange quality overtook him, and a look of unmistakable clarity met their gaze. The mirth seemed to drain from the room like air leaking from a pin-pricked balloon.

"Guys, I'll admit to the hand, but that was pretty obvious—rubber and ketchup—just meant to be funny, ya' know? But this other stuff...the broom and the note? I don't know what you are talking about...and I sure as heck didn't put anything on your porch tonight."

They all stood in confused silence. From a distance, the stark hoot of a Great Horned Owl pulled Becker's gaze away from Luke's earnest face. The blood moon hung silently against the black blanket of night, framed in the rigid frame of their front entryway. He followed movement as a bat flitted across the moon's face. At least he thought it was a bat. Funny, how it looked...more like...a shadowy human form, seated, hair flowing...than a bat. He shivered as an icy wind fanned across the open door's threshold and slowly sucked the house door closed with a dead and metallic *click.*

My Portrait
By Lou Blazquez

"MAKE SURE YOU GET ALL THREE OF ME," I told the artist, who already had begun brushing across the canvas leaning on an easel. I mused as he worked.

One of us is a 10-year-old who gives me wonder, curiosity, mischievousness, and naiveté. He is simple in a complicated world, doesn't understand it, or America, or his house in which things disappear and are found again later. He asks, "Why can Gene Roddenberry figure out warp drive but not NASA?"

Another is a 16-year-old with uncertainty, self-consciousness, and self-doubt who fears failure more than anything. He has impatient youthful energy, and he is shy. He wants to say, "Bite me!" to anyone who angers him and then thrust a résumé of knuckles into their throats for future reference. But, he has black belt discipline and is thus harmless. He has a lust that began with the urge of mitosis three billion years ago and believes that the process was fun even then. That was why life began. When he makes intimate advances to women, he hates it when they ask him to control himself. "Why can't women show this fabulous self-control and *increase* their sex drive?"

I'm the elder, with the experience and wisdom of 59 years who has to support the other two with food, shelter, movies, and dates. I'm the busy guy. I take mood disorder meds because my emotions can be overly capricious or confusing. I began a dedicated career of instructing children in 1972, but it's my daughter Jamie who is all-important. Teaching is what I do, a father is who I am.

Jamie displayed my 10-yearold self when she was four, walking her new puppy. A man was standing on his second story balcony when she called up to him, "Hey mister, do you want to pet my dog?" It made perfect sense, everyone was another her—is another me—and wanted to rush up to little Cinder and cuddle him.

The stranger called back, "No!"

"Okay," she replied brightly and happily moved on. I was puzzled with her cheerfulness at rejection. She knew something I didn't.

It took me a while to believe this, but I do now. In my life, I am allowed but one true relationship, and I had mine. My marriage changed me from an adult into a human being. Its ending is the biggest failure of my life, because I grew up wanting one person, one family, and one trip to the altar. My ex-wife's friendship is still my North Star.

After my divorce, I accumulated ten parrots and a girlfriend named Robin. I stayed at her house in Mesa on weekends. When I had my only modeling gig, I got up extra early to allow for getting lost. I needed to shave closely, and I panicked when I realized I forgot my travel kit. Robin handed me a brand-new Bic plastic shaver. I lathered up and began. Nothing happened. I stroked harder, but my stubble stood firm. I couldn't press too hard, because I feared tracks of moist scabs on my face. Exasperated, I told Robin that the Bic didn't work. She was puzzled. My electric razor was the dismal solution.

I left her house, got lost, and arrived on time. I went to the woman who does make up for the agency. "Do you realize you have two different-colored socks? I'll tug your pants lower to cover them."

I got through the job for Reality Executives to their satisfaction. That night I was in bed with Robin. She jumped up and exclaimed, "Wait a minute!" and ran to the bathroom. There was uncontrolled laughter. She came back holding the Bic razor as if it were a scepter. While she was still hysterically shaking and choking, she took off its plastic top.

I asked, "What's that?"

"It's a protector."

"From what?"

"From cutting yourself."

"I want to be cut. That's how I get the whiskers off." She doubled over.

"What's so funny?" She knew something I didn't.

When she could finally speak, she told me I looked like a little boy, just lying there bewildered.

I wondered, how do I turn the comical into the romantic? I read, or maybe someone mentioned, that girls get turned on if you talk filthy to them in bed.

Youngsters—even when they're 59—will believe anything that adults tell them. In the dark, I whispered dirty words to Robin. She went into gyrations of hilarity. I like amusing people, even when it's unintentional, but I also like being in on the joke. "Now what?"

"That was like my little old grandmother cursing."

So much for advice and so much for obscenities. I should have known better because it wasn't natural. I try to be respectful, kind, and caring to the woman I'm with. It was always that way with Robin. After five minutes of unrestrained guffawing, she noticed me watching her without guile. With quiet intent, she suddenly embraced me. She never refused my fierce passion, loved my innocence, and appreciated my good sense. In moments, four hearts beat as one and three of them were mine.

There is the mire of my faults. I don't know how dark or how bad they can be; I've never been tested in my fortunate life. I have a distressing amount of cowardice, deceit, selfishness, laziness, crankiness, and vengefulness—wait! I changed my mind about that last one. Vengeful is good. I'm tired of the innocent getting kicked around. Hurt the bad guys. I have some cynicism, but not too much. Mankind is basically good. I am, too, but my worst side is the bad decisions I have made for my daughter and will never forgive myself. In my quiet moments, the wound still trickles. My flaws are there in despicable amounts. I am ashamed as the artist works uninterrupted. But if a man must have faults, what's wrong with mine? Mrs. Shannon said in *Night of the Iguana*, "Nothing human disgusts me unless it is unkind or violent." I hold her standards.

I wonder if other guys are like me. I don't know because I can only be one male at a time. It's hard to believe females can be like me. I've been close to those who have been bashed, treated like meat, have had long-term hurts, or had ex-husbands who steal their possessions. These women occasionally wanted fatherly moments recreated, being warmly held unconditionally, and just be touched with a subliminal healing without payoff and receive an occasional kiss on the forehead. I like being sensitive in those quiet moments. My partner briefly becomes a 10-year-old, as she deserves to be for the rest of her life. I can feel my adult nurturing and caring for her as we are silent in a different way.

Among the three of us, the consensus is that we are in the wrong reality. Our heaven and our good day are the same. Each morning I would be with a blonde, each afternoon I would be with my daughter, and at night, me and Roger Rabbit would shoot up Toon Town.

"Did you get us all?" I asked as the artist finished the last stroke. He turns the easel. I inhale.

Persuasive Essay:

The Overweight American
By Pat Fogarty

YOU DON'T HAVE TO BE A DOCTOR to recognize a health problem when you see one. If you watch the evening news, you'll notice Americans of all races and ages are disproportionally overweight. Doctors, research scientists, and others in the health community have come up with dozens of reasons for this apparent epidemic. Every year there seems to be a new theory that explains the ballooning problem.

Lack of exercise and the propensity of the American public to dine at fast food restaurants are often touted as the root of America's obesity problem. But these unhealthy habits are just two of the most obvious sources for the expanding problem. Health experts also cite—lack of sleep, depression, antibiotics, pesticides, skipping meals, portion sizes, artificial sweeteners, stress, food addiction and numerous other reasons for the increasing waistlines of the American public.

Well, everyone is entitled to an opinion and here's mine. The U.S. government started America on the road to plumpness more than fifty years ago with its trade embargo on Cuba. I know that's a difficult statement to swallow but let's look at the evidence. On October 19, 1960, the U.S. government stopped sending American manufactured products to Cuba, and Cuba stopped exporting sugar, rum, cigars and dozens of other items to America. In retrospect we can clearly see; the almost instantaneous shortage of sugar became the catalyst that eventually paved the way for America's obesity problem.

You can witness Americans morphing from thin to chubby, simply by going to almost any "Old Photos" website on the Internet. Photographs of Americans, especially of American children, taken before 1961 show a lean citizenry, and photos of Americans from the mid-1960's to the present confirm the progression of the heavier and heavier American.

So, what caused Americans to go from a healthy weighted society in 1961 to the gargantuan mass of humanity it is today? I say it was the result of American based companies changing the way they sweetened their products. With the abrupt stoppage of Cuban sugar entering the American market, commodity prices soared and the large sugar consuming companies like Coca-Cola, Pepsi, Hershey, and Kellogg switched from using sugar to using the less costly corn syrup.

For a while, it seemed like everyone was happy with the sugar switch. The food and beverage manufacturers' that switched to corn syrup were making huge profits. Some American farmers who had never planted a stalk of corn in the past were now planting corn in every field on their farm. Farmers were getting rich and the demand for corn kept soaring. The race was on to make as much corn syrup as quickly and as efficiently as possible.

Corn syrup was relatively simple to make. Gottlieb Kirchhoff invented a process for extracting the sweet syrup from corn in 1812. Back then, cornstarch and hydrochloric acid were mixed together and heated in a pressure cooker. Today chemists use more sophisticated methods and produce a variety of much sweeter products. High Fructose Corn Syrup is the most recognizable product in the group. But, depending on what processes are used to extract the syrup, and what part of the world you are living in, the basic product can have a dozen different names. Besides calling it High Fructose Corn Syrup, some of the other names used are Glucose-Fructose Syrup, Isoglucose, Fructose-Glucose Syrup, Dextrose, and High Fructose Maize Syrup.

With all the different names for the seemingly same product, people were getting confused and it wasn't long before health-conscious researches started publishing studies in medical journals that demonized corn syrup in all its forms. They made the argument that no matter how you chemically tweaked corn syrup, it would always cause you to gain weight and it would always be harmful to your health. Well, the corn syrup producers were not about to let that kind of talk go unchallenged. They hired the best scientific researchers money could buy and studies praising the syrup began appearing in medical journals around the world. But for every paper or study produced extolling their product, another one would appear condemning it. The barrage of arguments from both sides convinced some and baffled others. And today, the dispute continues. At this very moment, someone somewhere is saying, "When I was a kid Coca-Cola tasted much better and no one got fat because they didn't use corn syrup to sweeten it. They used real sugar."

Well, it took more than half a century, but it finally looks as if the big food and beverage corporations are listening to their customers. If you walk up and down the aisles of an American supermarket today, you'll see all sorts of products marked with signs stating they are made with pure cane sugar and that they contain neither Corn Syrup nor High

Fructose Corn syrup. So, if you really want to lose a few pounds, take the first step and read the labels. You might be shocked when you read some of the stuff they put in their products. I know I was stunned when I read the label on a box of Plain Table Salt. It listed the contents as: "Salt, Sodium, Silco-aluminate, Dextrose, Potassium Iodide and Sodium Bicarbonate."

The Party
By Bill Lynam

MAC O'ROURKE PULLED HIS VOLVO up in front of the Victorian house with its two-story silo observatories, its crenelated scroll-work, and shingled-sided mansard roof and gawked at this mansion from a time. He pulled the doorbell that gave a faint ringing. Several minutes later, Geraldine Sommers answered and let him in. She knew he was coming. It was an insurance deal. The cops had already been there. What had gone on was over. Now, it was just the formalities. Paperwork.

"Come in Mr. O'Rourke," she chimed. He took off his fedora and put it on the sideboard.   "Come into the parlor. We can talk there. Would you like some tea?"

"No thanks just ate. Mind if I smoke?"

"Please do. Call me Gerry, Geraldine's too formal."

Geraldine, aka, Gerry, was one of two witnesses to the death of Hilda Hoover, owner of the house. The other witness, Brenda Postpistle, was in the hospital with a bullet wound. Gerry was at home where all three lived and Hilda was at the mortuary.

"Let's start from the beginning," Mac suggested.

"Us girls were having a party. You know? We had a little bubbly, actually, a lot.

When I woke up the next day, especially after the fire, the firemen, the cops and all; then I remembered Hilda was gone. She was sweet. So, yeah, we were partying when Brenda lit a cigarette, then fumbled it and dropped it on the bed and burned a hole in the sheets down to the mattress. Smoke started pouring out of the hole and nobody is really paying attention and whuff! up comes flames. Finally, we paid attention. Then, Hilda went over and was going to put out the fire, so she dumped half the bottle of brandy on the smoking hole in the bed. Shit! You can guess what that did. A fireball, more smoke and we all jumped off the bed as the sheets and mattress totally ignited and filled the room with smoke. Brenda got water and tossed it on the bed, then got some more. By then, the brandy burned out and the mattress was smoldering and stinking. There was still brandy left in the jug, so Hilda downed it, choked and I don't know if it was the liquor or the smoke. She looked kind of funny and went to get a cigarette. That's when it happened."

Gerry started crying and clamed up. I waited for a while then asked her if she wanted a glass of water or to sit down. Soon, she regained her composure, dried her eyes and continued with a little coaching.

"So, what went on next?" Mac asked.

"It was the cigarette lighter that did it." Gerry said. "It's shaped like a gun, almost like the derringer Hilda always carried. She was paranoid about strangers or something and only felt comfortable when she had her gun close by. When she pulled the trigger on the cigarette gun lighter, flame comes out of the end of the barrel. So, Hilda was half in the bag, woozy from either the smoke or the bubbly, she grabs a cigarette, fumbles for her cigarette lighter, gets her derringer instead, puts the cigarette in her mouth, aims the lighter at the end of the cigarette, pulls the trigger and no flame comes out, only a .223mm slug hits her cheek and blows out her brains on the left side of her head. When she fell, she still has the derringer in her hand and when she hit the floor, the two-shot gun went off and hit Brenda in the thigh or maybe it was her ass, I don't know for sure. She's in the hospital now. What a mess. Damn house is on fire, Hilda is mush and poor Brenda is screaming and bleeding. I'm holding my drink, smoking a doobie and baby, the party is definitely over."

"Where was the derringer that night?" Mac asked.

"On the dresser next to her lighter."

"Let's look in the bedroom. I'd need to see the scene and take photos."

Gerry pushed open the bedroom door after sweeping the crime-scene tape away the cops had put there. A fistful of stinky water, smoke, charred wood and soggy mattress hit our noses. Puddles of inky charcoal water spotted the floor. Mac looked over the bed, the dresser, the room and the carnage and took pictures. A wet piece of paper floated in a puddle. It looked official with a logo and said it was a receipt for an institutionalized…something or someone. Had more words but was waterlogged and bleeding ink. At the end, a signature by Dr. Joy L…and more wet smudge.

"You girls did a good job on this room," Mac said. "Gerry, you know Hilda took out a million-dollar life insurance policy four years ago. There'll be an investigation of her death. Keep the room locked. We'll have to go over it and gather evidence. And, we have to get Brenda's statement and the coroner's report before any decision is made on the policy."

Mac noticed there was no sign of the cigarette gun lighter in the room. Gerry had volunteered that the firemen had tossed the smoking mattress through the window and the cops had taken the derringer for ballistic tests.

At the hospital, Mac interviewed Brenda after finding her in room 232 on the second floor. She was lying in bed with IV tubes hooked to her and drains coming out of her raised, bandaged leg. She looked very uncomfortable propped up and watching a soap on the overhead TV.

"Brenda, I'm Mac O'Rourke from the Unlimited Life Insurance Company. I'm an investigator and need to talk to you about Hilda's death and the incident at your house. I hope this is a good time."

Without a pause, Brenda launched into her troubles. "That damn bullet hit my leg, went up my thigh and shattered my hip. Now they've got to dig it out and I have to have a hip replacement. How's that for dumb luck?" She went on for some time about her injury, her pain, what she was going to do, who she was going to sue, until finally, she focused on Mac and said, "Who are you and what do you want?"

"Brenda, you and Gerry are named as heirs to Hilda's estate in a million-dollar life insurance policy she took out."

"Yes, I know. We were partying last night because Hilda was just released after five years in the looney bin. She had a mental breakdown five or six years ago and after her family couldn't take care of her anymore, they sent her off to a private mental hospital for treatment. While she was there, Gerry and I lived in her house and took care of it, paid all the bills. Hilda was always saying she was going to end it. But, she never said what she was going to end. She was drinking a lot that night and seemed really happy. Sometime in the night, she snuggled up to me and whispered in my ear, giggling and said, 'They didn't let me out, I escaped.'"

"Poor Hilda. She was a good friend until she went around the bend," Brenda said.

"Thank you, Brenda, I believe I have all I need. But, do you know the name of hospital she was in?"

MEMO Case File 4326: In the matter of Hilda Hoover, age 32, deceased, of the address 458 Westchester Blvd., White Plains, NY, holder of Life Policy PO4738957394, dated August 4th, 1986, initiated by the same Hilda Hoover should be declared invalid, null and void as said policyholder on the date of the start of the policy date was being treated for drug and alcohol dependencies, depression and had made three previously unreported suicide attempts.

This recommendation is based on evidence of the subject's mental illness as substantiated by medical records subpoenaed from the files of

Dr. Jerome Whittaker, her physician. Dr. Paul Hume, her psychiatrist, Dr. John Mercer, her analyst, medical records subpoenaed from the Bright Star Treatment Facility (enclosed). All policy payments that have been made be reimbursed to the estate of the subject and should there be any claim on the policy, it should be denied based on the contestability and suicide clause. I.e. Mental Illness at the initiation of coverage and the demise of the insurer by her own hand.

Signed: MacArthur O'Rourke, Senior Investigator 15 December 1991.

Science Says Eat Dark Chocolate for Health Benefits
By Toni Denis

POPULAR FILM PORTAY CHOCOLATE as an aphrodisiac, as in the novels "Like Water for Chocolate" by Laura Esquivel, and "Chocolat." by Joanne Harris. In those two novels turned movies, the main characters seduce or are seduced by hot chocolate and a chocolatier's wares. While there is a scientific basis for the feeling of well-being quality cocoa and dark chocolate produces, recently studies also show that dark chocolate has an array of other health benefits when eaten in moderation.

The health benefits of chocolate have been touted since the days of Montezuma, the Aztec chief, who drank up to 50 cups of a cocoa concoction daily to give himself special powers. Considered the "food of the gods," the mostly bitter drink derived from fermented cacao seeds and flavored with cinnamon and herbs, was called "Xocoatl." Later, Spanish monks who settled in the New World derived the word "chocolate" from the Aztec word, and made it the drink more palatable by adding sugar.

In the many years since chocolate became a global taste sensation, scientific studies begun in the mid-'90s by the chocolate company MARS found that the cocoa butter in dark chocolate contains heart-healthy mono-unsaturated fatty acid, or MUFA, which is similar to olive oil. The MARS Center for Cocoa Health Science, formally established in 2012, as done extensive studies on how MUFA allows unsaturated fats easily glide through the bloodstream and help unclog and protect arteries from building up. Chocolate must contain at least 70% cocoa content to have this benefit—the definition of dark chocolate.

Dark Chocolate Is Heart Healthy

In recent years, a deluge of independently verified studies by international researchers have confirmed the MARS studies, such as a report in the British Medical Journal that found that eating dark chocolate could reduce the risk of developing heart disease by one-third. Also, the Journal of Nutrition found that plant sterols and cocoa flavanols are proven to reduce bad cholesterol and high blood pressure. Other reported benefits include:

Prevents Stroke

In a study of 44,489 people, Canadian researchers found that those who consumed dark chocolate regularly were 22% less likely to have a stroke than those who did not. Of those who had a stroke and consumed chocolate, they were 46% less likely to die as a result.

Reduces Appetite

Other studies have found that the MUFAs in dark chocolate help reduce appetite. This helps combat cortisol, a hormone that causes stress eating and induces cravings for sugar and fat.

Positively affects Insulin

Dark chocolate helps control insulin levels and relax blood vessels, lowering blood pressure.

Provides Minerals

There's a reason why women, especially, may crave chocolate. One dark chocolate square naturally provides important minerals, including magnesium, copper, calcium and iron. Women tend to need more calcium and iron than men in their diets.

Reduces Inflammation and Helps Peripheral Artery Disease Patients

Flavanols, a kind of antioxidant in dark chocolate, boosts good HDL cholesterol and reduces bad LDL levels, reducing inflammation. Flavanols are plant pigments found in dark green vegetables, berries, green tea, nuts, spices, red wine and chocolate. Antioxidants help the body's cells resist damage caused by free radicals. It's the anti-inflammatory qualities that offer protection against cancer, heart disease and type 2 diabetes. In addition, a study by the Journal of the American Heart Association found that Peripheral Artery Disease patients who consumed dark chocolate were able to walk farther, due to its artery opening qualities.

These benefits are not available in most milk chocolate, however. All chocolate starts out as dark chocolate, but when dairy is added it becomes milk chocolate. Dairy products, unfortunately, negate many health benefits of dark chocolate by reducing cocoa content in favor of adding unhealthy fats and a load of sugar.

Mass produced milk chocolate is derived from Belgian bulk chocolate, which is sold to many American chocolate makers. There are lots of problems with this chocolate from an ethical standpoint—often the cacao is picked and processed through child labor in West Africa. In addition, the cacao farmers are not paid a fair price for the product they sell. If they were, it would be called Fair Trade chocolate. Once this chocolate is sold in bulk, heavy processing and additives, flavorings, sometimes caffeine and a majority of sugar make it far less desirable. The first and main ingredient listed on most milk chocolate packages is usually sugar.

The healthiest chocolate is organic, Fair Trade dark chocolate. It comes from Central and South America but can also originate from such far-flung locales as Tanzania, Madagascar, Viet Nam and other tropical locations where cacao seeds grow.

Buying quality Fair Trade dark chocolate not only ensures that it's quality chocolate, but also can make buyers feel good about eating something that benefits many otherwise struggling farmers around the world—a psychological benefit that doesn't need a scientific study to prove. Many of these chocolate bars can be found in high-end grocery stores and health food stores.

Happy Birthday, William Shakespeare
By Steve Healey

KNOCK, KNOCK. WHO'S THERE? Why it's William Shakespeare. And *as good luck would have it*, today is his birthday! As a master of the *Queen's English*, Shakespeare determined that *all the world's a stage and the men and women are merely players*. Though many people walk around saying, "I never could understand Shakespeare. It *was Greek to me*," his work is timeless. To them I say, "*Mum's the word*." They *doth protest too much, methinks*.

I know my writing can't *hold a candle* to anything he wrote and *there's the rub*. How could I possibly come up with a way to honor him and take *cold comfort* in the fact that I will not become a *laughing stock* and make my friends declare, *"Off with his head!"*

The naked truth is that we writers, in our minds, sometimes believe *we few, we happy few, we band of brothers* and sisters are *the be-all and end-all* of the future of writing. That we are the indication of a *sea change* in the way literature will be written. That in *one fell swoop*, we will be the new Shakespeare. *The fatal vision* in this is that most of us refuse to realize that eventually, unlike Shakespeare, our works *will vanish into thin air.*

The long and the short of it is that a William Shakespeare only comes along every couple hundred years. And this simple fact puts us writers *in a pickle*.

We love our writing, but *our love is blind*. No matter how much we *night owls* burn the midnight oil, in the light of *the working day world*, the *daily bag and baggage* of life, we are required to be a responsible *tower of strength* while we wish to be *fancy free* and do nothing but write to our *heart's content*. There is no real *rhyme nor reason* to expect life to *budge an inch* and let us *play fast and loose* with *such stuff that dreams are made on*.

So, *woe is me*. Maybe it's *a wild goose chase* that I'm on, that my possibility of becoming a famous writer has *seen better days*. Maybe I *should be up in arms* about the way life has shown me nothing but *foul play* in this.

However, I will not continue to *wear my heart on my sleeve* and let Life *throw cold water* on *the method in my madness*. I will continue to *cry "Havoc" and let loose the dogs of war* on the literary world. I will not accept that *what's done is done* and will continue to write just as though *the world's mine oyster*.

For now though, I must say farewell. *Parting is such sweet sorrow*, but this little creation has become *too much of a good thing*. It's *high time* to end this piece. However take comfort in the fact that *all's well that ends well*.

So, to *come full circle*, I say once again, Happy Birthday to William Shakespeare, someone who really knew how to express *what a piece of work is a man*.

Dad Gets Buzzed
By Tom Spirito

During the Second World War my Father served in the Eighth Air Force and was based for a time in the London area of England. He experienced a period known as the V-Blitz. During the summer of 1944 Germany began raining down upon Britain a new terror weapon. The Nazi's called it Vengeance One. The Allies called it the Buzz Bomb. This was the granddaddy of the cruise missile, carrying a one ton explosive warhead, but with a guidance system so primitive it needed to be aimed at a target the size of a city. London became one big bullseye.

Between the more traditional night aircraft raids and this new menace, my Dad was getting a bit weary. Night after night his sleep was interrupted by the air raid sirens warning of the approaching enemy. These alerts required all the men in his Quonset hut, a sort of mini barn shaped building with a roof of metal, to leave the "comfort" of their improvised abode and head for the protection of a slit trench outside.

After many of these uneventful nightly interruptions, Dad decided it wasn't worth the effort to get out of bed. So, the next night, as the sirens began to wail, Dad decided to pull the covers over his head and stay in bed. It wasn't long before he heard a disturbing sound. It was getting louder, closer and sounded like a pulsing BUZZ. He next became aware of a noticeable vibration which began to shake his temporary home. The hut started swaying along with his cot. Dad jumped from and scrambled under his cot. The Buzz Bomb seemed to pass directly overhead and exploded a half mile away.

Dad always called his branch of the service The Air Corps. He would proudly sing and knew all the words to 'The Army Air Corps' song. He'd always loved the line "give 'em the gun" and would point both hands like they were guns and make a machine gun rat-ta-tat kind of sound effect.... what a character. He also emphasized the lines "they live in fame, go down in flames" and would make a motion with one hand of a plane going down. Not that he was ever in much danger of going 'down in flames,' but I think that night under the cot was as close as he wanted to come.

Dad did admit that after that night, when the sirens sounded their mournful warning, he was the first man out of his bed and into the slit trench. "Fool me once" he would say, as he pointed skyward with a twirling index finger, and smile a crooked smile, with his eyes wide open

My Last Deer Hunt
By Henry Nyal

"Come on," my cousin urged, "you owe it to yourself. And you'll have a real experience as a westerner. Don't be a wussie."

"I don't know," I retorted anxiously, "to kill a wild animal . . ."

"We need the meat, and I know you'll love roast venison—it's the most delicious stuff, and clean. It's natural—no hormones or antibiotics or transfats or crap like that." Wagging his finger in my face, cousin scolded, "the gods made these deer to be enjoyed by protein-deficient college guys, like us. Don't you know it's dangerous to disappoint the gods!"

"With that bit of pagan philosophy, I'm sure I won't go," I said.

"Well, I've got something that'll change your mind," cousin said as he pulled a rifle from behind the divan. "This is our grandpa's thirty-caliber saddle gun, lever action. Uncle Fred lent it to me. Says it has killed many a big buck for the family larder. Told him you were going to get some juicy venison with it."

Cousin handed me the rifle, carefully directing the barrel toward the ceiling. "It's not loaded," he said.

I have to confess I was impressed with this old cattleman's tool. The wooden stock was of fine-grained walnut, comfortably worn and an appealing color. The metal action and barrel were like dark nickel, beautifully finished. The lever action was placed perfectly and had just the right résistance as I shoved it down and pulled it back into place with a solid click. And it had a captivating smell. Was it machine oil or a subtle vapor of burned gunpowder? I was surprised at how familiar this gun felt in my hands, and I realized it was similar in size and weight to the pump action air rifle that I had owned as a teenager. I raised the gun sight and pointed it a fence post outside the window, sighting it confidently, and easing the trigger closed produced a solid click.

"Well?" cousin insisted.

A little embarrassed, I gave in and said, "OK, but you know I probably won't fire it at anything alive."

We made preparations during the week, buying the licenses and day-glow red caps. Throughout the week, I was possessed of a quiet excitement that I refused to acknowledge, even to myself. I liked the old gun.

Saturday, before dawn, we departed for the forest hunting grounds in cousin's old pickup, fresh hunting licenses expectantly nestled in our parka pockets. We parked in a clearing open to the road where three other pickups were already stationed. We strapped on our day packs. In mine, I had a small box of 30 caliber rounds, two boiled eggs, an apple turnover and some plastic bags. I had a small canteen of water on my belt, as well as a new handbook on safe hunting with a rifle. It had a section on dressing out a deer that told me to secure rope, bags and a knife. I had found a few feet of rope and my old pocket knife.

We hiked a mile or so into the forest along a trail that mostly mounted upward, cousin talking about the methodology of finding a killing a deer. It was clear to me that he didn't know much more than I did. After a half hour, he stopped and said we'd better choose a place to meet later, then go in opposite directions because together we'd scare away a any deer, making noise walking and talking together.

I headed south along a well-eroded secondary trail. Dawn had come up, so I could see all around clearly. I heard a bird give a shrill cry but couldn't identify the species. After a few minutes, I found myself in a grove of young pines with straight stems, interspersed with scraggly clumps of brush with dark green and gray leaves. I stopped and hunkered down to rest for a moment. My breath hung white in the cold air. I gazed back at the fading trail assuring myself that I could follow it back. I had also brought my ancient Boy Scout compass. The rifle was strapped over my right shoulder which was beginning to ache slightly. An unfamiliar sense of freedom and excitement mixed with anxiety filled me.

As I gazed from tree to tree, an indistinct shape emerged into the grove. It was a deer; no—it was a good-sized buck. I held my breath. He was looking in the other direction as I silently freed the rifle strap from my shoulder. Inch-by-inch I moved the barrel-sight in his direction. *What a magnificent animal!* I thought. From my squatting position, he appeared very large, and I was fixated on the contrasting colors of his tail, underbelly, and face. His nose was dull black, and he stood in what to me seemed a heroic pose. His rack of antlers was impressive, but I didn't try to count the points. A spasm of guilt hit my chest that I calmed as I told myself someone else will kill this buck if I don't---besides we need the food. I had just enough time to disengage the safety switch and aim carefully at his head. I squeezed the trigger. The rifle thundered and jumped in my hands, but the big animal did not cry out or fall. He stood paralyzed, then shook his head violently for at least two seconds before bounding away down the hill.

I was paralyzed for the moment too but seeing he had halted about fifty yards below I followed, trying to move quietly. The buck stood there in profile, so I could see his whole right side. He was vigorously rubbing an antler on a branch. When I reached a spot where I was hidden from him, I felt my hand automatically push down the lever expelling the spent cartridge which flew away. Instinctively I jerk up the lever and a new bullet was inserted into the chamber. The buck flinched at the sharp noises yet continued scrubbing his antler on the branch. The rifle was ready, and I aimed quickly—too quickly. I fired, hitting him again--this time I could see it struck the middle of his gut. He was stopped again for a second in which I worked the lever and fired off another bullet without aiming. This third shot hit him in the rump, in the right hind quarter. He rasped out a cry of pain and tried to run but was reduced to an awkward limp. He headed down again, into a shallow ravine. I followed, running over the broken ground, feeling sick with a realization of the fear and pain my victim must have been feeling. I soon reached him where he had fallen.

He was panting wildly. His wide bright eyes focused on me. Unable to rise and escape he seemed to be begging an answer, why? What have I done to harm you? I pulled down the lever, expelling the empty cartridge casing, feeling a stab of regret that permeated my scalp and the back of my neck. This time I would end his fear and pain. I leaned against the trunk of a larger tree just a couple of yards away and aimed at where I believed his brain would be. With the crack of the shot, his whole body trembled, and his punctured head dropped. Murdered was the first word that went through my brain; I tried to suppress it. Hunting is normal—is human.

As I stared at the inert body, I was impressed by his magnificent rack of horns and observed a big ragged-edged nick where my first bullet had struck. It was weeping blood.

I expelled a full breath and felt the worst of the tension flow away from me with it, leaving only a dead sorrow behind. Looking around, I realized that the big buck and I had descended into a ravine, perhaps a quarter of a mile below the ridgetop where cousin and I had parted. Assessing my victim, I guessed it weighed at least three hundred pounds, and I realized that I had no means to move its heavy body. A small branch projected about six feet up from a tree near where the wounded buck had fallen. I tied its hind limbs together and threw the rope over the branch.

Pulling with all my strength, I was able to hang its energy-depleted body up, with only its antlers and head resting on the ground. My pocket knife would hardly pierce the hide. All that meat and I hadn't even prepared myself with the sharp hunting knife.

Sitting on the damp ground, looking in random directions, I didn't know this alien forest. I felt lost—was lost—in so many ways. I understood freshly that I really had not expected success in my hunt.

Literary Genre: Steampunk.

Steampunk is a subgenre of science fiction or science fantasy that incorporates technology and aesthetic designs inspired by 19th-century industrial steam-powered machinery.

The Duello
By Bill Lynam

DOC HOLIDAY WENT TO the Palace Bar in Prescott, Arizona where he was banking the Faro table. When he left the hotel, his boots were freshly waxed by the bootblack in the hotel foyer. The handmade boots from top grade cowhide in Maryland were incised with his family motto: *Quarta Saluti* (Fourth Greetings). In the short walk to the saloon through the monsoon rain-muddied passageways of Montezuma Street, soil from horse manure, chewing tobacco spittle, roiled and wetted earth and tossed garbage smeared his footwear so that they looked like any cowboy's dusty, mud-entrenched foot coverings who entered the bar. He had to use the boot scraper at the entrance at the saloon's door to get the dough-like, congealing mess off before entering,

Walking up to the bar, he ordered a bourbon neat and proceeded to his Faro table. His dapper figure was confounded by fits of consumption and racked with coughs. He tamed his symptoms with whiskey and laudanum. He took out a small bottle of tincture of opium and splashed a dollop into his whiskey glass. The opium kept his coughing in check and the whiskey killed the tincture's lousy taste.

Jack, his case-keeper, had the cards laid out and set on the table, all thirteen spades arranged for the customers to lay off their bets up to the house limit. They were betting against the deck in the dealing box. Doc was banking the game today, using his own specially made two-card, gaffed dealing box. Instead of one card, it released two when he wished, one of which palmed off, gave him more than a slight edge in the game.

"Where's Timmy?" Doc asked. "He was supposed to be here an hour ago." Waiting for an answer from Jack, Doc adjusted the gold stickpin in his tie. It had a Cripple Creek gold nugget soldered on the tip with a small carved seal head from walrus ivory with diamonds embedded in its "eyes."

"He's sick boss. His kid came by and said he couldn't make it tonight. Probably two sheets, for all I know."

"Well, we'll need another lookout. Get ahold of one of the Earp brothers. They're good. See if you can find Morgan. You got your abacus all warmed up, Jack?"

"Certainly, boss," he replied. "I'll go down to the Bird Cage, Morgan hangs out there."

Doc twirled the ring on his pinkie. It was an old mine cut diamond set in a gold ring he'd cast with his own dental tools. The gold was from his Colorado adventures. On his other hand, he wore another gold ring with three semi-matched longitudinal gold nuggets stitched across the top. One of the nuggets had a chip missing, the result of a bar fight. Given Doc's slight build, he more often relied on his guns than his fists. He carried a Colt Single Action Army .45, not to mention the single-shot .41 Derringer he carried in his pocket and a five-inch knife in his boot scabbard

That night Doc was the dealer. He'd left Kate Harony, his sometime girlfriend, known as Big Nose Kate, back at the hotel. She didn't want to sit around the bar and watch a bunch of drunks roar over their winnings, or more likely, their losses since Doc was manipulating the cards.

As the card game began, more local cowboys and ranchers strolled into the Palace Bar. They'd heard Doc was running his Faro box and his reputation followed him. They whispered he'd shoot before he would discuss it if someone disputed him. Only twenty-nine, he'd wounded or killed several card players over wrangles. He also had a reputation for beating up his foes with his walking stick. Some were eager to go up against him in cards but were careful not to provoke him given his notoriety. Cross the man and you could wind up in boot hill, they said.

Others came sauntering in just to watch, but they had to sit at the bar. Sitting at the bar, though, was no free show. You had to drink. Let your glass sit too long, and you'd find a fresh glass with a new shot of whiskey in it with the bartender giving you the pay-up or get out look. No one was allowed to just sit or have an empty glass or idle whiskey.

After a half hour of play with Doc dealing all the cards for another round, one of the players, a local cowhand, Dilley Browne, who was losing his wages, called Doc on his dealing.

Dilley, a cowpuncher and farmer, liked to shoot his mouth off on just about anything. People who knew him let it pass. He just had a lot of wind to get out of his system, they said. What Dilley didn't know was

Doc was highly sensitive and didn't let the slightest affront go unchallenged.

Dilley, about thirty years old, wore a ragged, sweat-stained cowboy hat that was a little too small for his big head. His hay bale arms were loaded with freckles and he wore bib overalls that looked to be his only pair. He was one of six brothers who all worked the family's hardscrabble farm. They'd cleared the bush and trees on unclaimed Indian land and built the barns, sheds and a house where they lived together. Dilley was in town to have a little fun that Saturday night.

"Looks like you drew two cards instead of one but only one card surfaced when you dealt from the box," Dilley said.

Doc looked at him and said, "Farmboy, you think I'm cheating? 'Cause that's what you're saying." Then Doc emptied the box of the remaining cards and shoved it over to the cowpoke with a fresh deck of cards. "If you know how this thing works, show me."

Dilley got up and ambled over to the Faro box and looked inside, then over all the outside and pawed the inside some more to see if there was any contraption or spring that shouldn't be there. Then, he loaded it with a fresh deck of cards and dealt. Only one card came out. He dealt again and still only one card came out. He did it several more times with the same result. What he never found was Doc's pressure plate that ejected two cards at once when the correct spot was touched.

The accuser put the box down. Chagrined, he said, "Well, I guess I was wrong. Must have been the light."

Doc straightened his vest, pulled on his string tie and said, "You just called me a cheat, which you'll have to answer for. Noon tomorrow show up at the ballfield on Goodwin Street. You and I are going to have us a duello.

"What's that?" Dilley asked.

"That's Italian for a duel, hayseed. Be there. And bring your seconds and a doctor, if you can find one. The choice of weapons is going to be a little different. No swords, no pistols, just something my carpenter friend has worked up. You'll find out when you get there. We call it Preskitt Duello Rules."

"Wait a minute. I didn't do anything. I just asked...."

"Too bad, son. You just besmirched my good name. See you at the ballfield. Noon tomorrow. Don't be late, or else."

That ended the game and everyone at the table scattered out the door or over to the bar where they started talking about the duel and taking bets on the outcome.

The next morning, the principals walked up Goodwin Street and through the gate to the ballfield. They stared at a loud, belching machine that was hissing and letting off steam and sooty smoke from its stack as a fireman shoved lengths of wood into its maw and adjusted the gauges.

Two long rubber hoses came out of its side with gun-like implements at the end of each. The devices were identical, and each looked like a handgun with a large cylinder up by the front end. A whiff of steam was coming from the barrels of both. Closer inspection showed the cylinders held a clip of twelve objects in the steam guns. The objects were three-inch nails used in barn building.

The inventor, Elmer Hawkins, had made his fortune in the gold fields of California. He put together his device after thinking about it over long winter nights in the Sierras. He was a carpenter who'd quit work to find his fortune in the gold rush. A tinkerer by inclination, Elmer needed a way to build buildings and barns faster. With the number of immigrants coming west, there wasn't enough housing. Not everyone was a builder, so they wound up living in tents waiting for a few good carpenters to build them a house for the family and a barn and outbuildings for the livestock.

He came up with his steam-driven nail gun with a shuttle spindle and an automatic stop system, so that when the nails were used up, it could not fire. This device moved the construction process along faster than the old methods. It could fire one nail at a time with a trigger pull and could put a board in place in seconds. A replacement nail cylinder clip could be inserted as the first was exhausted.

Elmer was a card player and a friend of Doc, so the two of them cooked up the weapon of choice for Doc's duello—Elmer's steam-gun nailer.

Towards eleven o'clock the next day, crowds started coming to the ballfield. Someone was going to get shot. They showed up just like they did at the public hangings. They had to see the event, so they could say, they were there. And, they had money on the line. The odds were five to one in Doc's favor.

Dilley Browne knew this duello was not a good idea, but there didn't seem to be any good way to get out of it. At the ballfield, he brought his five brothers as seconds, thirds, fourths, fifth and sixths, but he couldn't find a doctor to stand by in case he was wounded.

At eleven fifty-five, Doc's second, Harry Cowlitz went to the center of the ballfield and dropped a white handkerchief and placed a stone on it so it wouldn't blow away. Then, he told the principals to take their positions. Harry went to the steam machine and brought the steam guns out and handed one to each of them. Moving to the side out of the line of fire, he explained how the steam gun worked. Then he reviewed the Preskitt duello rules to Doc, Dilley, and the crowd that had gathered.

"Starting at the dropped cloth, back to back, you will each pace ten steps away on my count. When I say *ten,* you'll take another step, turn and fire at will. Whoever draws first blood, satisfaction will be called, and you will shake hands and that will be the end of it. Agreed?" Harry said. The two parties nodded agreement.

On the count of ten, both stepped out and whirled. Dilley shot first, missing. Doc took only a second, aimed the steam gun and pulled the trigger a dozen times. Twelve nails flew through the air and whanged into Dilley's right leg. Dilley dropped his gun, started howling and hopped over to his brothers. "Kill that son of a bitch boys. Look what he did to me!" Dilley shouted.

"Hold it!" Harry, Doc's second yelled. He was holding a shotgun on the Browne brothers. "One move and you're going to be seeing Jesus."

"Yeah, Brownes, it's all fair and square," the crowd yelled as they stuffed their winnings into their pokes. The nails in Dilley's leg started to fall out. They'd only scratched him. At the twenty some paces between the duelers, the nails lost most of their steam, not to mention accuracy, and only stung a little bit.

Meanwhile, Doc walked over to Dilley, shook his hand and said, "You're a lucky cowhand Dilley. Usually, it's morticians you'll see next after my gun slinging. Today was just a bit of fun. Next time you're in a card game, watch your mouth. Now take your brothers and go on home."

When you focus on someone's disability, you'll overlook their abilities, beauty and uniqueness. Once you learn to accept and love them for who they are, you subconsciously learn to love yourself unconditionally.
—*Yvonne Pierre*

Tickets
By Shirley Willis

UP FROM WHERE I LIVE, Orion makes high siren sounds like an ambulance or a cop car. He also wears a too-big black hat like the bad guy in an old Western. I walk, and he weaves in and out of cars. Weaves between me and the other kids on bikes. He's all pointy sharpness and sinuous plasticity that spurt simultaneously from his compact self like cactus and orchids. Everyone honks and waves at him.

He tracks me, tells me how to be safe. "Don't go so fast." "Face the traffic." "Stay outta the road." He figure-eights' ahead and back. Rears his bike in front of me like a stallion. Pushes his hat back from his eyes. Spits off to the side like the big boys. Hands me a yellow stickie scrawled with, "Tikt for sped. 35 in 25 mi zun."

His numbers and letters are backward. Or upside down.

I put the "ticket" in my pocket, "Sorry, Officer. Won't happen again." Then maneuver past.

He follows, races ahead, circles back, tires slewing small rocks. "That stump? You know the one you took? My dad dug that outta our back yard."

I keep walking. Orion sizes me up, western style, hat askew.

"Bet you didn't know that when you took it," he yells. "Didn't know my dad dug it out."

For weeks, the stump reclined with disassembled seduction. Stripped branch-bare. In different lights, it was the Matisse Blue Nude, a muted Picasso I can't quite remember or, maybe the Ingres Odalisque. Distant. Compelling. All that. Begging to be staged. But not against the water tank in the no man's land at the end of the road.

I had to have it.

The boy points a gun finger. "Well. I saw that stump on your yard. Down the hill where you live."

I keep walking. "You need it back?"

"It's okay you took it." He follows along. "But it's really my dad's."

We move along the road together, him peddling, me stepping.

"Well, here's the deal," I say.

He slows. "Yeah?"

"Any time you want that stump back? Anytime. You come on down and get it."

"Owl."

"What?"

"My head hurts. Sometimes. Like, really owl!" He means "Ow."

"Now?"

"Yeah. They took that little piece outta my head." He rides his bike with no hands, pinches his forefinger and thumb to show me. "Little. Like this."

I slide my arm toward my left boob.

Cancer. His brain and my boob. He doesn't know it but we both paid the same ticket to keep on driving.

We move together toward the end of the road.

Traffic thins. From an open door, his gramma yells him to dinner.

His dad stands by the pickup in the driveway and waves. "Listen to your gramma. You hear now?" A world of sweet and sad drawls through his words.

The boy stops by his driveway. Shouts after me. "That ticket? It's just a warning."

If you're going to have a story, have a big story, or none at all."
—Joseph Campbell

The Spirits of Whiskey Row
By Howard Gershkowitz

THE HISS AND RATTLE of the kitchen radiator couldn't cloak the fearsome bellows of the gale threatening to shatter the windows. The wind howled through the gables as I waited for the water to boil.

I stared at the stove's blue flames which whooshed sporadically, emitting a pungent smell as dust motes vaporized. The steam from the tea pot swirled, mingling with clouds emanating from my mouth and nose. Without warning, the burner winked out and an eerie silence replaced the chattering of the pipes.

Stepping into the hallway, I listened at the cellar door. The boiler should have been shouting and clanging as it produced its meager heat, but all I heard was the hopeless clicking of the firing nozzle. I opened the door and the gloom of the basement rose to meet me. A pull of the chord at the head of the stairs and the stingy illumination of a single bulb cast shadows on the floor below.

Climbing down the wooden escarpment, an icy dampness oozed from the walls, attacking my nostrils like the cold steel of bayonets. My good sense urged me to flee, to risk the storm outside rather than descend one step further.

I took a deep breath to calm my nerves. I regained my resolve and hurried past the boxes and dust-covered furniture scattered about to the furnace. I checked all the obvious concerns, but no ready solution presented itself—there was no dislocation of the nozzle nor an indication the oil supply was exhausted.

Something flash behind me. The hair on the back of my neck stood instantly at attention. Turning slowly, I saw it. Seated squarely behind a roll-top desk was a man in top hat and formal attire. His face was ashen, his lips thin and colorless. Stringy, white strands of hair escaped his hat. His hook nose and wrinkled forehead betrayed old age. His eyes, however, were the most startling of his features, *for he had none.* No iris or pupil inhabited the hollow sockets. In their place, a reddish tinge of supernatural light escaped their empty confines.

Unable to move, I stared as the specter pointed a long, emaciated finger at me. Its mouth opened and from the depths of hell came a single word, *"DOOM!"*

Thousands of stinging, red ants crawled inside my skin. I breathed deeply, trying to stay conscious. Then the macabre image blinked out of existence, nothing left except a floating retinal image. I tried blinking it away to no avail. A thunderous cackle shattered the silence behind me and I whirled around, a scream at racing through my throat like a desert wind. I fully expected to see the ghoul on the attack. Instead, the boiler erupted back to life, the smell of sulfur heavy in the air. I turned tail and raced up the stairs, slamming the door behind me.

I leaned against it, my heart pounding in my ears, as the house returned to life. The pipes shook once more with their familiar clanging as hot water surged through them once again. Hidden subtly within the metallic chords of the old copper coils, however, was something different, something new; a sound I'd never heard previously.

It grew steadily louder, originating in the living room. I rushed into the kitchen towards the back door when the cacophony ceased abruptly. The unexpected silence caused me to look back. Another apparition appeared in the archway.

This poltergeist was ethereal and shifting, with no discernable features. I could see the stairs behind it through its silken folds as it hovered above the floor.

"Who are you? What do you want of me?" I asked, my voice trembling.

In response, it coalesced, churning and whirling like astral cotton candy. No longer transparent, images formed at its center, and I found myself staring at downtown Prescott, as if through a lens. The town's clock tower clearly displayed the time; 5:30. People were hurrying along Main Street.

As I watched, a fireball burst forth from the St. Michael's hotel obscuring the street with roiling orange and yellow flames. When the blast subsided, the hotel was engulfed in fire, the thick, black smoke rushing out splintered windows. Bodies lay on the ground and cars were ablaze up and down the street. The neighboring buildings caught fire as well. In the blink of an eye, the entire downtown was a roaring inferno.

The image faded, replaced by a new scene as if the ghoul had pressed fast forward on some celestial remote. Devastation was everywhere. Skeletons of vehicles threw off wisps of smoke. The clock tower, by some miracle, had survived, standing guard defiantly, frozen at 5:31.

The cosmic lens clouded over, and like the fog of melting dry ice, it floated to the ceiling, disappearing through the rafters.

I stood transfixed, blood pounding once more in my ears. The echoes of *doom* reverberated in my mind as I replayed the astral hologram over and over. Was it a curse? A premonition? And if so, what was I supposed to do about it? I could spread the alarm, but who'd believe me? Mayor Jessup was unlikely to evacuate the town on my say-so, not without proof.

I looked at the digital clock on the wall, the bright red numerals reminiscent of the first specter. It was past midnight, but I couldn't sleep now. The spirits had chosen to retire, at least temporarily, and I needed a plan.

"A bomb, you say? At the St. Michael's?" Tom Jessup said, eyeing me with skepticism. Mayor for the last six years, his family had been early settlers, operating the Bar J ranch on the Southern edge of the Yavapai River since the1890's.

"I said maybe. I don't know for sure. It could be the gas lines are rigged to rupture," I said, sticking to my hastily contrived script.

"And tell me again how you know this?"

"Like I said, I stopped for coffee at the cafe and overheard two men talking. They were behind the partition between the restaurant and lobby. '*It oughta blow at 5:30. It'll be a heck of a sight, I figger,*' one of them whispered. The other one said, '*we'd best be long gone. I don't want to end up no crispy critter.*'"

"So, you figured they meant the hotel was going to blow up tonight at 5:30?"

"Wouldn't you?"

"Why didn't you tell Jake? I'm sure he would have investigated immediately."

"I *did* tell him! He didn't believe me—thought I was telling tales."

"Are you? Cause if I order an evacuation and nothing happens, you're going to be in big trouble, Bill."

"I'm not telling tales and I'm not telling you what to do. I heard what I heard. If something happens and people die, it'll be on your head, not mine."

He scratched the stubble on his chin.

"It's only 10:30. I'll call Sam down at the Sherriff's, have him meet us at the hotel. No use alarming the guests just yet. We'll evacuate if we find anything suspicious."

"And what if we don't find anything right off? What then?"

"Then it'll just be your imagination gone wild, understand? I don't want a panic, and I expect you to keep this between us till I say otherwise, understand?"

"Understood," I said.

The St. Michael was built soon after the fire on Whiskey Row in 1900 which destroyed a good portion of the town. The furnace and feeder lines for all the modern, gas-fed fireplaces ran in a grid below the main floor, located behind a solid oak door leading to the basement, a sturdy behemoth with a modern steel lock intended to last another hundred years.

Tom, Sam and I methodically traced the pipes and wires lining the beams above us. We picked through the graveyard of long-forgotten furnishings and spittoons. It felt like the catacombs of France, though less musty and without the requisite piles of decaying bones.

"What exactly should we be looking for?" I asked.

"Anything out of place," Sheriff Sam Goldstein said. "Keep your eyes open for recently disturbed furniture or signs of fresh sawdust. Tom and I will check out the boiler."

"What about the gas company?" I asked.

"Already called them. A repair team is on standby just in case."

"You know," Tom said, "the town was nearly destroyed a couple of times by fire. The first one in 1900 was caused by a careless miner who left his mining candle burning near a wall in one of the saloons. You think some laid-off, disgruntled miner is trying to repeat it on purpose?"

Sam didn't answer directly but turned to me instead. "You have any idea who those two fellas were you overheard, Bill?"

"They didn't sound familiar."

"And you didn't think to peek around the partition to get a look?"

"I did, but they were gone before I could."

"And you don't remember anything else that might be useful?"

"If I did, I'd tell you, wouldn't I?"

"Keep thinking—maybe something will come back to you." He and Tom headed off to check out the boiler.

'*There were these two ghosts, you see...*'

Two hours later, having found nothing suspicious, Tom called the search off.

"Looks like you sent us on a wild goose chase, Bill," Sam said as we stood outside of the hotel.

"I'm telling you, I heard what I heard. Something bad's gonna happen here tonight. I feel it in my bones."

"Well, I can't order an evacuation because you've got arthritis," Tom said. "Just be glad I don't have Sam arrest you for wasting our time. Next time you hear voices, go see an ear doctor. I have a council meeting to prep for." With that, he turned and stomped away.

The clock tower chimed 1 pm.

Back in the hotel, I found the bellhop who'd unlocked the door to the lower sanctum. "Sorry to bother you again," I said, "seems I left my cell phone downstairs."

He nodded and unlocked the basement door again.

"Thanks. I'll find my own way out."

In the main furnace room, I repeated my search for obvious problems, as I did in my own basement the previous evening. There were no observable misalignments or frayed wires and no tell-tale odor of rotten eggs to indicate a gas leak.

Next, I meticulously retraced the gas lines crisscrossing the basement paying careful attention at each junction disappearing through the floor above me.

Glancing at my watch, I realized two more hours had passed. I removed a dusty sheet from an old wicker chair and sat down to gather my thoughts. Stretching my neck, I noticed a wisp of smoke around the pipe just above me. It didn't dissipate however. It casually floated there, suspended in space. Then a second wisp appeared, and then another, like strands of cotton candy forming around the copper. The tingling at the back of my neck returned. The strands condensed into a long, thin rope, wrapping itself around the pipe. It moved along its length like a snake. I followed, staying a good twenty feet back. Finally, it stopped and formed a small, white ball around an elbow joint I'd surveyed ten minutes ago. The ball brightened sharply, then exploded like a sun going nova. Then it blinked out entirely leaving me momentarily blinded. When my eyes readjusted, the smoke creature was gone, but in its place, I saw a bulge in the joint just below the floorboards.

4:15 pm.

I jumped the stairs two at a time, nearly smashing my face when the knob turned but the door didn't open. It took a second to realize it was locked. I shouted for help, pounding on the wood.

4:18 pm.

Then it hit me—it was check n time! Everyone was at the front of the hotel with the arriving guests. Racing down the stairs I searched for another exit. Breathing deep to control the panic, I found no unexpected doors or boarded windows. I scoured the floorboards above me for a trap door or hidden, collapsible stairs.

In desperation, I started overturning the furniture and boxes along the walls. I worked furiously but stopped when a flash erupted behind me. Turning, I spotted an old desk on the south wall. A figure sat there, this time with its back to me. I could make out the top hat and scraggly, white hair. It didn't turn to face me this time. I watched as two beams of red light shot from its hidden eyes, forming a slender laser beam. It glinted off something on the wall, splitting into a crimson spider web.

Then it vanished again.

I walked towards the desk, finding death by haunting preferable to death by fire. It was empty, but on the wall where the beams converged was a rusted nut and bolt. Pushing the desk aside, I found several more holding a rusted steel plate in place. *Of course!* There were no gas lines here in 1901, but there was plenty of coal.

Scouring the immediate area for something to pry the plate from the wall, I tripped on a wooden box. Opening it I found several shovels and a pickaxe, rusted but functional. Grabbing it, I struck the flat blade against the first bolt, snapping it like a dry twig. Three more swings and the remaining nuts broke off.

Stepping back, I swung the pointed end of the ax at the top of the place. There was a loud, metal clang and a small separation appeared. Placing the flat end into the opening now, I leaned heavily on the handle. It moved slowly at first, but then gave way with an ear-splitting shriek.

Sunlight framed the ax handle in my hands. I looked up the exposed shaft; a wooden hatch covered it, some eight feet above me, the dusty rays streaming through the weathered boards.

The sides of the chute were too slippery to climb so I reached up with the ax and hooked it between two of the planks. I pulled myself up, wedging against the sides by pushing with my legs to keep my back secure against the opposite wall. I broke apart the boards, one by one before dropping the ax and pulling my body through the opening.

I was in the alley behind the hotel. Racing around the corner, I emerged on the street and came face to face with the town's clock tower.

5:10 pm: There wasn't time to find Tom or Sam. The gas company's office was up on Sheldon Street, two blocks away so I sprinted up the sidewalk. I was winded in less a block and a half, so I half walked, half jogged till I reached the front door and pushed on it.

When it didn't open, I cursed. *Damned banker's hours.* It was after 5 pm and they were closed for the day. Peering in a side window, I spotted an employee sitting at a desk. He looked up when I rapped on the glass but just shook his head and pointed at this watch. I stepped back towards the street and found a suitable rock. The window shattered with a loud bang as the glass shards erupted from the casement. The man appeared at the window, shouting, but I shouted louder and with more enthusiasm;

"There's no time to spare. There's a gas leak at the St Michael's, and it's likely to blow any second. You have to shut off the gas any way you can. There are hundreds of people in that hotel, and they'll all be dead if you don't act *right now!*"

"What?" he said, and then it sank in. He rushed back to his desk and picked up the telephone. By his arm gesticulations, I could tell he was belching orders to someone on the other end of the line.

Exhausted, I turned back towards the street. I was about to check my watch when I heard a loud bang and cried out, collapsing to the ground. *Too late.*

Something touched my shoulder and I nearly jumped out of my skin. I jerked my head around to see a young boy staring down at me. "Don't be scared, mister. My Dad's car always backfires like that. He says it has to do with the carb'rator or somethin'."

I stared at him in disbelief. Getting up, I rushed back to Gurley Street. The hotel was unharmed; no fire or smoke spewing from its windows. Several utility vehicles were pulling up along with a police cruiser.

The hands on the clock tower announced it was 5:32pm.

Seated at the massive, formal dining table at the Bar J Ranch, I exchanged pleasantries with Sam and his lovely wife, Diane.

"Your quick thinking saved a lot of lives, Bill," Tom said as he joined us at the table. "But one thing still bothers me. That crazy story of yours about a bomb…"

"I told you— they never said 'bomb.' I stuck to my story."

"Okay, so how'd they arrange for the gas line rupture? The fire marshal's report cited metal fatigue. Pure circumstance, and pure luck you found it."

"How should I know? I mean, after all…"

"But you said '5:30'. You were very specific. What aren't you telling me?"

"Nothing. I'm telling you the tru…."

My eyes caught a picture on the wall behind Bill. He caught my stare and turned to look.

"Oh, that old picture? That's my great granduncle, Eldon and his wife, Clarice. I found it in the attic recently and decided to put it up."

Eldon looked serious and dapper sitting at an accountant's desk, dressed formally in a tuxedo and top hat with gray hairs protruding. His eyes, focused on the camera, appeared reddened from the flash. Clarice stood beside him, elegant and ethereal in her flowing, white gown with lace accents.

"They look like a happy couple," I muttered.

"So, I've been told," Tom said. "I never met them. They died in 1900, during the great fire."

Narrative Essay:

Bolder Demolition
By Howard Gershkowitz

There was this boulder in my way. I kept bumping into it, but it wouldn't budge. I cursed at it. I hit it with my pen and whacked it with my journal, but it just stared at me, stone-faced.

So, what was the problem? Apparently, the problem was me. My "boulder" was my pre-conceived notions of how things ought to be. Conditions to write had to be right, the inspiration some universal truth only I could see. It never occurred to me that, perhaps, nobody cared what I thought.

My son had a suggestion; "Why don't you take a creative writing course at one of the local community colleges?"

What? Go back to school? Hah! I'd rather be boiled in oil.

He was right, of course, wise beyond his ego.

So, I signed up. The professor, an expert in boulder demolition, immediately began eliminating the obstacles her students faced. "We're a community of writers. Like Vegas, what happens here, stays here."

Clichés were banned. Next came target practice; "Take 'white,' 'lake,' and 'apple' and write a love poem. Make me smile or cry or both."

Finally, a terrifying exercise called "workshop."

So, I wrote a poem about unrequited love.

There was silence at first, and I thought it a good time to shrivel and die. Then, one by one, hearts and mouths opened. *That happened to me!", "I felt it too!", "This is a whole new side of you, where's it been hiding?"*

Now I know. I am thankful for an intelligent son and appreciative of the capable professor who skillfully smashed that boulder to smithereens.

"This above all to thine own self be true," the Bard said, "and it must follow, as the night the day, thou canst not then be false to any man."

My Casita
By Christy Powers

I WILL NOT BE RETURNING to my place by the sea, the place I call My Casita. It was a dream that became a reality and now it will be stored away tenderly in my memory.

I have another month here and I must use it well. But there is reality to deal with and that detracts from the magic. Taxes and newsletters take energy.

This place began as a dream, an unreality, a moonbeam worth grasping. Walking around the vacant garage, above which houses a dream too obscure, I pictured myself within those walls overlooking the ever-changing water and placing wonderful words into stories that would secure my place on the bookshelf.

I had always longed for this kind of opportunity of time, of place, of peace, and of nature. To me, it would prove whether I had that skill with words that could make a difference.

What I learned through it all, is what I have always known, but have shoved aside. One does not need a place except in the heart, and soul. and mind. My place is where I am and while changing my home may change the outlook for a minute or an hour, it does not change what I am, nor who I am, nor how well I write.

I love my place here overlooking the bay. I listen night and day to the sounds that I do not hear at my other place. The birds here are different and the trees have a different sound from the wind. The wind blowing in off the sea has a personality all its own.

Walking along the beach, I see and hear and smell the world around me in a way foreign to those from the world of mountains or lakes or deserts. Strolling on the beach can open my eyes if I will allow them to open. My early morning and evening walks help to infuse me with the smells and sounds and pictures that I treasure. My hope is; if I store them deeply enough and remember to call upon them frequently, the misty fragrance smells and the tidal lapping sounds of small waves will stay with me until my final days.

The fact is; this place which I love severs my life and keeps me from really belonging anyplace. I often think of the things that I am missing at my other place, like spending spring in my garden and waiting for the first robin to arrive. Or the joy of watching the leafing of the trees outside my sunroom window. I love it there. And thankfully, my life there is not one of total solitude. I allow the distractions of phone and news and email to chop my day like garlic on a cutting board.

I also love *My Casita*, the place overlooking the bay. But the financial burden is far too great, and I worry and wonder why I ever thought I could do such a thing in the first place. I am grateful for the years of having *My Casita*, my place overlooking the bay. I have loved it and will store the view of the bay in my mind as I travel through the rest of my life. And, if in my writings, I should ever feel stuck for words, I will remember my place by the sea. And, in my mind, I shall sit in front of the window by the sea and watch the changing mood of the water through the trees now bare that reach skyward in the awkwardness of youth. I will listen and smell the world that I loved and experience glorious thoughts, except they'll fade like a dream in the wind when the reality of money and taxes and newsletters come to attack its magic.

If I thought it would be the answer, I could move here I suppose. But I know I would grow stale and lazy with this peace because that is my nature. I would have to work away from my place at the window if I lived here and that would chip away at the magic.

During the next month, I will suffer through the reality of taxes, the bustle of another holiday and the creation and distribution of another newsletter. Will I have time enough to dream and finely chisel the memories I want to take with me? This is my place and I love it here. But I do not belong here and my life is on hold waiting for my return. I have never had such a dream as this Casita before that I was able to turn into reality. The change from dream to reality spoils the magic.

I do not really know whether I am sad about this dream turned into reality. New people have come into my life and they will remain in my life. The way of life is different here and yet the same. It is the differences that I want to cling to and dream about and always remember.

In a month I will pack up and move on. I will cry a little and wonder if I should have done this in the first place. It was never a practical idea and mostly I am the practical sort. I will always be grateful that this opportunity presented itself and I dared to grasp it and cling to it through all the times of self-punishment and condemnation that come with allowing a dream to become reality. I hope I can hang on to the magic, the view from this window, the wonder of the world as I walk the beach in the morning and evening. The gentle breezes that float in off the sea and the fine mist from the small waves make certain that my walks are never the same from one time to the next.

But mostly I hope I have learned that to write is a gift of the heart and the soul. If the talent be mine, I need to practice and nurture and dream my dreams wherever I may be. The place is inside of me. The magic is inside of me. The love to write is balanced with the need to write. If this gift be mine, never let me make an excuse of place or time or worldly commitment. If this gift be mine, may I use it wisely.

I will not be returning to *My Casita* that I love except through the magic of imagination, dream, and memory. In my heart and in my soul, I know I made the right decision, but still, I feel as if part of me will always remain at *My Casita* by the sea.

Does that mean I will not write? Only if I cease to live. For to write and to live are one.

Nobody
By Bruce D. Sparks

GROWING UP IN A SMALL TOWN, I wanted to be a lot of things. A happy man never really was part of those dreams. I thought as long as you were something, happiness would be yours. Being something or nothing was all I thought about. Something would be what everybody else was, and nothing would be what nobody was. The more time I spent on the subject the more I realized I wanted to be a nobody. Nobody could do anything he wanted to 'cause he wasn't locked into being somebody like everyone else. Once I had my mind made up, I started off to become a nobody.

The first step to being a nobody was to become a paperboy. Nobody knows their paperboy. He is just the nobody that delivers the newspapers they read—so they can be somebody. He never reads them 'cause that would tend to make him a somebody. Even when he comes to your house to collect the paper bill, he is still a nobody. Yuma Daily Sun for 75 cents a week or $2 a month--not a bad deal to learn all you need to know to be somebody. Mary Ann Palmer didn't know who I was when I came to her house to collect. She was somebody to me and I noticed her right away, even at my young age. Absolutely gorgeous, and she was always nice to me. I thought we had a connection once upon a time. Guess I was daydreaming 'cause it turns out I was nobody to her.

I came up with an idea to buy a crystal radio set and listen to late-night radio out of Texas or Oklahoma. So, I got me one and put it together. Each night I would tune in to some show on the airwaves and listen to the music of the day through the earpiece. I really thought I was a nobody then 'cause nobody listened to the radio in the middle of the night.

One night I went outside with my radio to try to get better reception and found it was 10 times better out there. Mom got mad at me for being up past bedtime and for listening to God knows what on that radio. She took it away from me saying, "You must think you're somebody to do that sort of thing." She got me to wondering if maybe I was turning into a somebody.

Used to borrow my dad's .22 rifle and go out shooting on the desert. Long as I kept the rifle clean for my dad to use, I could use it anytime I wanted. In Yuma, summer days would get well over 100 degrees, but I didn't mind a bit. I'd go out on the desert a mile or two from the house and hunt snakes and rabbits. I figured I must be a nobody 'cause nobody goes out on the desert in Yuma in the middle of the day.

Always had a natural eye, as my dad would say, to shoot things dead center every time. Never feared getting bit by a snake 'cause I could see for miles in all directions at once, so it seemed. Nobody could do that.

I told my brother that I could shoot really good and I always hit the snakes in the head.

He said, "That's because the snake has such keen eyesight he can look right down the barrel of the gun when you point it at him and see the bullet coming. Snakes are so fast they actually strike at the bullet as it nears 'em."

So even if I was a bad shot I would get my fair share of head shots, too. He was my older brother and stood there lying to me as big as you please. I guess he thought I was a nobody and it didn't matter if he lied to me. I didn't care 'cause I was truly becoming a nobody.

With two older brothers, my clothes were hand-me-downs all my life and already somewhat threadbare. Just the clothes a nobody like me would wear, but always clean from the homemade lye soap that Mom used to wash our clothes. My dad believed that boys didn't need hair while growing up. "High and tight" was his motto and he owned the clippers in our house. So I was a real nobody in clean, ironed, faded-out clothes and no hair.

Took on the task of working for extra spending money by cleaning up back yards and throwing out trash for people. While cleaning up the back yard of old Mr. Webster, a man that went to our church, I found something of interest. It was wrapped in burlap bags and wired up tight like a mummy, as if it could get away if not treated in such a manner. When I asked about it, he said it was of no importance to him and that I should just throw it out with the other unwanted junk from bygone years. Like any boy my age, I had to know what it was, and what I found when I unwrapped it was breathtaking. It was a 1946 Matchless 750cc one-cylinder motorcycle with the chain missing, and no wheels or tires. It was beautiful, like nothing I had ever seen before. It had a little brass plaque stuck on the gas tank that read: "Track Record - Salinas, California - 1950-1951 - 98 MPH."

I asked if I could have the motorcycle since he was going to throw it out anyway. He looked at me like I was crazy. "Boy, this is the machine that took my brother from me. Hell, this machine is a killer and it sure isn't for children to be playing with even if it will never run again. Just you throw it out and forget about it." I told him I would take it in pay for my work, and I would even clean out his shed and straighten up everything for it. He looked at me for a long time, then at the motorcycle.

"I know of two other people that died riding that God-forsaken machine. As sure as I'm standing here, it will kill you, too. But if you think you can get it started and ride it without going to meet your Maker, you're welcome to it. Just swear you will never try racing it." I swore that I wouldn't, and I really thought I had the better end of this bargain. Nobody had one of these, I thought, and away I went dragging it home, much to my dad's dismay.

I tried real hard to get it running. Engine came apart easily enough and I could tell even with my limited ability that the rings were shot, so I could get no compression when trying to start it. Dad, being an auto mechanic, looked it over and decided DeSoto rings of that size would work. So, I bought a set and put the engine back together with a new gasket here, and new tapped and threaded bolt there, hoping it would start, but secretly praying it wouldn't. I did not want any part of going 90-plus miles an hour on this old beast with very little in the way of brakes. But then brakes wouldn't make it run. One thing at a time, I thought, and put brakes at the end of my fix-it list.

I figured that a somebody wouldn't even try to fix this old relic, but a nobody like me was perfect for the job. Cleaned out and reset the carburetor. Adjusted the old magneto, drained and refilled the crank case and transmission. Then came the clutch—all I could do was clean it, sand it a bit, and hope it would work. Then with everything ready I gave her a stomp with the old kicker. I remember yelling as the beast roared to life, "Holy Sh—!"

Run it did and very well for an old hunk of metal that had been in captivity for some 15-odd years. I could tell I had a handful with this machine. Time after time it fired right up and ran like it was brand new and breathing fresh air for the first time after being bound and gagged all those years. Now all I really needed were tires, wheels, and a chain to make her go. I also needed brakes to make her stop, but that was still at the bottom of my list.

My dad, having been a motorcycle rider in his youth, was just as interested in getting the thing going as I was. Took a while but soon the bike was together and ready to ride. I had Harley Davidson wheels and tires, a new chain and drive sprockets. Dad was taking no chances and took me out to the desert on the hardpack to ride the machine, away from everyone and everything. Said if I killed myself he would bury me right there on the spot and bring Mom by on my birthday to visit. Fitting for a nobody, I thought, and it just might happen.

I had no choice in the matter, you know. Men, and boys, too, sometimes put themselves into situations like this without thinking. It's a macho thing we do, the rite of passage to manhood. I wanted to be a man even if a nobody type of man. So, with an old army helmet I had found and a beat-up pair of welding goggles, I fired up the machine and sat on it while it warmed up. A slight adjustment to the fuel mixture and I was ready to ride. With clutch in I stomped it into first gear and got ready to go. I looked at my dad with one last look. You might know the look I'm talking about. The look that says, "I don't really want to do this, but if you're not going to stop me then I'll have to do it." He didn't do or say a thing, and the silence from him was almost louder than the motorcycle.

I still remember that feeling as the bike took off and I was hanging on with every bit of strength I could muster. The hand throttle went to full open and stuck in that position, which was something I had not counted on. Here is where I mention two points about speed. One is fast and can take some time to achieve. The other is quick, which takes no time at all to achieve. I had never been to 90-plus miles per hour in my short life, not ever, and certainly not as quick as that machine between my shaky legs was taking me there.

We were absolutely flying, and I was on my way to the ride of a lifetime for sure. Having bought my ticket to ride, I was going to stick it out. I swear death was approaching me as fast as I was approaching the horizon. That little brass plaque kept running through my mind about the 98 miles per hour record in Salinas, California, the three dead riders that went before me, and the everlasting reminder of how brakes should not be last on anyone's list of needed parts. The brakes didn't work, and the clutch would not disengage. The increase in speed was happening faster than I could handle, and even with goggles firmly in place I was losing my ability to focus.

Then I had a brainstorm. I reached down and pulled the fuel line from the gas tank and held the clutch in for all I was worth. I swear it took what seemed like a lifetime, but it died for lack of fuel and finally came to a stop, after covering the other half of Yuma County.

I got off of that silent machine, laid it down none too gingerly, walked several steps and collapsed on the ground near it, but not so close that it could touch me. Dad drove up in the truck to where I was. It took him a while—I must have covered five miles. He said, "Damn, Boy, that thing is a rocket." I looked at him and said, "I want to go home." We loaded up the bike in the truck and drove back home. Dad never said a word all the way there. I didn't mind; I had some thinking to do. I needed to evaluate my decision to be a nobody.

Dad adjusted the throttle, so it would work right, and fixed the fuel line and brakes. He rode the bike several times around the block and back and forth to work and told me the bike ran just fine. That was as close to dying as I had come in my young life. I saw the face of death and had lived to tell the tale. I knew that if I ever rode that machine again, it was going to kill me. I looked at it many times after that, but I never did ride it again.

I recounted the event to the man who gave me the machine, and he went into the story of how it had killed this guy, and mangled that guy, and so on. Said that motorcycle was the cause of at least three deaths that he knew of. He looked me straight in the eye and said, "Son, you are a very lucky boy." I knew for certain that death could be cheated. There would be other times in years to come.

I have had other motorcycles in my life and I was a motorcycle policeman for a number of years. Riding motorcycles for pay was easy and challenging with the right training. Riding them for fun and pleasure is exciting if you know what you are doing. Riding a motorcycle because you want to prove you are a man, or a nobody for that matter, is stupid and childish, especially if you have never done it before. My dad knew that, but it was something I had to learn on my own. Some things in life are like that.

That old motorcycle and the ride it gave me changed my thinking. To be somebody wasn't a bad thing, and happiness can be yours if you put in the effort required. To be a nobody takes a lot of work and most of it amounts to nothing. I decided I was just too lazy for that. At 14 years old I figured out something that I had been working on for some time. I was getting to know the person I was becoming. I even had thoughts of doing something great with the time I had left to live, and it felt pretty good. Hell, I might even turn out to be somebody--that is, if I can live long enough.

Monster Under the Bed
By D. August Baertlein

MY SISTER AND I SHARE a bed wit the monster that lurks underneath.

"Girls put your PJ's on," Mama calls.

"We can't," I say. "If we hop off the bed, the monster will get us!"

"Sillies." Mama laughs. "Hop wide. He can't get you then."

But we know better. The monster has long, hairy arms and sharp, sharp claws.

I stretch way out and grab my froggy umbrella that leans near the closet.

I use it to poke at the blanket where it hangs down by the floor. "Are you there, Monster?"

The blanket flies up and thwacks Froggy on his big, green eye.

"Eeeee!" My sister and I squeal and bounce on the bed. "Eeeee!" We melt into giggles and hold each other tight.

"P.J.s!" Mama yells.

I use Froggy to snag our P.J.s off the dresser. We put them on, careful to stay in the middle of the bed, far from the monster with long, hairy arms and sharp, sharp claws.

"Slurp!"

"Did you hear that?" I say. My sister nods, her eyes big.

"Slurp, slurp."

"He's hungry," I say. "He's licking drool off his lips."

"Eeeee!" We hug and jump even higher than before.

"Girls brush your teeth," Daddy calls.

"We can't," my sister says. "If we hop off the bed the monster will get us."

"Sillies." Daddy smiles. "Must we go through this every night?"

He comes in and scoops us up, one in each arm. Over his shoulder we see the monster take a swipe at his heels.

"Brush well," Daddy says. "Monsters don't like girls with stinky teeth." Then he leaves.

"Daddy!" we yell. "You have to carry us back to bed or the monster will get us!"

Daddy's chair groans and his newspaper crackles. He's not coming back.

We spit and slosh and spit again, then tip-toe back to our room.

"The monster's going to slash at our feet," my sister whispers. So, we put our bunny slippers on for safety.

We stand just inside the door, holding hands.

Finally, I say, "I'm not afraid." (I say it like I'm really not.)

I pull the belt from my robe and RUN past the bed, dragging it all wiggly across the floor.

Two long, hairy arms with sharp, sharp claws whip out from under the blanket and snatch at it. Snag it! Lose it!

"Rrrrow," the monster complains.

"Ha, ha!" I dance around the room. (Far from the bed, of course.)

"I want to try!" my sister cries. I give her the cloth belt, and she's off! Running. Zigging. Zagging. The claws reach and slash and miss.

"Nanny, nanny, nanny," she teases and shakes her slipper under the bed.

"NO!" I scream.

She yanks her foot back. Bare.

"He got Left Bunny!" she cries and leaps up on the bed.

I leap after her, but I slip.

"Eeeee!" She grabs my arm and drags me up.

"Girls!" Mama yells. "It's time for you AND that monster to go to sleep."

Mama comes in and stands right by our bed – our bed with the monster underneath! She tucks us in and kisses our foreheads.

The monster bats at her ankles.

"Monster!" she scolds, "knock it off." She lifts the blanket and reaches under. She grabs that monster under his furry armpits and pulls him out.

"Neee-ow?" he asks.

She says, "Yes monster, now!"

She kisses him on his furry forehead and plops him in the middle of our bed.

Monster yawns, stretches out a long, furry leg and slurps it down to the neat, white claws. Then he works his small, pink tongue all up and down the whole rest of his furry self.

When his bath is done and every inch of him is clean, he curls up round and soft, teeth and claws all tucked up safe and purrs himself to sleep.

My sister and I share a bed . . . and the Monster, who sleeps between us.

S.A.P.
By Dawn Watson

I AM A SAP. I've been a **S**ocially **A**nxious **P**erson for most of my life. Oh, I'm great at public speaking, which is more like talking at a crowd, as opposed to talking to and interacting with people. But, if you walk into a room filled with animated adults, I'm the one cowering in a corner, clutching my purse as though it contains an envelope with secret information from a foreign government.

Being an SAP can be funny, although only to others. I often give inappropriate answers to simple questions. For example; at a social event a seemingly friendly person might say to me, "Hello, my name is Ananda, what's your name?"

Inevitably in any kind of social interaction with another; my jaw will go slack, my tongue would cease to function, and most times, by the time I am able to force a word or two from my mouth, the other person would have by then smiled, nodded their head, and moved on to speak with another guest. Besides the onset of vocal cord paralysis at such functions. I also sweat uncontrollably at social affairs. I've been known to disperse a crowd with one shake of my head. Some folks even look up towards the ceiling wondering if there is a leak.

Plus, in all fairness, I should mention that normally I am fairly agile. But, put me in a roomful of other people and, you guessed it— my clumsy gene takes control of all my movements. Hand me a full platter of food and the show's on.

Did you know you can roll forty feet on one meatball?

Olympic events aside, I'm certain that I'm not the only **S.A.P.** in the world. I wonder what it would be like to host a gathering of fellow suffers?

It would certainly have to be held at a place with enough corners to shield the number of guests, attending. And there would be no point in serving food because nobody would volunteer to be the first in line. Also, it would be good to have a couple of those machines that start your heart back up again when you die of fright. And, it would be important for guest to be given a complimentary towel for perspiration purposes. And, it might be wise to provide each attendee with their own oxygen tank, or at least a paper bag, for the inevitable moment when one guest makes eye contact with another. I have found that best the way to remedy my situation is to invite people to my home instead of attending social gatherings. In sports, this is called the Home Court Advantage. In real life, it's called Being Comfortable on Your own Turf.

For me, this involves cleaning the house and praying that my dogs don't get loose and gnaw on the guests.

Over the years, I've learned to live with **S.A.P.** and have carved a life for myself, even if I'm forced to overcome quite a bit in order to enjoy life fully.

I have close friends who support my efforts and forgive my failures. I also have a supportive a family who insist on interaction at family gatherings. However, they know to stand back when I break into a monsoon-type sweat. And fortunately, for all of us, they are wise enough seat me at a table before handing me a platter of food. Their support allows me to live an almost normal life. And, while I probably won't create a new Olympic event with them by my side, at least I'll be able to answer the occasional question appropriately and not need CPR, afterwards.

Stirring the Memory
By Judith A. Dempsey

A recent conversation with my baby brother Marty, who is in his seventies, brought to life some buried memories.

Lately, due to poor balance, I have experienced a series of falls. In the first fall I broke my left hip. In the second spill I broke my favorite angel statue. Then, I really hit the deck, all left side of me landed on the bathroom tile floor. At Sunday church several males suggested that I tell others, "You should see the other guy. Well not being a guy I prefer to just say, "I hit the deck, and this is the result."

Before retiring, my brother Marty was a county prosecutor in Ohio. He is very conscious of small details. Marty's next statement hit me right between the eyes. He said, "Judith, may now be a Dempsey but remember we are Aubry's and Aubry's tend to get in trouble."

How could I have forgotten some of the adventures my two brothers and I engaged in as children. I smiled at Marty and said "Really, still an Aubry?"

Then my mind started turning back to incidents of my childhood. As a young girl I had sticky hands, especially for chocolate bars that were not paid for. When a nun asked for flowers for the May altar, having none of our own, I stole Mrs. Treason's irises. Unfortunately, I dropped a few on my walk to school.

My older sister, Pauletta found them and reported the situation to Mom. Upon my arrival back home, Mom was waiting and told me in no uncertain terms I must go next door and confess my misdeed to Mrs. Theason and ask for forgiveness.

Once I told my story to Mrs. Theason, she bent down and gave me a hug for being so honest. Then to my surprise and delight she told me I could have as many irises as I wanted. I am now in my 80s and to this day I have irises in my yard.

As children, both of my younger brothers joined with me in raiding the alleys behind our home. I remember finding cast off lumber to build a play shed which we not only used for ourselves but shared with other neighborhood kids. We also used that rickety old shed as place to hide when we needed to be alone.

Then there is the case of the sway back black sedan down the street from us. On a hot summer day, the three of us took a walk and stopped to watch a group of kids enjoying themselves sliding down the top of the car as if it were a slide. It looked like so much fun when they invited us to join them there was no hesitation on our part. However, it was not so much fun when our father asked if we had destroyed the neighbor's black sedan. We told our father that the other kids asked us to join them and they did the damage. It seems the other kids told their father it was the Aubry kids up the block who did the damage. I have no idea what our father had to pay for the damage that was caused but it was a lot and yes, we were sorely punished for our misdeed. We weren't bad kids, just active and imaginative. Yes, we Aubry's did get in trouble. But, for all the follies we committed, every one of us got advanced degrees and served society as adults: two attorneys, two counselors and one accountant. Yes, there were five of us. My two older sisters never got into as much trouble as my two younger brothers and me. At least, that's what our parents and our older sisters always told us.

Seven Hours Fine Except for Mothers
By Dolores Comeaux-Everard

London psychiatrist Jane Gomer believes "too much rest can shorten your life." The author of "How Not to Die Young" suggests that seven hours or less of sleep is ideal.

What a heavenly hypothesis for new mothers who practice demand feedings, and late-night TV addicts. Wide-eyed sufferers can now boast rather than curse insomnia.

Last week I had a bout with inadvertent insomnia. The symptoms became acute. A look in the mirror set off a chorus of high-pitched voices chanting, "ring-around-the-eyeballs."

A family health guide says abnormal wakefulness can be caused by poor sleeping conditions. Noise, light, someone moving around and worries are all indicative of the ailment.

The problem began at about 1:30 a.m. on Saturday when my husband began pacing the floor in anticipation for our daughter's cast party being held after the production of "Fiddler on the Roof."

Probing real and imagined fears, we discussed everything from wrecks and abductions to crazy snipers lurking on the highway. The talk proved a catharsis for him but not for me. Twenty minutes passed before the car bumped up the drive. Our Cinderella entered to a round of parental applause.

By 2 a.m., I gave in to saucer-sized eyes and trudged toward the typewriter where I pecked away until my peepers pooped. The vigil led to a sluggish next morning. No sooner did my head hit the pillow that night than Z's began dancing.

A rapping at the front door stifled my slumber. I pried open sleepy eyes to note the digital clock was blinking a hazy 5 a.m. As I dragged my body aft, I wondered why the "Gestapo" was in my town. I remembered voting in Saturday's primary, but only once. Yesterday when the children burst two bean bag chairs that released trillions of polystyrene beads in the house, I threatened to kill them, but thoughts don't equal deeds.

Clad in a nightgown, I crouched behind the banging door then slowly opened it. As laser beam struck my terror-filled eyes. Shielding my face from the flashlight, I recognized the "storm troopers" to be the new milkman and his wife. To guarantee future delivery, they explained, I must pay our overdue bill.

As I searched for a checkbook, I wondered what company psychologist had drummed up this choice piece of behavior modification.

"When and how do we get bills?" I queried.

"Oh, we slap them on the milk bottle, the couple answered.

That explains it. One of our boys has the job of bringing in the milk. Sometimes he becomes engrossed in early morning cartoons, and he forgets about his job until returning from school by which time the milk has soured. There was no doubt in my mind that the bill had met its fate fluttering about in the dawn dew.

Back in bed, my drowsy husband interrogated me about the knocking.

"Oh, go back to sleep…that commotion was only Elmer and Elsie hoofing-it-up over some green stuff."

I'll Have One More
By G. Williamson

SHE WAS SITTING AT THE BAR drinking a dirty martini. I walked over and sat down beside her.

"Can I buy you a drink?" I asked innocently.

"Wow. Does that line ever work? Try another." She said sarcastically.

Her strawberry hair had purple streaks in it. I was still formulating my answer when a cowboy sat down on the other side of her. He was built like Hoover Dam.

"What's up darling? Would you like to dance?" the cowboy said.

"No." She answered and turned toward me.

I was still trying to remember my stellar pickup lines as I gazed at her perfect profile. This could be someone's angry girlfriend, so I was cautious. I picked up my mug of beer and started to get up. She blocked my exit with a pair of gorgeous all-the-way-up legs. I put my beer back on the bar.

"Still want to buy me a drink?" Her eyes widened as she raised her brows.

"Sure. What are you drinking?" I asked.

She gave the barkeep her order and then sat staring into her drink. After about ten minutes, I concluded that she had only been interested in the free drink. I looked at her and then I said, "I believe I'll have one more."

About four drinks in for each of us, something broke. I was looking at her via the mirror above the bar when I thought I saw water on her face. I spun her stool around, so she was facing me. There were tears on both cheeks and mascara running down. I said, "What is it? Tell me."

"I think I'm getting a divorce." She responded between sobs.

I put my hand on her shoulder and she leaned in to me. I waited for the sobs to subside. When they did, she got up and went into the ladies' room. I almost left right then. That would have been the smart plan. Of course, I was way too drunk by then to be smart. I perched on the edge of my seat and waited for her to come back out. Finally she emerged. I stood and waved to her, thinking she might have forgotten what I looked like. She raised one hand and waggled it at me. We were both pretty well lit. We were trying to have a conversation, but it didn't seem to be going anywhere. It had been my experience that women hate questions and that seemed to be all I had. So, I shut my mouth.

I asked the barkeep for some coffee and he brought a cup for each of us. We enjoyed the silence and the hot coffee for almost an hour. The jukebox kicked out one slow song after another, all of them sad and romantic. I don't know exactly how it happened, but her hand touched mine. It gave me a small electric shock and I jumped. She laughed and that was it. We started talking. We were simpatico. Her eyes danced as she told me about her dog and the tricks it could do. I told her about my cat and how he exercised himself every evening by tear-assing up and down the stairs. Time flew by.

We had everything and nothing in common.

At two a.m. the bar closed, and I walked her outside.

"Where are you parked?" I asked.

"I'm dizzy. I think I'd better get a cab." She replied.

"Can I call you sometime?" I asked.

Immediately I wanted to take it back. I didn't know this person. But she was writing her number on my palm before I could say anything else. I looked at my palm and then into her deep brown eyes. And I knew I would call her.

"I'll go wait inside for the cab." She said.

As soon as I got home, I grabbed my cell. I didn't realize until then that the ink on my palm had run and it was all just one big blue spot. Well, guess it was just fate.

Jesus in the Kitchen
By Lena Hubin

HE HUNG IN an oval frame on an oblique wall in our Iowa kitchen. Wavy brown hair caressed his shoulders; his warm dark eyes looked toward a far corner of the ceiling.

I faced him from my place at the round oak table as we ate. "I fold my hands, I bow my head; I thank thee, Lord, for this good bread," we said, and as I lifted my young head from the prayer, I wondered: Was Jesus responsible for the bread my mom slapped into being each Saturday with her fine-boned hands? If so, how?

"Jesus loves me," this I was supposed to know, according to the song, but the Bible never did tell me so—at least not so I'd believe it. With those Middle-Eastern eyes of his, JC gazed upward, dark and golden-aura'd—consumed by reverence, and heedless of the likes of me.

He was *Mom's* Jesus, this guy on the wall, not mine. I know Mom loved him. She'd hung his portrait; she went to church and prayed "in Christ our Lord." And she'd married my dad, who was JC's spitting image, with shorter hair—a dark-haired, dark-eyed, gentle farmer.

But I would seek and find that same soft, raw-umber allure in men whom I'd love fiercely. The first was dark, soulful-eyed Richard Cohen, whom as a teen I dreamed in vain of kissing beneath the pines during ice-skating parties. In Arizona, Armando Garcia's chiseled cheekbones drew me into many kisses before he told me he was married. I met handsome, charismatic Raj Patel at a San Francisco party; we married within a month, and two years later we divorced.

Just like my mother's, none of my JC look-alikes had stuck.

Serene and silent, always looking the other way, neither Jesus nor any of his facsimiles would ever know me, nor I them. I traded them off for a lasting relationship with a tall, talkative, flaxen-haired Scandinavian who looked my way and smiled, showing his white, even teeth.

~~~~

When Mom died, Dad left Jesus hanging on the bedroom wall of their little house in town. The oval portrait was there when he passed nine years later, and it fell to me to figure out what to do with it. I had it in a Goodwill pile till Aunt Jean, Mom's sister, came by and claimed it for her bedroom wall. Her husband—gruff, dark-haired Uncle Reuben—had died from heart problems a few years before. I suspect Jesus has taken his place.

Narrative Essay:

The Notorious Jumping Cholla
By Fedora Powell Williams

I had recently moved from Hawaii to the Sonoran Desert, and I was awestruck by the towering majestic saguaros and the beauty of the desert. I had always been drawn to the desert and the dry heat was just what I needed.

My first adventure took me to the Saguaro National Monument which gave me lots of photo opportunities to capture these magnificent giants. I found myself on a 10-mile curvy one-way road out in the middle of nowhere! Then a beautiful saguaro skeleton caught my eye and I pulled over to get a closer look. The saguaro skeleton was so tall, I squatted down to take a vertical shot and boy did I ever let out a SCREAM! A notorious jumping cholla had poked patches of tiny needles into my tender buttocks! I walked back to my jeep stooped over in agonizing pain and very carefully got back in the driver's seat. I drove the remaining 9 3/4 miles holding my butt up off the seat while trying to steer and brake at the same time. Halfway into the drive, I had a good laugh at myself which helped me forget about the stinging pain!

When I finally arrived at the Information Center, I explained my situation to the ranger on duty, and he declined to assist me due to the sensitive location of the needles. He suggested I wait for a woman ranger who was scheduled to arrive in one hour. "One hour!" I yelled. "Please can you take these out now?" I pleaded. "You'd better wait for her" he replied in a matter of fact tone of voice. So, I retreated and waited. The female ranger finally walked through the door and I shouted, "Thank God you are here!" I said relieved. She led me into a small room and had me lie across a desk where she very carefully plucked out each tiny needle with a pair of trusty tweezers. During the procedure, the good-humored ranger laughed and told me some of her desert stories. "I am from the mid-west, and the first time I took a group of visitors out on a walk, she chuckled, I casually leaned up against a saguaro with my hand and I acted like it didn't hurt until the talk was over!" We both laughed at how we had been initiated into the desert and had great respect for it.

Twenty-seven years later, I look back at the experience and have a great laugh! I enjoy eating delicious cholla buds, but I avoid squatting in the desert at all costs!

Nineteen Forty-Four
By Joseph Babinsky

Excerpts from the Memoir: "Climb the Mountain – A Path Taken

IT WAS NOT THE BEST OF TIMES. In our family, it was a horrible time. As for me, a nine-year-old boy, it was a nightmare. This was the day everyone cried, especially mom, dad and my older siblings. If I had looked around (which I didn't dare do) I might have seen other people in the room also crying. I did hear the noise—people blowing their nose and loud moans.

At the front of the room, there was black cloth draped over a table. His photograph was on the table. Large baskets of flowers were on the floor. We were in church—the church where my father was the pastor. I was sitting in the front row with my family.

I really didn't understand what was going on. I only knew that Charles, my favorite brother, was killed during the War in 1944.

We first heard about the death of Charles at Christmas. I came into the living room and saw my mother crying. She was wiping away tears with her handkerchief, and with her other hand, she was removing ornaments from our family Christmas tree. Dad was standing near the fireplace, holding a yellow paper in his hand. He was crying really hard. Never saw anything like this before. They received a telegram from the War Department. It was news telling us that Charles was killed in action. All the kids heard the commotion and were told what happened.

After church, we went home and ate a meal. I recall that all my siblings were home. Two brothers were still in the army; they were home. When we finished eating, dad started a conversation about what each of us would do when the war was over. The older ones knew what they were going to do. They spoke first and explained plans for their lives. Several in the family were in high school and told their plans to go to college. Everyone but me was standing.

I sat in the high-back chair and tried to hide I wanted my dad to forget that I was in the room. I was wrong. He turned and spotted me sitting in the big chair. *Ghee whiz, what was I going to say? Don't ask me, please!*

Dad looked directly at me: "Alright, Joey, you're last. What about you? What do you want to do when you grow up?"

To tell the truth, the first thing that I wanted to say was that I dreamed to be a soldier, like Charles, and go shoot people—shoot them like they shot and killed my brother.

I didn't say this. No way! I squirmed in the chair, and merely stammered: "I don't know."

Memories of this time period are vague, not only because I was a young boy, but I have a lot of mixed feelings and emotions about this period in my life. I'm telling it here only because of what happened after the Memorial Service at the West Side Hungarian Church located in Buffalo, New York. The thing that happened was the question asked by my dad. His words stuck with me the rest of my life. In the years ahead, what he said lingered and became a huge influence.

This narrative is purposely placed at the beginning—it serves as a prologue to this book. As the story develops, it will be shown that the question asked was remembered and remained an abiding presence to assist various decisions and changes during my long life. The death of Charles, and the question asked by my father, merged into one experience and colored my life in such a way that it followed me both as a shadow and a guide.

Within the story I tell, an answer to the question slowly emerges.

No Common Abiding Place

By the time I wanted to know more about my family, we were all old—even me. When I started to write this book (2014), all but three had already died.

A sister, nearly ninety, offered to provide information about the early life of our family. When she began to tell family stories, she quickly realized that buried memories remembered brought on sleepless nights. Thus, she did the thing she felt best for her to do, which meant that she quit sharing stories with me.

At this writing, I have one additional sister still living. Dorothy is close to me in age; our birthdays are only fifteen months apart. Many years ago, she made it clear that I didn't know our family history. We were having a conversation with a mutual friend. The talk drifted to our family, and I mentioned: "there were twelve in our family, seven boys and five girls." Dorothy quickly interrupted and corrected me: "No, that's not right! There are eleven in our family!" I laughed and answered: "Dorothy, why don't you ask mom how many children she had!" Mother was still alive, but to my knowledge, Dorothy never asked mom.

Over the years I did what research I could. I found that Dad kept records of the family in his Bible. He recorded the date, name and place of birth of each child. There are twelve births listed in his Bible. He wrote a note that a daughter died one day after birth, July 2, 1924.

For the longest time, I carried the opinion that we had two families. There were four in the first family, born between 1916 and 1920, three boys and one girl. In the second family, there were eight—four girls and four boys, born between 1924 and 1935. The two families were separated by four and a half years, a period when no children were born.

It is a mystery when and how I became aware of the number in our complete family. A few weeks after I was born the two eldest sons left home for good. One brother went off to college, and the other went to live with his aunt, my mother's sister. I did not have much of a memory of either of them until 1944 when they came home for the funeral of Charles. Even then, they seemed more like strangers or distant relatives than brothers. And the same thing applies to my eldest sister. She left home when I was only one-year-old. And the third brother left home when I was three. So, in essence, my view of our family was that there were seven of us—three brothers and three sisters.

There might be more to this story than I am telling, but I'll never know. I say this because I heard my sisters whisper things about the subject of children, and why there were so many births in our family. I was a snoopy boy, and they probably didn't see that I was close enough to hear their conversation. I heard them say that mom went to a doctor to ask how she might stop having more children. I do not know when this took place, or if it happened at all. If mom did go to a doctor and ask advice about birth control, when did she do it? Did mom do this after the first four were born (what I call the first family)? Perhaps she did it after I was conceived and took matters in her own hands and stopped having sex with dad—the only birth control information she had. I'm guessing, of course. I say this because it helps explain, to an extent, why I never felt that I was really wanted.

I had a curiosity to know more about our family origins, and when older turned to genealogical research for answers. I already knew that we were Hungarians, and I wanted to know if we were related to the famous neurologist, Dr. Josef Babinski, born in France. My oldest brother, Elmer, told the story which he called a family legend. He said that there were three brothers that lived in Poland, and during a threat of war they fled Poland. One brother went to France; he became the father of the famous doctor. A second brother went to Czechoslovakia and drifted to

Brazil. The third brother went to Hungary and became the grandfather of our dad. I like this story and often tell it, but my genealogical search did not prove it. On the other hand, the research did not prove the legend false. It is mentioned here as a story, and it is the way that I tell it when asked by anyone about my surname.

My dad was an immigrant; this much I know to be true. He came to America in 1910 from Hungary, the place of his birth. My mother, Julia (Kayati), was born in Youngstown, Ohio, but both her parents (Andrew Kayati and Suzanna Pastor) were born in Hungary.

Dad was a teacher when he lived in Hungary, and this is what he did for a living when he came to America. Later, he attended theological school, and was ordained a Christian minister. After several different cities and churches, he moved his family to South River, New Jersey. They lived here during the heart of the Great Depression, and when things grew desperate, he found a solution. When I was two years-old, dad once again decided to move the family. Where? The family moved to an orphanage in Pennsylvania.

His plan was supposed to be a move for the good of the entire family. What began as a good idea became a nightmare for nearly everyone—at least for me it did.

A question could be asked as to why my father chose to move the family to an orphanage. The only answer I am able to provide is what little I know of the early life of our family, gathered in pieces and bits from older brothers and sisters and this, coupled with the slim knowledge I possess of the social and economic situation existing during the 1930s in the United States. One answer I have come up with is simple, and it is not an exaggeration: Our family was poor—very poor.

The older sister, mentioned above, shared information with me about the conditions of our family life while living in South River. Our dad was the pastor of a small church that had few members. He did not have additional employment and source of income. Many times, the people of his congregation had no funds to share with the church, and to pay his salary. The people did the best they could, and often gave help only in the form of food. They gave the family things like apples, peaches, pears and fresh garden vegetables—carrots, beets, potatoes.

This same sister said that when we arrived at the orphanage, we were immediately instructed that the children were not permitted to address our parents as mom, dad or in any other personal way. For the benefit of those who were truly orphans, we were taught to call dad, "Mr. Teacher," and mom, "Mrs. Teacher". We became orphans—though, of course, in name only.

When I consider the stories about our family, a move to an orphanage seemed to be my dad's only choice. Knowing this makes it understandable but provides little relief to the young child that I was. Eighty years later I can't imagine a two-year-old child not saying *mommy*. How can you undo a boy's relationship with his mom and dad? Who suckled him when he was sad or sick? Did she take the boy along with her when she went to her duties as the cook for the orphanage? Was the little child scolded (or worse, punished) when he was heard to say *mommy* or *daddy*?

The stories of my "beginnings" tell a great deal about certain factors that went into the formation of my basic personality, and the underlying loneliness and unsettledness that I have experienced throughout my life. I make no attempt to speculate how it was for the ten siblings older than me. However, I cannot help but wonder what their experiences were. When I study the list of births in our family, dates, places born, I see the number of times the family moved from place to place, city to city, and each child still very young, I sense that we all share a common thing, namely, we had no stable home—no roots. Our common root, in addition to the same father and mother, is a picture of a family continually on the move, similar to gypsies.

I do think that if each sibling were asked to tell his or her story, I guarantee that eleven very different books would be written. This is as it should be. Even though we were members of the same biological family, we are, after all, individuals, and each one has a story to tell. This is my story.

The Bus Stop

I would have enjoyed having him as my older brother. I was young, of course, but I saw Charles as a giant, not just physically tall, but tall and strong. After I grew older I discovered that he was also intelligent, an honor student in high school, and an outstanding athlete. Also, I learned that he helped the family by working as a salesman in a clothing store, Riverside Men's Shop, located in our neighborhood near the Niagara River in Buffalo.

Our family was devastated by the news that he was killed in action—mom, dad, my brothers and sisters, other relatives, members of our church, many friends and neighbors.

The scene is clear in my memory. When I heard the news, I ran upstairs to my bedroom. I threw myself on the bed, cried out loud and yelled: "No, no! It is a lie! It is not true! You'll see; he'll come home." I refused to believe that Charles was really gone.

Often, I sat alone outside on the front steps of our home, watching for a city bus. I waited and watched for a bus to come along on Tonawanda Street, and stop near our house. I knew that I would see Charles get off the bus, smile and wave to me. That's what I believed would happen. I believed it strongly and knew without a doubt that he was coming home. They tried, but nobody could convince me otherwise.

There were two funerals for Charles: The first was a Memorial Service, which was soon after we received the news in the telegram that he was killed in action. This was the same time that my father asked the question: *What are you going to do when you grow up?*

The second funeral happened years later. His body was shipped home in a sealed casket. I was one of the pallbearers. When I touched the casket, I knew his body was not inside. That's why I used to sit on the steps and watch for a bus. I did this for a long time. But it never happened. Charles did not come home. He never came home. And one day, I quit watching city buses on Tonawanda Street. Instead, I watched the girls walk by. But that is a story for another day.

Lest I Forget
By Carol A. Rotta

DUST MOTES FLOATED LAZILY in the afternoon rays of California-sunshine that poured through the windows, across the blue Formica table top, and onto the darker blue-patterned linoleum floor. I loved this corner of the cheery yellow and white kitchen that mother referred to as, the "breakfast nook." Tucked at one end of the room, it was always pleasant, especially when the sun was shining through the large windows facing southwest at the front of the house.

I flopped in one of the S-shaped chairs upholstered in bright yellow vinyl and tucked my feet under me. I glanced at the delft-blue and white Dutch clock that hung at the end of the upper cabinet. *It's almost time for my program to start.* Daddy had already looked over my homework. He'd given me an ultimatum in September when I started seventh grade, "You can't listen to any of your radio programs 'till you've finished all your homework." And that meant weekends, too.

Turning around, I reached over and turned the knob of the small, black rectangular-shaped radio that sat against the white tiled sink. I listened to the announcer extol the virtues of the product that sponsored the program, then the familiar deep, rolling laugh from Throckmorton P. Gildersleeve—*The Great Gildersleeve.* I smiled with pleasure and chuckled right along with him and squirmed to settle more comfortably in my seat, ready to be entertained for the next half-hour.

Suddenly to my annoyance, an unfamiliar, somber-sounding voice cut in with the announcement, "We interrupt this program to report the Japanese have bombed Pearl Harbor." The program came back on and I was able to catch up on the plot of the story as it continued.

Again, there was the announcement, "We interrupt this program to report the Japanese have bombed Pearl Harbor."

The broadcast resumed, but with the same intrusion continued. Soon, I'd lost the thread of the storyline. My twelve-year-old self-was irritated when the entertainment I'd looked forward to, was spoiled.

I reached over and turned off the radio, stomped out of the kitchen, and slammed the back door.

"Mama?" I queried, as I leaned over the metal railing on the back porch.

"I'm back here." Her voice came from behind the garage.

I scrambled down the cement steps to the driveway and walked along the path between the garage and the geranium-filled planter next to the patio.

When I rounded the corner of the garage, I spied her small frame, clad in a red-and blue-plaid button-down-the-front housedress, topped by a faded red sweater, a hedge against the chilly winter air. Her short-cropped, wavy dark brown hair ruffled slightly in the breeze that always seemed to blow through the space along the side of our garage. A wicker clothes basket at her feet was nearly filled with neatly folded towels topped by an assortment of white underwear and colored socks.

"Mama," I said, anxiously. "I was listening to *The Great Gildersleeve* and it kept being interrupted. The announcer kept saying the Japanese have just bombed Pearl Harbor. Are they going to bomb us?"

"No," she replied in a calm voice. She continued to pluck clothespins from the crisp, dry garments and drop them in the basket. "They're a long way away. We don't have to worry." She paused. In a convincing tone, she added, "They aren't going to bomb us here."

I walked back into the house reassured by her words. But still disgruntled I hadn't been able to enjoy my favorite Sunday program.

Little did I know—or understand—but the world had changed that day—that historic Sunday, December 7, 1941

Monday morning began as usual. Mother fixed oatmeal with raisins and brown sugar and a sliced banana. She was adamant that we needed to begin the day with a nutritious breakfast.

We ate together as a family in the cheery kitchen. Daddy finished first, then left to walk down the hill to Colorado Boulevard and take the streetcar. He worked in downtown Los Angeles, in the Planning and Zoning Department in the City Hall.

Mother packed our lunch pails and sent my younger brother, and me off to school: Bunky with his pal, Bob Lawhan, (both in the fifth grade) for Dahlia Heights Elementary School, while I made my way down the street to my best friend Phyllis' house. We were both in the seventh grade and walked together to Eagle Rock Junior/Senior High School on Yosemite Blvd.

This was December 8th—the day after the Japanese had bombed Pearl Harbor.

We arrived at school shortly before nine o'clock, when our first-period class started. We sauntered towards the entrance and stood at the fringe of a group of girls clustered there. One of them, Lois, was telling the others, "My mom's *really* upset. Yesterday, when she heard the Japs had bombed Hawaii she tried to reach my sister, who lives in Manilla. And she's been trying ever since."

Someone interrupted. "But it was Pearl Harbor that was bombed."

Tears glistened in Lois' brown eyes. "They also bombed Manilla."

I knew Pearl Harbor was in Hawaii but hadn't a clue about Manilla. In fact, I had only a vague idea where Japan was located.

In mid-morning, the principal, Miss Babson, called for an assembly. The combined junior and senior student body squeezed into the auditorium. She announced to the restive audience, "The United States has declared war on Japan." A hushed silence instantly descended over the gathering, like a sound-proof blanket. Not a foot shuffled. Not a whisper of clothing was heard. No one coughed. Nothing. No one moved. Then there was a collective gasp followed by scattered sounds of crying.

Hardly daring to move, I glanced furtively around and saw teachers dabbing their eyes as tears trickled down their cheeks. Others had their arms around some of the older girls holding them close while they sobbed. Even some of the older boys wrestled to maintain a "manly" stance and swiped vainly at escaping tears.

"Quiet. Please sit down. May I have your attention. Quiet," the principal implored, as she struggled to regain control. Finally, her pleas were heeded, and a modicum of silence returned to the now tense assembly.

She paused until quiet was restored, then continued. "To comply with safety regulations I received this morning, you can expect regular safety drills, and you may be directed to certain areas designated as bomb shelters. I'll be sending a note home with you today informing your parents of the measures the school will implement to ensure your safety."

Thank you for your attention. You are dismissed to go back to your classes. Please leave in an orderly manner."

We filed out, quiet and somber-faced—a contrast to the laughing, lively group who entered just a short time earlier.

Later, during the junior high lunch hour, Phillis and I were seated at a table outside, in the lunch quad. She looked over at me and asked, "Do you know *Patty Matthews? She's not in our class, she's still going to Dahlia Heights. But she lives near us, over on Dahlia Drive."

"No. I don't know her but I know who she is. What about her?"

"Well, she has two older brothers, one's a senior, and I think the other's a junior. Anyway, I heard her father's in the navy, and he was killed in the bombing yesterday in Pearl Harbor. Isn't that awful!"

I agreed. It was awful. But what does a twelve-year-old know about death? I did know it would terrible if it was my dad who had been killed.

This was just the first day of the United States' involvement in World War II. In the days that followed, there were many changes at school and school bus service was discontinued. All those affected had to take public transportation. There were no field trips. My friend Pat Bury, had to leave home very early in the morning to get to school since she came by bus and had to transfer several times.

The wood shop closed when the teacher was drafted. There was no one to replacehim.

Air raid sirens became a familiar sound. We ducked under our desks and huddled there with our arms over our head until the all-clear sounded.

Inter-mural sporting events: basketball, baseball, football, and track were discontinued. All large gatherings were discouraged.

"Victory Rallies" were held weekly on the steps of the cafeteria that faced the lunch quad to encourage us to buy defense saving-stamps. The denominations of stamps were: 10- and 25-cents and were sold to help fund the war. A full booklet was worth $18.75, the price of a $25 war bond.

Some of the older girls married before their boyfriends went into the service and were sent overseas.

My Social Studies period always incorporated current events. We perused the newspaper for maps relating to battles in Europe and the Pacific and gained a knowledge of geography from them. An understanding of United States history was acquired by learning about its past wars. And I soon learned the location of Manilla—and Japan.

The teachers and staff were zealous in their efforts to provide as traditional a school experience as possible. They sponsored varied recreational activities: dances and sock-hops in the gym, athletic competitions between juniors and seniors on the football field, music and drama productions in the auditorium, and classic movies.

Only the fondest recollections spark my memory of those high school days. On the other hand, perhaps this is due to the mellowing effect of the passing decades. Certainly, they were "different" when compared with those of the previous and following generations. However, to those of us who were teenagers during those war years, they were *our* normal.

The mid-August sun made squiggly patterns on the flagstone patio as a barely perceptible afternoon breeze fluttered the leaves of the elm tree that shaded it. I was engaged in my favorite summertime "activity"— stretched out along the length of the comfy patio swing, a few library books beside me, one read and one to-be-read, and another open to the mystery I was engrossed in. A small bunch of icy cold green grapes on a napkin sat atop my belly. Mechanically, my fingers reached for a grape and plopped it in my mouth. I savored the refreshing juicy fruit and sighed with pleasure.

Suddenly, I stopped reading, fingers poised mid-air about to pluck another grape from the bunch. I sat up, surprised to hear Daddy's excited voice getting louder as he walked up the driveway.

"Carol? Bunky? Where are you?" he shouted.

"I'm out here," I called back. "On the patio. What's wrong? You're home early—it's only 4:30."

"Nothing's wrong," he answered as he bounded up the steps. "Nothing's wrong at all. In fact, everything's all right." I saw the huge smile that lit his face and his blue eyes twinkled with happiness.

"The war's ended! *That's* what's all right! Now, where's your Mother?"

My brother came up beside Daddy and asked, "Hi, Daddy. What's wrong?"

Daddy, usually on the reserved side, beamed as he repeated the news to my brother.

"Let's find your mother. We're going downtown to celebrate. Tootie," (Daddy's nickname for her) he called as he turned and went into the house. "Tootie. The war's over! The Japs surrendered. Let's drive downtown to watch the festivities."

After a quick dinner, we headed off. What should have been a half-hour drive took over an hour. We saw jubilant people gathered on street corners shouting and flashing the V for Victory sign at the passing cars. In response, they slowed, honked and flashed their headlights while the riders gestured back. Daddy grumbled under his breath about "all the traffic," and later as we neared the downtown, mumbled to no one in particular, "I'd better look for a place to park where we wouldn't be blocked in. I don't want to sit in a parking lot all night."

Dusk was falling as the distinctive, white tower of the 27-story city hall, where Daddy worked, came into view. It towered above the other buildings downtown, an icon of Los Angeles.

"Oh, my gosh," I said as I viewed it against the backdrop of the darkening sky. "Look at the city hall. The windows are all lit up, and there are outside lights are shining on it again. Doesn't it look beautiful? Wow!"

"Look! There are lights in *all* the buildings downtown!" Bunky said, in awe. "I almost forgot what the city looks like, all lit up like that."

"It's been a long time," Daddy said. "Almost four years. It looks like the blackout's over." We drove a few blocks in silence, dazzled by the sight of our hometown illuminated once more.

Spotting an empty space in a parking lot within walking distance of the inner city, Daddy hurriedly pulled in. As we exited the car, bedlam surrounded us. There were people everywhere. Happy people—laughing and shouting and waving. They rang bells and blew noisemakers. They linked arms and danced on the sidewalk and down the street.

"Stay together," Daddy hollered above the din. He took Mother's arm and hooked it into his own. "Carol, take my hand—Bunky, you hold on to Mother. We need to stay together. If we get separated, we'll *never* find one another in this crowd."

Off we went, south down Broadway. Exhilarated, we melded into the melee of slow-moving, exuberant humanity. The crowd grew as it moved toward the heart of downtown—like tiny trickles of water that merge to become the rushing torrent of a thunderous river. Except this was a virtual wave of revelers that filled the street. I felt like I was absorbing the sights and sounds, the sheer energy that surrounded us.

The sidewalks teemed with merrymakers. They walked shoulder-to-shoulder and overflowed into the street. There was barely enough room in the middle of the street to allow passage of horn-honking vehicles that inched forward. They overflowed with shouting passengers wildly waving small American flags out of the open windows or making the V-for-Victory sign with outstretched fingers. Some belted off-tune songs at the top of their lungs as they toasted America's victory with raised bottles of beer or whiskey. Euphoric hangers-on balanced precariously on the running boards, and clung, like leaches, from their perch on the front and back bumpers.

In the buildings that lined the street, people leaned from open windows, waving and shouting and throwing handfuls of confetti that wafted downward in the balmy summer air like misplaced snowflakes.

Windows in some of the stores must have been broken, as a deafening clang of activated burglar alarms added to the cacophony. A few policemen stood nearby but seemed disinclined to do anything about the triggered alarms. I guessed they were probably only there to protect the compromised property from vandalism.

Strangers hugged and kissed one another. Daddy, ever watchful, protected me, his almost sixteen-year-old daughter, from the overzealous and amorous clutches of one obviously intoxicated merrymaker. He good-naturedly remarked as he peeled the man's fingers from my arm, "Go find yourself a girl your own age, young man." The rebuffed man complied without a word and stumbled into the surging crowd to find a more willing subject for his euphoric advances.

As we were pushed and shoved along, we watched with fascination a conga-line of hundreds of chanting, swaying dancers. Like a giant reptile, it undulated as it zigzagged its way back and forth across the jammed street. It wove between the revelry-filled vehicles that moved at a snail's pace, jockeying for space amidst the crush of people.

Groups of servicemen seemed the most boisterous. They shouted the loudest and grabbed any willing body, male or female, within arm's reach to bestow a bear hug and a smooch. A cluster of sailors whooped and hollered and threw their caps in the air, seemingly oblivious of the plainly identified, but grinning, shore patrol and military police scattered throughout the crowd.

Block after block we shuffled along jostled and drawn forward by the riptide of the citizenry. The push and shove finally became too great. Daddy managed to herd us around a corner and down a side street for a few blocks.

"It's time we head back to the car," he bellowed above the pandemonium. Mother nodded in fervent agreement.

Like salmon headed upstream, we shouldered our way north on Main Street until we reached the parking lot. Fortunately, our car wasn't hemmed in, as some were, by an illegally parked vehicle. Daddy unlocked the doors and we dropped wearily onto our seats.

"Well!" Daddy said with a deep sigh as we sat for a moment in the idling car. "That was quite a celebration."

"It sure was," Mother said, her voice sounding tired. "But I wouldn't have missed it for anything."

Bunky and I merely nodded in agreement. We were too worn out by the festivities to reply.

The war in Europe had ended in June. But this was the country's final victory, the end of the war in the Pacific, and we had celebrated with all the energy and passion we could muster. Looking back, it may also have been the zeal of a people ready to forge ahead into a world at peace—not one driven by war.

The year was 1945. During the intervening years, I've watched many events on TV, but nothing has generated the unequivocal emotion and joy that marked that occasion on August 14th.

Could it be because I was part of it?

The Story Ranch
By Amber Polo

THE CABIN WASN'T CHARMING or particularly cute, just a step up from ordinary. Didn't even look particularly lived in it. Her map indicated the Story Ranch was the only building in the vast Story Desert.

Rumors told her that burying her story would lift memories from her mind and heart. She'd be able to sleep and go on with her life. She hurried around to the back field. She wanted this over. She had to be rid of it.

Behind the cabin, she saw piles of soft dirt as if an army of gophers had advanced to attack the cabin. She couldn't falter now. Choosing a serviceable spade from an assortment of shovels, she began to dig in an untouched spot. The ground was hard. But no harder than she'd expected. Leaning her entire weight on her shovel, at last the blade broke the surface and she lifted out a scoop of brown sandy dirt. A few more shovelfuls and the hole was a foot deep.

She removed a think stack of papers from her bag, placed them in the hole, and smoothed them flat. Refilling the hole with a sigh, she stomped down the dirt, turned, and left with a step lighter than she'd felt in years.

~~~~~

A few hours after the woman left, a man walked into the field. Looking over his shoulder, he moved quickly, following what he called his Inspiration, took up his regular shovel, strode to the freshest mound of dirt, and uncovered the papers. Holding the sheets up, he shook off the remaining earth. There were few rules here, but the one that could not be broken was that once he touched the pages he couldn't put them back, nor could he return for a year and a day. But he'd learned to trust his first judgment and today as he scanned the first page, knew he'd chosen well. This woman's story would become a bestselling novel like all his others.

Stories have three parts: a beginning, a middle, and an end. And although this is the way all stories unfold, I still can't believe that ours didn't go on forever.
—Nicholas Sparks

Poetry Section

Funky Friend
By Dolores Comeaux-Everard

Funky Friend,
Fabulous, flamboyant, fluid.
Creativity oozes from her very fingertips,
Splashing colors, fabric, and fashion
Into designs that dazzle, daze and delight.

Funky Friend,
Hair tipped with tinsel
Nails bright deep red,
Shoes fantastic fuchsia begging an eye-
A fashion statement extraordinaire.

Funky Friend,
A Renaissance retro woman
Channels rainbow renditions
Of delight to tickle our palettes
For enlightened life and art.

Funky Friend.
Open to Divine Ideas of pleasure
Channeled from her Source of Being,
Gifting us with breathless beauty-
Art and song serenade us through her efforts.

Untitled
By Sherrie J. Lyons

Where are you, John?
I look into your eyes, searching for something I can recognize,
But the man I loved is gone.

You stand there at attention, gazing down at me,
Your back as straight as it can be,
Saluting an unseen commander,
Reliving the life you loved the best.
And I sit here in my wheelchair,
Saluting you for a job well done,
But needing you to be here—in *my* reality.

I am old, John. *We* are old.
My body has forsaken me, as your mind has forsaken you.
I would have preferred the opposite to be true.
Seeing your mind disintegrate over time
Has been the most painful thing that I have ever endured.
And I have suffered much pain, John. And endured. And endured.

Once, in another lifetime, we had each other,
And that was enough.
Now I am alone.
Even though you stand beside me,
You have abandoned me.
We vowed to stay together, " 'Til death do us part,"
But something worse than death has taken you from me.

I am tired, John. I am so tired.
I can no longer care for you,
And I no longer care for you.
You are not the man I loved.

Where is my John?
My John is gone.

A Wedding in Connecticut
By James Raymond Thacher

Has it already been
thirteen billion life years
since I've conceived this
image of you shimmering
walking down the aisle
of ten thousand universes
existing in an area as big as
a grain of sand held arm length out
in the pulsating hand of God
which is without a doubt
smaller and larger
taller and thinner
than anything I can perceive / than anything I can achieve
and can you believe / and two can believe
the size of that rock / this side of that rock
a diamond on a finger / door locked
your finger
touching mine
glowing in the dark of light
dressed in yellow
blessed in white
curtains drawn infinitely tight

The Wall
By Joe DiBuduo

I have learned sharks can live for four hundred years or more. It appears turtles live that long too, unlike humans who can't see any light after a hundred years have passed. I must ask "Why?"

Why, we have to die so soon? I don't have a clue why other creatures
live so many more years than we? I become afraid and scared when I
think about going through death's door. If I have a soul, where will it go?

What will I owe after all the years I've been here? There are so many worlds
out there that I like to believe we're here to train how to behave on the one
we'll go to when our spirit leaves our body here and ascends up there.

After we meet our end, will I comprehend, or twiddle my thumbs for fun while I
wait my turn for my soul to soar up to a planet chosen for me by the one
who sent me to live here? Once I go, I'll become an alien like him.

It's true; I believe God is an alien being, unlike you and me who are never free.
Where God came from, no one knows, but many suppose and believe what
the scriptures say, "God was here before the moon and stars."

God created Earth and everything in it, but he wasn't born in the USA, or anywhere
else on this world, so If I happen to see God, should I call the police or ask for his
green card because he's the one alien the wall can't keep out?

Chiropractor Engraving Scars on People's Backs
By Dan Dražen Mazur

I'd like to sigh my own air

And have my own precarity

If I was Hilary I would honestly reveal my sister's chest

So nobody would remember my scary face

I would try to look aside

So nobody would glimpse my eyes

If I was Hilary and a woman chiropractor

I would carve a long skinny scar on your back

So you will remember me by something else

And I would like to be seriously invisible

So nobody would have even a chance

To do bad things to me

You're never going to kill storytelling because it's built into the human plan. We come with it.
–Margaret Attwood.

My Maiden Aunt
By David Nicoll

Oh Lord, please let me not grow old the way my maiden aunt has done;
Her bitterness is uncontrolled—she takes it out on everyone;
And though she needs a helping hand to get her through her every day
She doesn't seem to understand she's driving everyone away.

Finding fault is her domain and she will likely misconstrue
My actions, and then she'll complain of every little thing I do.
My patience tried, I bite my tongue and contemplate what made her thus
Just what went wrong when she was young that made her so
cantankerous?

Sometimes I think that it must be because she can't control her life
She focuses on little needs and turns them into daily strife
Making helpers want to leave. So it's so hard to comprehend—
Despite the treatment we receive we keep on to the bitter end!

Oh Lord, my maiden aunt has died—I should be glad that she has gone.
I know in every way I tried to ease her life e'er she passed on.
It was not fun and by the end, while there's no need to wonder why,
She lost the chance to be my friend—a thing for her in scarce supply.

It seems to me when we depend upon another for our needs
It's better not to mar our end by biting off the hand that feeds!
I grieve that she has passed away and wonder why it matters so
But it is such a subtle grade, the line twixt love and duty owed!

Assault
By Brenda Whiteside

Being alone isn't so bad
Warm, cocooned in her bed.
She burrows deeper, chin tucked.
Satin-bound cover rests across her nose and cheeks.
Drawing her knees up to her chest, she tugs on her
nightgown
Until even her toes are tucked, snug under flannel.
Night is quiet,
A veil of stillness.
Gossamer navy darkness.
The faint glow of moon drips from the bottom of the
curtains.
Smiling into her pillow of night sensations, she
surrenders to slumber.
Half-sleep dreams fill subsiding consciousness.
Then a sound,
Where none should be.
Eyes wide peer into shadows.
Dark scarcely melts, reluctant to reveal shapes of insipid
hue.
Her breath catches on inhale.
She strains an ear on the void.
Her lips parted, body rigid.
The creak of the back-door hinge, then silence.
The deafening quiet drowns out her pounding heart.
Short gasps, clenching satin, crouched within covers,
She seeks more than warmth.
Impending footsteps,
Nameless intrusion looms.
Mouth dry, face hot, her chest aches from her
pummeling heart.
She prays for invisibility, prays to be shadow in
blackness.
Fear scrapes her throat, bathes her body in numbness.
She is no longer alone.

Desert Night by Firelight
By Bruce D. Sparks

Old wood we found in a wash, good for nothing but burnin'
Let's drag some in 'n make us a fire, start some old stories a churnin'

Friends and family all gathered 'round, feel alive as the embers glisten
Wind dies down but the fire burns on, and stories too good not to listen

Parts of our lives from a bygone age, kindled like old wash wood
Chilly winter night yet warm by fire's glow, times and tales so good

Put on another piece of old wood to burn, get us a blaze a goin'
Stir up those coals a bit, old pard, old wood and stories a glowin'

Tell a tall tale but don't you dare lie, we know the truth when we hear it
We want to be taken away for a while, stretch it and make us believe it

Cold desert night with a fire for our light, good food, good drink and good friends
Here we share the joys of the hunt, before the night comes to an end

These are good times that will end one day, we all have that for the learnin'
Gone soon the stories to tell 'round the fire, like the old wash wood we are burnin'

A poet can survive everything but a misprint.
—Oscar Wilde

Goldie's Love
By Sherrie J. Lyons

Like a Down-syndrome child, who try as she might
Just doesn't comprehend,
You look trustingly into my watery eyes
Thinking that I'm your friend

But what kind of friend sends prayers up to God
Begging for you to die?
And what kind of friend takes steps on her own,
Ignoring God's reply?

The tears that I shed are not for you—
They selfishly roll for me
For you'll move on, but I must remain
With the truth you do not see:

I never truly loved you, dog
Though I walked and groomed you and such
For I saw you as a ditzy pooch
Who'd never amount to much

A retriever that wouldn't chase a ball
Or swim or even wade
And couldn't learn to speak or shake
Just didn't make the grade

Still, I would have found a place for you
To grow within my heart
If only you'd done that simple thing
That was keeping us apart

The iceberg that loomed in front of me
Was your passive attitude
You never smiled and wagged your tail
To show your gratitude

So I didn't see that your heart was pure
Loving children; strangers; all
And I didn't see your love for me
From behind that monstrous wall

But I see it now in your clouded eyes
Through my salty, raindrop tears
As the vet awaits my signal nod
To end your fifteen years

I stroke your head one final time
And turn to look away,
But a tiny flicker catches my eye—
And I curse this beastly day

Dedicated to Goldie, age fourteen;
Not because it's true—but because it might have been . . .

Elegy for a Dying Planet
By David Nicoll

It may be inconvenient; the truth
And Al Gore's famous chart won't change some minds
For though his graphic rose to touch the roof
There's always those with attitudes enshrined.

The frozen North—the Pole—for what it's worth
Is now a summer route to distant shores
And snow-melt to the far side of the earth
Is quicker, cheaper passage than before.

Though icebergs break from ancient arctic sheets
And polar bears are stranded without snow
There's none so blind as those that will not see
Or deaf as those who do not want to know

Tornadoes blasting houses from their roofs
A swath of peoples' lives gets blown away
But climate change—though who could want for proof -
Is not the work of man, the skeptics say.

Records broken in the evening news
From New York City, down beyond The Keys,
Show hurricanes destroy familiar views
And most is lost by those who have the least.

Then California trembles as each shake
Could be the looked-for one that starts the fall
As earthquakes with Tsunamis in their wake
Show just how easily we lose it all.

We're faced with vital issues everywhere
And bumper-sticker wisdom says "Enough!"
As T-Shirts on a prudent group declare
"Don't trash the earth—it's where we keep our stuff!"

The sky is melting, shrinking, turning brown
And everywhere you look we're on the skids.
Our common global house is breaking down.
"Preserve the world—it's borrowed from our kids!"

What is Love?
By Darlis Sailors

LOVE is fragile,
Like a flower in bloom.
Nurture it carefully,
Let it grow.

LOVE is challenging,
Like a trail in the woods.
Explore it slowly,
Discover its joy.

LOVE is valuable,
Worth effort and time.
Invest it thoughtfully,
Reap the rewards.

LOVE is emotional,
Up, down, twirled around.
Buckle your seatbelt,
Risk the ride.

LOVE is sharing,
Both laughter and tears.
Open your heart,
Widen your world

Sweet Nothings
By James Raymond Thacher

As old as the ocean
Violin
This memory
I have
Of you
And the waves
Rolling in
On a vibrating
String
Of wind
And this
Thing
Called love
All Einstein
Eon
Sand
And science
Dissolving
In defiance
Reforming
The way weigh words
Written
On a fogged bathroom mirror
Are good
For remembering
Sweet nothings
Floating
On a stream
Of subconscious
Ionic
Extreme

Unfit
By Joe DiBuduo

I supposed you were the only one under the sun, who would rather die than cheat or lie, but like all the others you found a way to make me believe. Like me, you aren't worthy of love.

Even though I know that's how you are, I want to believe it's not true,
I try to accept as accurate that you'd be truthful, but I know that will never
be, because you want someone younger than me before your life is through.

I understand, and I search above and below for another too. It doesn't matter to me, just so she's younger and prettier than you. I have a need for love I can't have.
So, if my feelings for you were returned, you'd be spurned, and I'd soon
tire and dispose of a woman so senseless she could love a man like me.

Unlike you I'm the perfect one to avoid because I can never return what
you feel because that's the way I am, and love isn't programmed into my
DNA, unless it's for a dog or a cat.

I can love an animal like that, but never a woman like you for more than a day or two. Behind your façade you're as unfaithful as
a Bonobo and desire whiskey and sex like a lioness in heat.

Loving you isn't worth all the pain I'd feel in the days that remain.
My life is only a dream where someone like you is faithful to me and make
all my pains go away, but we know that'll never be, because like
you, for love,
I'm unfit.

Paper Child
By Shirley Willis

The paper child goes to Paper-Ruled School.
She sits in the corner, sorting paper cards at the little table, her
fingers long like a pianist, candle tapered.
She smiles her half-flirt, half-hurt smile.

The seven consultants consult at their big table,
coffee cups flashing,
pencils lashing,
their presentation smashing
for each other.
They can't say "retarded—retarded from birth."
They can say, "PDD/NOS,
Pervasive
Developmental
Delay
Not
Otherwise
Specified. PDD/NOS."

Her future is bleak, that child in the corner at the little table, life
compressed to initials.
She could be running.
Swinging.
Singing.
Touching blades of grass with candle-slim fingers.
Lighting the world with skyward smiles
Instead, she moves meaningless symbols where she won't
bother other learners.

At the big table by the window, the consultants seek words for the
non-verbal child—words for
parents
and peers.

It's best," they say,

"for Sarah to sit, to sort colors,
to match numbers while we consult."

Sarah sits. Not bothering anyone but herself.
The consultants use reams of paper in order to not say
retarded.

They only treasure
what can be measured—their shiny hubcaps of tiny
learnings

They count progress in decimals,
not seeing the child in corner who yearns to touch, to run .
Sarah's motor idles joy. Her fingers reach for data instead of the real
girl.

Sarah speaks.
No one hears.

The consultants squeak at each other and,
in their astuteness, they describe the child's muteness.
Their presentation shines
for each other.

The child soils herself.
Shifts in her chair.
That, the consultants hear.
They mark their charts.
The child has met the day's expectation.
Only one clothing change today.

Paper success. Paper child.

Friend
By Mike Doyle .

. .to all my friends with love, Mike

I whispered your name as I awoke
I saw you in a dream
We were hiking up a mountain trail
Along an alpine stream.
The odd thing was
I wasn't sure
Just who you really were
And yet, I felt I knew you
From another place…
Sometime before.
I turned around,
looking down
To see where the water flowed
A sleepy hamlet down below
With stories…
yet untold.
I looked back up
And you were gone.
Where?
I didn't know.
And so I thought
Keep hiking on
to the source
of the waters flow.
It was a blissful place,
so serene,
Impossible to believe.
I felt I was
in a state of grace
I didn't want to leave.
And that was when
my big fat cat
Landed on my chest
As he leapt
from the windowsill
ME-owing

"feed me! get up! get dressed!"
Obedient cat-dad that I am,
I did as I was told.
Then I showered, shaved
On my way to work
Wondering
how my day would unfold.
I was sitting in traffic
Lost in my reverie,
Stitching together
Fragments of my dream.
Then the car behind me
honked its horn
The light had turned to green.
A gulp of coffee, NY strong
Jolted me awake
Now, armed and ready to right the wrongs
And to deal with the day's fate.
It's 5 O'clock
The work day's done,
I'm on my way back home
Suddenly, my dream
sprang back to life.
With a mind all its own
My head was flooded
with thoughts of you
as a wave washed over me
tossed and turned and upside down
very much like a tsunami.
And then it all became crystal clear.
I realized just who you were.
You are every friend
That I ever knew
Of that, I'm very sure.
You are Bryan, Diane, Carol D
Jimmy, Meg, Ray and Joe Ali.
A montage of faces
From distant places
alive within my brain
It's the memories of all of you

That helps to keep me sane.
Many of you are still here,
Some of you are long gone.
I hope that you
who have gone before
can guide us from beyond.
Just by being whom you are
Has made me rich beyond all measure
Yes, you are a guiding light
and your friendship
I will always treasure.
If perchance, when I dream tonight
I hope to find you
near that crystal stream.
And if I don't,
I'll again search tomorrow
In another realm of my dreams

Poetry on the Runway
JamesRobert Platt

The prestigious literary review announced its upcoming literature festival, and promoted a featured author's scheduled appearance and credentials: *Poet, Instagram star and model.*

Once upon a time we saw Hollywood stars, TV stars, and sports' stars; some folks long ago amazingly looked to the heavens to find stars. Apparently, our star search has become unlimited, and less intense. Stars are discovered and declared everywhere (far too many being self-proclaimed). Now we have Reality Show stars (let's keep on script, please), Op-ed Talking Head stars (making me believe in fake news), YouTube stars, Twitter stars, and not to be ignored or under-marketed—Instagram stars.

Exactly how trite has stardom become? Is there no longer a need, a place, for simple hardcopy poetry publication, paying your dues, or possibly learning to write (excuse me, tweet) using more than 140 or 280 characters? How about having to actually "pen" a lyric line? Today, would Emily Dickinson, Robert Frost, e. e. cummings, and Sylvia Plath be texting while catwalking a fashion runway, followed by posting original poetic compositions (plus photos, of course) on their websites and blogs? Is the look or the book what's important?

It must be the number of "friends" and "hits" that matters; or is it the number of friends you hit? (Poetry should always come at you hard!) My cynicism is probably unfair. Yes Heraclitus, I know, change is the only constant. It's just that the writers that I respect, read, and purchase, describe themselves as poets—period. Any resume embellishments may include novelist, playwright, storyteller, activist, teacher, student, parent, or anarchist. Not celebrity; not star. Clearly, my own social-networking aptitude was sidestepped at the passing of the previous century. Perhaps there actually was a Y2K millennium bug. (I do vaguely remember feeling somewhat ill on New Year's Day 2000.)

My rambling discourse leaves me wondering if even I could become a world-renowned star (I mean poet). But I'm left to ponder how much weight my work might really have. A gram? (Which equals 0.035274 ounce.) Upon reviewing my poetry (and my looks), maybe a gram is fitting for a star that truly would shine only for an instant.

Temp's Lament
By Sherrie J. Lyons

Consigned as relief to understaffed places
Prepared to change jobs on a daily basis
You try to look and perform your best
Outwardly smiling, inwardly stressed

Wherever the job, it's always the same
Your badge bears a number—never your name
Your training consists of one or two tries
The desk you're assigned has been stripped of supplies

The copy machine is an albatross
When questions arise, you can't find your boss
You can only make calls from a special phone
And when lunchtime arrives, you eat alone

As the days wear on, you start to fit in
You're thankful not to move on again
But you're barred from training, meetings, reviews—
You're always the last to hear vital news

Then after weeks of working late
Just when you think things are going great
Down comes the final indignity
The ultimate corporate malignity

Of being "released" with no explanation
No handshake, no "thank you," no personalization
Disposed of like trash thrown out on the street
You take a day off to climb back on your feet

Then ignoring foreknowledge of what to expect
And suppressing the pain of lost self-respect
You move on to another similar place
Recycled again, with that same smiling face

Poetry is language at its most distilled and most powerful
—Rita Dove

Portulaca
By Maureen Norcross

she gathered us when
we were full of the future
saving for another season
to greet all
with exclamation of life
receiving with sweet smiles

we take our time
we are tiny seeds
with aspirations
to glow with blooms
exploding with fanfare
to greet your eyes
for another season of color

we are planted with watchful eyes
we are tendered with care
we send forth our flowers
till it's time to gather once again.

I want to encourage women to embrace their own uniqueness. Because just like a rose is beautiful, so is a sunflower, so is a peony. I mean, all flowers are beautiful in their own way, and that's like women too.
—Miranda Kerr

Peonies
By Maureen Norcross

white with a strike
of dark wine
dashing through
the snowball

heavenly
fragrance
feathered with
angel kisses

Poetry can be dangerous, especially beautiful poetry, because it gives the illusion of having had the experience without actually going through it. —Rumi

Child's Play
By David Nicoll

Provide a child a box of bricks
And see him make a pile
Then hear him chuckle as he makes
His pyramid collapse and break
And clatter on the tile.

Give a child a rubber ball
To throw across the floor.
He laughs with glee at once because
A throw which uses little force
Comes bounding off the wall.

Observe a boy with stones and rocks
In some neglected place.
He picks a grimy window-frame
And takes it out with just one aim -
To leave an empty space.

And thus it goes from boys to men
The pleasure's still the same.
A pyramid of empty cans,
And bottles broken in the sand,
Upon the desert range.

Or later, shooting at the club
He practices his skill
The most effective way he can
Destroy the outline of a man
If he has need to kill.

Give a man a gun that fires …
Five shots a second should suffice …
To fill the empty outline in
And decimate a human life.

To chuckle as they hit the floor
Delighted that such little force
Will knock them down and leave their lives
In pieces on the floor.

Three Examples of English Haiku
By Mark Wenden

5-7-5 Syllabic Form

Haiku I

I cannot be lost
When all roads have the same name
I'm always right here.

Haiku II

≈≈≈

Silently speaking.
Unearthed ancients testify
Present will be past

Haiku III

≈≈≈

Hydrangea lovely
in rain, dream of a sun-kissed
moment before death.

Her Mom
By Pat Fogarty

On Sundays cluttered halls
play host to warm metal meal bins
sitting idle while vile
canvas laundry baskets vex
harried nurses pushing locked
narcotic carts stocked to
sedate strident clients who
behave like craving addicts

That Sunday her mom leaves
with my bride holding the hand
that wiped her childhood tears
and walked her to school
and punished and protected
and was all that mattered
to the daughter who could not
let go of the woman she lost

That Sunday my words fell
like futile bombs on numb
ears that shutout the muttering
promises of a well meaning
groom who like a callous fool
begged his bride to refrain and
to compose and to be calm and
to cease her niggling babble

This Sunday at Serenity Hills
another daughter weeps and
another daughter begs and
another daughter prays and
another daughter pleads and
another daughter cries for
a mother whose love and loss
will sear her heart forever

Making Wine for Tryion Lannister
By Janice Shanks

These are flora,
fragrant grapes,
minuscule purple, black as a bruised eye.
Small grapes, ripe, a vintage for a tiny man with large hands.
My small hands pluck each blue berry off its stem
and drop each broken skinned orb
into the wooden barrel,
sending up a rare perfume.
This task is endless,
plucking each bead on the rosary,
revealing spring green pulp,
leaving stained fingertips, inked cuticles, pruned skin.
Lifting another bunch from the vat,
nimble fingers journey up the river of amaranthine nectar,
working each bunch of prayers,
breathing violets and cloves.
Small hands roll grapes off the stems,
fermenting in seconds.
In yonder times Tyrion drank
this rich magenta wine
to excess.
Large hands cupped his goblet.
Tiny man had his fill,
then sought revenge after the drunkenness,
killed his own,
and took up his manly journey.
Broken and sober
he now seeks his allies clearheaded,
shrugging the haze of waste.
As I perch on a lowly stool,
plucking,
thinking of him unleashed,
I wonder
what alliances,

what strength and power,
what courage will this valiant prince
allow himself?
Will he, the victor, sit on the Iron Throne
drinking my vintage?
Dare he lift the chalice
to honor my people?

"Don't use the phone. People are never ready to answer it. Use poetry." —Jack Kerouac

The Cast
By Pat Fogarty

Father, in our living room, I remember reading
"The Lady or The Tiger" to my siblings.
In our kitchen, mother inhales a deep breath
and wipes her brow with a worn dish towel.
Then, like magic she prepares a meal
fit for your majesty.

It's payday and you are late again.
The wall clock ticks away the minutes.
And panic, like a spreading virus, soaks the air.
A door slams and I keep reading.
You stagger towards the trail of my voice.
Your shoes pound like war drums.
Your little girls behave like frightened kittens.
They squiggle and squirm with no place to hide.
Your angry eyes stare and your daughters scatter.
Then, for no reason at all, you charge at me.

I tremble and wriggle as far away as I am able.
My arms rise over my head.
My legs pull up towards my small chest.
And, as your fist strikes my young knee,
I feel the punch and I hear your scream.
But, your broken hand and the agony in your face
delivers a strange comfort to my young mind.
And today, a half century later, I still wonder
What did you tell your friends?

Weather's Role
By Sherrie J. Lyons

I want to be a millionaire
The gestating woman proclaimed on the air
'Orange' is the fruit with vitamin C
My final answer's decidedly 'D.'
And so, she continued to play the game
But the more she won, the less brash she became
'Haboob'? . . . 'Tsunami'? . . . I just don't know . . .
But I'm sure the answer is not 'Big Blow.'
I'd like to phone a friend of mine.
Sure, the host said, It's your last life-line.
Who's the friend you'd like to call?
Her name is 'Dot Com,'—she's a know-it-all.
Dottie, my friend, the question's on weather.
I hope that your mojo is all together.
By jinkies, Christine, our connection is bad
It's starting to sprinkle and thunder like mad.
I think we're in for a cyclone, my dear—
I'm sorry Christine—I simply can't hear.
'Cyclone' Dot said! That's letter 'A'
And good fortune shined on Christine that day.

Simplicity is the glory of expression.
—Walt Whitman

Time
By Susan Grant Fogarty

Our Past
Never returns
Our Today
Never leaves
Our Tomorrow
Never comes
Our Eternity
Never ends

The life of the dead is placed in the memory of the living.
—Marcus Tullius Cicero

Mia
By Susan Grant Fogarty

You were . . .
The sole redhead to capture my heart
Who knew you would leave me so soon
You were my shadow and comfort
At times of stress or sadness
On that dark day we said goodbye
Emptiness filled my heart
Tears flowed like a dam had broken
Part of me went with you
The moment you crossed over
The Rainbow Bridge

"We cannot tell the precise moment when friendship is formed. As in filling a vessel drop by drop, there is at last a drop which makes it run over; so in a series of kindnesses there is at last one which makes the heart run over."
—Ray Bradbury

So long, Tami
By Sherrie J. Lyons

So long as you are alive
I want to be part of your life:
To chat with you over the phone
To sit with you alone—or not—
In a car or at a restaurant
At my house or at a park
Anywhere your spark
Flames or flickers or faintly glows
Because my heart knows
That your life fuels my life.

The smile in your voice brightens my day
Your sunny spirit shows me a way
To live my life better
And whether or not I achieve this end
I can't thank you enough for being my friend
For so long, Tami—forty years or more—
And no matter what life holds in store
I'll always feel blessed
Because you possess
A warmth that can't pass away.

Dedicated to Tami Knapp (1959-2017)

Tetter
By James Robert Platt

Voicemail beckoned. I listened to the
message from my little sister, her love and
best wishes to one and all. And then the news,
the news she knew I would sadly need to hear:
"Jim Tetter has died."
A brief, brave, cancer battle ending just a few days
past Christmas, before the rest of us celebrated a
fresh start, time's annual rebirth. My niece and Jim's
daughter are friends, another bond from adolescence.
Without pause, I phoned my youngest sibling.

I last saw Jim when I attended the Junior Miss Pageant
at our old high school. A wonderful program which
showcased the talents of Jim's daughter and my niece.
I spotted him on the stage after the final curtain,
embracing and praising his child. A proud father,
happy husband . . . and rightfully so. Climbing
the stairs, I walked toward him with extended hand,
calling his name and announcing mine, re-introducing
myself across the aged planks, decades of separation.
Smiles, congratulations, small talk,
brief reminiscences, and laughter.
The handshake goodbye.

Living on the opposite side of the continent, I never saw,
nor spoke to, Jim again. My sister's words awakened
the memories of youth; both of us stirred to melancholy.
He was a frequent visitor, in and out, going through our
parents' house. I winced, certain I felt the body aches
we long ago inflicted on each other, playing tackle football
on the perfectly manicured grass of Green's Farm. When
he got wheels, I hitched rides with him to school, sharing
early morning glee club, history, English, study hall, and
last-period music class. Jim advancing above my poor
trumpeting to become the master tuba/sousaphone player

of the high school marching band.
Graduation.
Each life's road veering its own course.
He stayed rooted; I became a vagabond. Jim hired me
once as a summertime security guard at the local department
store. A generous gesture to a struggling college friend
by the up-and-coming assistant manager. Later, boots on,
he served. The army, Korea, eventually returning to family
and finding his place, pleasure, and career, completing his
appointed rounds for the Post Office in our hometown.
I headed west.
Today, my sister's call, her heart draped at the outset.
The holidays had brought the loss of her dear cat, "Biscuit."
An abandoned tabby kitten she rescued from the dumpster
near her office, more than fourteen years ago. Jim's passing
encircled tearful days. And yet, this season also gave my sister
the joy of grandchildren, being able to steal their magic.
Somehow there is balance.
As we talked, my thoughts rewound to New York City. Not
the traditional wild New Year's Eve celebration, but the
Easter vacation taken by two seventeen-year-old schoolboys,
alone—no chaperon. My first plane trip was to the Big Apple.
My first hotel stay and skyscraper elevator ride were in
Manhattan. My first visit atop the Empire State Building, the
Statue of Liberty, the sidewalks of Times Square, and my only tour
negotiating the corridors and assembly hall of the United Nations.
Two teenagers sitting in a studio audience watching the filming
of Allen Funt's (and Durward Kirby's) television show, impatiently
waiting for the TV camera to scan our faces and hear Allen shout:
"Smile, you're on Candid Camera!"

The first great adventure of my life.
Jim Tetter and I.
No reservations, no concrete plans. Too young to get into
the bars, and into trouble. That is why my father said yes
over my mother's protests. That is why a couple of small-town
boys returned conquering heroes with exaggerated tales and
gaudy Batman ties. A feat unmatched even by our school's elite—
the athletes, the cheerleaders, the moneyed, and the in-crowd
Me and Jim.

A memory that has survived a lifetime and binds me to him now,
and forever. Jim, you helped set in motion the urge to travel,
to move about, to explore and experience beyond our backyard.
To try new things despite fear, and often common sense.
You were there when a door opened, and I would not let it close.
Thank you, friend. Godspeed.

lost years find comfort
knowing kindness defies death—
good deeds (and men) last

Hunting Turtles
By S. Resler Nelson

Beneath overhanging ledges of foliage
And unclear rippling of clear water,
Turtles hide in muskrat caves.

My brother and I,
With long hooked poles,
Like blind men, feel the dark river banks.

My pole thuds against a log,
Heavy and solid,
Then cracks
On the turtle with the bounce of a ripe watermelon.

I snag his shell and pull his clawing body
Into the sun.
His head rolls, snapping the air as if he knew
About the dark, musty barrel on the back porch…

Where he'll be kept alive
On buttermilk and flies until the junkman
(Who deals in various other things)
Comes to buy our catch.

"With me poetry has not been a purpose, but a passion."
—Edgar Allan Poe

City Corn
By Pat Fogarty

Carefully tap tap tapping in
time counting silent steps in
his mind a red tipped cane in
hand and hurrying to buy corn

While traffic horns blare in
ears tuned to scary sounds in
alleyways teeming with rats in
garbage chewing on rotten corn

In a ghetto of foreigners living in
a place where no one can speak in
his native tongue he stands mute in
serenity at a red light corner for corn

Gentle hands petition his elbow in
gratitude he steps yet feels a sigh in
pity from this giving stranger who in
no way perceives of his quest for corn

Proves acceptance belies all faith in
others to shrink by an utterance in
foolish compassion for a man in
a rush to purchase perfect corn

With money he knows the sign in
a window states in six languages in
God we trust all others please pay in
cash and no checks permitted for corn

The man swings a white stick in
an arc intending to hit a hydrant in
front of his greengrocer his dealer in
an early summer harvest of sweet corn

An accented clerk places produce in
a canvas bag and says thank you in
English to a man tipping his hat in
reply and heads out with his corn

Home to a roach infested apartment in
a neighborhood with blind people in
every tenement watching others in
distrust without a handful of corn

From fire escapes stoops and roofs in
kitchen sinks tenement faucets leak in
soot filled ash cans along cellar walls in
tubs of rubbish rodents feast on dead corn

Poetry is thoughts that breathe, and words that burn.
—Thomas Gray

Earth, Wind and Fire
By C.L. Lynne

Sputtering jolts disrupt a day
where calm began.
Windows rattle, shelving shakes—
Treasures fall and figurines break

Hearts beat faster;
dishes tremble
pulsating ground, machine-gun sound.
Land rebelling, land releasing

Calm again where gentle wafts of air
distinct as branches sway
with leaves a jiggle,
Whoosh and wiggle.
Zephyrs ascend

until drifts of smoke emerge
from orange glow, crackling flames
flurry and grow
to burning furor—

Consuming brush and dry debris
into rhythmic inferno, diminishing
upon hydration and chemical warfare.
Rage is overpowered in defeat.

Trying to Explain
By Bruce Paul

Standing on a highway,
Riding on a train,
Trying to understand,
Trying to explain.
There are many ways to be alone.
Listen to the wind whisper and moan.

A crazy riddle:
The windowpane—
Caught in the middle—
Was broken in vain.
There are many ways to be alone.
Listen to the wind whisper and moan.

The man in the moon
And I never know
Why some die,
Why some grow.
Lost in the moment,
We find what we need,
And—truth or lie—
We plant every seed.

I stood on a highway,
She rode on a train,
Unable to understand,
Unable to explain.
There are many ways to be alone.
Listen to the wind whisper and moan.

Beggar
By Elaine Jordan

His hand extends
For a coin
A veteran
Head shaved
Stalks me
Among candies
And toasted corn
In the Juarez market
His American eyes
Raging
At my prosperity.

Combat boots drum
Entreaties
Spilling succulence
Ripe with nothing
I need.
He shouts
I hope
You'll find yourself here
Some day
A curse from Hell
For a Christian tourist.

Frantic guitar
Blasts of brass
Mock my scurry
A guilty lizard
Hiding between stalls
Safe behind
Piles of golden mangos
Mounds of chilies
Baby iguanas tied with ropes.

Acrid odor of urine
Drenches my heart
While Jesus
Begs for deliverance
With desperate hand.

Virture of Verde
By C.L. Lynne

Land of freshness
vast and blessed,
where junction of
earth and sky surround

Small brush on
gentle inclines—
a winding highway
leads to iron profusions

Where roundabouts and
populous now preside,
yet beauty speaks
and thrives

Since nothing manifest
from man
can ever override
this pure domain

Men
By Sherrie J. Lyons

What is it about a distressed woman
That compels a man to make promises
That he has no intention of fulfilling
That he hopes will fade with time
And be forgotten in three months or six
But when she doesn't forget, he ignores
the gift, and the mail, and oh
why did she have to call today, his first
day back from a trip?

What is it about this distressed woman
that draws from him
sworn secrets?
The desperation in her voice?
The vehemence that drives her soul?

I do not despise you for reneging
Nor do I harbor hard feelings
For you tried and you failed
But the more important is that you tried
And I also tried and failed
So we are a pair of unlikely
bedfellows
Or perhaps we are only human

Ode to My Old Roman Nose
By Carolyn Jones

As far as I know
all humans have noses. We use them to smell garlic and roses.
Essential to breathe, fresh air is the best—
no pollutants to clog one's nose or chest.
Tempting it may be
to see what can fit in those tiny chambers just north of the lip.
Neither BB's nor peas nor Halloween candy
should be stored in your nose, no matter how handy.
Told not to pick it—
you secretly do, in lots of places you think out of view.
But it's better to blow, and <u>please</u> use a hanky!
They come in all colors, some rather swanky.
Bugs flying about,
without detection, can enter the nose—lead to infection.
You try every cure bandied about,
including the ones you snort up your snout.
Your poor schnoz reddens—
it doubles in size. It throbs when you blow and you agonize.
With tissues nearby, you dab every drop
and wonder aloud, *Will this ever stop?*
Straight-edged or sloping,
bent like a ski-jump. Flat as a pancake—reshaped by a fist-bump.
Beak-like or bulbous, fleshy or pointed,
no matter its shape, we're STILL disappointed!
Cyrano once thought
his nose a real blight. He feared the ladies would not treat him right.
Cursed with that honker, he didn't pursue
the lovely Roxanne he wanted to woo.
Standards of beauty
change over time; a hook in one's bill was once thought sublime.
But these days you're teased…as happened to me,
so I changed my look with rhinoplasty.
The irony is

I now understand, my old Roman nose was really quite grand—
and beauty that's of the physical kind—
it's soon surpassed by one's spirit and mind.
So, friend if you have
a nose that's freaky, it's better than one that's always leaky.
Remind those who jest, and poke fun at you,
what's given is got…goes right back…*ah-choo!*

My Special Friend
By Kaya Kotzen

I want the wind to carry me out into the universe when I'm gone.
I want it to blow my ashes around mountains and into streams.
I want it to sweep me inside of the base of a mesquite tree
and up into its center so that I could be part of the dancing branches
that I always see, that are so very magical to me.

I want the freedom of the wind to blow my restlessness away,
to carry my fear away from my being along with any doubts.
I want it to blow me across oceans and to
hold up the planes that I ride in while I cross the vastness of
countries that I long to see.

I want my writing to flow like the wind across the page with
no punctuation or capital letters.
I want to not care how it looks, only how it sounds.
I want the wind to breathe words into my soul for the things
I don't have language for yet so that I can share them all.

I want to discover and uncover so much of the world I have not yet
seen.
Would that the wind could levitate my body when I become tired
or my legs and feet sore that I can still carry on.

I ask the wind not to blow chairs off my porch or damage my home
while I'm gone, this summer, but rather be like an aura of protection
around it,
swirling gently and lovingly to protect it from storms and heat.

I would ride the wind like a stallion if I could,
saddled and holding on to the horn for dear life
as it galloped through the sand.
Like the whale rider, I would become one with it
and trust where it took me into places unknown

The wind is a woman,
constantly changing, softly caressing, and
carrying me forward in this life.
I want her to hold me up as my body ages and let the feel of her
remind me of when I was once young without a care in the world,
with grasshoppers for daily pets,
remembering the time when I'd find lightening bugs in the dark at nite,
when fears of the forbidden and strangers
had yet to be thrust into my face,
causing me to both wonder and rebel at the world I lived in.

The wind blows away worries, and welcomes my dreams,
supports my intuition, and embraces me when I need her
in the dark of the early morning when I walk my dog.

The wind is a gift and a welcome friend.
I invite her to be a part of all my days.

Cyberspace with Sleepytime Tea
By James Raymond Thacher

I'm tired of contemplating
Myself
This Earth
Those stars
The universe
Accelerations
Spinning in my head
Intergalactically wired into
You
And everything
We have been through
As beings do
I'm tired
In reverse
Crickets
Peep toads
Highway traffic
Buzzing by
Across the Magellanic sky
My meandering eye
Driving fast forward
In hypothetical statement
Imperatives in a net
Compromised
Of categorical probabilities
Commanding
I close my mind
Shut down
Go to sleep
As I am bound
To do

Not in weakness
Not in strength
In fact
That I am
Wired
Intergalactically
Into you

Tornado
By Carol Bolinski

Its bad tempered fingers
reach out, whip
counterclockwise,
then knead the earth
twirl it around
and drop debris
into the hands
of prayer.

Eclipse 2017
By Carol Bolinski

It was so brief
so fast
so very very far away

walking on half moons
the anticipation more exciting
than the actual event

but after the darkness
a sliver of light
beamed some hope, that
the world would be right again

Heartbroken
By Bruce Paul

Who gets lost in romance,
After the wine and the candlelight
And the last slow dance?
Who gets lost in romance?
It breaks my heart to think about it,
But I've been heartbroken before.

And who gets hurt in love,
After the last sacrifice
And the last flight of the dove?
Who gets hurt in love?
It breaks my heart to think about it,
But I've been heartbroken before.

Disappointment and betrayal—
Turmoil at every turn.
We study every detail,
But do we ever learn?
Do we ever learn?

And who gets killed in war?
Christians, Muslims, and Jews.
Is there any hope anymore?
Tell me, who gets killed in war?
It breaks my heart to think about it,
But I've been heartbroken before.

Vaquero Solitario
By Bill Lynam

I'm a vaquero, amigo.
My name is Juan Prospero.
I live down the street from
you, but you can't see me.

You look off into the hills,
The Bradshaw's, from your deck,
but you can't see the barbed-wire
and the extent of *el rancho*.

All you can see is mesquite, Alligator juniper,
Ponderosa pine, scrub, gamma grass, the silhouette of the hills.
Look closer amigo, there's a man on a horse,
he's rounding up strays, its auction time.

There're 300 head wandering the bush,
down in the ravines, not far up the slopes.
They like the draws where water ponds,
and grass grows better in the catchment.

There's a bunkhouse out there, behind the big house.
Me and two other vaqueros tend *el rancho,*
We mend fence, deliver calves,
look for sick steers, and put out licks.

We get to go home, *hogar,* once a year--
Guatemala, Mexico, San Salvador.
Mostly, we go to Western Union, that is
our peso connection to home, *hogar*.

Mi espousa y los chicos
go to the store every month—no mucho dinero.
She keeps chickens and maize and trades
with the cow farmer--milk for *los ninios*.

Mi caballo, my horse, only speaks en espanol.
He talks to me, we sing the old songs, *la concion,*
together. No giddiup, it's "hi, *arriba, arriba*"
He came with me in his trailer from home*, hogar*
He is my only love here.

The Mole People
By Jude Crump

Under the damp clay soil live families of moles
Not for them, the arid earth of the desert
Thirty-four years living just above their burrows
Amidst forests of fir and fields thick with ferns
Never having left these places encased in fog
The valley rife with pollens and mold spores

Chronic grey cloud cover
Holding fast its coveted position
Moving ever inland to cross from the Pacific yet
Unable to scale the higher Cascades
Cities and towns trapped in dismal light

Moss encroaches ten months of the year
On roofs and the dark side of houses
Mold claims the interiors of unheated buildings
Finding no relief month after month
The dampness infiltrates aching arthritic joints
People turn inward or lash out

Cold creeps around the edges of me
Seeking entrance through the fibers of my clothing
Until neck deep in a steaming tub and slowly, slowly
The cold driven from the marrow of my bones
Leaving only flushed and wrinkled skin

Engines groaning, the plane lifts skyward
On my first flight away from moles
I see only grayness through the window
And tiny droplets skittering over windowpanes
Hopelessly blank like an empty screen
I settle back in my seat, expecting nothing more

The gray mass wicked away now
We are soaring high over a downy white quilt
The valley of green no longer visible
A spirited sun reigns over clear turquoise sky
Eyes smarting from the brilliance of it

The only home I've ever known and yet there is
The world, replete with sun drenched places
Long forgotten by valley residents with umbrellas
Awareness now settling as a soft cloak around my shoulders,
I was never intended to be one of the Mole People

The Conductress
By Janice Shanks

lifting her hand, fingers motion for softness
music up
strings and keys
begin her symphony
she sees beyond the things
she's seen
dreams beyond the dreams
she dreams
lifting her head, eyes in signal and approval
tones sound
brass and skins
concerto in fullness
she hears more music
than an ear can hear
she feels more rhythm
than a heart can bear
lifting her arms, batons swing the tempo
hypnotic expression
notes and chords
melody transcends us
to the places of
brightness
sadness
comfort
peace
at a crescendo
we travel back
lift our hands and hearts
the music will linger into the night
the songs will ride home with us
because the conductress
so fine tuned
orchestrated it just so

and even though it seemed
it was over
a flick of the wrist and a downward move
and the music ends
it never does

Genuine poetry can communicate before it is understood.
—*T. S. Eliot*

All Things Must Die
By Joe DiBuduo

You have a soul you know.
I agree and say, I have two, not one
and point to the bottom of my shoes.
Not those soles you fool echoes intimately inside my skull.
A fist grips my heart and the beat suddenly stops.
Now that you're dead, you can see where your soul resides
echoes throughout my corpse with a still functioning brain.

I know, but why do I have to go long before I want,
and when I do, where will I go?

Is there really pie in the sky?

It has been said, life is better after death, but I want to live
while I'm alive, to put ice cream on my pie and have one
more chance to have sex.
I search through all my body parts, but there is no soul
to be found. I'm a soulless man," I cry to the skies above.
When you don't believe in me, that's the price you pay, the
crashing voice resonates throughout my dead body, causing it
to move. Unfair, unfair, my lifeless form declares.
Tell me which God you are? Are you Achtland, the Celtic
Goddess of wanton love?"
Love is a word falsely attributed to me. If I loved, would your
world be such a mess?" the voice assumed I understood.
Tell me then, are you be Xtabay, the Mayan Goddess of Seduction
without love in your heart?
Or are you an evil being who made me and the rest of humanity so
you'd have someone with whom to play?"
For a soulless man you should be begging for clemency instead
of questioning me.
You must be the Son of perdition," I exclaim. The antichrist,

the deceiver, chief of demons, Beelzebub, the father of lies.
Laughter shook the entire sky and I got a preview of my soul being
carried away by birds of prey. Wait! I cry, I see my soul.
Laughter shook the sky and the Earth. Too late my boy,
it's gone now and will never return. You're doomed to the
bottomless pit for eternity since you didn't know my name.
One more chance, I cry and see dark clouds fluctuating
throughout the darkening sky, merging into an image of a
terrifying old man with an unpleasant face.

The mouth made of clouds opens and releases crashing thunder
clearing all other clouds from the sky. You'll never have another
chance, I'll see to that, booms round the heavens.
I gather all the electro-mechanical energy within my brain's
limbic system and send it to my amygdala to project my
thoughts onto the only cloud left in the sky, causing it to burst.
Screams fill the air as my mental powers disintegrate the God
who has made me and all others.

He should have known, because he made the rule, all things must
die.

Poetry is an echo, asking a shadow to dance.
—Carl Sandburg

Summer Memories
By Pat Fogarty

Cotton candy
At the beach
Saltwater
On your feet

Boardwalk splinters
Walk with care
Vendors hawk
Everywhere

Roller coasters
Often fly
Funhouse mirrors
Always lie

Guess your weight
Two hoops win
Frozen custard
On your chin

Kites and birds
Fill the air
Spandex males
Folding chairs

Dainty Ladies
Craving shade
Younger men
Surfing waves

Sandy children
Splash and play
Crafted castles
Melt away

Ocean tides
Rise and fall
Summer memories
Some recall

"Everything has to come to an end, sometime."

–L. Frank Baum, The Marvelous Land of Oz

Biographies

Lois Elizabeth Allbright: Born in Shanghai, China, daughter of a journalist and a stenographer from Portland, Oregon. Parents had to evacuate to the United States, due to Japan's invasion. Elizabeth spent her childhood in Hawaii and was in Honolulu during the bombing of Pearl Harbor. Elizabeth has six children who are artists, writers and musicians. She is a graduate of Mills College.

Roger Antony grew up in Maryland and began writing stories at an early age. He graduated from the University of Maryland with a Bachelor's degree in Civil Engineering and a MBA. Early in his career, he had the opportunity to spend four years in Columbus, Mississippi working on the locks and dams along the Tennessee-Tombigbee Waterway. Columbus is the setting for three of his twelve novels. His genres include science fiction, historical fiction, mystery, suspense/thriller, young adult and romance.

Joseph Babinsky attended the University of Buffalo. He is a Veteran and graduated from Monmouth College (Illinois), B.A., Philosophy. He matriculated at Union Theological Seminary and was ordained as a minister in the Presbyterian Church. He worked as a Plumbing Designer and after retirement, began to write and became a self-published author. His online bookstore is at: www.lulu.com/spotlight/josephbabinsky

D. August Baertlein grew up in the Tucson, Arizona desert. She's now settled in the wilds outside of Prescott where she enjoys watching animals, wild and domestic. She also can't help making stuff up. It's not called lying when you're a writer. Twenty years ago she joined the Society of Children's Book Writers and Illustrators, picked up a pen and started scribbling. She hopes you enjoy reading her flights of fancy as much as she enjoyed writing them.

CR Bolinski has published poems in a number of literary journals, anthologies and state poetry society websites. Her poems have placed first and second in a number of poetry contests and she co-published a poetry book, Pearls Beneath The Rind, with her brother, Richard Seldin. Bolinski also co-facilitated poetry classes for OLLI through Yavapai College in Arizona

Gretchen Brinck (Phelps) began writing at 6. In college she majored in Creative Writing. After working in a mental hospital, then as a VISTA volunteer, she got her Master's in Social Work, married and lived/worked in a native Alaskan village. Three children and a divorce later, she worked in San Francisco hospitals and wrote stories published in obscure journals. In 1999, her true-crime book The Boy Next Door came out. In 2010, retired, she moved to AZ for family and writing. She's a volunteer editor for Cirque Journal of Alaska. The Alaska University Press is publishing her memoir The Fox Boy.

Dolores Comeaux-Everard retired as an instructor at Lone Star College in Montgomery, Texas, teaching Counseling Skills and Family Intervention classes prior to moving to Prescott two years ago. She is an expressive therapist, who earned a doctorate in counseling, creativity and addiction treatment. Before teaching at LSC, she taught at the University of Alaska and later at community colleges in North Carolina and Montana. In her twenties, she worked for a daily newspaper in Baytown, Texas as a reporter then columnist. Her hobbies are writing and "clowning around." A trained hospital clown, she's taught clowning and wrote a clowning manual.

Cordell Compton is a retired Management Services Division Manager from the Town of Prescott Valley, Arizona. Originally from Kentucky, Cordell has lived in the Prescott Valley area since 2005. He enjoys writing and researching data for his historical fiction short stories.

Toni Denis moved to Prescott in 2008 after a long career in journalism as a writer, editor, then publisher of an internet company she founded with her husband Andy. She is a member of the Professional Writers of Prescott and the Society of Children's Book Writers and Illustrators. She has a master's in English from the State University of New York at Stony Brook and a bachelor's in journalism from the University of Illinois.

Joe DiBuduo's stories and poems have been published online and in print anthologies. In 2015 his memoir, "A Crime a Day" was published by Jaded Ibis Press. Also, Joe has published 2 volumes of sci-fi, a collection of "flash fiction" poetry, 4 novels, and one nonfiction book. Joe was awarded the 31st Jerry Jazz Musician New Short Fiction in 2012 and an Alto Saxophone Award in 2013.

Pat Fogarty is an award-winning author and poet. He writes creative non-fiction, historical non-fiction, memoir, literary fiction, and poetry. Born and raised in the Bronx, his works are infused with personal experiences from his childhood. He is a graduate of Yavapai College's Creative Writing Program. His stories have been published in many magazines in the USA and abroad, including Threshold—the literary magazine of Yavapai College, Inscape—the annual literary magazine of Washburn University, Tincture—Australia's Literary Journal, plus, dozens of his Short Stories and Poems have been published by other magazines, in-print and online.

Howard Gershkowitz is 61, married (38 years) with one child (age 31), and two grand-children who provide extraordinary inspiration. He has lived in Arizona since 1981 but at age 55, he decided it was time to get serious about his poetry and started taking classes through Maricopa Community Colleges and the ASU/Piper Creative Writing Center. To date, he has had a dozen short stories published, the most recent, 'A Christmas Story,' and 'Ghost Stories,' published by Zimbell House Publishing in December 2017, as well as two dozen poems published in a variety of both on-line and print magazines and collections.

Wendy Picard Gorham completed her Master's Degree in American Literature and has had a fascination with books and writing all her life. She lives out her love of words daily by teaching high school literature and writing. She co-authored the Becker mystery series novels, Keepers of the Sandbox, and Old Bones. She lives in California with her two daughters.

Melody Huttinger was born in Oregon, but raised in Prescott, Arizona when it was still a little Cowtown. After graduating from college, Melody and her husband traveled extensively throughout the world. She now, once again, resides in Prescott, Arizona. Melody is the author of three Young Adult novels, loosely based on her early life growing up with horses. Second Chance is her first published Short Story.

Elaine Jordan is retired from ministry in Arizona where she now writes and muses. Her memoir, Mrs. Ogg Played the Harp: Memories of Church and Life in the High Desert (Two Harbors Press) was published in November, 2012. An excerpt from that book appeared in the Dec. issue of Sharing the Practice.

Bill Lynam is a writer and teacher. He is the author of central Arizona histories for a local newspaper and his works have been published in numerous magazines. His Steampunk Mashup, a collection of science fiction short stories was published in 2017 on Amazon and Kindle. He co-authored Footloose Pilgrims, a coming of age travelogue published in 2014 also on Amazon and Kindle. Soon to be published are two children's books, Bernie, the Flying Squirrel and another about the adventures of two foxes. Bill and his wife, Maria, live in Prescott, AZ.

Sherrie J. Lyons' passion is playing with words. She enjoys penning poetry, novels, and songs. Her poetry has been published in Khamsat, Blue Collar Review, and Anthology. Her manuscript for The Macava earned third place in the Arizona Authors' Association's writing contest. Her greatest literary challenge was writing a 3-act play in rhyming iambic pentameter, "The Tragedy at Cambria," which was published in the Oregon Literary Review. She recently retired from Lyons' Pride Editing, her small business, and is currently writing a Western novel. She lives in Tempe with her husband but grew up in Prescott, Arizona where her heart remains. Email: Sherriejlyons@cox.net

John Maher is a native New Yorker, born and raised in Manhasset, a small town on Long Island's North Shore. After John graduated college with a BA in English, he wanted to write the Great American Novel. Then he had dinner with his father, who'd spent 40 years in book publishing and was then the national sales manager at Random House. His father gave John life-changing advice. He said if he wanted to be a writer he had to do two things: 1) Pick up a job as a bartender, waiter or cab driver. *That way he'd be exposed to all sorts of characters, and characters drive storytelling; 2) Buy a mirror...to watch yourself starve. Professional writers make no money. John put his writing aspirations on hold and followed his brother into the advertising business. He spent the next 40 years mollycoddling petulant clients but never gave up his writing ambitions. After being kicked to the curb for being a dinosaur in the youth-dominated ad game, he retired and started to write. Eight years later, John has written 45 short stories and begun but not finished three novels. But he hopes to put out his memoirs as a collection and completing at least one of his mystery thrillers. But there's no rush. He took 40 years to get to this point. It'll get done.*

Dan Dražen Mazur is a self-published author. His works include, Inside the Horse, Mad Bag Tales, and Short Stories of the Third Kind. In 2015 he established Loose Moose Publishing, a small company which is releasing noteworthy manuscripts by writers across the United States. He is currently working on his first book of poetry written in English, entitled (Divine) Tragedy.

S. Resler Nelson is the author of three novels in the popular Luke Hudson Mystery Series. The first book, MORE THAN DEAD, challenges Detective Hudson through two different cases in Northern California. The second, MORE THAN GONE, finds him embroiled in a unique mystery on an African safari. And the third book is MORE THAN BAD, but readers say it's "more than good." It leads Hudson to Arizona. The author has also written award-winning poetry and short stories. Her novels are on Amazon and Kindle. Sandy lives near Prescott, Arizona, with her husband and two Shetland sheepdogs.

David Nicoll is a member of the East Valley Poets and Changing Hands Bookstores in Tempe, Arizona.

Bruce Paul studied creative writing at Ohio University. After graduating with honors in 1967, he traveled to San Francisco and lived in the Haight/Ashbury district. Bruce has been a singer-songwriter in a folk-rock band, an elementary school teacher in the Virgin Islands, a taxi driver in Denver, a social worker in a maximum-security prison, an investment advisor, a real estate developer, and a riverboat bartender. Bruce is the author of many songs and The Artama Legend series of books. He now lives and writes among the ponderosa pines in the mountains of central Arizona.

Greg Picard finished his Bachelor's in English, specializing in creative writing. After getting his Master's, he worked as a teacher, law enforcement park ranger, and firefighter/medic as well. He co-authored the Becker mystery series novels and makes his home in the mountains of Arizona.

James Robert Platt, a native of Batavia, New York, lives and writes in Arizona. Email: Jplatt3@cox.net JamesRobert—(Without a space between James & Robert is my preferred manner for authorship of my writings)

Christy Powers is a freelance writer. Christy lives in Prescott, Arizona and claims that it is the greatest place to live because it's beautiful, friendly, and perfect. Mostly, Christy enjoys writing about pet care and training. But, she also loves to write opinion pieces. Today, Christy sits at her big window looking out at the pine trees and homes on a high hill in Prescott and realize it is as wonderful and inspiring as "Her Casita" by the sea.

Carol A. Rotta was born and raised in The City of Los Angeles, California. Three years ago, Carol and her husband of 52 years, moved to a Senior Retirement Community in Prescott, Arizona. One of the activities offered is a memoir writing group. Carol began to chronicle her stories of homesteading in Alaska in the early 1950s. Carol's first book, Where the Williwaws Blow was published in August, 2018.

Dennis Royalty is a retired reporter/editor/columnist who moved to Prescott Valley with his wife, Ginger, in 2016. A business-journalism graduate of Indiana University, he was a sportswriter for three years for the former Bloomington (Ind.) Courier-Tribune, and then worked in several capacities for The Indianapolis Star for 27 years, including as a reporter, city editor, and columnist. As city editor of The Star, his staff won numerous honors, including the Pulitzer Prize. He is a member of the Professional Writers of Prescott. dennismroyalty@gmail.com

Darlis Sailors enjoys reading and writing stories for children. At the library she often gets lost in the children's section. She also writes short inspirational stories for adults. They are published weekly on her blog, New Day by Darlis. She is the author of Reflections: Inspirational Stories from Everyday Life.

Joanne Sandlin is a retired educator, lifelong reader, multi-genre author having published two children's books, as well as contributed to four anthologies. Other works include magazine articles in Country Woman, Country Decorating Ideas, Colorado Country Life, Maitre D', And Country Discoveries. Her first published work was a cookbook entitled The Front Burner featuring recipes from 17 years of writing recipe columns for the Tehachapi News, Tehachapi, Calif, and the Prescott, Az. Daily Courier.

Janice Shanks likes to write poetry, loves all music, and is a retired librarian. She spends her time with family, traveling, enjoying the outdoors, and volunteering. You can find her in the kitchen testing a new recipe and contemplating which wine to pair with it.

Bruce D. Sparks was born and raised in Yuma, Arizona. After serving in the military, he became a law enforcement officer, followed by a 30-year career with United Parcel Service. Now retired, Bruce makes his home in Prescott, Arizona where he enjoys writing the vivid details of his life as a boy in Yuma, and the outdoor life in Arizona as he experienced it.

Georgia Sparks resides in Prescott, Arizona and is the author of three children's books, including The Perfect Rock, an allegory about the twists and turns of life. A mother of four and grandmother, Georgia's *writing is inspired by life experiences and incorporates positive messages through lively characters. She believes we all have a story to tell, and there is someone, somewhere who needs to hear it. Her books are available on Amazon.com.*

Tom Spirito is a retired New Yorker who moved to Prescott six years ago. He has been a dude wrangler, bartender, bouncer, short order cook, waiter, salesman, teamster, telephone man and wrangler again. Tom is in his 69th year and professes that he still doesn't know what he wants to be when he grows up. Tom writes what he has lived.

Fredora Williams enjoys journaling and writing children's stories. She lives with her two cats in Prescott, Arizona. Fredora also loves nature and enjoys hiking and kayaking.

*Some authors chose not to include their biographies.

Great is the art of beginning, but greater is the art of ending.
—Henry Wadsworth Longfellow